Shadows of the Opera:
Retribution in Blood

BY THE SAME AUTHOR

Adaptations:
Judex (by Arthur Bernède & Louis Feuillade)
The Return of Judex (by Arthur Bernède & Louis Feuillade)

Fiction:
The Last Vendetta (in *Tales of the Shadowmen* No. 1)
Dr. Cerral's Patient (in *Tales of the Shadowmen* No. 2)
The Lady in the Black Gloves (in *Tales of the Shadowmen* No. 3)
Corridors of Deceit (in *Tales of the Shadowmen* No. 4)
All Predators Great and Small (in *Tales of the Shadowmen* No. 5)
Incident in the Boer War (in *Tales of the Shadowmen* No. 6)
Will There Be Sunlight? (in *Tales of the Shadowmen* No. 7)
Vampire Renaissance (in *Tales of the Shadowmen* No. 8)
Gods of the Underworld (in *Tales of the Shadowmen* No. 9)
Acolytes of the Shadows (in *The Shadow of Judex*)
Judex Rules (in *The Shadow of Judex*)

Shadows of the Opera:
Retribution in Blood

by
Rick Lai

A Black Coat Press Book

ISBN 978-1-61227-188-0. First Printing. August 2013. Published by Black Coat Press, an imprint of Hollywood Comics.com, LLC, P.O. Box 17270, Encino, CA 91416. All rights reserved. Except for review purposes, no part of this book may be reproduced or transmitted in any form or by any means, electronic or mechanical, including photocopying, recording, or by any information storage and retrieval system, without permission in writing from the publisher. The stories and characters depicted in this novel are entirely fictional. Printed in the United States of America.

Table of Contents

Introduction

Rick Lai's most obvious gift lies in his ability not only to envision obscure connections between diverse works of fiction, but to embellish those connections and weave a tapestry that proves enthralling as a literary work able to stand independent of the celebrated originals. Along with his peers, Win Scott Eckert and Christopher Paul Carey, Lai has distinguished himself as an heir to Philip Jose Farmer, the originator of the Wold Newton concept that first sought to connect the fantastic fiction of the past three centuries.

Having the second volume in Rick's *Shadows of the Opera* series be published by Black Coat Press is doubly appropriate since the imprint is rooted in the Wold Newton universe and many of Rick's stories first appeared in Black Coat Press' *Tales of the Shadowmen* annual anthology series. The difference between the stories that first appeared in *Tales of the Shadowmen* and now appear in *Shadows of the Opera* is that readers are now able to enjoy the author's original vision of the work freed from the strictures required by the celebrated anthology series. These are Rick's purebred creations grown from a lifetime devoted to the fantastic and esoteric.His director's cut, if you will, of his contributions to the Wold Newton universe.

I first learned of Rick's name from his work as a literary scholar. Wold Newton seemed like a peculiar cult to me as a kid growing up in the 1970s. Much like the Cthulu mythos, it was something Roy Thomas frequently invoked in his scripts for Marvel Comics. Its value and growing attraction for me was the remarkably thorough degree of scholarship that was evident in the work. This was quite uncommon in those days long before the internet where the luck of what might be held in a local library or used bookshop were one's only recourse to discovering such works. It was a bit like stumbling across the secrets held by an Adept of some Gnostic order. Here was a box of delights beckoning to be opened…promising to send one on further quests for still more obscure Holy Grails.

I believe I was about 20 years old when I first found a reference to one of Rick's articles published in a fanzine that I had no idea how to obtain. This would have been in the early 1990s. I hastily scribbled down the author's name, the article's title, and the fanzine's volume number for future reference. Here was a scholar so well-versed in the works of Sax Rohmer and other writers I only knew of only by reputation at the time that my blood boiled in envy. I had amassed at the time what I thought was an impressive home library of fantastic fiction and here was a scholar who not only knew more, but knew so much that the ideas were clearly overflowing from his fertile imagination. My desire to plumb the depths of that knowledge and absorb it all was unrelenting. It burned

7

within my breast like Saul Bellow's Henderson always being driven to find something more.

The advent of the internet freed me from the constraints of local resources. Suddenly the works of Wold Newtonians and fellow kindred spirits such as Will Murray were obtainable. I recall quite vividly the afternoon I stumbled upon a Wold Newton website and discovered article upon article in an online repository. I printed as much as I dared at work and then retreated to the library. It was a seemingly endless project, but it sent me on a hunt for more and more.

Soon I learned that some of these articles were being printed in book form similar to the binders of printed articles I had already compiled for my own study. Eventually my binders gave way to floppy disks and then flash drives with downloaded or cut and paste copies of the same. There was a satisfying sense of fulfillment when a speculative article would align with a thought that had struck me when reading the work. The joy upon reading an article's footnotes or a character's chronology and learning of titles one never knew existed is beyond compare.

The concept of crafting fiction set within the continuity of an existing series appealed to me more and more. I knew writing for the Wold Newton universe wasn't quite what I wanted, but the idea of creating works that would fit in that fabric and possibly find acceptance among its number became an ever-growing desire. The well-researched chronologies and articles opened up endless possibilities for filling in gaps in ways that previous continuation authors had never imagined. It was a bit like discovering a university for fantastic fiction existed in which one could study the works of the finest scholars and emerge better-prepared to embark on the task of embroidering the works that caught and transformed one's adolescent imagination.

So that brings us to the second volume of Rick's *Shadows of the Opera* series. His scholarly speculations having given rise to the need to tell the very stories he had researched for so long. Rick is still overflowing with ideas. It is all too obvious that there can never be enough time or space to capture all that his mind holds. Readers will find many of the stories contained within whet the appetite for still longer works.

Rick is a unique storyteller in that his fiction constantly opens unexpected doors into corners of the imagination one never suspected existed. Like most Gnostic magicians, exposure to his Black Arts is at one's own peril. Once observed by untrained eyes, there is no turning back. The reader's world will be transformed and familiar tales and characters will now loom larger, becoming more dangerous, more real than the safety promised by the well-read classics where they first appeared. You will see a world that always existed but was just beyond your reach. You will see Technicolor where before was only monochromatic shadows and light.

This is no dream, dear reader; you will not awaken back in your arm chair safe in the realization that the escapism was only fantasy. You will instead realize you have entered another realm existing alongside our own. Like Adam and Eve before you, you will have eaten of the Forbidden Fruit and found the price of becoming gods and goddesses. You will realize Rick Lai wasn't the creator of this realm, but he was the navigator you willingly chose to follow. The pleasures to be found are undeniable, but be warned. You will never safely walk among the Garden again ignorant of your nakedness.

William Patrick Maynard
Fort McMurray, Canada
April 5, 2013

The Story So Far
A Summary of the Revenant's Earlier Adventures

The Revenant's previous exploits were collected in *Shadows of the Opera* (Wildcat Books, 2011). What follows is a brief synopsis of those events.

In 1879, the European underworld was dominated by the crime syndicate called the Black Coats. An internal power struggle had broken out between two factions. The organization was led by the All-Father, a shadowy personage claiming to be the immortal Colonel Bozzo-Corona. His chief lieutenant was Count Salvatore Corbucci, the head of the Camorra in Naples. An insurrection against the All-Father's authority was launched by Jim Nemo, the chieftain of the British branch of the Black Coats. Nemo's primary agent in Paris was a woman known as Gloria Scot, an anagram for Cagliostro.

Gloria Scot was actually Joséphine Balsamo, the great-granddaughter of the notorious adventurer, Count Cagliostro. An earlier female member of the Cagliostro family, a heroic vampire hunter, had bore the same name. Nevertheless, this current Joséphine Balsamo was the very epitome of treachery.

In order to advance Nemo's schemes, Gloria Scot framed Darlla Rassendyll, an agent of the French police, for treason and murder. Darlla was left by Gloria to drown in the lake beneath the Paris Opera House, but the detective was saved from a watery grave by a mysterious recluse. Darlla's rescuer was Erik, the enigmatic Phantom of the Opera. Taking an interest in Darlla, Erik offered to train her in order to seek revenge on Gloria and the Black Coats. Accepting Erik's offer, Darlla found herself falling in love with her new mentor.

Gloria's main accomplice was her lover Leonard. He seduced Valorie Varno, an impressionable acrobat in her teens. Posing as Leonard's sister, Gloria tricked Valorie into burglarizing Count Corbucci's villa near Naples. Valorie was apparently slain by a poison needle hidden by Corbucci. In reality, Valorie was thrown into a cataleptic trance. Revived by the All-Father, Valorie was "brainwashed" by the Black Coats into becoming an assassin called the Green Lamia.

Pretending to be a man, Darlla assumed the identity of the Revenant, a vigilante who preyed on the Black Coats. Mimicking a ploy originated by Vautrin, a legendary master criminal, Darlla recruited a person contemplating suicide to act as her principal assistant. This recruit was Julia Orsini, a passionate Corsican whose ancestors had been persecuted by the Black Coats. Also aiding the Revenant was Charles Blanton, a coachman indebted to Erik. The Revenant and her two assistants called themselves the Acolytes of the Shadows. As Acolytes, Julia and Charles adopted the respective aliases of Lady Judex and Lord Charon.

During a confrontation in a graveyard, Nemo and Gloria learned of the existence of the seemingly male Revenant and her female Acolyte. Although the Revenant foiled the Black Coats in this encounter, her two principal adversaries escaped to fight another day.

Count Corbucci then ordered the Green Lamia to target Gloria through her two daughters. The older sibling, then only 11 years old, was also named Joséphine, but everyone referred to her by the nickname of Josine. Her father was an American munitions dealer, Arthur Gordon. Sabine, the other daughter, had been raised under the false impression that her father was the same as Josine's. The father of Sabine was actually Théophraste Lupin, a master thief who committed crimes under the anagram of Lothaire Stepphun.

Slaying Josine's governess, the Green Lamia abducted Josine as a hostage. After Gloria was unable to persuade Nemo to halt a major assault on the All-Father's assets, Corbucci ordered the Lamia to slay Josine.

Because her vendetta did not extend to innocent children, the Revenant intervened to rescue Josine. In the course of a battle in which the Lamia was supposedly killed, Josine saw the Revenant unmasked. The young girl did not recognize Darlla because she had never seen her before. In exchange for a promise not to reveal her true sex or her appearance to anyone, the Revenant agreed to return Josine to her mother. Josine scrupulously kept her word.

In 1880, the Queen's Necklace was stolen from the haughty Countess de Dreux-Soubise by Arsène Lupin, the six year old son of Théophraste. When the Necklace fell into Théophraste's hands, he intended to use it as a gift to win back Gloria's affections. Learning of Théophraste's intentions, the Revenant manipulated Gloria into an ambush. In the course of her deceptions, the Revenant not only tricked Théophraste into believing that Gloria intended to murder him, but also fooled Gloria into thinking that Théophraste had betrayed her.

Fatally wounded, Gloria died in Josine's arms. Before she perished, Gloria made Josine swear an oath of vengeance against the Revenant and Théophraste and his children. Although Gloria revealed Sabine's true parentage secretly and exempted her from this pact of vengeance, the vendetta extended to Arsène and his older sister, Irene. While Théophraste never learned the Revenant's real identity, he did deduce that she was a woman.

Under the impression that Sabine was also his child, Arthur Gordon gained custody of the two Balsamo children. He enrolled them into the Marie Gilbert School run by benevolent nuns. When Leonard left for London, Josine and her sister became forgotten by the Black Coats.

Falling in love with opera singer Christine Daae, Erik resisted Darlla's romantic entreaties. Obsessed with Christine, Erik brutally slew anyone who interfered with his romantic designs during 1881. He embarked on a murder spree that resulted into the death of three innocent people. Because of her complex feelings for Erik, a tormented Darlla refused to halt Erik's rampage.

Reports of the violent occurrences at the Opera House drew Nemo's attention. The mastermind constructed a false theory that wasn't far from the truth. Concluding correctly that Darlla had survived her drowning in the lake, Nemo wrongly concluded that she was the female Acolyte seen at the cemetery. As for the Revenant, Nemo wrongly identified the apparently male vigilante as the Phantom of the Opera. Nemo instructed Feliciana Sorelli, a member of the Black Coats who was also the lead ballerina at the Opera House, to verify his suspicions.

Feliciana surprised Erik in his underground sanctuary. The Phantom was about to kill Feliciana when Darlla interfered. Unable to countenance another murder, Darlla slew the man she loved to rescue the ballerina. A grateful Feliciana revealed her connection to the Black Coats. Utilizing Erik's corpse and a wax image of Darlla, Feliciana then fooled Nemo into believing that she had killed the Revenant and the female acolyte. Nemo falsely believed that his original theory was the truth.

Celebrations among the Black Coats over the Revenant's alleged death ended when Darlla appeared in a new costume. Darlla now made no effort to hide the true sex of her masked alter ego. The Black Coats wrongly concluded that the "new" Revenant was another female Acolyte who had assumed the persona of her dead master.

Feliciana and Angelique LaSalle, young woman whose twin sister had been murdered by the Black Coats, were recruited into the Acolytes of the Shadows as respectively Lady Leopard and Lady Tocsin. Feliciana was ordered to withhold the truth of Erik's death from her fellow Acolyte, Lord Charon, due to the coachman's fierce loyalty to the Phantom. Charon was told that Erik had died from a broken heart stemming from Christine Daae's rejection.

Julia Orsini became engaged to Pierre de Trémeuse, Théophraste's best friend. Since Pierre's cousin was married to a prominent Russian dignitary, the wedding reception was hosted by the Russian Embassy. Countess Yalta, an insane Nihilist allied to Colonel Bozzo-Corona, wanted to assassinate everyone at the reception with a bomb. Assisting her in this diabolical enterprise was the Green Lamia, who had miraculously survived a vicious attack by the Revenant.

During the foiling of this bomb plot, Yalta lost her life while the Revenant captured the Green Lamia. "Deprogramming" her captive, Darlla made Valorie Varno realize the horror of her crimes as the Lamia. A repentant Valorie them joined the Acolytes of the Shadows as the Jade Seraph.

Legacy of the Phantom

Inside the underground catacombs of the Paris Opera House was a secret sanctuary. It had been constructed by an enigmatic genius who called himself Erik. Months ago in this year of 1881, Erik had perished. He had been buried secretly elsewhere in the subterranean labyrinth. Present at his funeral had been two women

One was Christine Daae, a young opera singer. Erik had envisioned her as his Disciple of Life, a woman who was the embodiment of his desire to celebrate existence through music. Christine's rejection of Erik had ignited a series of events that culminated in Erik's death.

The other female mourner was Darlla Rassendyll. Two years earlier, Darlla had been a trusted member of the French police. Her activities offended a member of the Black Coats, a European crime syndicate based in Corsica. The motto of the sinister brotherhood was "pay the law." This doctrine was interpreted thusly: "Give the courts a *guilty party* for every crime committed." In reality, the "guilty party" was a scapegoat, often an innocent person, whom the Black Coats desired to eliminate. After framing Darlla for treason and murder, the Black Coats left her to be drowned in the underground lake near Erik's sanctum.

Rescued by Erik, Darlla found herself faced with an unusual choice. Erik had roamed Asia years earlier as an assassin and a pirate. He had learned many lethal skills. Wishing for his murderous knowledge to be preserved by another human being, Erik had a parallel ambition to train a Disciple of Death. He originally intended his pupil to be a man, but his unexpected encounter with a woman presented an extraordinary opportunity. Darlla was given a choice. She could leave Erik's abode and take her chances in the outside world, or she could become the Disciple of Death in order to seek vengeance on the Black Coats.

Accepting Erik's offer, Darlla underwent vigorous training to become a formidable combatant. One condition of Darlla's tutelage was that she must never seek to view the face beneath Erik's mask. Under the alias of the Revenant, she became a masked vigilante. Scores of criminals were slain by her weapons, a Thuggee pickaxe and a Punjabi lasso,

Darlla fell hopelessly in love with Erik, but his obsession with Christine blinded himself to a fundamental truth. Unlike Christine, Darlla loved Erik without any reservations. As he lay dying, Erik removed his mask. A tearful Darlla kissed him on the lips. She revealed that she had secretly gazed upon his face two years earlier. As death overcame him, Erik realized he had squandered his one chance to find true love.

After Erik's death, Darlla questioned the violent trajectory of her life. While still pursuing her brutal war with the Black Coats, she sought to create her own Disciple of Life. This incarnation of the Disciple would temper the Revenant's justice with mercy. The Disciple would act as the Revenant's conscience.

Whereas the Revenant had only executed agents of the Black Coats in the past, she rehabilitated one of their most formidable assassins. The role of Disciple of Life was bestowed on Valorie Varno, a young girl who had been the subject of bizarre experimentation by the Black Coats. Injected with a rare South American poison, Valorie's skin was turned green. Valorie's mind had been twisted by the All-Father, the allegedly immortal patriarch of the Black Coats. With the assistance of a Persian sage, Darlla had re-instilled in Valorie respect for human life. In order to make amends for her earlier murders, Valorie swore never to kill another human being.

As the Revenant, Darlla wore a black and red costume consisting of a hood, shirt, pants, gloves, and boots. Inside her clandestine refuge, she had divested herself of her flamboyant apparel to wear a scarlet robe. The flame-haired Darlla has an attractive face with a singular flaw. Her mouth drooped slightly. When she had appeared in the stage during a brief stint as an actress, noted journalist Leon Fauchery had described her mouth as "the embodiment of cruelty."

Seated at a table, Darlla was writing in a large bound journal. Erik had advised to record all her exploits for future reference. These records were the private annals of the Revenant.

Valorie Varno was seated at an organ. As Darlla transcribed her adventures, her Disciple of Life had been playing one of Erik's musical compositions. Her dark hair was piled upwards in a bouffant style. A thin blade of hair was pointed downwards between her slanted eyebrows.

Valorie was clothed in green robe. A chain encircled her neck. The neckwear ended in a jade pendant in the shape of a seraph, an angel with three pairs of wings. The necklace was a gift from Laurent Remy, the secretary to the Director of the Paris Opera. Valorie and Laurent were passionate lovers.

"I'm going to my room," said Valorie. "You should retire as well."

"I only need to make a few more entries." Darlla scribbled a few more sentences. "I'm done!"

"You really should find some better way to secure those journals, Darlla."

"They're locked in a cupboard. Only you and I know where the key is hidden."

"Locks can easily be picked. Imagine if our sanctuary was discovered by an enemy. It's a pity that Erik didn't design a secret vault."

"Actually, he did, Valorie. It's way in the back of our sanctuary. I haven't been able to figure out the combination."

"Can you show it to me?"

"I can, but I'll need my pickaxe."

After Darlla had retrieved her pickaxe, she escorted Valorie through the corridors of the underground haven. Inevitably, they reached a wall containing a large circular illustration. A red skull with black teeth was painted in the middle of the circle. Hidden inside the lines between the teeth was a thin key slot.

Darlla's pickaxe was a three-pronged weapon vaguely resembling a crucifix. Unlike a normal pickaxe, this instrument featured a sharp blade extending from the head. Inserting the blade into the slot, Darlla twisted the pickaxe. The wall slid to the right revealing a chamber with a large vault.

"I found this secret vault shortly after Erik died, Valorie."

Valorie scrutinized the door. There were eight circular rings on which were inscribed the letters of the alphabet. Next to the eight circles was a large handle. Valorie tried to turn the handle, but it wouldn't budge.

"If you examine the door, you will discover an alphabetic lock," volunteered Darlla. "I don't know the correct combination."

"What combinations did you try?"

"Erik would have wanted me to open this. The combination must be a word made up of eight letters. I tried 'Revenant,' but it didn't work."

"But you were Erik's Disciple just as I am yours. 'Disciple' also has eight letters."

Valorie arranged the rings to spell the word "Disciple.' Valorie was able to open the door.

Inside the vault was a painting on a stand. It depicted a young woman with blonde hair and blue eyes. The portrait bore the signature "Erik."

"I knew that Erik was a musician and an architect," stated Valorie, "but I wasn't aware that he was a painter."

"I didn't know," replied Darlla. "Erik kept this part of his life secret from me."

"The woman in the portrait. She's very beautiful. Who is she?"

"She's Christine Daae, Erik's Disciple of Life."

Next to the portrait were several sketchbooks on the floor. Valorie inspected them.

"There must be a hundred drawings here, Darlla."

"Valorie, could you please look through them while I get my annals."

Darlla left only to later return with a wheelbarrow containing her notebooks. Valorie helped her move the annals into the vault.

"I looked through all the sketches," said Valorie. "They're all of Christine."

"Please help me put Erik's sketchbooks in the wheelbarrow."

"What are you going to do, Darlla? These sketches are beautiful works of art. They belong in a museum."

"I'm going to burn them."

"Burn them! That's not right! What are you going to do about the portrait! It's a masterpiece! It's worthy of the Louvre!"

Darlla picked up her pickaxe. She slashed the painting in half.

"The masterpiece is now firewood."

Following a fiery conflagration that consumed Erik's artwork, Darlla was alone in her bedroom. She held a red hood that Erik had worn to disguise his ugliness. Tears ran down her eyes.

"Oh, my darling, why couldn't at least one of your hundred sketches been of me!"

The Fire Eater

"I must choose a woman to be my husband's mistress," said Madame Nemo.

"I don't understand," replied Leonard Scot. "Why should the wife of the Lord of the Night create a rival?"

This unusual conversation transpired one night during 1883 in the living room of a London residence. Both the speakers were members of the Gentlemen of the Night, the predominant crime syndicate of the British Isles. The woman, a slim brunette with black eyes, was married to the secret society's leader, the Lord of the Night. She wore a turquoise robe with golden birds embroidered on the sleeves and collar. Scot was an elegantly dressed man with a beard. His hands rested on a sword cane as he sat across from his hostess.

"A rival is inevitable," resumed Madame Nemo. "Jim only married me because of my father's influence among the gangs of New York. My husband is a man of great ambitions. He will use the Gentlemen of the Night to secure dominion over Europe and then turn his eyes on the United States and even Asia."

"If an American alliance is so important to Jim Nemo, he can't afford to cast you aside."

"Yes, but he limits my influence. He clearly does not love me. Otherwise, he would publicly acknowledge me as his wife. In his real identity, Jim still pretends to be a bachelor. He isn't with me tonight because he's at an academic conference. If I could grant him a son, I would be in an invulnerable position. Unfortunately, the doctors told me a stark truth after Trickie's birth. I can have no more children."

"If you choose his mistress, how do you benefit?"

"I secure the future of my daughter. Trickie has inherited her father's brilliance. She's a child prodigy. At the age of seven, she can compute mathematical equations that would perplex an adult. Jim plans to create a new scientific subsidiary, the Neptune Society. Trickie should eventually assume leadership of the Neptune Society, but there is an obstacle."

"Trickie's half-sister, Urania."

"Urania has recently turned twenty-one. Jim intends to place her at the helm of the Neptune Society. That would be a disastrous choice. She's scientifically brilliant, but lacking in managerial skills. Urania has no sense of frugality. She'll lead the Neptune Society into bankruptcy."

"Doesn't Jim see this?"

"He does, but he still dotes on Urania. Jim's well aware of my budgetary and accounting skills. He hoped to have me tutor Urania."

"You refused."

"No, I didn't. Urania rejected any thought of accepting my help. She hates me. Urania sees my marriage as an insult to her late mother's memory. Her animosity extends to my daughter. Urania has strengthened her position by granting Jim something he has long coveted – a male heir. The child is named after his grandfather."

"Jim has a grandson! I didn't know Urania was married!"

"She isn't, but that doesn't bother Jim. He never wedded Urania's mother. In order to spare his precious little bastard's feelings, Jim tells Urania that he was secretly married to Emily Caber. He wasn't."

"Trickie's inheritance is now threatened by another bastard. Leonard. I need to secure my daughter's future. Jim will only turn against Urania if her place in his heart is supplanted by another woman. I must form an alliance with that woman."

"Describe to me the ideal candidate for your husband's mistress."

"First, she must be young. Probably about the same age as Urania. Jim must feel that the woman is helping him recapture his youth. Second, she must have drive and ambition. Third, she must prove herself worthy of his affection."

"In what way?"

"She must have talents beneficial to Jim's endeavors. For example, Jim admired my ability to curb wasteful financial expenditures. I see my last comment has rubbed a sore wound, Leonard."

"I haven't forgotten how your frugality impoverished my nieces."

"Joséphine and Sabine Balsamo really aren't your nieces, but you do have genuine affection for them. In addition to your own fee, I'll create a trust fund for them." Madame Nemo wrote figures down in small memorandum book. She showed it to Leonard. "Are these acceptable?"

"Yes. May I ask why you chose me as your collaborator?"

"I had to find someone who Jim wouldn't suspect of being in league with me. Your resentment concerning my treatment of your 'nieces' is well known."

"Does this candidate have any other qualifications?"

"Jim is locked in a massive struggle with the All-Father for control of the Black Coats. My family's connections aid him in this battle. It would be advantageous if the mistress had a pedigree helpful to Jim's revolt against the All-Father."

"If I find such a woman, what am I to do?"

"Submit her for my approval. If she interviews well, then you merely have to introduce her to Jim."

"When would I be paid? When would my nieces get their trust fund?"

"Your compensation and your nieces' will be authorized as soon as Jim enthrones the woman as his mistress."

"Then I have a suitable candidate. I've been hiding her until her talents were needed. Let me describe her."

The Gentlemen of the Night was part of a larger tapestry of crime. Allied with the Camorra, the Brotherhood of the Seven Kings, the Companions of Silence and other murderous associations, the Gentlemen formed a confederation collectively feared as the Black Coats. The center of Black Coat activity had long been Paris. Many families of petty criminals owed allegiance to the Black Coats. Representative of these generational felons were three young bandits. Their names were Cocotte, Piquepuce and Landerneau.

Cocotte had planned a profitable robbery tonight with his two compatriots. Two ladies from the Cesarine Popinot Charities were delivering money to needy families. The criminal trio intended to ambush the envoy and steal the money.

A satchel of cash was being carried by Chantal Lebrue, a brunette of 24 years. She was accompanying her middle-aged superior, Marie de Sales. The two ladies were passing a dark alley. Piquepuce grabbed Chantal and hustled her into the darkness. Landerneau did likewise with Marie.

As Piquepuce held Chantal, Cocotte tried to pry the money bag out of her fingers. The brunette refused to relinquish it.

"Give me the money," threatened Cocotte, "or we'll strangle your friend." Chantal released the satchel.

"I am the Jade Seraph! Surrender or face my wrath!"

The speaker was a woman attired in a green leotard with black gauntlets and boots. A chain was looped around her thighs. Her black hair was elevated in a bouffant. A thin stroke of hair pointed downward between her slanted eyebrows. Her face and neck were green.

The three robbers laughed. "She's dressed for Mardi Gras!" shouted Landerneau. "The necklace!" yelled Piquepuce pointing at the Seraph.

Encircling the Seraph's neck was a metal chain with a jade pendant in the shape of an angel with six wings.

"I'll break the arm of anyone who touches my necklace!" threatened the Seraph swiftly unhooking her metal belt.

The felonious trio rushed the Seraph. Swung like a club, the Seraph's belt smashed into the face of the three ruffians. They all dropped senseless to the ground.

"Thank you!" said Chantal. "Is there any way we could repay you?"

"I saw a gendarme about six blocks away." said the Seraph. "You and your friend can fetch him."

After the two ladies left, the Seraph vanished into the night.

Unfortunately for the interests of justice, the policeman initially refused to believe the story of the two women. He thought their claims about a green woman were the result of too much liquor. The gendarme's doubts were overcome when Chantal opened the satchel and showed him the money. However, the patrolman's hesitation allowed Cocotte, Piquepuce and Landerneau to awaken. They were gone by the time the gendarme arrived on the scene.

A French journalist, Sigismond Trottier, learned of this incident. After interviewing Chantal and Marie, Trottier embarked on a series of articles for *L'Epoque*. In his first article, the female vigilante was described as "the Green Angel." In subsequent articles, she was identified properly as the Jade Seraph. Artistic renditions of the Seraph accompanied the articles. Soon other newspapers mimicked *L'Epoque*. The Jade Seraph had become a newspaper sensation.

A London newspaper sought to exploit this story to increase circulation. Trottier's articles were summarized in an English translation with the original illustrations. This newspaper was read by Leonard Scot. He saw an excellent opportunity to promote Madame Nemo's plans.

Leonard requested an audience with Jim Nemo. Seated inside Nemo's study, Leonard was struck by a painting by Jean-Baptiste Greuze on the wall behind Nemo's desk. The sun coming from the window was in Leonard's eyes while Nemo sat comfortably in the shadows. Nemo had the appearance of an ascetic scholar. Seated to his right was a short stout man with a faint white scar on his forehead. He was one of Nemo's most trusted lieutenants, John Clay.

"Having read yesterday's newspaper, I can deduce the reason for this meeting," said Nemo. "You want to discuss Valorie Varno."

"Your deductions are correct as always," replied Leonard.

"Young Clay here is unfamiliar with Varno's background. Please enlighten him."

"Four years ago, we received information that the All-Father was entrusting the Scapular of Mercy to Salvatore Corbucci. The Scapular is the symbol of the All-Father's authority over the Black Coats. If he were to lose it, the chances of overthrowing him would increase."

"The worshippers of the All-Father are fools," interjected Nemo. "They blindly imagine the current holder of the office to be Colonel Bozzo-Corona."

"Haven't all the All-Fathers throughout history pretended to be the Colonel?" asked Clay.

"You're forgetting the Sword-Swallower," reminded Nemo. "I hope to emulate him."

"Acting on the Lord of the Night's instructions," resumed Leonard, "Countess Cagliostro and I planned to steal the Scapular. The information might have been leaked to lure us into a trap. We decided to recruit an expendable pawn. I was apprised of the existence of Valorie Varno, a young acrobat at Ronder's Circus. She was 19 years old at the time. I easily seduced her. After she eloped with me, I told her a cock and bull story about being a British spy. The little fool naively believed that I needed to burglarize the home of a foreign agent. I tricked her into volunteering to break into Corbucci's home. Our suspicions about the All-Father were warranted. It was indeed a trap. Varno was infected with a deadly poison."

"The Mato Grosso Pestilence," added Nemo. "It turns the skin of its victim green. One strain of the toxin is fatal, but another only imposes a catalytic trance. Varno was exposed to the latter."

"The Countess and I mistakenly left Varno for dead. After reviving her, the All-Father forced Varno to submit to his will. He trained her to be an assassin. As the Green Lamia, Varno terrorized the French supporters of our rebellion against the All-Father. In Paris, she murdered at least seven people including the governess of my nieces. The Lamia even kidnapped my older niece, Joséphine. Somehow Joséphine escaped. She refused to talk about her ordeal, but my niece did claim the Lamia was dead. Joséphine also hinted that the Lamia perished at the hands of a woman."

"Joséphine was mistaken," said Nemo. "A spy in the All-Father's camp later told us the truth. The Lamia had been horribly beaten. The woman mentioned by Joséphine must have been responsible."

"Do we have any suspicions regarding the identity of this woman?" asked Clay.

"I have a theory," indicated Nemo, "but let me make you cognizant of certain facts. According to our informant, it took two years for the Lamia to recuperate from her injuries inflected by the nameless woman. When the Lamia recovered in 1881, she severed all ties with the All-Father. Shortly hereafter, I began to receive reports that the Lamia was interfering with our operations in Paris. Furthermore, the Lamia was now fighting alongside the Revenant."

"The female vigilante!" exclaimed Clay. "Now I comprehend your theory. It must have been the Revenant who pulverized the Lamia in 1879."

"Precisely," confirmed Nemo. "As you must have guessed, the Lamia is the Jade Seraph depicted in the newspapers."

"Pardon me for raising an objection to your theory, My Lord," commented Leonard. "The Revenant in 1879 was a man. He was replaced by a woman in 1881."

"I'm well aware of that fact. The current Revenant professes to be a disciple of the late unlamented original. In whatever guise in 1879, the second Revenant must have vanquished the Lamia."

Nemo was only partially right. There had actually been a single Revenant. Early in her career, the Revenant had pretended to be a man. Later the Revenant faked the death of her male persona and abandoned all ploys to hide her true sex.

Nemo turned towards Clay. "Analyze the character of Valorie Varno."

"She has the psychology of a slave. She can only obey a person whom she truly dreads. Both the All-Father and the Revenant nearly killed her. Their cruelty instilled fear in Varno's heart. She served them fanatically."

"What course of action do you recommend?"

"We must capture Varno and gain her subservience through torture," advocated Clay. "Besides being a resourceful assassin, she will provide us valuable intelligence on the Revenant. Varno may even know the Revenant's true identity.

"We may not be able to break Varno," observed Nemo. "The third time may not be the charm."

"Then we simply kill her," advocated Clay. "We leave her body in a public place as a warning to the Revenant."

"I agree with John's assessment," concurred Leonard. "I have the ideal person to apprehend Varno. I took the liberty of bringing my candidate here. She's waiting outside in the living room."

"She?" uttered Clay in surprise.

"To paraphrase a cliché, it takes a woman to catch a woman."

"I'll need to interview this woman," decreed Nemo. "Summon her."

Leonard left the study. When he returned, he was accompanied by a young woman in a pink dress. She had red hair and blue eyes. Her cherubic face smiled at Jim Nemo.

"My name is Ida Similor."

Jim Nemo's brown-haired daughter, Urania, lived in a separate London residence. She had been estranged from Jim since his marriage to her stepmother in 1875. Over the last few years, she reconciled with him. A major factor in the reconciliation was Urania's academic brilliance. She was one of the few people to fully comprehend her father's book on asteroids. Jim was also filled with pride when Urania at the age of twenty passed the medical exams at St. Swithin's. Rather than the Nemo alias or her father's genuine surname, Urania employed her mother's surname, Caber.

Dr. Urania Caber gazed at the sleeping infant in the crib. She heard the door open. John Clay walked in. He took Urania into his arms and kissed her.

"Rani, you won't believe what happened in your father's study today!"

"Shh!" whispered Urania. "You'll wake our son."

The father of the young infant gave the mother all the details of the meeting with Leonard Scot.

"When Ida revealed who her father was, you could have knocked Jim over with a feather. I think that sealed the icing on the cake."

"My father gave her the Varno assignment?"

"Yes, but I'm not talking about that. Your father's fallen heads over heels for Ida."

"That American woman is bad enough! Now I have to worry about some trollop!"

"She's nothing like your stepmother. Ida's only two years older than you. She's got a vibrant personality. If Ida was an actress, she would be perfect to play Queen Elizabeth."

"You're making me jealous."

"Don't worry about me, Rani. Your father nearly killed me when he discovered your pregnancy. Now that he's warmed up to us, I'm not chasing after some bird that he's ogling."

"I can't see how this new complication can help us!"

"I do. I invited Ida to lunch with us tomorrow."

"Are you serious?"

"Ida may be the proper pawn to counter your stepmother. Your father only married her because your grandfather forced him. It's inevitable that Jim select a mistress. There's no harm in being friendly with Ida. Your stepmother keeps pressuring Jim to cut your stipend. Let her worry about all the loot being showered on Ida."

"But what if my father divorces that American harpy? Ida could become my new stepmother!"

"Jim can't divorce the American. Brendan McGinty is her maternal uncle. Her sister is married to Armand Zeck. Your father doesn't want to anger those New York bosses."

"What if Ida gives birth? If I had a half-brother, Jimmy's future may be in doubt."

"Our son doesn't need to inherit his grandfather's empire. Just a slice of it. I'm not sure we want Jimmy to be running the Gentlemen of the Night. In the old days, men like me and your father only had to worry about the police. Now we've got the Pinkertons in America and the Revenant in France. By the time Jimmy grows up, we may have a plague of private detectives and masked vigilantes. It won't be easy for Jimmy to play the Emperor. It's better for him to be a Royal Duke. Get Ida to agree to your control of the Neptune Society, and little Jimmy's inheritance will be safe."

In a third home in London, there dwelt Madame Nemo and her young daughter. Although Jim Nemo had no affection for his American spouse, he did respect her skills as an accountant. She kept the financial books for the entire organization. As Jim played mathematical games with Trickie, Madame Nemo recorded the revenues and expenses for the current quarter.

"You always say, Jim, that each quarter is our most important quarter. This quarter will be our most expensive quarter if you authorize miscellaneous expense entries like this. Where is all this money going?"

"I bought a French circus."

"What? Who's running this new business for you?"

"The matter need not concern you. Just record the entry."

Madame Nemo had no need to ask the question. She knew the answer was Ida Similor. The redhead had already secretly informed her. Jim Nemo's reluctance to discuss Ida made Madame Nemo confident. Leonard's plan was working.

25

"Madame Nemo expects me to be her ally just as Marguerite Blakeney befriended her husband's mistress," said Ida Similor. "She will discover that I am playing Anne Boleyn to her Catherine of Aragon."

"Be careful with your analogies," cautioned Leonard. "Anne Boleyn lost her head. A more apt analogy would cast you and Madame Nemo as respectively Marie Louise of Austria and Joséphine Bonaparte."

"I shall not be as unlucky as Boleyn. I've already charmed Urania. She is easily manipulated. Urania will be the ideal ally to checkmate Madame Nemo."

"You need to warm Nemo's bed first. You haven't done that yet."

"It's only a matter of time. Nemo has promised to reward me once I deliver Varno."

Chantal Lebrue was sleeping in her apartment. At three o'clock in the morning, Chantal felt her shoulder shook. She woke up to behold an unexpected intruder.

"The Jade Seraph!"

"Chantal Lebrue, I humbly beseech you to be my Acolyte."

"You recruited an Acolyte without my permission!"

The angry speaker was a red-haired woman with a mouth that slightly sloped downwards. She was Darlla Rassendyll. When fighting crime as the Revenant, she was attired in a black costume consisting of a hood, shirt and pants. In the privacy of her underground sanctuary beneath the Paris Opera House, she wore a red robe.

"I'm not your slave, Darlla!" said Valorie Varno. "I'm capable of making my own decisions!"

"What value will Lebrue bring to our organization?"

"Organization? You call the Acolytes of the Shadows an organization! If you haven't noticed, we're severely understaffed."

"That's only because Judex left when she got married."

"It's been two years since Judex left. You've done nothing to replace her."

"That's not true. I recruited you."

"As your Disciple of Life. Not as an Acolyte. Chantal is filling Judex's vacancy."

"Judex was an expert lip-reader. She could spy on other people. What talents does Chantal have?"

"Due to the newspaper coverage of her rescue, she knows a lot of reporters. It will not be surprising to anyone if she embarked on a similar profession."

"You wish Chantal to quit her job as a charity worker and become a journalist."

"Not exactly, Darlla. I want Chantal to open her own news agency. To the outside world, she will be publishing a weekly news digest of articles gleamed from other newspapers. This will allow her to pump other reporters for information. She will also be subscribing to every major newspaper in Paris. Her primary duty would be to read the morning editions and clip articles of potential interest to us."

"Like stories of crimes and so forth."

"Exactly."

"Do you have a name for this proposed news digest?"

Valorie handed Darlla a piece of paper. On it were written the French words "Valeurs Sûres," which literally translate in English as "Sure Values." Valorie was also engaging in an elaborate pun. "Valeur" could be translated into English as "value" or "valor." The Jade Seraph's English first name was related to the word "valor."

"You enjoy wordplay," commented Darlla.

"So do you, A. L. Lard." Valorie was citing the mail drop employed by the Acolytes. It was a deserted law office rented under an anagram of "Darlla."

"Did you tell Chantal about my bogus law office?"

"Not yet. I wanted to clear such disclosures with you."

"I've have to meet Chantal first before we let her know our secrets. Arrange a meeting."

"That might be a problem, Darlla. Chantal doesn't know yet that I work for the Revenant."

"Why didn't you tell her? Are you ashamed of me?"

"Of course not, but you have to remember how frightening you are to the French public. You used to carve into the corpse of any criminal that you killed. Remember when we first met?" Valorie rubbed her neck. "You nearly killed me."

"I'm not like that anymore. You changed me."

"Just as you changed me." Valorie paused before continuing. "Can I tell Chantal about the law office?"

"The office is used by Tocsin and Leopard. At this stage, we can't trust Chantal not to jeopardize them." Darlla was referring to two Acolytes who spied on the Black Coats.

"Then how will we receive Chantal's reports?"

"We'll set up Chantal's news bureau in the building that houses the law office. It's within walking distance of here. Her reports can be manually picked up."

"I'm confused. The only person who can pick up Chantal's reports is Lady Leopard. You said that Chantal can't be made aware of her."

"You'll pick up Chantal's reports, Valorie."

"Darlla, I'm not exactly inconspicuous."

"You've operated in the daylight before wearing a thick dress with a veil and gloves. You can do so again."

One floor above the A. L. Lard office, another office was rented by Darlla Rassendyll. The Revenant handled the transaction disguised as an elderly spinster, Augustine d'Erlette. The sign on the office door of the business read "Agence Valeurs Sûres."

The proprietor of this new endeavor was Chantal Lebrue. At 1:30 every afternoon, Chantal was visited by a veiled woman who always left with an envelope full of clippings.

Once Valorie was late by five minutes. She found Chantal juggling three balls in the air.

"Where did you learn those tricks?" asked Valorie

"When I was a young girl in Normandy, a carnival would come every summer. They had a game where you could win prizes by throwing balls to knock down wooden pegs. I was extremely good at playing that game. I was so good that the game's operator handed me heavier balls to throw off my aim. I figured out the trick being played on me. For the next year, I practiced with balls of all shapes and sizes. When the carnival came around again, I couldn't be prevented from winning. I also practiced juggling."

"It's too bad that you didn't join a circus."

"Why would I do that? Circus performers are just as dishonest as that carnival operator."

"That's not true! Circus performers are wonderful people."

"I'm sorry if my remarks offended you, Seraph."

Despite their disagreement, Chantal and the Jade Seraph remained on cordial terms in the days that followed. Finally the Seraph decided to take her Acolyte into her confidence.

"I work for the Revenant," admitted the Seraph.

"But she's a bloodthirsty maniac!"

"No, she isn't. The Revenant kills criminals for a reason. Her life was ruined by the Black Coats. They falsified evidence accusing her of murder."

"Who are the Black Coats?"

"They are a gang of criminals with tentacles throughout Europe. Their leader is the All-Father."

"You shivered when you spoke his name."

"I've met him, but I never saw his true face. He claims to be an immortal named Colonel Bozzo-Corona."

"How long have the Black Coats existed?"

"Since the early 1800's."

"And their leader has always supposedly been this Colonel?"

"No, there was a brief period in the 1860's when the position of All-Father was filled by two men. Neither of them posed as the Colonel. One was a negligible Vicomte. His successor was the Sword-Swallower, a man with a reputation for doing the impossible."

Two weeks later, Chantal's eye caught a full page advertisement in one of the morning newspapers. It was accompanied by a photo of a young woman with long black hair. The ad read as follows.

Have you seen this woman? Her name is Valorie Varno, the daughter of Garth and Marta Varno. She disappeared from Ronder's Circus in England during 1879.
Description: 23 years old. Black hair and blue eyes. 1.63 meters in height.
If you have any information, contact the Circus of the Impossible.
Her best friend misses her.

On the opposite page was an advertisement for the Circus of the Impossible. It was situated near the Palais des Tuileries. In the center of this ad was a drawing of a young woman surrounded by depictions of animals, clowns and acrobats. The woman was wearing a ringmaster's outfit and holding a torch. A caption under the female figure read "Ida the Fire Eater."

The photo in the Valorie Varno ad resembled the Seraph. The description fitted her as well. Chantal recalled how her disparaging remarks about the circus upset her benefactor. Also the "Valeurs" in the agency's name could be derived from the name Valorie.

When the Seraph arrived at the agency, Chantal showed her the advertisement. Admitting her identity, Valorie was overcome by emotion. She gave a summary of her life to Chantal. Valorie mentioned her seduction by Leonard and her transformation into the Green Lamia.

"I was a vicious murderess, but the Revenant captured me and redeemed my soul," concluded the Seraph. "I swore never to take a human life."

"Who's the best friend in the last line of the ad?"

"Ida Similor." Valorie pointed to the drawing of Ida the Fire Eater.

"Tell me about her."

"Her mother was a fire eater. When Ida was an infant, she and her mother were deserted by her father in France. Settling in England, Ida's mother joined Ronder's Circus. Ida and I are the same age. We were raised together. We use to watch each other practice our acts. She used to always critique my razor."

"What do you mean? Razor?"

"It's an acrobatic move where the performer extends his legs forward and then pushing them upwards toward his head."

"Like folding a razor or a pocketknife."

"Correct."

"There probably wasn't much constructive criticism you could offer a second generation fire eater."

"Ida's talents are not confined to fire-eating. She trained to be a knife-thrower. I helped her develop a sensational act."

"Did she do it blindfolded?"

"Ida always felt that blindfolds were too risky. She created a spinning wheel. Her assistant was strapped to it. As the wheel revolved, Ida would throw knives close to the assistant's body. When Ida was about to debut, her assistant panicked. She refused to be in the act. I took her place. Ida performed brilliantly. All her knives were close, but I wasn't even scratched. The audience gave her a big round of applause. After my release from the wheel, I jumped into the air and did a somersault. The crowd applauded even louder. This should have been our greatest triumph as friends, but my mother ruined it. She complimented me on upstaging Ida."

"Did Ida hear that?"

"Yes, but she was very gracious. She said friends like us could never be rivals."

"Her hair seems to be light in the illustration. Is she a blonde?"

"She's a redhead like her mother."

"What are you going to do about Ida's ad?"

"I'm going to see Ida tomorrow after the circus ends its performance."

"Doesn't this ad strike you as a little odd? You vanished in England four years ago, and now Ida is looking for you in Paris."

"There's a very logical explanation. It all stems from the news coverage of your rescue."

"It isn't credible that Ida would publish this ad based solely on an artist's rendering. Your hair is totally different for one thing. If I hadn't seen you in the flesh, I wouldn't have seen the resemblance to the photo in this newspaper."

"It isn't just the rough resemblance. The newspapers identified me as the Jade Seraph. I was part of an acrobatic troupe called the Flying Seraphs. The newspaper portrait together with the Seraph name must have made Ida suspicious."

In their sanctuary, the Seraph briefed the Revenant on Chantal's discovery. Darlla was happy that about Valorie's upcoming reunion with Ida.

"I'm planning to dine tomorrow night with Judex and her husband as Augustine d'Erlette. You can have Lord Charon for the entire night. I'll take a cab to Judex's home."

"Thank you, Darlla. This means a lot to me."

"You say Ida is a knife thrower. We could use an Acolyte with that skill."

"I won't recruit her! I don't want Ida risking her life!"

"But you recruited Chantal."

"She's confined to clerical research."

"Ida's very important to you."

"I love her like a sister, Darlla."

Tomorrow afternoon, the Seraph paid her regular visit to the news agency.

"Can I come with you tonight?" asked Chantal. "I would like to meet Ida."

"Certainly not," ordained Valorie. "The Acolyte of the Jade Seraph must be invisible."

"I could wear a mask. I have a white mask from Mardi Gras." Chantal pulled a white mask out of her purse. "It would go very nice with my dress." Chantal wore a white skirt and red blouse.

"I'm sorry, Chantal. I forbid you to go."

"Will the Revenant be going with you?"

"No. I don't want a chaperon."

"There must be other Acolytes. Can't one of them go with you?"

"I have no need of their services."

That evening, the Jade Seraph wore a thick dress over her costume. Her gauntlets looked like ordinary gloves due to her wide sleeves. A veil hid her face.

Lord Charon was the only male Acolyte. His real name was Charles Blanton. He drove a coach that transported the Revenant and the Seraph throughout Paris. Tonight he drove the Seraph to the Circus of the Impossible. The veiled Seraph brought a ticket for tonight's performance.

Seated in the stands, Valorie Varno's eyes were riveted on the female ringmaster. She was clothed in a white lace shirt covered by a tight pink jacket. Pink pants and brown boots completed her ensemble. Her long red hair hung freely over her back and shoulders.

The mistress of ceremonies introduced herself as Ida the Fire Eater. In between acts, she juggled thin torches. Ida then extinguished them by putting them in her mouth. Later in the evening, she seemingly lit her torches by breathing on them. She even invited men from the audiences to come down and have their cigarettes lit by her breath.

After the performances were over, Ida retired to her private wagon. The Seraph knocked on the door. Answering the summons, Ida beheld her veiled visitant.

"I have information about Valorie Varno," announced the Seraph.

"Please come in."

As soon as Ida closed the door, the Seraph removed her veil.

"Ida, don't you have a hug for your best friend."

"Valorie! I knew you were the Jade Seraph!"

As Ida embraced her, there were tears in Valorie's eyes.

Chantal Lebrue was dining with Sigismond Trottier, the author of the Jade Seraph articles.

"There's a new circus in town, Sigismond."

"You mean the Circus of the Impossible. It's actually an old circus. It was originally called Madame Canada's French and Hydraulic Theater. The owner was an extraordinary woman. She was a lion tamer and a bearded lady. Following Madame Canada's death, her heirs couldn't keep the circus profitable. They sold it to Ida the Fire Eater."

"Do you know anything about her?"

"Nothing. Not even her last name."

"It's Similor. Her mother was a fire eater as well. "

"She must be related to Saladin Similor. He was a performer at Madame Canada's. Saladin was a superb showman but also a scoundrel. He got involved with some criminal gang in the 1860's. If I remember correctly, they were called the Black Silk Bonnet Club. Ida may be Saladin's daughter. It makes sense for Saladin to have romanced a fire eater."

"What do you mean?"

"Saladin was a sword-swallower."

Over the last couple of hours, Valorie had given Ida a guarded account of her life after she left Ronder's Circus. She was particularly circumspect regarding the Revenant. Valorie withheld from Ida the Revenant's true identity and the location of her sanctuary.

"Where did you get that lovely pendant?" asked Ida.

"It's a gift from the man I loved."

"I imagine that he's athletic and graceful."

"Actually he's frail and awkward, but I love him all the same. What about you, Ida? Any men in your life?"

"I'm being courted by a wealthy scholar. I'm not sure of his intentions, but I should know by tomorrow."

"I'm surprised that you didn't give a demonstration of your knife-throwing tonight."

"I can't find an assistant with your courage. No one else is willing to be strapped to a spinning wheel."

"Do you still have the wheel?"

"I even modified it to spin faster. Would you like to see it?"

"Yes."

"It's in one of the storage tents. Before we leave, let me take off this tight jacket."

As Ida removed her jacket, Valorie replaced her veil.

"Won't you be cold outside?" asked Valorie.

"I'll wear this." Ida reached for a large pink coat hanging from the wall. After putting on the coat, she threw a lengthy white scarf around her neck.

Leaving the wagon, Ida escorted the veiled Seraph outside. When they reached the tent, Valorie was in for a surprise. Her eyes beheld parallel bars with a height of ten feet.

"My bars! You kept them!"

"Remember how I always scolded you about your razor moves?" asked Ida.

"I've perfected my razor."

"Maybe you can give me a demonstration later."

Ida motioned Valorie toward a large upright wheel connected to a large pole.

"Would you care for a spin, Valorie?"

"Only if you promise not to throw any knives at me."

"Oh Valorie! Don't you trust me?"

"Of course I do!"

Doffing her veil and dress, Valorie's Jade Seraph costume was exposed. There was a small shelf on the bottom of the wheel. Turning around, Valorie put her feet on the shelf. Valorie's back reclined on the wheel's surface. Her arms rested by her sides. Ida secured leather straps around Valorie's wrists and ankles.

"And now I have another surprise for you," proclaimed Ida. "You can come out now!"

From behind a large crate appeared a bearded man with a cane.

"Leonard Scot!" screamed Valorie.

Leonard smiled. "When we were last together, you were in agony from poison and I was making love to Countess Cagliostro. I run the danger of sounding plebeian, but it's a small world."

Valorie's shocked eyes beheld Ida brazenly opening the sides of her coat and revealing ten knives in sheaths on both sides. Ida distanced herself several feet from Valorie.

"Start the wheel!" commanded Ida. Leonard turned a lever on the post. The mounted wheel containing Valorie spun swiftly.

"You're entitled to an explanation. Valorie," said Ida. "Listen carefully as I throw my knives. Leonard didn't come to Ronder's by accident." Ida's knife landed near Valorie's right knee. "Leonard came to find me." The second knife was adjacent to the left knee. "I'm the daughter of the Sword-Swallower." The third knife was imbedded next to the right forearm. "Leonard was also looking for a naive dupe." The fourth knife was next to the left forearm. "I recommended you." The fifth knife was near the right elbow. "Remember my debut as a knife thrower." The sixth knife was next to the left elbow. "You upstaged me!" The sixth knife was next to the right shoulder "You stole my moment of triumph!" The seventh was next to the left shoulder. "I said I forgave you!" The eighth knife was near the right ear. "I lied!" The ninth knife was near the left ear. "I've hated you ever since!" The tenth knife was above Valorie's head. "Stop the wheel!"

The wheel slowed down after Leonard adjusted the switch. When it finally stopped, Leonard manually adjusted the wheel in order for Valorie to be standing upright.

A gleeful Ida approached her captive

"Four years ago. You were reluctant to elope with Leonard. You asked my advice. I filled your head with romantic notions about true love. I knew very well that your elopement could result in your death."

Valorie was in tears. "You were my friend. I loved you like a sister."

"I'm not your friend. I'm not your sister. *I'm your conqueror.*"

Ida pulled out the knife above Valorie's head. "This time I won't miss," declared the fire eater. "My knife will hit right here." Ida touched the dark forelock of hair between Valorie's slanting eyebrows.

Ida resumed her position. She threw the knife. It smashed into Valorie's forehead just as the fire eater promised.

Chantal Lebrue was overcome with anxiety. Ida Similor was linked to the Black Coats. The Seraph must have walked into a trap. Chantal didn't know how to contact the Revenant or any of the Acolytes.

Jim Nemo was staying with his bodyguards at the Royal Palace Hotel. He was awakened by Larry Parker, a trusted subordinate.

"We received a message from the Circus of the Impossible."

Parker handed Nemo a note. It read "The angel has fallen."

"Ida has been successful," said Nemo. "As I earlier agreed with Ida, we'll arrive at the Circus shortly after dawn."

Nemo showed an expensive necklace to Parker.

"A little gift for my fire eater, Parker."

"You're very serious about this woman, sir."

"She will play the role in my life that Theodora did in Justinian's."

When Ida Similor threw her last knife, she had hurled it backwards. Only the flat handle had struck Valorie Varno's head. Rather than slain, Valorie had been knocked unconscious. When she awoke, Valorie found her arms extended over her head. Her wrists were tied together from the center of the forward parallel bar. Her feet dangled above the ground. Her ankles were also bound with ropes.

Leonard took an apple from a basket on a table. He sat down on a chair facing the Seraph. He crunched on the apple held in his right hand. His left hand rested on his sword cane.

Ida Similor was holding her scarf. She was twirling it in the air.

"Valorie Varno, you shall be my passport to a great destiny. When Leonard first met me, he revealed to me the truth about my father. Leonard wanted to recruit me into the Black Coats, but Countess Cagliostro vetoed the idea. She viewed me as a potential rival. Her death freed Leonard's hands. He waited for the proper moment to unveil my existence to his colleagues. That moment has arrived. Soon I will be installed as the reigning Queen of the Black Coats!"

"The All-Father would never permit it," challenged Valorie.

"The All-Father is in decline. The Lord of the Night is the future. Monsieur Nemo smiles with favor upon me. He needs a young woman by his side to govern his expanding empire."

Valorie had heard rumors of Nemo's domestic situation from Lady Leopard, the Revenant's spy inside the Black Coats.

"Madame Nemo will oppose you."

"Let me worry about Madame Nemo."

"You overestimate your importance to Jim Nemo."

"Do I? In the entire history of the Black Coats, only two men held the mantle of the All-Father other than Colonel Bozzo-Corona and his impersonators. One of them was my father, Saladin the Sword-Swallower. When he was a performer working for Madame Canada, he secretly married my mother. Madame Canada would have become enraged if she had learned of the marriage. When my mother became pregnant, the Sword-Swallower gave her money to travel to England. My father was supposed to join her there, but he never did. My alliance with the Lord of the Night will fortify his claim to the throne of the Black Coats. He'll be here at dawn."

"You may kill me, but the Revenant will hunt you down!"

"I hope to avoid killing you. I have a more preferable fate. The Revenant is not the only one to study Thuggee. So have I. The Thugs employed a scarf like mine. It has a weight at the end. It's a more effective weapon than your Revenant's pickaxe. Let me prove it "

Ida stepped behind her prisoner. "Valorie, your back needs a massage." *Whack!*

Ida was elated. "A most effective persuader!" *Whack!* "The All-Father almost killed you!" *Whack!* You became his slave!" *Whack!* "The Revenant almost killed you!" *Whack!* "You became her slave!" *Whack!* "Fear me as you feared them!" *Whack!* "Become my slave!" *Whack!* "Pledge your loyalty and I'll stop!" *Whack!* "Prove your loyalty!" *Whack!* "Answer these questions!" *Whack!* "Who is the Revenant?" *Whack!* "Who are her Acolytes?" *Whack!* "I'm not without mercy. I'll stop to hear your answer."

Ida stepped in front of Valorie and stared into her eyes. The Jade Seraph's response was to spit in Ida's face.

Ida wiped away the spittle. "A foolish gesture, Valorie Varno. You are the Revenant's slave. Why can't you be mine?"

"I'm... not... the... Revenant's... slave... I'm... her... friend. "

"Delude yourself if you wish. If you refuse to accept my sovereignty, I'll have no choice but to beat you to death. The Lord of the Night is willing to accept your broken corpse as the price for my elevation. If you won't be my slave, be my victim!"

"I am the Jade Seraph's Acolyte! Surrender or face my wrath!"

Those words were shouted by Chantal Lebrue wearing her white Mardi Gras mask. Deciding to search for Valorie at the Circus of the Impossible, she had hired a cab to take her to the Palais des Tuileries.

Rising from his chair, Leonard unsheathed his sword.

Chantal grabbed one of the apples in the basket on the table. She threw the fruit with all her might. It hit Leonard squarely in the forehead. He dropped unconscious to the ground. There were two more apples in the basket. Grabbing the apples, Chantal threw them at Ida. Whirling her weighted scarf, Ida easily swatted both missiles aside. Chantal retrieved Leonard's sword from the ground. She rushed at Ida. The end of the fire eater's scarf smashed into the blade. The sword snapped. Chantal threw the hilt with the broken blade at Ida. As the redhead's scarf batted the partial blade aside, Chantal ran behind the Jade Seraph. Ida twirling her scarf stood facing the duo.

"I'm going to smash your skull in, Acolyte!"

"Razor!" yelled Chantal pushing the Seraph from behind. The Seraph jackknifed her legs. The soles of her feet crashed into Ida's jaw. The redhead collapsed.

When the fire eater woke up, she was strapped to the wheel. Leonard's ankles were tied to the front rod of the parallel bars. He hung upside down with his hands bound behind his back. A gag was tied covered his mouth.

The Jade Seraph stood some distance in front of Ida. The fire eater's ten knives sat on a table in front of her.

"The Revenant taught me to throw knives. I'm going to give you a demonstration. Please forgive me if my aim is off. Through no fault of my own, I have a severe backache."

"You swore never to take another human life!"

"I'm not trying to kill you, Ida. I'm trying to miss you. My oath does allow for random accidents."

The Seraph picked up a knife. The masked Chantal handed Ida's scarf to the Seraph. With a slice of the knife, the Seraph cut the scarf in half. She gave the half with a normal end to Chantal. The Seraph picked up five knives in her left hand.

"Acolyte, please do the honors."

Chantal tied the severed scarf around the Seraph's eyes.

"I promised my Acolyte to wear a blindfold. Since I'm blindfolded, I only use half your knives."

The fire eater began to scream.

"Good idea!" said the Seraph. "Screaming will help me determine your position!

Start the wheel, Acolyte!"

Chantal hit the switch As Ida screamed, the wheel whirled her around. The Seraph counted as she grabbed a knife and threw it. "One! Two! Three! Four! Five! Stop the wheel!"

Removing her blindfold, the Seraph saw her knives perfectly placed. Two were above Ida's shoulders, two next to each of her head, one over her head. When the wheel stopped its spinning, Ida was upside down.

"Should I turn her right side up?" asked Chantal.

"No," replied the Seraph. "She must look her worse for Nemo."

"You can't leave me like this!" pleaded Ida. "Nemo will *cut the branch!*"

"What does pruning trees have to do with all this?" inquired Chantal.

"She's using Black Coat parlance for the execution of an underling who failed," explained the Seraph. "Ida, you can be very charming and manipulative when you put your mind to it. If you beg for mercy, Nemo will spare your life. However, your dream of being Queen of the Black Coats has been shattered. Once Nemo witnesses your humiliation by my hands, you will be relegated to the lowest echelon of the Black Coats."

"Someday I'll kill you!" swore Ida Similor.

"I'll never be your victim! I'll never be your slave! *But I am your conqueror!*"

After those words, the Seraph stuffed the blindfold into Ida's mouth.

The Seraph and her Acolyte reached Charon's coach before dawn. Valorie Varno instructed Charon to take Chantal Lebrue home. After dropping off Chantal, Charon's coach proceeded towards the Paris Opera House.

As he promised, Jim Nemo arrived at dawn. He was not amused by what he found. Nemo spared the lives of Ida and Leonard, but the pearl necklace became a peace offering for his wife. Madame Nemo unexpectedly benefited from this debacle. The Lord of the Night concluded that a competent wife was superior to an unreliable mistress. The couple reached a compromise. In exchange for accepting Urania's dominion over the Neptune Society's research activities, Madame Nemo would administer the division's finances. The only person unhappy with this arrangement was Urania.

At their sanctuary, The Seraph briefed the Revenant on the whole affair. Darlla Rassendyll sought to console her Disciple of Life.

"You've been through a horrible experience."

"My body will heal, Darlla."

"Your emotional wounds worry me. Ida was like a sister to you."

"My true sister lives under the Opera House."

Since Charon's coach arrived at her home in the early morning, Chantal Lebrue didn't go to work that day. She took a well-deserved rest. The next day, she returned to her news agency. In the afternoon, Chantal didn't receive a visit from the Jade Seraph. Instead, an elderly woman with a large bag appeared. She introduced herself as Augustine d'Erlette. Closing the door, Augustine made a startling admission.

"I'm really the Revenant in disguise."

"The Revenant!"

"Chantal, you have both my apologies and my thanks. I apologize for ignoring you. I thank you for saving the life of my best friend. All your fellow Acolytes know my true identity. I now unmask for you." The Revenant removed her disguise. "I am Darlla Rassendyll."

"Darlla Rassendyll!"

"You know my history. I swear by God that I'm innocent!"

"You don't need to explain. I trust the Seraph. She told me that the Black Coats chose you to *pay the law*."

"Thank you. There are some changes to your work routine. You will put all your news clippings and summaries in an envelope every day before one o'clock. You will place the envelope in the door slot of the A. L. Lard law office one floor below. If the Seraph chooses to visit you, it will be mainly to socialize. Your regular instructions will come from Feliciana Sorelli, a fellow Acolyte whose alias is Lady Leopard."

"Acolytes have aliases? I don't have one."

"An oversight to be remedied immediately. I will formally induct you as an Acolyte." Darlla took her pickaxe out of the bag. "Chantal, please honor me by kneeling before me."

Chantal did so.

Darlla raised the pickaxe high in the air. Her head gazed upwards.

"We are the Acolytes of the Shadows! We are the dispensers of justice! We are the punishers of the guilty! We are the executioners of the sinful! Yet we must remember one fundamental truth. We must never become as monstrous as the criminals we chase!"

Darlla looked into Chantal's eyes.

"You were born Chantal Lebrue. As an Acolyte of the Shadows, you must adopt a new name. Just as I, the Supreme Acolyte, call myself the Revenant, you must choose a name that strikes fear into the souls of the wicked."

"The Jade Seraph said that I should be invisible. I take the name Invisible."

"Arise, Lady Invisible."

The Heir of Pistolet

1. Woman of Bronze

"She was that terrible woman of bronze
who passes by amid our laughter
like the afterthought of fatality."
Paul Féval. *Heart of Steel*

Lying on the ground, André Maynotte struggled against the ropes binding his wrists behind his back. One evening in 1848, he had been overpowered by ruffians on the streets of Melbourne. After knocking him unconscious, the assailants had transported him to an unknown location. He was surrounded only by darkness.

The door of the cell opened. A woman of 36 years entered. Clad in a red dress, her attractive face was crowned by chestnut hair.

"Who are you?" asked André.

"I am the Woman of Bronze," pronounced the woman. "I first earned that nickname because of my hair, but it reflects my implacable nature. You killed the greatest love of my life. I shall commemorate his death by washing the ground with your blood."

"What are you talking about?"

"Have you forgotten a certain night six years ago? You tricked my lover into robbing a massive safe! You publicly exposed him as a thief! When my lover tried to escape, you slammed the door against his head! His head was crushed like an egg!"

"Lecoq! You're his mistress! You're Marguerite Sadoulas!"

"You didn't recognize me at first because you only saw me in Paris disguised as a nun. Address me properly. By marriage, I am the Countess de Clare."

"You violated your marriage vows with Lecoq. Your husband should kill you. No French court would punish him for a crime of passion."

"Much has happened since you fled Paris for Australia in 1843. Count Joulou du Bréhut de Clare acted as you suggested one year after your flight. He grabbed two pistols. Joulou blasted my skull open while he blew out his own brains."

"But you should be dead!"

"I would be if another of my admirers, Dr. Samuel, hadn't stolen the Purple Sacrament from Colonel Bozzo-Corona. The Sacrament grants incredible

39

powers of self-healing." Turning her head, Marguerite shouted to two men waiting outside the door. "Remove the prisoner!"

Raising André to his feet, the henchmen pushed him into an outside chamber. André beheld a guillotine with a basket in front.

"So this is my fate, Woman of Bronze."

"Rather fitting, André. You'll die in a manner like my lover."

"I'm not afraid to die."

"Be warned! My vengeance is twofold!"

A door opened. Two men propelled a struggling woman into the presence of the Countess de Clare. Like André, the hands of the female captive were tied behind her back.

"*Julie!*" gasped André. "Leave my wife alone!"

"You shall see her die," promised Marguerite. "You shall suffer just as I suffered when you beheaded Lecoq. Then you would join your precious Julie in the embrace of my instrument of justice." Stroking one of the guillotine's posts, she grinned at her reflection in the raised blade of polished steel.

Marguerite signaled her minions to place Julie in the guillotine. Forcing Julie on her knees, they placed her neck against the base of the murderous device. The horizontal stock was locked around Julie's throat.

"*I beg you!*" pleaded André. "*Have mercy!*"

"Mercy? Am I a nun? I am the Woman of Bronze!"

Marguerite pulled the guillotine's lever. The blade slammed downward and sliced into Julie's neck. Her head dropped into the basket. André screamed.

Reaching into the basket, Marguerite grabbed Julie's black locks and raised the head in front of a tearful André.

"Dr. Samuel claims that a disembodied head can survive on a supply of oxygen stored in the brain for up to two minutes," noted Marguerite. "Do you have any words of comfort for your pitiful Julie, André? She probably can still hear you. Alas! You're too overcome by grief." Marguerite dropped Julie's head back into the basket. "Perhaps you will comfort her in the next life. Feed André to the guillotine!"

Two days later, the headless bodies of the Maynottes were found in an alley in Melbourne. A police investigation resulted in the arrest of an innocent aborigine for the crimes. He was quickly convicted and hanged.

Two years passed before news of the fate of the Maynottes reached France. In 1850, Dr. Abel Lenoir and his wife Rose became fearful for their safety. Leaving Paris with their two young children, they eventually settled in Zagreb, capital of the Austrian territory of Croatia.

In early January 1851, a luxurious costume ball was held in the mansion of Vladimir Donevitch in Zagreb. During 1848-49, Hungary had attempted unsuccessfully to secede from the Austrian Empire. The rebellion had been suppressed by the Austrian authorities with the assistance of Croatian troops. The Donevitch family claimed to be an offshoot of the House of Trpimirović, the last Croatian dynasty. When the dynasty became extinct in 1091, Croatia was absorbed by Hungary, which centuries later fell under the dominion of the Hapsburg Emperors of Austria. Vladimir had made an ambitious proposal to Emperor Franz Joseph. In recognition of its loyal support for the Austrian Empire against the Hungarian separatists, Croatia should be allowed its own King subordinate to the Emperor in Vienna. Of course, Vladimir had himself in mind for the role of this proposed royal vassal. In order to impress Franz Joseph with a display of indigenous support, Vladimir held this elaborate celebration.

Seated at one of the tables were four French expatriates. They were Abel and Rose Lenoir, and their close friends, Roland and Nita Fitzroy de Clare. The Lenoirs were dressed as Harlequin and Colombine, the popular comedic characters. Roland was attired as Captain Buridan, the chief protagonist of *La Tour de Nesle*, a historical drama by Alexandre Dumas. Nita's elaborate costume resembled a summer cloud. The Lenoir children were not present. They were in the care of a Croatian governess.

Both ladies were attractive women in their twenties. Rose was a brunette while Nita was a blonde. Their husbands were older men in their thirties. Roland was the Duke Fitzroy de Clare. In addition to being a French Duchess by marriage, Nita also inherited via mediatization the title of Princess from her Austrian mother. Nearly all of her mother's property had been confiscated by the Austrian government, but Nita still owned a house in Zagreb.

"I'm surprised at your brazenness, Nita," stated Rose. "Both you and Roland are wearing the same costumes from Marguerite's ball."

"They're quite appropriate," argued Nita. "Don't you know what today is?"

"Of course!" exclaimed Abel. "It's the anniversary of Marguerite's 1844 costume ball! You're tempting fate, Roland. You may bring down the wrath of the Black Coats!"

"That gang of cutthroats no longer exists," contested Roland. "Colonel Bozzo-Corona is dead and buried. So is Lecoq."

"You're forgetting Marguerite!" warned Rose. "The Woman of Bronze!"

"The Woman of Bronze became a fitting sobriquet for Marguerite," said Roland. "Worse than dead, she's now as motionless as a statue. Marguerite's in a coma as a result of her head wound during the ball. She was still a bedridden invalid when Nita and I left Paris in 1846. She paid a high price for her murderous designs on my inheritance."

"I've heard rumors," added Abel. "She recovered soon after your departure. Dr. Samuel took her on an ocean cruise "

"She still would be little more than an imbecile," observed Nita.

"Don't be so sure," cautioned Rose. "Have you forgotten that strange explosion that wounded Marguerite months before her costume ball? Not only did Marguerite fully recuperate within weeks, but she bore no scars or injuries."

"What are you suggesting?" questioned Nita. "That Marguerite is some sort of sorceress?"

"I put nothing pass that she-devil," professed Rose. "Not even witchcraft."

"Nor the brutal murders of the Maynottes in Australia," interjected Abel.

"Enough of that nonsense!" pronounced Roland. "The Maynottes were butchered by an indigenous savage. Your suspicions about the Black Coats have consumed you, Abel. You had a flourishing practice in Paris, but you threw it all away in a panic to join me and Nita here."

"You also fear the Black Coats!" countered Abel. "For what other reason would you and Nita bury yourselves in Croatia!"

"Our exodus from France had nothing to do with the Black Coats," confessed Roland. "Our exile was caused by the plague of liberalism that has overwhelmed France."

"You never told us that!" said Rose.

"We wanted to avoid another intense political disagreement," volunteered Nita. "Our politics have diverged since our joint wedding in 1845. You and Abel have been corrupted by the writings of Armand Carrel."

Nita had cited a prominent French liberal philosopher slain in a duel during 1836.

Rose briefly hesitated before replying.

"If you sought to escape democratic liberalism, you didn't succeed. 1848 saw revolutions erupt in both France and the Austrian Empire."

"But the liberal contagion was contained here," proclaimed Roland. "This ball is a celebration of the defeat of Kossuth and the Hungarian liberals. Unlike King Louis Philippe, the Hapsburg Emperor understood how to crush opposition with bayonets."

Recognizing that the conversation was becoming increasing divisive, Abel changed the subject.

"Our host seeks to exploit the Emperor's victory. Look at him over there." Abel pointed to Vladimir Donevitch's table across the ballroom. "Vladimir has the boldness to masquerade as Demetrius Zvonimir, the great monarch of Croatia."

A woman arrived at Vladimir's table. She had striking chestnut hair. Attired in a bronze Grecian gown with gloves, the skin on her face, neck and arms was painted the same metallic hue.

"Look!" shouted Rose. "A Woman of Bronze! *Mon Dieu!* It's Marguerite!"

Jumping up from her seat, Rose headed towards Vladimir's table. Abel immediately left his seat. Seizing his wife's right arm, Abel spun her behind him.

"Rose, you're making a scene!"

Quickly a man from an adjacent table stood up. His garb was that of an executioner.

"Death to the Donevitchs! Long live a free Hungary!"

The executioner threw a round object at Vladimir. Catching the object, Vladimir threw it back at the attacker. The executioner dodged the projectile. It landed on the table occupied by Roland and Nita.

An explosion rocked the ballroom.

The shapely body of the Countess de Clare has been immortalized twice on canvas. Joseph Bridau made Marguerite the subject of his 1839 masterpiece, *Diana the Huntress*. In 1841, she posed as the goddess Venus for *The Javelin of Diomedes*, a painting by the great-grandson of Colonel Bozzo-Corona. Vladimir Donevitch was savoring Marguerite's physique in a far different manner than those two artists.

"Roland and Nita were killed instantly," said Vladimir. The Donevitch patriarch was lying naked in his bed. His arms wrapped around an equally nude Marguerite.

"What about the Lenoirs, Vladimir?"

"Abel received minor injuries. Djanko's body shielded him from the force of the blast. Poor stupid Bartol Djanko! He believed my lies about the range of the bomb. Djanko really expected to escape in the confusion after the detonation."

"Djanko had his talents, my love. He impersonated effectively a Hungarian patriot. Bartol also wore his executioner outfit rather well. I'll miss him. What of Rose? Is she dead?'

"She's still in the hospital. The doctors have amputated her right arm."

"Good! I hope that she lives!"

"Why, Marguerite? You hate Rose more than the others. She was the true architect of your setback at the 1844 costume ball."

"Dr. Lenoir is so predictable. He will inevitably return to Paris seeking vengeance. Lenoir will hide his wife and children from me somewhere in France. A one-armed woman with two children will be easy to trace. In time, I'll exterminate the entire family."

"You haven't forgotten your promise, Marguerite?"

"Of course not, Vladimir. Once I find the Colonel's Treasure, I'll use it to finance your bid for the Croatian throne."

"Once I'm crowned King, I'll make you my Queen!"

Leocadie Samayoux hailed a cab in Paris during 1852. She was a massive figure. Under her stage name of Amadine Canada, she was a lion tamer and a circus strongman. Although her current husband bore the surname of Echalot, Leocadie continued to utilize her maiden name. As she seated herself in the cab, the door was opened by a man with an unlit cigarette in his mouth. His name was Coyatier.

"I'm sorry, Monsieur, this cab is taken," said Leocadie.

Coyatier's response was to blow on his cigarette. It was actually a blow-pipe. An anesthetic dart imbedded itself in Leocadie's neck. After Coyatier entered the cab, it galloped off into the street.

Leocadie awoke in a remote area of the forest called the Bois du Boulogne. She was lying bound and gagged in an open coffin. The coffin was next to a freshly dug grave. Standing over the captive were three men including Coyatier. There was also a woman, the Countess de Clare.

"Leocadie Samayoux, you have sabotaged my schemes for the last time! You will be buried alive! This is your punishment for interfering with my search for the Treasure of the Scapular years ago! This is the penalty for helping your foster daughter, Valentine, to escape the Black Coats!"

The Countess ordered her henchmen to secure the lid on the coffin. After the coffin was lowered into the grave, the three underlings shoveled earth over the oblong box. Once the grave was covered with earth, the Countess and her satellites entered a coach. As the vehicle sped away into the night, none of its occupants noticed a shadowy figure observing them behind a tree.

When Leocadie failed to return home for several days, Echalot knew that his wife must be dead. Staring at her umbrella, Echalot would often burst into tears.

In his house at the Rue de Bondy in Paris, Dr. Lenoir conferred with a member of the police. Lenoir's guest was Joseph Clampin, alias Pistolet. He was a short handsome man with tightly curled blond hair and grey eyes.

"Your wife and children are now safely secured in Avignon, Doctor."

"How is my wife adjusting to her new mechanical arm?"

"Very well, I must commend you on your inventiveness. So long as she wears gloves, no one would imagine that she is missing her right limb."

"What alias did Rose decide on?"

"A variation on Armand Carrel's surname. Rose reversed the vowels."

"Madame Cerral. Very ingenious. We need to move to other matters, Pistolet. Marguerite du Bréhut de Clare has helped the Black Coats to reorganize."

"But she and her fellow members of the High Council are at the mercy of a cruel master, Cadet-l'Amour. His dominance is so pervasive that the Black Coats have been rechristened the Cadet Gang."

"We can use the resentment against Cadet-l'Amour to our advantage. Remember Reynier?"

"Colonel Bozzo-Corona's great-grandson. Reynier's an honest man, Doctor. He's nothing like his great-grandfather, the founder of the Black Coats."

"Exactly, Reynier has contacted me. He has conceived an elaborate strategy to hurl the Cadet Gang into confusion. The High Council was in awe of the Colonel until his death. They viewed the Colonel as an incarnation of Satan. Reynier will prey on their superstitions. He'll pretend to be his great-grandfather miraculously resurrected from the grave. Reynier has even stolen the Colonel's body to enhance the illusion. The skeleton of a greyhound now resides in the Colonel's tomb. When the Colonel perished in the early 1840's, the Treasure of the Scapular seemed lost. Reynier will use the Cadet Gang's greed for the Treasure to disrupt their plans."

In early 1853, the personage known as Colonel Bozzo-Corona confronted Marguerite and her accomplices. The Colonel was a thin wizened man. He looked over a hundred years old. His blue eyes mockingly scanned the faces of the Cadet Gang. He opened a golden snuffbox bearing the image of a Russian Czar. The Colonel's aquiline nose sniffed a few gains of tobacco before he spoke.

"My foolish children, you have been very naughty in my absent. You listened to the entreaties of the incompetent Cadet-l'Amour. He is absent from our little gathering. Cadet has been punished for his defiance. His lifeless body is encased in a block of ice.

"Your carelessness, my little imps, had made you vulnerable to Dr. Lenoir and Pistolet. Your enemies have been deceived by me. They naively believe me to be my great-grandson Reynier. The imbeciles! Reynier is dead by my hand. I have been impersonating him. I used Lenoir and Pistolet to help me punish Cadet.

"You all desire a share of my Treasure. For over a century, I accumulated my golden hoard. Even before the Black Coats were born in 1807, the Brothers of Ajaccio and the Camorra plundered Europe on my orders. My sweet children, you must earn the right to share in the spoils of the Treasure. You must make it even larger. For one year, you must follow my dictates. Together we shall unleash a new series of crimes. The Black Coats will regain their former glory!

"I am Colonel Bozzo-Corona! I am Bel Demonio! I am Fra Diavolo! I am the Master of Silence! I am the All-Father! Grovel before me!"

The other members of the Cadet Gang looked at Marguerite du Bréhut de Clare. With Cadet's death, she was the natural leader of any opposition to the Colonel. The Woman of Bronze went down on her knees. She lowered her head as a sign of submission.

"Thy will be done, All-Father. We are your slaves. Command us!"

"Reynier has betrayed us!" declared Dr. Lenoir at Pistolet's abode.

"I suspect our false ally isn't Reynier," replied Pistolet. "This version of the Colonel must be some secret descendent of the original."

"What are we going to do?"

"I can't trust anyone at the Sûreté. The late Cadet-l'Amour had infiltrated the police with informants. The Colonel has inherited this network of turncoats. We must recruit allies outside the police. In order to oppose the High Council of the Black Coats, we must form our own Council—a Council of Vigilance."

"Vigilante justice? Pistolet, you can't be serious!"

"I'm not joking. You're familiar with *pay the law*."

"It's the Black Coat doctrine of covering up crimes by planting evidence against innocent men."

"I've reviewed the Sûreté files looking for men who must have *paid the law*. Three men made scapegoats by the Black Coats were recently released from prison. They will be our colleagues on the Council of Vigilance."

"What are their names?"

"Leonard Manfred, Georges Poiccart, and Ramon Gonsalez. My butler will join this trio as a fourth man of justice." Pistolet opened the door to a nearby room. "Come in, my servant." A muscular individual entered the room. The bearded figure resembled a veritable Hercules. "This is Amandus," revealed Pistolet.

"You did an excellent job, Manchot, of eliminating Cadet-l'Amour," said the Colonel. "His death was particularly painful."

The Colonel was addressing an ugly man with a missing right arm. He was called Le Manchot ("the One-Armed"). His face was a mass of scars,

"The swine deserved to die. He caused the loss of my arm!"

"Today's your birthday, my child. How old are you?"

"25."

"Would you like a new arm for your birthday?"

"Only God could make it grow back."

"I'm not God, but I'm just as bountiful." The Colonel opened a large trunk. Inside was a metal arm that terminated in a smooth round metal stump with a hole in the center. "This was made by Master Chun, a young Chinese artisan in my employ. Let me strap it on."

When the Colonel had finished connecting the arm, Le Manchot swung it with great dexterity.

"This is wonderful, All-Father, but shouldn't there be a hook at the end."

"Examine the box, my lad, you'll find a hook, a sword, an axe and a mace. All nice new toys for you, my son. What shall you do for your kind All-Father with these shiny toys?"

"I'll kill for you!"

For the next year, a violent clandestine war plagued the streets of Paris. Scores of criminals were found with their throats cut. Next to each corpse was found the number "6" written in the victim's blood. Various newspapers received letters from a mysterious group claiming responsibility for the slayings. These letters were signed "The Six Vigilant Men." Pistolet, the leader of the Six Vigilant Men, had ordered the killings to weaken the Black Coats. The assassinations were performed by Manfred, Poiccart, Gonsalez and Amandus. Never were any of the members of the High Council targeted by the Six Vigilant Men.

Pistolet had formulated a deliberate strategy to divide the leadership of the Black Coats. All the High Council members had rebelled against the Colonel in the past. If Pistolet could show the Colonel to be powerless to protect the rank and file of the Black Coats, the High Council would once again turn against him. Many members of the Black Coats left France because they feared the Vigilant Men. The Colonel's weapons designer, Master Chun, fled as far as New Orleans to elude the wrath of the relentless avengers.

The Vigilant Men slew their quarries with razor blades. These weapons had been suggested to Pistolet by a notorious case in London where a barber cut the throats of his patrons. As a member of the Sûreté, Pistolet was able to mislead his fellow policemen into following false leads. He also tipped of his fellow Vigilant Men when they were in danger of apprehension by the law.

Never directly involved in the killings was Dr. Lenoir, but he provided medical assistance when a Vigilant Man were wounded. There were times when Lenoir doubted the wisdom of the Pistolet's methods. The other Vigilant Men sensed the surgeon's discomfort.

"You have qualms about our methods, Doctor," asked Ramon Gonsalez while he was being treated for a knife wound.

"Yes, I think they're deplorable."

"But you still help us? Why?"

"When I waiver in my resolve, I remember certain things."

"Such as?"

"I remember the mangled bodies of Roland and Nita. I remember my wife in agony on the operating table. I remember Julien and Remy."

"I know nothing of those two men. Who were they?"

"Julien was my brother. His death in a duel was contrived by the Woman of Bronze in 1830. Remy d'Arx, my closest friend, was an examining magistrate. His father was strangled by the Black Coats when Remy was a boy. Once Remy reached adulthood, he tried to destroy the entire organization in 1838."

"The Colonel must have ordered Remy's death."

"The Colonel did much worse. He murdered Remy's soul."

"What do you mean, Doctor?"

"The Black Coats abducted his sister when she was only three years old. The Colonel had her re-christened Valentine. He arranged for her to be raised by others. She grew into a beautiful brunette with large eyes. When Valentine was eighteen, Remy was threatening the Black Coats. The Colonel arranged for Remy and Valentine to constantly meet socially. Inevitably, Remy fell in love with her."

"But she was his sister!"

"A fact the Colonel arranged to be revealed to Remy at an appropriate time. Remy was devastated by the knowledge that he had incestuous feelings for his own sister. He took his own life."

"And Valentine? Was she party to this depraved scheme?"

"She was as much a victim as her brother. Valentine had only vague memories of her early years as a child. She's entirely blameless."

"What happened to her?"

"Her heart really belonged to Maurice Pagès, a gallant lieutenant in the French army. Like you, Maurice was made to *pay the law* by the Black Coats. After breaking her lover out of prison, Valentine fled France."

"A courageous woman. Where is she now?"

"Somewhere in South America."

Elsewhere in Paris, the Colonel privately conferred with Marguerite.

"Marguerite, my dove, you've been misbehaving. You've been organizing another challenge to my authority."

"You have only yourself to blame, All-Father. Your efforts to neutralize the Six Vigilant Men have been futile."

"I've decided that this shall be my last affair. I shall finally divide the Treasure. The others on the High Council are unworthy. Only you shall share in the spoils."

"Let me guess. In exchange for a share of the Treasure, I must divert our partners on the High Council while you secretly send your gold to Brest."

"You know about Brest!"

"I know many things. For example, you had a message forged in Dr. Lenoir's handwriting."

"My forger has been indiscreet. I'll have Le Manchot teach him the virtues of silence."

"A messenger took that letter to Brazil. It was delivered to a certain French woman. Her husband had been falsely charged with murder 16 years ago. The false letter claimed that Lenoir has evidence proving her husband's innocence. This woman will be arriving in Brest in matter of weeks."

"Leave Valentine out of this!"

"I shall not. I recall vividly how you looked at her years ago. You secretly lusted for her, but your countermeasures against her brother took precedent."

"Even if what you say is true, what difference does it make?"

"You intend to abduct Valentine to satisfy your own perverse desires. In order for me to trust you, All-Father, you must surrender someone you value to me. Give me Valentine."

"What will you do with her?"

"I intend to strangle her in your presence."

Leonard Manfred was a handsome man who knew how to charm members of the opposite sex. He had successfully wooed a maid at the residence of the Countess de Clare. Manfred's paramour kept him fully appraised of her employer's movements.

"Marguerite has left for Brest," Manfred announced at a meeting of the Six Vigilant Men in May 1854.

"Perhaps she is planning an ocean voyage," mused Poiccart.

"In my opinion, she's arranging an assignation," resumed Manfred.

"Why do you believe that?" asked Pistolet.

"The Woman of Bronze has been acting strangely. She keeps cutting heart-shaped designs out of paper with scissors. Her maid remarked that St. Valentine's Day has already passed. Marguerite's response was that she would soon be meeting an old friend named Valentine traveling by sea. Valentine must be an old lover arriving from England."

"A logical assumption for an Englishman," quipped Amandus. "Valentine is a man's name in England, but it's a woman's name in France."

"Doctor!" exclaimed Gonsalez. "Could it be Remy d'Arx's sister?"

"It must be she!" contended Lenoir.

"You're jumping to wild conclusions," cautioned Manfred.

"Dr. Lenoir is being very sound," professed Pistolet. "If Marguerite's intention was to meet an Englishmen, he would most likely disembark at Dieppe or Calais. Brest would be the most likely port for a person coming from across the Atlantic."

"In the past, we've refrained from targeting the High Council," said Lenoir. "That restriction must now be lifted. Marguerite not only butchered the Maynottes, but Roland and Nita. We can't permit Valentine to suffer the same fate. Just as four musketeers engineered the execution of Milady de Winter, we must end the rampage of Countess de Clare. "

"We never killed a woman!" protested Poiccart.

"Forget that we are dealing with a woman," said Pistolet. "The time for chivalry is long gone."

The Six Vigilant Men departed for Brest.

Vladimir Donevitch was traveling incognito in France. He was staying with the Countess de Clare at a house rented by her in Brest.

"You understand the plan, Vladimir."

"Yes, Marguerite, the Colonel plans to transport his treasure to Martinique aboard Captain Pattu's *Fanchette*. After you depart with him, I shall follow on the *Stefan*.

"Pattu will find excuses to slow down the *Fanchette*. Your *Stefan* should easily overtake us."

"Are you certain that the Colonel won't kill you before I arrive?"

"Once I dispose of Valentine, I'll be the only woman on the ship. The Colonel has certain needs. He won't try to kill me until we reach Martinique."

"My crew will overrun the *Fanchette*. The Colonel will finally meet his long-delayed death. The Treasure shall be ours, my future Queen!"

Hours later, Le Manchot had an audience with the Countess.

"The Colonel is deserting you, Manchot. Switch your allegiance to me, and I shall grant you a share of the Treasure."

"I'm your man on one condition. I want the Colonel's head."

Valentine Pagès was met by a carriage upon her arrival in Brest. For the past few years, she had been living in Pernambuco, Brazil. Because he was wanted by the French authorities, Maurice had remained in Brazil. With Valentine were Isidore and Jacinta Salazar. They belonged to a family who had been leaders in Pernambuco for generations. Having befriended Valentine in Brazil, the Salazars had insisted on accompanying her.

Valentine and the Salazars were transported to Marguerite's abode. Valentine was under the false impression that she would be visiting Dr. Lenoir. As soon as they entered the house, the three travelers were over powered by six of Vladimir's henchmen.

Each of the captives was held by a pair of Vladimir's underlings. Marguerite followed by Vladimir and Le Manchot then entered the living room to inspect the prisoners. Le Manchot, wearing a hook on his artificial arm, carried a suitcase that contained his other deadly implements.

"Countess de Clare!" said Valentine.

"When we knew each other in Paris 16 years ago, you never suspected how much I vehemently hated you. My boldness and beauty earned me the title of Woman of Bronze. I rose through the Black Coats because men were susceptible to my charms, but one man proved impervious to my beauty. Yet you were able to solicit his lust without any effort."

"Who are you talking about?"

"Colonel Bozzo-Corona. His passion for you remains unabated."

"The Colonel is dead!"

"He's very much alive. You shall shortly be reunited with him. I must remove unnecessary encumbrances. Manchot, Vladimir would like to see a demonstration of your swordsmanship."

Le Manchot opened his case. Unscrewing his hook, he replaced it with the sword.

"The Salazars have no value for me," decreed Marguerite. "Start with the woman."

To the shock of Isidore and Valentine, Le Manchot drove his sword into Jacinta's stomach. The blade sprang out of Jacinta's back. Le Manchot pulled his sword out of his dead victim

"The husband is acing hysterically, Manchot," commented Marguerite. "Please quiet him."

"May I use the mace, Countess? I like variety in my murders."

"As you wish."

Substituting the mace for the sword, Le Manchot raised his arm up in the air. It came down on Isidore's skull. The two henchmen holding Isidore let his lifeless body fall to the ground.

Marguerite turned towards Valentine.

"You're speechless, my dear Valentine. This is only a foretaste of the bloodbath that is yet to come, daughter of Mathieu d'Arx. Your entire family shall pay for its defiance of the Black Coats. Following your own demise, Le Manchot shall visit your husband and children in Pernambuco. Le Manchot has great plans for your daughter. What's her name? Leocadie? You named her after your beloved foster mother. Leocadie Samayoux is dead! I buried her alive!"

"Woman of Bronze!" shouted Valentine. "You shall die by my hand!"

"No, Valentine, you shall die by my hand. Do you really hope to kill me? A bomb shattered my body. A bullet exploded in my brain. Yet I still live!"

"You must be a witch! There are proven ways for dealing with a witch!"

"You'll never get a chance to try them."

"Marguerite and Valentine should be here soon," predicted the Colonel on the *Fanchette*. "You did well, Captain Pattu, to inform me of her treachery. Is the cannon securely aboard."

"Along with the gunpowder and ammunition below deck, Colonel. When the *Stefan* tries to intercept us, we'll blow her out of the water."

"Once Marguerite witnesses Donevitch's defeat, I shall send her to a watery grave."

The sun had set when a coach carrying Marguerite and her prisoner left for the Brest harbor. Two of Vladimir's hirelings went with her. Inside the house, Le Manchot and Vladimir were discussing how to dispose of the two corpses with the help of the Croatian's four remaining subordinates.

"The best remedy is to chop up the bodies in small pieces." suggested Vladimir.

Le Manchot attached his axe to his stump.

"My family has long had an appreciation for well-crafted blades," said Vladimir. "May I examine your sword?" Le Manchot nodded in assent. Vladimir picked up the sword from his accomplice's case.

Outside the house, another coach arrived. It was driven by Dr. Lenoir. Inside were Pistolet and the four other Vigilant Men. They all wore black hoods with the number six etched in white on the forehead. Every one of the occupants was armed with a razor except for Amandus. His weapon was a meat cleaver. The Countess de Clare was a celebrated socialite. It had been easy to trace her.

Pistolet kicked open the door of the house. He immediately spied Le Manchot engaged in his grisly work. "Murdering filth! Prepare to die!"

Pistolet fatally slashed the throat of the nearest man. Manfred, Poiccart and Gonsalez engaged the three other minor underlings. With his axe raised high, Le

Manchot sprang towards the intruders. The massive killer was met by Amandus. Le Manchot's axe clashed against the bearded avenger's meat cleaver.

Waving Le Manchot's sword in an artistic flourish, Vladimir advanced from the other side of the living room at Pistolet. "Your razor is no match for a sword."

Pistolet's response was to throw the razor like a knife. Slamming into Vladimir's right eye, the blade drove into his brain. The Croatian died instantly.

With the exception of Le Manchot, Vladimir's other allies had all been slain by the Vigilant Men. Amandus swung the meat cleaver at Le Manchot's right shoulder. The cleaver imbedded itself in Le Manchot's shoulder. Amandus pushed the cleaver deep into his opponent's arm before withdrawing it. The cut was three-quarters of the way through the shoulder. The partially severed arm dangled uselessly. Overcome by pain, Le Manchot collapsed. Amandus raised his cleaver to deliver a beheading blow, but Pistolet grabbed his comrade's arm.

"We need to find out about Valentine! Talk, Manchot! Tell us where she is, and we'll leave you alone!"

"You've to do better than that! I'm bleeding to death! I need a doctor!"

"A doctor is waiting for us outside. I could easily fetch him."

"Valentine's boarding the *Fanchette* at the harbor! Get the doctor!"

"I said that I *could* fetch a doctor. I never said that I *would*."

After the Vigilant Men exited the premises, it took Le Manchot forty minutes to bleed to death.

Holding a gun on Valentine, Marguerite forced her to board the *Fanchette*. Valentine's hands were bound in front of her. Captain Pattu raised anchor as soon as the women were aboard. Pattu instructed his crew to stay away from the boat's right side. His employer had private business to transact there.

On the dark deck, a shadowy figure waited. He stood next to a lantern hanging from a cabin's wall. Prodded by Marguerite, Valentine approached him.

"Closer, closer, my dove," ordered the apparition. "Let me look at you. You've grown into a lovely woman." The speaker emerged into the light.

"Colonel Bozzo-Corona!" grasped Valentine.

"Here, let me untie your hands. Marguerite, my sweet, you should apologize to our guest. There was no need to tighten ropes around her pretty wrists. That's better, your hands are free. Do you have anything to say to your former patron?"

Valentine spat in the Colonel's face.

The Colonel delivered a vicious slap to Valentine's face. "You ungrateful whelp! You're only alive because I spared your life as a child!"

"You killed my father! You drove my mother to a madhouse! You used me unspeakably against my brother! You expect me to be grateful! There's only one word in our language to describe you! *Merde!*"

Swinging Valentine around, the Colonel looped the rope around her neck.

"Marguerite, my angel, I made you a promise concerning this insolent slut. If you let me throttle her myself, I'll increase your share of the Treasure by ten percent."

"Will you slowly choke the life out of her?" Marguerite's right hand lowered the gun.

"Yes, my Woman of Bronze."

"Consider our agreement amended."

The Colonel tightened the rope.

Discovering the *Fanchette* departing, the Vigilant Men quickly rented a large row boat. Manfred, Poiccart, Gonsalez and Amandus paddled while Lenoir steered from the back. Carrying a rifle, Pistolet stood in the front of the boat. His keen eyes perceived Marguerite, the Colonel and Valentine on the side of the boat. Seeing Valentine's peril, Pistolet aimed his rifle and fired.

The bullet smashed into the Colonel's skull. His head exploded in a shower of blood that swept into Marguerite's eyes. As his fingers released the hold on the rope around Valentine's neck, the Colonel fell backwards.

Valentine pulled the cords from around her neck and threw them on the deck. She leaped at Marguerite. Valentine's left hand squeezed the right wrist of Marguerite while her right gripped her adversary's throat. The momentarily blinded Marguerite dropped the gun.

"If I break your neck, you still might survive, witch!" yelled Valentine. Throwing Marguerite contemptuously to the deck, Valentine kicked the gun away. She pulled the lantern off the hook. Swiping the blood from her eyes, the sprawled Marguerite saw a gleeful Valentine holding the lantern.

"Burn, witch, burn!" shouted Valentine as she threw the lantern with all her might into Marguerite. The lantern broke igniting a conflagration. As the flames engulfed her body, Marguerite screamed in torment.

Running to the side of the ship, Valentine jumped into the ocean. She struggled to swim towards the boat of the Six Vigilant Men, but an undertow was pulling back towards the holocaust. Amandus leaped into the waters. The bearded athlete reached the struggling Valentine. Grasping the young woman, Amandus managed to reach the small craft of the Vigilant Men. Pistolet helped the duo into the boat.

The wet beard of Amandus suddenly fell to the bottom of the boat. It had been a disguise loosened by the water. As the true visage of Amandus was exposed, Valentine yelled "Mama Leo!"

For Leocadie Samayoux had not perished in the coffin. Pistolet had followed the Countess and her Black Coats to the Bois du Boulogne. Rescuing Leocadie, the detective had disguised her as his manservant.

Turning to face the burning ship, Valentine muttered a final epitaph. "Roast in Hell, Bozzo-Corona."

On board the *Fanchette*, the sailors struggled to extinguish the fire. A spark fell through a crack into the cargo hold below. It landed on the gunpowder.

As the Vigilant Men were distancing themselves from the *Fanchette*, the Colonel's ship was wracked by an explosion. The *Fanchette* swiftly sank. There were no survivors.

Following a tearful reunion with her foster daughter, Leocadie returned to her husband. She explained to Echalot that it had been necessary to sever all contact with him for his own protection. Leocadie didn't want her precocious Echalot slain by the Black Coats. She resumed her circus career as Amandine Canada.

Valentine embarked for Brazil. After escorting the feisty brunette to her vessel for the homeward voyage, Lenoir discussed the recent events with Pistolet.

"Valentine can't be right. That couldn't have been the real Colonel."

"She's very adamant, Doctor, and I believe her. Bozzo-Corona may be the Anti-Christ from *Revelations*."

"Was the Treasure really on the *Fanchette*?"

"We'll probably never know. The Colonel could have been pulling an enormous bluff to ensnare Countess de Clare. It's quite possible that the Colonel had the Treasure transported out of France by another ship."

"I'm leaving Paris, Pistolet. I'll be rejoining Rose in Avignon."

"I assume that she'll drop the Cerral alias."

"No, I've proven unworthy of the Lenoir name. As a member of your Vigilant Men, I participated in dishonorable acts. I'll be adopting the Cerral surname. Promise me two things, my friend, before I go."

"Name them."

"Disband the Council of Vigilance. History has proven that all secret vigilante societies inevitably descend into criminality. If the Vigilant Men continue, some horrible atrocity like a political assassination will be committed by them."

"I accept your logic, Doctor. What is your second request?"

"Sever all connections with Manfred, Poiccart and Gonsalez. They exulted too much in their roles as private executioners."

"That won't be too difficult. Manfred is planning to return to England. He's trying to convince the others to join him there."

Joseph Clampin, nicknamed Pistolet, rose through the ranks of the Sûreté. By the 1860's, he was the head of the organization. During this time, he had to deal with the Black Silk Bonnet Club, a new revival of the Black Coats. For once, the All-Father was clearly not Colonel Bozzo-Corona. The mantle of All-Father fell on a young charismatic felon named Saladin. However, Saladin's career terminated very quickly when he inexplicably disappeared.

After the *Fanchette* affair, Pistolet married an American woman, Dora Marley. He fathered an heir, Francis Clampin.

The years 1870-71 saw major changes in the fortunes of both France and Pistolet. The Franco-Prussian War saw the collapse of Napoleon III's regime and the rebirth of democracy in the Third Republic. A brief left-wing revolt, the Paris Commune, caused the Sûreté headquarters in the Rue de Jerusalem to burn to the ground. Pistolet's wife died in the fire. Blamed for the police's inability to maintain order, Pistolet was forced to resign.

The absence of Pistolet in the Sûreté led to ominous developments. The first sign was the construction of a tomb for Marguerite Sadoulas in the Père-Lachaise Cemetery. Some unknown personage had taken advantage of the chaos in 1870-71 to create this edifice even though Marguerite's body was never officially found. Soon rumors spread through the dark alleyways of Paris that Colonel Bozzo-Corona had returned from the grave.

In his retirement, Pistolet devoted himself to raising his only child. By 1881, Pistolet's health had severely deteriorated. As Pistolet laid on his deathbed, he asked his heir to make a remarkable pledge.

"Francis, my heir, it is up to you to succeed where I failed. You must find Colonel Bozzo-Corona. You must kill him in the way prescribed in this ancient manuscript. Only then will his soul be permanently consigned to Hell.

"In order to locate the Colonel, Francis, you must infiltrate the Black Coats. You're young, but so was I when I first fought the Black Coats in 1834. My mentor then was Inspector Francis Badoît, the man whose name you bear.

"I have contacted the children of my former collaborator, Dr. Cerral. His son, Anatole, wants nothing to do with this holy quest, but the daughter, Rolande, has agreed to assist you. Let her be your conscience as her father was mine.

"Don't contact the families of the other Vigilant Men. The promise that I made concerning Manfred, Poiccart and Gonzalez extends to their descendants.

"You've read of the Revenant. Don't seek out this vigilante as an ally. The methods of the Revenant are just as deplorable as those used by me as leader of the Council of Vigilance.

"The Black Coats have made many poor souls *pay the law*. Have compassion for those unfortunates whenever you encounter them.

"Promise me, Francis, that you will follow these instructions, Promise..."

Joseph Clampin, alias Pistolet, never finished the last sentence. These were the last words that he uttered upon this earth. He never heard his heir's reply.

2. The Bounty Killers

In a deep cavern in Corsica, a figure sat on a throne. He was clothed in a long black robe with a hood. The hood was drawn over the head of the enigmatic personage. Inside the hood, the face was totally covered by a black mask. This was the All-Father, the supreme leader of the Black Coats, in the year 1884. He was known by many other names including Fra Diavolo.

The throne was behind a table. Covered by a long black cloth, the table gave the impression of an altar. Next to the All-Father's right hand were two golden jars.

The subterranean chamber was lit by torches, Black drawn curtains behind the throne hid a passageway leading further underground. A rotund man with a bushy mustache, Count Salvatore Corbucci, approached the All-Father.

"Come closer into the light, Salvatore. You have amusingly written novels about the American West, my son. Explain to me the concept of bounty killers."

"They hunt down men wanted by the law, Fra Diavolo. A reward has been posted for these outlaws dead or alive."

"Most of these wanted men must be delivered dead by the bounty killers."

"Generally a corpse is delivered to the local constabulary."

"In your novel about the Navajos, you described a similar profession, the scalp hunter."

"The scalp hunters were essentially bounty killers who worked for the American government. They collected a bounty on every American Indian killed. As proof of their killings, these slayers delivered the scalps of their victims to a government agent."

"The Black Coats are plagued by a rebellion, Salvatore. The leader of these insurgents, Jim Nemo, has ordered his followers in Paris to revive an old *nom de guerre* from the 1820's. They styled themselves Mohicans."

"I suspect Nemo's resurrected the Mohican alias to mock my passion for the American West, Fra Diavolo."

"You flatter yourself, my son. I originated this nickname. I told my followers to resist the police as fiercely as American Indians. Nemo mocks me not you. If Nemo wants his partisans to resist me like Indians, then they should be treated like Indians. Post a bounty of 500 francs for each Mohican killed."

"A scalp would be insufficient proof of a true Mohican's death, Fra Diavolo."

The All-Father reached inside the golden jars and pulled an object out of each. "This should be sufficient proof, Salvatore." Each of the All-Father's hands grasped an embalmed human head. "Your men in Paris should be able to recognize the face of a genuine Mohican. Do you recognize my two friends?"

Corbucci shook his head.

"They're André and Julie Maynotte, my son. Marguerite Sadoulas gave them to me as a gift before her immolation by Valentine. Because of this gift, I forgave Marguerite for her constant betrayal. I built her a monument in the Père-Lachaise Cemetery even though I had no carcass to bury. I even transplanted her soul into the body of Countess Yalta. Alas! Marguerite was cremated again! Who was responsible for this atrocity?"

"The Jade Seraph and the Revenant!"

"Andre and Julie are lonely. They desire company. Post two additional bounties, 5,000 francs for the Jade Seraph and 10,000 francs for the Revenant."

"The head of the Jade Seraph will be easy to recognize, Fra Diavolo, but the Revenant's presents a problem. No one knows what she looks like. Anyone could decapitate a woman and dress her head in a Revenant mask."

"The Revenant's bounty shall be paid by me personally. The Revenant's killer must present her head to me. I'll know if the bounty killer is lying. Any attempt at deception will merit death. Make your killers aware of this."

The All-Father dropped the heads back into the jars.

"Bring me the head of the Jade Seraph! Bring me the head of the Revenant!"

The sign of a bleeding severed human ear hung over the Parisian tavern called *L'Oreille Cassée*. Two men exited the alehouse into the street. They belonged to the gang of street toughs called the Mohicans. Members of this criminal fraternity often adopted the names of famous Indian warriors. These two felons had respectively adopted the nicknames of Puma, the courageous Comanche, and Two-Knife, the Apache chieftain.

They spotted a woman fashionably dressed with a fancy hat. She was an attractive brunette of 25 years.

"Sirs, can you help me?" asked the lady in an American accent. "I've lost my way."

"That's not all you're going to lose," promised Two-Knife. He grabbed her purse. "Puma, I'll take her money. You can have her virtue."

Puma responded by grabbing the woman and pulling her into an alley. Two-Knife followed his cohort to watch the assault. Suddenly a soft click was heard. Puma fell backwards. His shirt was covered in blood. Before Two-Knife could move, a blade chopped into his neck from behind. His decapitated corpse dropped to the ground.

Standing over the dead Mohican was another woman. Her height was six feet. The newcomer was dressed like a sailor. She wore a blue outfit consisting of a Guernsey-style shirt and pants. Her muscular physique was draped in a coat. Black boots protruded under the cuffs of her pants. Her brown hair was pulled back from the face and held by a chignon. Gold earrings hung from her ears. Her lovely face was marked by high cheekbones and blue-gray eyes. Blood dripped from a gold-plated sickle grasped in her right hand.

This imposing female was called La Bouchère ("the Butcher's Wife"). Despite her sobriquet, she was an unmarried female of 23 years. Her well-dressed companion was known as La Richarde ("the Rich One").

La Bouchère reached into her coat pocket with her left hand. Pulling out a handkerchief, she wiped the blood off her weapon.

"Your sickle is cumbersome," commented La Richarde. "It's very difficult to conceal. You should use an instrument like mine." La Richarde opened the palm of her right hand. Inside was a circular disk with a small protruding barrel in the front and a metal handle in the back. This instrument of death popularly called "a squeeze gun" could fire up to ten small caliber bullets.

"As you're well aware, Richarde, my sickle is easily concealed in the large pocket sewed into my coat." La Bouchère illustrated her point by secreting her blade inside her coat. From the same pocket, she removed a large sack. Picking up Two-Knife's head, she shoved it into the sack.

"Another 500 francs!" exclaimed La Bouchère as she proceeded to walk away.

"Aren't you forgetting something?" said La Richarde. "We flipped a coin to see which one of us would always collect the heads. You chose heads. It came up tails."

"The coin had two sides with tails!"

"Bouchère, don't act so innocent. Your original coin had two heads. Django replaced your two-headed coin with my coin!'

"Your deception backfired! Django felt guilty over tricking me. He used to be your lover! Now he's mine!"

La Bouchère decapitated Puma's carcass. The head of La Richarde's victim joined his fellow Mohican's in the sack.

L'Epi-Scié was not only a rival establishment to *L'Oreille Cassée*, but also the traditional gathering place of the Black Coats. Criminals loyal to the All-Father and Count Corbucci frequented *L'Epi-Scié*. Its name meant a sawed off ear of corn.

In an upstairs room called the "Confessional," Count Corbucci and his assistant, Dr. Antonio Nikola, discussed a pair of posters. Nikola was a lean man of 28 years. He stroked a black cat.

"David Burtoni did an excellent job with these illustrations," said Corbucci.

Both posters had "Wanted - Dead" emblazoned on the top. In the middle of the first poster was the picture of a woman with a bouffant hairstyle. A blade of hair spiked downward across her forehead between her slanted eyebrows. Her face was painted green and her hair black. Her eyes were blue. Below her portrait were the words "The Jade Seraph" and "5,000 francs." In small letters were these words:

Description: Approximately 1.63 meters in height. Wears a green leotard covering her arms, legs and torso. Black gauntlets and boots. Has a necklace with a jade pendant in the shape of an angel with six wings latched around her neck. A metal chain is looped around her thighs.

The second poster depicted a woman wearing a black hood with an opening for the mouth. A crimson skull insignia adorned the forehead. Underneath the illustration were the captions "The Revenant" and "10,000 francs." The lower portion of the poster read thusly:

Description: Wears a black shirt with a V-shaped neckline outlined in red. Also attired in red gloves, black pants and boots. Armed with a pickaxe and a strangling lasso.

"I must compliment you, Antonio, my boy, on assembling a contingent of bounty hunters so quickly. Tell me about them."

"There're five of them in all; three men and two women, Excellency. Major Marcus Huret was an assassin reporting directly to President Diaz of Mexico. He's an expert pistol shot. Jack Capper kills with a crossbow. Supposedly his ancestor was an assassin for the House of York during the War of the Roses. Alain Sanson dispatches his targets with an axe. Slaughter is part of his blood heritage."

"I'm familiar with the illustrious Sanson family. They were the government executioners of France from 1688 until 1847. Tell me about the women, Antonio."

"La Bouchère is a native of Magna Sark, one of the Channel Islands. Her real name is Meaghan Cullin. She claims to be the illegitimate product of a brief romance between a barmaid and an English earl. La Bouchère's a modern Amazon, a woman with great beauty and the strength of an ape. Her weapon is a gold-plated sickle."

"She must be familiar with the Druidic rites involving a golden sickle."

"The other woman is Paris Mason, alias La Richarde. She's an American from West Virginia. She got into a bit of trouble three years ago. On the anniversary of the surrender at the Appomattox Court House, she hung up a Confederate flag. When an irate Union veteran tore it down, she shot him. Of course, Paris was arrested. One of her relatives was a prominent attorney from the prestigious firm of Mason, Smith and Mason. He was able to secure bail for her. Rather than face trial, she fled the country. Her parents named her Paris because they honeymooned here. Their daughter felt it natural to flee to the city whose name she bares."

"La Richarde emulated Belle Boyd."

"The Confederate spy? I don't understand, Excellency."

"Belle became a spy due to a similar altercation with a Yankee soldier over Confederate and Union flags."

"Didn't Belle become a spy because her father was murdered by abolitionists?"

"Antonio, my boy, don't believe everything in print. That story about the abolitionists was a flagrant lie invented by Jon Dest, a fanatical apologist for slavery. Belle's father actually died of an illness while she was in Richmond. You should read Belle Boyd's autobiography."

"I'll do so, Excellency."

"How does La Richarde kill?"

"She uses a modified version of the Protector gun patented in 1882 by Jacques E. Turbiaux."

"A squeeze gun? Turbiaux didn't originate it. An ex-Confederate gunsmith named Lee Bailey made such a weapon in the 1870's, American shootists such as Gunsight Eyes and Linus Jerome Carradine utilized Bailey's invention."

"An intriguing observation, Excellency. La Richarde's squeeze gun has a unique feature. Attached to the barrel is some sort of silencer. She refuses to identify the designer of this attachment. Perhaps it was Bailey."

"Where are our bounty killers now?"

"The women are stalking Mohicans near *L'Oreille Cassée*. The men are acting upon an interesting rumor. One of the Mohicans has been publicly boasting his intentions to steal a barrel of La Frenaie wine from the local bottling plant."

La Frenaie was the most expensive beverage sold at *L'Epi-Scié*. It was a blood-red wine cultivated in the south of France, The winery producing La Frenaie was owned by a French count. In medieval times, the nobleman's ancestors had been Satanists. The current Comte de La Frenaie was a member of the Black Coats. He worshipped the All-Father.

A quartet of Mohicans had planned to hijack a keg of wine from a bottling plant owned by Comte de La Frenaie. The theft had not gone off as planned. The foursome had been surprised by Valorie Varno, alias the Jade Seraph.

Valorie had formerly been an assassin trained by the All-Father. A South American poison had transformed her skin green. Under the influence of the Revenant, Valorie had rebelled against the Black Coats. In order to make amends for her former crimes, Valorie had sworn an oath never to take a human life.

One of the Revenant's agents was Angelique LaSalle, alias Lady Tocsin. Angelique worked as a waitress at *L'Oreille Cassée*, the gathering place of the Mohicans. An expert lip reader, Angelique had observed the four Mohicans discussing their proposed robbery. Alerted by Angelique, the Jade Seraph had ambushed the Mohicans at the bottling plant. Due to her superior fighting skills, the Seraph easily knocked all the Mohicans unconscious. Using ropes stored at the plant, she tied the wrists and ankles of the criminals. She intended to send an anonymous message to the police to pick up the perpetrators.

Leaving her prisoners inside the plant, the Seraph exited by the front door. She unexpectedly met Major Huret and Alain Sanson. The Major pulled a gun. The Seraph kicked it out of his hand. A further leg kick smashed into the Major's face and sent him sprawling on the ground.

Sanson swung his axe at the Seraph's head. Dodging the blow, the Seraph quickly unbuckled the chain around her thighs. Sweeping the chain across the sidewalk, the Seraph hit Sanson's feet. He fell backwards.

From somewhere in the darkness, a crossbow twanged. A black arrow shot into the Seraph's left arm. Another arrow creased the lower right side of her neck. Concluding flight was her only option, the wounded Seraph threw her chain up in the air. A hook on the chain caught on a rooftop gutter. The Seraph swiftly scrambled up the chain. As she was reaching the roof, another arrow pierced her left leg.

As the limping Seraph retreated on the rooftops, the Major and Sanson rose to their feet, Jack Capper, the wiry archer, joined them.

"We just lost 5,000 francs," announced the Major, a stocky man with a beard.

"But we do have a prize," said Capper picking up an object."My shot that missed the Seraph's neck broke the chain on her necklace." Capper held the image of a jade angel.

"This night will still be profitable," prophesied Sanson, a massive man nearly seven feet tall. "The Seraph generally leaves her victims tied up for the police. The Mohicans must be inside."

Entering the building, the three bounty killers found the bound Mohicans.

"Shall you do the honors, Sanson?" asked the Major.

"No, not here," replied Sanson. "Comte de La Frenaie is friendly with the All-Father. We'll gag the Mohicans and take them to Tanja."

"I'll fetch Django," said the Major.

The Major walked four blocks. He came across a delivery van. Holding the stirrups of the horses in the driver's seats was a boy of 17 years.

"Do we have merchandise to deliver, Major?" asked the boy.

"Yes, Django. We have fodder for Dr. Samuel."

The Jade Seraph had broken the shafts of the arrows shortly after reaching the safety of the rooftops. With the two arrowheads imbedded in her flesh, the wounded vigilante made her way to a rendezvous with two allies.

Charles Blanton, alias Lord Charon, was the only man among the Revenant's agents. He was a coachman. It was his primary duty to transport the Revenant and the Seraph throughout Paris. After dropping off the Seraph near *L'Oreille Cassée* in order for her to secretly be briefed by Lady Tocsin, Charon had taken the Revenant to a different location. Once the Revenant had concluded her mission, she returned to the coach. Charon then proceeded to pick up Seraph where they had initially left her.

After Charon reached the predetermined destination, the Revenant looked outside the coach for any signs of the Seraph. Spotting the injured Seraph struggling to reach the coach, the Revenant immediately rushed outside to help her.

Count Corbucci and Antonio Nikola had debated the wisdom of leaving a string of headless corpses scattered throughout Paris. Corbucci had argued that the bodies must be found to demoralize Nemo's Mohicans. Nikola had countered that too many cadavers would lead to public pressure for the police to thoroughly investigate the crimes. Therefore, a compromise was reached. Only a small percentage of the slain Mohicans would be left to be discovered. The majority of the corpses would be taken to the house of Tanja Samuel for disposal.

Tanja professed to be the daughter of the Prussian physician who had been a treacherous member of the High Council decades earlier. At the age of twenty-eight, Tanja not only ran a funeral home but she also had a medical degree. To be more accurate, she had a piece of paper that looked like a medical degree from the University of Jena. Her detractors doubted its authenticity. While the original Dr. Samuel had been a homely man, this female namesake was quite beautiful. She was a statuesque blonde. Her hair had been cut short in order to easily wear *le bonnet rouge*, the red cap made famous during the violent days of the French Revolution.

The van carrying the captured Mohicans and the bounty killers arrived at Tanja's funeral parlor. Alain Sanson knocked at the door. When the mortician answered, Sanson swept her off her feet in a huge hug and kissed her on the lips.

"Another delivery, darling," said Sanson.

"How many?" asked Tanja.

"Four, and they're still alive!"

"Wonderful! I'll get to see the beheadings!"

After the bounty killers moved their captives into the basement, the Major had a question for his hostess.

"Why are you so excited about witnessing the executions?"

"There has long been a theory among doctors who examined the heads of those condemned to die by the guillotine. The majority of the victims died instantly from shock, but some heads survive on oxygen stored in the brain for a few minutes. Some heads moved their mouths and eyes. Of course, this could only be a misleading reflex action like the movements of a snake whose head had been crushed."

"Couldn't these living heads talk?"

"No, the vocal cords have been severed. I'll need to examine the heads of these Mohicans after separation."

Sanson used his axe on each of the Mohicans. After each man was decapitated, Tanja scrupulously examined the head. She took special care not to allow any blood to drip on her white blouse and black skirt. Tanja was bitterly disappointed by the result.

"No movement in any of the heads. These numbskulls most have all succumbed to shock. Why can't Mohicans have the will to live longer?"

"I'm sorry, Tanja," consoled Sanson.

"It isn't your fault, Alain. At least I saw your strong muscles in action."

Sanson and his fellow bounty killers transported all four headless corpses to a large rectangular container. Made of glass, the receptacle had a length of fifteen feet, a width of five feet and a height of ten feet. Two rows of four bottles were on hinged benches each side of the glass chamber. After the bodies were deposited in the glass cell, Tanja pulled down on a cord hanging from the row of bottles. The benches rotated forward and poured the liquid inside the bottles into the container. The liquid was a flesh-eating acid.

Underneath the Paris Opera House was the secret sanctuary of the Revenant. The wounded Seraph lied in a bed. The Revenant had used a knife to remove the arrowheads. She then bandaged the wounds of her injured comrade. The arrows had contained a poison fatal to an ordinary human. However, the Seraph's physiology had been altered years ago by the Purple Sacrament. As a result, the Seraph was able to fight the effects of the poison, but she was in a half-delirious state.

"I lost my pendant," moaned the Seraph. "Laurent gave it to me. I need to get it back."

"I'll find it for you," said the Revenant.

"Promise me, Darlla, promise me."

Darlla Rassendyll was the real identity of the Revenant. No longer wearing her mask, the Revenant was a red-headed woman with world-weary eyes and a cruel mouth.

"I swear by all that is holy, Valorie, to find your pendant."

Mercifully, the Seraph fell asleep.

"All who harmed you shall die," vowed Darlla Rassendyll.

The Major, Sanson and Capper delivered their four heads to Corbucci and Nikola at *L'Epi-Scié*. Also present was Stefano Baldi, Corbucci's manservant. A combined bounty of 1,500 francs was paid on three of the heads. The money was divided equally among the three bounty killers. Regarding the fourth head, there was a minor dispute.

"I've never seen this man before in my life," asserted Stefano.

"He was discovered in the company of the other Mohicans," said the Major.

"Don't worry, my friend," assured Corbucci. "We have anticipated difficulties of identification arising. Stefano has corrupted a barmaid at *L'Oreille Cassée*. She should be able to identify your trophy. Your reimbursement will merely be delayed a day."

"We wish to collect another bounty," stated Capper placing the jade pendant on the table.

"The Seraph!" exclaimed Nikola. "Where's her head?"

"She ran away before we could collect it," admitted Capper, "but I wounded her with two of my poisoned arrows. A third creased her."

"The Seraph could survive the effect of your venom," elaborated Nikola. "Have you heard of the Purple Sacrament?"

"Marguerite Sadoulas used it twice to cheat certain death," answered the Major.

"The Seraph once received regular doses of the Sacrament," explained Corbucci. "She has the capacity to survive injuries ordinarily fatal."

"Hey, there's something wrong here!" objected Sanson. "If the Black Coats have the Sacrament, why don't they give it to us? We'll be on an equal footing with the Seraph!"

"The All-Father's supply of the Sacrament is limited," replied Corbucci.

"The drug also has the disadvantage of driving its recipients insane," added Nikola. "Those dependent on the drug have made careless mistakes in the past when combating the Revenant."

Corbucci raised the pendant in his hand. "I'll need time to fully analyze the value of this trinket. It may be the key to netting the biggest prize of all! The Revenant!"

Shortly before dawn, Stefano Baldi was visited at *L'Epi-Scié* by his female informant. She was a petite woman with brown hair. She was able to identify the head of the unknown Mohican.

"He used the nickname of Wolf Hunter," said Angelique LaSalle.

After the sun had set, Angelique made out a report of all she had witnessed. Sealing her summary inside an envelope, she traveled to an office building on the Rue de Provence. Angelique deposited the envelope into the mail slot of a locked office ostensibly rented by a lawyer named A. L. Lard. Sometime this afternoon, the Lard office was opened by Feliciana Sorelli, the leading ballerina at the Paris Opera House. Like Angelique, Feliciana was one of the Acolytes of the Shadows, the secret agents loyal to the Revenant. She utilized the alias of Lady Leopard. Feliciana's dressing room had a secret passageway which was a route to the Revenant's sanctuary. The ballerina delivered Angelique's report to the Revenant.

While Valorie Varno slept. Darlla Rassendyll perused Angelique's communiqué.

....Although Stefano didn't explain why he wanted the head identified, I saw two posters hanging on the wall. They were like those "Wanted" posters described in the popular novels of Stanley Corbett. The posters depicted the Jade Seraph and you in your Revenant mask. There was a 5,000 reward for the Seraph and a 10,000 reward for you. The Black Coats seem to be employing bounty killers against both the Mohicans and our organization.

During her time with the Black Coats, Valorie Varno had learned that Count Corbucci composed adventure novels set in the American West. While these novels were published in Italy under the Count's real name, they were issued under the pseudonym of Stanley Corbett in foreign countries. Valorie had communicated her knowledge of Corbucci's literary endeavors to Darlla.

"So Corbucci seeks my head," murmured Darlla. *"Perhaps I shall send him the heads of his hired killers."*

One year ago, the raven-haired Chantal Lebrue had been a worker at the Cesarine Popinot Charities. While delivering money to a starving family, she and a co-worker had nearly been robbed. The Jade Seraph rescued Chantal and her colleague from the thieves. The Seraph later contacted Chantal secretly and recruited her into the Acolytes of Shadows. Quitting her job as a charity worker, Chantal now spent her days supposedly running a news bureau, the Sure Values Agency, in the same building housing the A. L. Lard office.

Known to her fellow Acolytes as Lady Invisible, Chantal's primary duty was to read newspapers for stories or advertisements of possible interest to the Revenant. She then posted her findings in a report delivered to the A. L. Lard office. Any orders from the Revenant were communicated to Chantal by Feliciana Sorelli. That afternoon, Chantal was instructed to pay particular close attention to any possible reference to the Seraph's missing pendant in the newspapers.

In her early forties, Rolande Cerral was a handsome woman with auburn hair. One afternoon, her brother visited her at her house.

"Things are going very badly at the medical school, Rolande. Those idiots had the effrontery to compare my theories to those of Moreau! I may have no choice but to resign within the coming year."

"Where will you go, Anatole? Have you discussed this with your wife?"

"Veronique wholeheartedly supports me. We could take the children back to Avignon. I'll be able to find a position at the Countess Yalta Memorial Hospital scheduled to open next year. It's dedicated to the replacement of limbs lost in accidents."

"Our late parents would be proud of you, Anatole. I don't know what they would think of me."

"You should abandon your vendetta against the Black Coats. You're manufacturing instruments of death. You're a doctor like me and father. You should be seeking ways to preserve human life."

"I'm worried about Francis Clampin. See what I'm reading." Rolande held up a copy of Jabez Marriott's *The Eradication of Thuggee*.

"At least it's an improvement on those books you used to read about weapons. What does the cult of Thuggee in India have to do with Francis?"

"Marriott was a *London Times* correspondent in India. He described an English officer who was instrumental in exposing the vicious activities of the Thugs. This officer infiltrated the horrible cult. In order to prevent the Thugs from suspecting him, the officer had to commit murder. The officer came to exult in the bloodshed. He nearly went insane."

"Francis seeks to destroy the Black Coats from within. You fear your friend is being seduced by a life of violence like this Englishman."

"Yes. Francis is being seduced in another way. Young Clampin has also fallen in love."

L'Epi-Scié was famous for its five billiard tables. The bounty killers had gathered around them to play various matches against each other. La Bouchère had challenged La Richarde to a game, but the latter declined because she wanted to savor a glass of La Frenaie. Tanja Samuel offered to take La Richarde's place.

"I understand, Bouchère, that you've been showing Django around Paris," said Tanja in the middle of their game.

"I took him to visit the graves at the Père-Lachaise Cemetery."

"You must have visited the tomb of our hidden master, Colonel Bozzo-Corona. Of course, he didn't really die in the early 1840's. Nor did he die in 1854. He's alive in Corsica."

"Actually, we visited the Sadoulas Mausoleum. Django and I did something naughty. We opened up Marguerite's stone coffin. There's no one buried inside!"

"Of course, Marguerite's body was lost when the *Fanchette* blew up. I know all the details."

"I never heard the full story. Enlighten me, Tanja."

"It wasn't until the 1870's that the Colonel explained what actually happened. The Colonel was being pressured by the High Council to share the Treasure of the Scapular with them. At the same time, the Colonel was being threatened by the Six Vigilant Men. The Colonel decided to kill two birds with one stone. He secretly shipped the Treasure through Marseilles to his stronghold in Corsica. Then he tricked Marguerite."

"How did he do that?"

"The Colonel pretended to dispatch his Treasure from Brest aboard the *Fanchette*. He fooled Marguerite into believing that she would share in his loot. She joined the Colonel on the *Fanchette*. The Colonel then leaked his supposed plan to the Six Vigilant Men. They attacked the *Fanchette*. After lighting the fuse of a bomb, the Colonel swam to safety. Both Marguerite and the Six Vigilant Men perished in the explosion."

"I never knew that the Colonel killed the Six Vigilant Men!"

"It's the only possible explanation, Bouchère. The Six Vigilant Men inexplicably disappeared after the *Fanchette* sank. Later The Colonel felt guilty about his betrayal of Marguerite. He constructed the Sadoulas Mausoleum to honor her memory."

"Django was so sweet when we opened the coffin."

"What did he do?"

"He said that only a great woman like me deserved such a burial place."

"You'll never rest in the Sadoulas Mausoleum," interrupted La Richarde. Her left hand was holding a glass of Frenaie while her right flipped a golden object like a coin. "I'm seriously considering buying it as my own future resting place."

'You could never afford to purchase the Sadoulas Mausoleum," said Tanja.

"Why not?" said La Richarde. "My family keeps me amply supplied with funds."

"You lazy pig!" shouted La Bouchère. "You remittance woman! You always flaunt your money! Your fancy dresses from Van Klopen's! Your glasses of La Frenaie! The little gold bauble you're tossing!"

"It's not a bauble," remarked La Richarde. "It's a golden bullet. It's my good luck charm."

"Your little charm is powerless!" claimed La Bouchère. "Your luck ran out with Django! You lost him to me!"

"You're merely a temporary fling," asserted La Richarde. "Django will soon realize the terrible mistake he's made. He'll be mine again."

At this point, Django entered L'Epi-Scié. The women immediately ceased their conversation about him. Django approached La Bouchère.

"May I see you in private?" he asked.

Django looked very nervous. La Bouchère was worried. Was Django about to break with her and return to La Richarde's bed?

Django handed La Bouchère a tiny box. She opened it. A beautiful diamond ring was inside. The gold setting had an eagle etched on one side and a bee on the other.

"There's no woman in the world as remarkable as you, Bouchère. This was my mother's engagement ring. Will you honor me by becoming my wife?"

"Yes!" Hugging Django, she lifted him off his feet. She planted a huge kiss on Django's lips.

Looking at La Richarde, La Bouchère was exultant. "Django and I are going to be married!"

Tanja congratulated the young couple. The blonde doctor then escorted La Bouchère to show her ring to the other female regulars at L'Epi-Scié.

"You wouldn't be so happy if you knew the truth about La Bouchère's family," La Richarde said to Django. "What do you know about her father?"

"He's an English earl. She showed me a photo of him from a London newspaper."

"Did you notice how ugly he is? He looks like an ape!"

"That doesn't matter. La Bouchère takes after her mother."

"Except for her muscles. She got those from her father. La Bouchère also has a twin brother. You've also seen his photo, he looks like their father. "

"Not all twins resemble each other."

"The blood of the Albino Ape Priestess runs in her veins!"

"What nonsense are you saying?"

"In the 1700's, an English earl mounted an expedition to the Congo. He stumbled upon a hidden city of intelligent albino apes. Being a degenerate libertine, he took an ape priestess for a bride. The nobleman hid his wife when he returned to England. La Bouchère's father is a descendant of that explorer. In the family estate in Mayfair, La Bouchère has a monstrous half-brother who resembles a gorilla. He's kept locked in a shuttered room!"

"This can't be true!" shouted Django.

Hearing Django's distress, La Bouchère rushed back to the billiard tables.

"Swear, Bouchère, swear to me that it isn't true!" pleaded Django.

"What isn't true?"

"La Richarde says you're descended from albino apes!"

La Bouchère's face contorted in rage. "Trickster! Pig! I'll have your head!" Reaching into the secret pocket in her coat, she pulled out her sickle.

"Bouchère, calm down!" begged La Richarde. "What will the Black Coats do if you kill me?"

"They'll thank me!"

La Bouchère raised her sickle in the air. Suddenly a bullet struck the blade. The force of the impact caused La Bouchère to drop her sickle. La Richarde had drawn the squeeze gun from her purse. Django grabbed La Richarde's arm and pried the gun from her hand. He placed the firearm on the billiard table.

"Django, you're my fiancé," said La Bouchère. "This woman libeled my family. If you love me, *you'll kill her*."

"Well, I'm your fiancé, and I do love you. Hand me your sickle, darling."

Picking up the weapon from the floor, La Bouchère gave it to Django. The young thug placed the blade against La Richarde's throat. Richarde's eyes were filled with fear.

"There's only one reason why I don't take your pretty head, Richarde," said Django. "You could have fatally shot my beloved, but you merely disarmed her. Now, speak the truth. Where did that story about the Ape Priestess come from?"

"I heard the story from an English sailor," gasped La Richarde, "but it was about an unnamed English baronet. I replaced the baronet with an earl."

"There's no basis to believe that my betrothed has an ape as an ancestor. You lied!"

"I lied."

"Someone please bring me a chair," requested Django

Major Huret placed a chair behind Django. The young man promptly sat down and pulled La Richarde over his knees. Reversing the sickle, Django gripped it upside down by the handle.

"You've been behaving like a spoiled brat, Richarde. You're going to be punished like one. I'm going to spank you."

As Django hit her backside with the sickle's handle, La Richarde wriggled her feet as she yelled. Laughter erupted throughput the tavern.

Count Corbucci was watching La Richarde's chastisement with great glee from the railing of the upper level of *L'Epi-Scié*. Standing next to him were Antonio Nikola and Stefano Baldi.

"That young man below is quite talented," observed Corbucci. "He defused a potentially fatal confrontation. What's his name?"

"Django," answered Stefano.

"An aficionado of your novels, Excellency," observed Nikola.

"While the activity below has been quite entertaining, I need to interrupt it," declared Corbucci. "Stefano, fetch Django for me. Antonio and I shall wait for him in the Confessional.

Nimbly walking down the spiral staircase, Stefano soon reached Django. Stefano whispered in Django's ear.

"Your punishment is over, Richarde," pronounced Django. Released by her tormentor, La Richarde scampered sway to everyone's amusement. Django followed Stefano upstairs.

Entering the conference room, Django spotted Corbucci and Nikola seated behind a table.

"Do you know who I am, young man," asked Corbucci.

"You're Count Corbucci," replied Django.

"I have other names as well. One of them is Stanley Corbett."

"You're the writer! I love your novels about America!"

"So it would seem by your alias."

"I took my nickname from the hero of *The Undertaker's Big Gun*. Of all your works, it's my favorite. You really have a great imagination."

"My book was actually based on fact. Your namesake really exists."

"Was his real name Ignacz Djanko?"

"Yes. The Americans have an unfortunate tendency to change the pronunciation of non-English names. Djanko evolved into Django."

"Your book mentioned that Djanko fled Croatia because of some political problem."

"I was very vague in the novel. The true story is that Djanko's older brother became involved with the Hungarian rebels. His brother was killed while trying to assassinate a Croatian dignitary. Ostracized by his fellow Croatians, Ignacz Djanko sought a better life in the United States. But enough about Djanko! Let's talk about you!"

"What do you want to discuss."

"You're truly a remarkable young man. You have captivated both La Bouchère and La Richarde. Let me complement you on your taste in women."

"La Bouchère and I are engaged to be marrying."

"Congratulations! That brings us to another matter. Your wife shall have to take your name. What is your real name?"

"I can't tell you that"

"Stefano!" yelled Corbucci,

Grabbing Django from behind, Stefano placed his knife against Django's larynx.

"When His Excellency asks a question, you answer," demanded Stefano.

"Understand, young man, there's nothing personal in my actions," said Corbucci. "I have to protect the Black Coats. Decades ago, a young scamp romanced the female residents of these halls. He was really a police spy named Pistolet. I must assure myself that you're not another Pistolet."

"Pistolet?" said Django. "He must have packed a small gun. I'll carry a big gun like the real Django."

"Don't you comprehend your plight? A mere raise of my hand will cause Stefano to slit your throat. What is your real name?"

"I refuse to answer."

Corbucci was about to raise his hand, but Nikola gently covered it. "Wait, Excellency. Let me look into his eyes." Rising from the table, Nikola moved towards Django.

"The good doctor has studied Asian mysticism," claimed Corbucci. "He sometimes can read a man soul. What do you see, Antonio?"

"I see great ambition and great desire."

"Spies like André Maynotte have wormed their way into the Black Coats for revenge. Do you see any need for vengeance?"

"No, Excellency, He's quite capable of vengeance, but no thoughts of revenge consume his spirit."

"What do you recommend, Antonio?"

"Spare this exceptionally brave man."

"Remove your knife, Stefano." Corbucci addressed Django. "I complimented you earlier on your taste in women. Now I commend your courage. However, your choice of an alias is exceptionally unoriginal. Even before the Civil War, the real Django established a formidable reputation as a killer. Men of lesser ability frequently assumed his name to enhance their own reputations. I will not allow this atrocious practice to be exercised among the Black Coats. If you must conceal your origins behind another name, choose a different one. You have a week to inform me of your choice. Dismissed."

Just after Django departed, Corbucci issued another directive to Stefano.

"Collect all five bounty killers and bring them here."

Minutes later, the quintet of assassins were gathered before Corbucci and Nikola.

"Gentleman and ladies," began Corbucci. "We're about to begin on a grand enterprise, the final destruction of the Revenant. I expect all of you to put aside personal differences and cooperate with each other. You all shall share equally in the spoils."

"10,000 francs equally divided is only 2,000 francs a piece," computed the Major. "It's not worth the risk."

"I have the All-Father's authority to raise the bounty to 30,000 francs," divulged Corbucci. "That raises the stakes to 6,000 francs per person."

"The All-Father won't release the money until he personally inspects the head," indicated Sanson.

"If you're successful, His Excellency will arrange for you all to accompany the Revenant's head to Corsica," added Nikola.

"I was once part of a trio of assassins in Mexico," recalled the Major. "I returned to France after my two comrades died seeking Benito Juarez's gold."

"What's your point, Major," asked Corbucci.

"Some of us may die tomorrow."

"The shares of any unfortunate casualties will be divided among the survivors," decreed Corbucci.

"What if someone's wounded?" said Sanson.

"Django's van could be posted a block away," proposed the Major. "He could transport anyone wounded to Dr. Samuel."

"An excellent idea!'" proclaimed Corbucci. "To quote General Sherman: 'An army is a collection of armed men obliged to obey one man. Every change in the rules which impairs the principle weakens the army.' I'm your general. You must obey my dictates to the letter."

"Command us, General," concurred the Major.

Corbucci displayed the jade pendant. Its chain had been repaired. "I've arranged for an advertisement to be posted tomorrow in the personal columns of every major newspaper in Paris. It suggests that the pendant will be available for recovery at the place where it was lost. This newspaper item will draw the Revenant into a trap tomorrow night."

"How can we be so sure that the Revenant will take the bait?" asked La Bouchère.

"A group of Black Coats once assaulted a pair of charity workers. The Jade Seraph interrupted the robbery. During the ensuring struggle, she threatened to break the arm of anyone who touched her pendant. Clearly this object has value for her. All our intelligence confirms an intense friendship between Revenant and the Seraph. The Revenant will surely want to recover the pendant for her friend."

"What about the Seraph?" said Capper. "She might have recovered from the poison by tomorrow. We might be facing two opponents."

"Based on my medical knowledge of the Purple Sacrament, the Seraph won't recover for at least three more days," replied Nikola.

"Do you own a white dress, Richarde?" asked Corbucci.

"Yes."

"Wear it tomorrow night at the entrance to the bottling plant. White will make you more conspicuous in the dark. You shall also be wearing this pendant."

"If you want me to act as decoy, then my share of the bounty should be greater," suggested La Richarde.

"What a greedy pig!" shouted La Bouchère

"You stupid ape!" howled La Richarde.

"Cease this bickering!" ordained Corbucci. "Richarde, do as you're told, or I'll *cut the branch*." Corbucci used the Black Coat euphemism for murdering a subordinate whose services were no longer needed.

"Forgive my impertinence!" implored La Richarde.

"You're forgiven," said Corbucci. "Are any of you familiar with concept of running the gauntlet?'

"I am," asserted the Major. "It's when a person is forced to run through a group of warriors."

"I intend to create my own version of the gauntlet. There are four stories in the bottling plant. The bottom level has the offices and equipment while the upper levels are mainly used for storage. Four of you will be assigned a floor. After luring the Revenant inside, La Richarde will take the stairs to the top floor. As the Revenant enters each floor, the posted bounty killer will attack the Revenant."

"We could all attack the Revenant at once," recommended Sanson.

"You'll only get in each other's way," contended Corbucci. "Of course, the bounty killer at the highest level should have La Richarde to assist him. Those in the higher levels will have a greater chance of survival." He pulled out a deck of cards. "In order to be fair, the four of you will each pick a card. The floors will be assigned from highest card to lowest."

The Major, Sanson, Capper and La Bouchère picked cards. La Bouchère drew the high card.

"Can't I try to shoot the Revenant with my squeeze gun at the entrance?" asked La Richarde.

"Give me your gun," ordered Corbucci.

La Richarde surrendered her weapon. Corbucci examined it.

"A squeeze gun is only really effective at short range. If you try to kill the Revenant at the entrance, we run the risk of our adversary executing you quickly. If the Revenant removes the pendant from your corpse, she will have no reason to run the gauntlet."

"I understand, Count," said La Richarde. "May I have my gun back?"

"No, you may not. You may panic and try to kill the Revenant prematurely. Your colleague will be holding your gun for you on the top floor." Corbucci handed La Richarde's gun to La Bouchère.

"The Count is just trying to help you, Richarde," said La Bouchère. "Unarmed, you'll have greater incentive to run for your life."

After the bounty killers had left, Corbucci made an observation.

"Both women will be waiting at the last level. The animosity between them could help the Revenant "

"I disagree," retorted Nikola. "I believe it guarantees your plan's success."

"How so?"

"Ever since my training by the Oracle of Benares, I've been having vaguely prophetic dreams. I once dreamt that the Revenant was lying covered in blood with a shadowy figure standing over her. The figure was laughing. The voice belonged to a woman. The Revenant must be destined to be slain by a woman."

Late that night, Django made love to La Bouchère in her bed. A book lay on the floor. It was a verse play that La Bouchère had given her lover to read. Its title was *Le Roi en Jaune*.

"I have the top floor," revealed La Bouchère.

"You always want to be on top."

"You're like the Phantom of Truth in the play, Django. You unlock all my secret cravings."

"I'm more than a Phantom. I never told you about my parentage. My father was a most extraordinary man."

So far Chantal Lebrue had read six morning newspapers and found the same posting in the personal columns:

JADE SERAPH – a valuable pendant was lost Tuesday night. Made of jade, it depicts an angel with six wings. If the owner wishes to reclaim this article, be at the place where it was lost at midnight.

Chantal cut out the advertisement. After she finished typing her report for the Revenant, she included it and the newspaper clipping in a sealed envelope delivered to the A. L. Lard office. In the afternoon, Feliciana Sorelli took Chantal's report to the Revenant at the Paris Opera House.

Dr. Nikola's diagnosis had underestimated Valorie Varno's recovery. Her recuperation had been speeded up once the Revenant summoned Laurent Remy, Valorie's lover. Laurent was also the personal secretary to the Director of the Paris Opera. Although he had originally held that position under Firmin Richard, Remy currently answered to Pedro Gailhard, the new Director. In addition to being a famous opera singer, Gailhard was also Laurent's distant cousin. Because of their family bond, Remy had been able to secure from Gailhard a week of unpaid leave. While he was supposedly handling some private financial matter, Remy had been inside the sanctuary nursing Valorie back to health.

"Don't worry about the loss of the pendant, my precious Valorie. Our love resides in our hearts not inside external objects."

As Laurent consoled Valorie, Darlla Rassendyll contemplated her strategy in her private chambers. She stared long at her pickaxe. She had deliberately kept secret from Valorie the advertisement unearthed by Chantal. Darlla had promised earlier to retrieve the pendant. She changed into her Revenant costume. Holstered in loops in Darlla's belt were her pickaxe and her Punjabi lasso.

On the top floor of the bottling plant, La Bouchère patiently waited. She had discovered hidden under a canvas a large barrel of La Frenaie. She also found a pair of glasses. Some workers in the bottling plant must have concealed the barrel to secretly sample the wine.

Near the entrance was La Richarde in a white dress. Valorie's pendant graced her neck. As midnight passed, La Richarde noticed a coach approaching She memorized the features of the driver holding the reins. As La Richarde's eyes were focused on the driver, a dark-clad passenger leaped out of the passing coach. The Revenant tackled La Richarde.

Pinned to the ground, La Richarde felt the Revenant's red-gloved hands around her throat. "You stole something from my friend," hissed the Revenant. "Tell me why I shouldn't snap your neck."

La Richarde was missing her squeeze gun, but she had a small pepper shaker hidden in her right palm. She sprayed the pepper into the Revenant's face. The irritation in her eyes and nose caused the Revenant to loosen her grip. Pushing the Revenant aside, La Richarde leaped to her feet. She ran into the bottling plant.

Regaining her senses, the Revenant pulled her pickaxe out of her belt. She entered the site of Corbucci's gauntlet. Her pursuit of La Richarde was blocked by Alain Sanson.

With his axe, Sanson swung at the Revenant's head. She blocked the blow with her pickaxe. The handles of the weapons were locked together. With all his might, the gigantic Sanson pushed to the side. Wrenched from the Revenant's hands, the pickaxe went flying on the floor as the Revenant was pushed against a table of empty bottles. Reaching behind her to grab a bottle by its neck, she hid it behind her back.

"You're not the first woman to be killed by my family," said Sanson. "My ancestor slew Marie Antoinette and Charlotte Corday." The giant raises his axe high in the air, "I'm going to spit your skull!"

The Revenant broke the bottle. She slashed at Sanson's throat before he could strike. Sanson fell dead from a severed jugular.

On the second floor, John Capper waited with a quiver of twenty poisoned arrows.

Reaching the top floor, La Richarde breathed a sigh of relief. "That mad-woman nearly killed me! Hand me my gun!"

The Revenant took the stairs to the second floor.

A black arrow swooshed out of the darkness. She knocked it aside with her pickaxe. Another arrow followed. The Revenant deflected it again with her pickaxe. On her tenth deflection, the Revenant knew she was weakening. She gambled by throwing her pickaxe in the direction of the archer. Another black arrow zoomed from the shadows. Slapping her hands together, the Revenant caught the arrow's shaft before its head could pierce her heart.

The flood of arrows ceased. The Revenant pulled Capper's corpse out of a blackened corner of the room. The tip of her pickaxe was imbedded in his skull. Pulling out her pickaxe, she went toward the stairs.

Two levels above, La Bouchère tightened her hold on her sickle while La Richarde clutched her squeeze gun. Because the room was stuffy, they had opened a window.

As soon the Revenant reached the third floor, two bullets blasted into her body, The Revenant fell forward. The blood of Darlla Rassendyll soaked into the ground.

Holding a smoking gun, Major Huret stood over the fallen vigilante. "You were overrated," he said. Standing at the bottom of the stairs leading upward, The Major shouted to his two female collaborators.

"The Revenant's dead! Come down, ladies!'

On the top floor, La Richarde put down her squeeze gun on table. She lift-ed the lid off the wine barrel and tilted it on the side. La Richarde slipped one glass into the wine followed by the other. Holding both glasses, she offered one to La Bouchère.

"Let us put pass arguments aside and drink to our good fortune," said La Richarde.

"Give the other glass to the Major. He deserves it."

Still holding her sickle, La Bouchère went downstairs. With both glasses in her hands, La Richarde trailed behind her.

On the third floor, the Major took the glass offered him by La Richarde. "A toast, my dear ladies, to the bounty. 10,000 francs each!" La Richarde and the Major drained their glasses.

"Are you sure Sanson and Capper are dead?" asked La Bouchère. "They may only be wounded "

"Why don't you go below and see," suggested La Richarde.

"Have you forgotten our coin toss? I have to remove the Revenant's head."

"All right!" La Richarde walked towards the stairs. "I'll do it."

As La Richarde discovered the bodies below, La Bouchère turned over the blood-soaked Revenant.

"Shouldn't you unmask her first?" questioned the Major. "I want to see the face underneath—"

The Major never finished his sentence because the point of La Bouchère's sickle penetrated his heart.

"I'm sorry, Major, but I want all the 30,000 francs for me and Django, I'll blame your death on the Revenant."

La Richarde returned. She saw the slain Major and La Bouchère's bloody sickle.

"You're next! Richarde!"

La Richarde rushed up the stairs into the room where she had left her squeeze gun. Her bloodthirsty nemesis stampeded closely behind her.

On the top floor, La Richarde seized the circular lid near the wine barrel. She quickly turned around to use the lid as a shield. La Bouchère's sickle smashed into the lid. The blade got stuck in the wood. La Bouchère's twisted the lid out of La Richarde's hand. With the sickle still jammed inside, La Bouchère dropped the lid.

"I'll kill you with my bare hands!"

La Richarde turned around towards the table where her gun rested, but her opponent was quicker. La Bouchère gripped La Richarde from behind in a brutal neck hold. Pushing her captive's head down towards the open barrel, La Bouchère ranted,

"You greedy pig! You love La Frenaie! Greedy pigs drown!"

"So do stupid apes!" snarled La Richarde's as her hands went behind La Bouchère's head to grab her chignon. La Richarde flipped La Bouchère in front of her. La Bouchère was propelled into the wine barrel. Her legs extended upwards in the air. They writhed helplessly. Grabbing her rival's legs, La Richarde pushed downwards.

"Drink! Drink! Enjoy the wine!"

The legs of La Bouchère ceased thrashing. La Richarde pulled her foe out of the barrel. Gazing down on the asphyxiated Amazon, La Richarde smiled.

"The wine will console your thirst in Hell! I now have both the 30,000 and Django!"

Some distant away, a shiver went down Django's spine. He had a premonition that something awful befell his fiancée.

During her tenure with the Black Coats, La Richarde had learned the concept of *pay the law* all too well. In order to win back Django, she would have to blame La Bouchère's demise on the Revenant. La Richarde intended to move the Revenant's body upstairs.

The false story would be as follows. The Revenant slew the Major with her pickaxe. She then ran to the top floor. The vigilante knocked the squeeze gun out of La Richarde's hand. As La Richarde scrambled to retrieve her weapon, La Bouchère and the Revenant fought. The battle concluded with La Bouchère's drowning. La Richarde then fatally shot the Revenant.

On the third floor, La Richarde grabbed the Revenant. Before she could move the body upstairs, La Richarde heard cries of "Bouchère!" from downstairs. Django had arrived! La Richarde quickly amended her plans. She hid the Revenant behind a bunch of crates. La Richarde ran down the stairs. She met Django between the first and second floors.

"They're all dead!" yelled La Richarde.

Django rushed to the top floor. He knelt beside the body of his fiancée. Cradling La Bouchère's head in his lap, Django wept.

La Richarde entered the room.

"How did it happen?" asked Django.

"The Revenant knocked my gun out of my hand. Before I could retrieve it, she drowned La Bouchère. I shot The Revenant twice, but she jumped outside."

La Richarde pointed at the open window. "The Revenant must be lying dead somewhere outside. If you go outside and look for her, I'll split the bounty with you!"

"Bounty! I don't care about money!" Django's tearful eyes looked at La Bouchère's face. "I only cared for her." Django put his arms under La Bouchère. Although only a male of medium height, he lifted her off the floor.

"What are you doing?" asked La Richarde.

"I'm taking her to Tanja."

"Tanja can do nothing for her!"

"Tanja can embalm her. I don't want her beauty to decay."

Cradling La Bouchère in his arms, Django went down the stairs to deliver his burden to the van outside.

La Richarde pried La Bouchère's sickle loose from the barrel lid. She went down to the floor where the Revenant was. Locating the Revenant behind the crates, La Richarde bent down. Yanking the Revenant head upwards, she pulled off the Revenant's mask.

"Darlla Rassendyll!" La Richarde recognized Darlla because her photo had appeared in the newspapers when she had been falsely accused of murder and treason.

La Richarde placed the sickle under the Revenant's neck. This was the moment that the Revenant moaned.

Charles Blanton's carriage was parked four blocks away. An observant man, Blanton saw the woman in white from the bottling plant approaching him. She walked up to the coach.

"My name is Francis Clampin," said La Richarde. "I'm not your enemy. The Revenant has been gravely wounded."

Blanton knew all the subterranean entrances to the Revenant's sanctuary under the Paris Opera House. Early the next morning, Laurent and Valorie were surprised by the coachman.

"The Revenant is dying!"

Valorie quickly donned a dress with a thick veil and gloves. Together with Laurent and Blanton, she left the sanctuary.

Blanton's coach arrived at the house of Dr. Rolande Cerral. Inside Valorie and Laurent were taken to the Revenant's bedside. An unconscious Darlla Rassendyll rested with a bandaged shoulder.

"She was shot twice in the shoulder," explained Rolande. "I removed the bullets, but your friend lost a lot of blood. I fear that she'll expire in a few hours."

"I won't let her die!" said Valorie. "Can't you give her a transfusion?"

"Transfusions are unreliable. They often result in the death of the patient."

Rolande spoke the truth. The year was 1884. Even though the first transfusion occurred in 1818, Karl Landsteiner didn't discover human blood groups until 1901.

"We have to risk it!" argued Valorie. "I'll be the donor."

Rolande performed the transfusion. Fortunately, Valorie was a compatible donor for Darlla. Valorie's blood had been enhanced by the Purple Sacrament. The recuperative powers of that drug circulated in Darlla's veins. Darlla didn't die. She embarked on the slow road to recovery.

As Darlla rested, Rolande talked to Valorie and Laurent.

"Francis left this with me." Rolande handed the jade pendant to Valorie. "Let me apprise you both of my friend's true past. She promised at her father's deathbed to kill Colonel Bozzo-Corona. In order to gain access to the All-Father, Francis penetrated the Black Coats in the false identity of Paris Mason, alias La Richarde. It wasn't difficult for her to pose as an American, Her mother, the former Dora Marley, was the daughter of a prominent lawyer. Francis took the surname Mason from this book on the American legal system by Randolph Mason. Francis also read *Belle Boyd in Camp and Prison*, the autobiography of a Confederate secret agent. Francis modified an incident in Belle Boyd's past to justify the flight of her La Richarde persona from America. Besides being a doctor, I'm a competent mechanic. I equipped a Protector gun with a silencer for Francis."

"Where is Francis now?" asked Laurent.

"After she and Blanton brought the Revenant here, Francis returned to *L'Epi-Scié* to report to Count Corbucci."

As La Richarde, Francis told the distorted tale of a seriously wounded Revenant escaping by a window. She demanded to be awarded the bounty, but Corbucci refused. He would need the Revenant's head to confirm her death. Corbucci dispatched Stefano Baldi and other Black Coats to clean up the mess at the La Frenaie bottling plant. The bodies of Huret, Capper and Sanson were taken to Dr. Samuel's funeral parlor. The cadavers were fed to the acid vat.

Tanja Samuel also embalmed La Bouchère's remains. One night, Django secretly visited the Sadoulas Mausoleum in the Père-Lachaise Cemetery. He placed his betrothed's corpse inside Marguerite's empty coffin. Before replacing the lid, he kissed the forehead of La Bouchère.

"Rest, my darling, in a memorial worthy of you."

As a result of the blood transfusion, Dr. Cerral's patient survived. After Darlla Rassendyll regained conscious, she was made cognizant of the true facts by Rolande. A day later, Francis visited Darlla's bedside.

"Before his death, my father gave me a medieval manuscript identifying a demon of avarice who visits the earth at certain times in history. This demon promotes the worship of gold. The All-Father is this demon. Just as a werewolf is vulnerable to a silver bullet, this gold-demon can be slain by a golden bullet such as this."

Francis showed Darlla the bullet that she tosses as La Richarde.

"With all due respect to your father, Francis, he allowed superstition to warp his judgment. The All-Father is just as human as you and I."

"But the All-Father is over 150 years old. In 1854, my father shot him in the skull. An explosion then decimated his body. Yet he revived the Black Coats in the 1870's."

"The All-Father has been impersonated by various men throughout history. Your father must have really killed one of these pretenders. A totally different man is the current All-Father."

"Are you so sure? Marguerite Sadoulas survived a bullet wound and an explosion. Could not the All-Father have done the same?"

Darlla Rassendyll didn't have an adequate retort.

"When the All-Father offered a bounty on your head," resumed Francis, "I saw an opportunity to finally meet and slay the All-Father, I became a bounty killer. My profession was rather appropriate because one of my American cousins is a bounty killer in Arizona. I excused the killings of Mohicans on the grounds that they were criminals. I viewed you as a fanatical killer no better than the felons that you pursued. Your head would be my means to fulfill my oath to my father."

"Yet you saved me. What changed your mind?"

"When I unmasked you, I recognized you."

"But I've been publicly branded a criminal."

"Like the Vigilant Men organized by my father, I realized that you had been made to *pay the law* by the Black Coats. I couldn't take a life ruined by the Black Coats. My father wanted me to show compassion to those forced to *pay the law*. My dual life was turning me into someone evil. A strange madness engulfed me. Sparing you allowed me to regain my sanity."

"What do you intend to do now?"

"I'll continue to fraternize with the Black Coats, but I'll no longer be a bounty killer."

Darlla and Francis had other talks in the days that follow. Three weeks after her initial arrival at Rolande's abode, Darlla was ready to leave. She made a final farewell to Francis and Rolande.

"My father forbade me to associate with you, Revenant, but I must use my own judgment," said Francis. "Rolande and I have reached a similar conclusion. May we join your Acolytes?"

Darlla Rassendyll instructed the two women to kneel before her. Her pick-axe, which Francis had removed from the bottling plant, was raised high in the air. Darlla began the rite of initiation.

"We are the Acolytes of the Shadows! We are the dispensers of justice! We are the punishers of the guilty! We are the executioners of the sinful! Yet we must remember one fundamental truth. We must never become as monstrous as the criminals we chase!"

The Revenant gazed downwards into the eyes of Francis Clampin.

"You were born Francis Clampin. As an Acolyte of the Shadows, you must adopt a new name. Just as I, the Supreme Acolyte, call myself the Revenant, you must choose a name that strikes fear into the souls of the wicked."

"I choose to honor my father. I shall be Pistolet."

The Revenant shifted her eyes towards the other candidate.

"And you, Rolande Cerral, who was born Rolande Lenoir. What name do you choose?"

"I am a surgeon. Evil is a disease that must be extinguished with fine precision to avoid harm the innocent. My profession uses a scalpel to cut accurately. I shall be Scalpel."

"Arise, Lady Pistolet and Lady Scalpel."

The Acolytes of the Shadows were not the only group who enhanced its strength that day. The Black Coats made a momentous decision that would affect scores of lives.

After a prolonged absence, Django reemerged at *L'Epi-Scié*. He requested an audience with Count Corbucci and Dr. Nikola. It was granted.

"You deserted your post on the night of the gauntlet," scolded Corbucci. "When an aide-de-camp of the Black Coats decamps without permission, I would normally *cut the branch*. However, I am not without compassion. I too lost the woman of my dreams prematurely. Your dereliction of duty is forgiven, young man."

"Thank you, Excellency. When last we talk, you wanted to choose a new name. I have taken the surname of Boucher."

"An admirable choice, young man. You seek to honor the memory of your late lamented lover."

Corbucci was commenting on "boucher" being French for "butcher" just as "bouchère" means "butcher's wife."

"What about your first name?"

"I would have been killed by Stefano if not for Dr. Nikola. With his permission, I would like to take the French equivalent of his first name."

"Granted," said Nikola.

"Antoine Boucher!" announced Corbucci. "Truly the name of a great man! When Stefano visited the La Frenaie premises, he retrieved this object. Since it was the property of your late fiancée, I'm surrendering it to you."

Corbucci handed over Meaghan Cullin's sickle.

"I'm afraid that the gold plating has been damaged severely," stated Nikola. "You should either have the blade re-gilded or scrape off the remaining paint."

"I shall have the gold paint scrapped off," decided the newly christened Antoine Boucher. "I want the blade pure when I baptize it with the blood of an enemy."

Nikola stared into the young man's eyes.

"I now see vengeance in your soul, Monsieur Boucher. Perhaps, Excellency, this is the man we seek for our little project."

Corbucci made a startling proposal.

"Young man, Antonio and I have longed discussed taking a talented fellow and training him to be the perfect assassin. Are you interested?"

"Shall I be taught how to properly use this?" asked Boucher holding up the sickle.

"That and many other weapons as well," guaranteed Nikola.

"Your sole goal in life will be to spread terror!" promised Corbucci.

The young man's face became grim. All color drained out of it. His visage resembled a pallid mask.

"I accept the destiny you and the Black Coats offer, Count Corbucci. *Make me a Lord of Terror!*"

The Face of Fu Hsi

Approaching the age of thirty in 1863, Emily Caber was an unmarried woman with three young children. Five years ago, she had been a singer at the Grayson Music Hall in London. Emily had originally been engaged to a railway station master. The nuptials never happened because Emily had been romanced by her fiancé's older brother, a professor at the University of Manchester. Having made prudent investments in the stock market, the professor was much wealthier than his younger sibling. Installed in a house in Manchester, Emily was the scholar's secret mistress.

Emily was an extremely attractive redhead, but her judgment didn't match her beauty. She was extremely impractical. Kept cloistered by her lover, she craved human companionship. While her housekeeper minded her children one afternoon, Emily had gone grocery shopping. At the market, she had befriended a younger woman. Giving her housekeeper the night off, Emily had invited her new friend, Minnie Warrender, to have dinner with her. Minnie had been accompanied by her servant, Mola Singh.

After their meal, Emily and Minnie sipped tea together. Minnie was a dark-haired Eurasian woman of 21 years. As the two ladies conversed, Mola Singh played with Emily's two sons, James and Emile. They were three-year old twins. Emily's youngest child, a one-year girl, was asleep in another room.

"That's a lovely pin in your hair," said Emily. She was commenting on a piece of jewelry adorning the front of Minnie's raven locks. The ornament was a golden circle intersected by a scepter.

"My pin is a family heirloom from Syria," explained Minnie. "Before the birth of Christ, one of my ancestors was training to be the high priestess of Astarte in Damascus. A rebellion led by a follower of Jehovah forced my ancestor to flee Syria. Eventually settling in India, she became the priestess of a different goddess."

"Your ancestors came from Syria and India, but your surname is English."

"My mother was an Englishwoman, Her name was Sarah Warrender. I have taken her surname during my sojourn in Europe."

"And your father?" asked Emily.

"He was Achmet Genghis Khan, a distant cousin of the Mogul Emperors."

"Was he a Maharajah?"

"He was a deposed Maharajah. Our ancestral kingdom is in northern India near the Yamuna River. My father belonged to a religious sect persecuted by the British authorities. In 1828, an intolerant army officer, Colonel Savage, slew my grandfather. My father was then a young boy. Denied his ascension to the throne, my father was forced to flee with loyal retainers to the Central Provinces. Are you familiar with the Sepoy Revolt?"

"It happened some years ago. The Indians rebelled."

"I was 15 years old at the time. My father was able to regain possession of the royal palace in northern India. For one brief glorious moment, he was Maharajah. Unfortunately, he perished in combat against the colonial government. In the chaos of the fighting, my mother disappeared. A German merchant took pity on me. He took me to Europe to act as a companion to his own daughter. Poor sweet Gretchen! She was very fragile. Gretchen died at a young age."

"How did you come to England?"

"Following Gretchen's death, I answered an advertisement for a governess in Yorkshire. I tutored three young children. Alas! One of my charges, Ethel, was just as fragile as Gretchen. Her life was very short. Last year, I was contacted in Yorkshire by Mola Singh. His uncle had been my tutor in India. My father's colleagues have been looking for me. For the last year, I have been living with Mola in Liverpool. Arrangements are being made for my journey to India. We shall be returning to the land of my ancestors very soon to claim my inheritance."

"Will you be allowed to sit on the throne?"

"The British Raj won't permit it, but my father's associates will allow me to succeed him as the Supreme Soobehdar."

"Soobehdar?"

"It's a religious title. That's why I've come to Manchester. I must perform a ritual of thanks to the divinity that I revere."

"What does this ritual consist of?"

Minnie fingered a scarf of bright colors wrapped around her neck. "I must place this scarf on a worthy subject. Will you honor me, sweet Emily, by being the subject of this ceremony?"

"It will be my pleasure."

"May my servant perform the same ritual with your two boys?"

"Of course."

Mola Singh removed a similar scarf from his neck.

Holding the scarf in both hands, Minnie draped it around Emily's neck.

"You're holding it too tight," pleaded Emily. "You're hurting me."

Minnie's dark eyes burned with intensity. "I'm honoring you, Emily. You are a sacrifice to the Great Mother! Kali is life! Kali is death! Kali is all!"

A quick flip of Minnie's wrist snapped Emily's neck. As Minnie lowered Emily's corpse gently to the ground, two similar snaps sounded in the house. Minnie saw Mola standing over the bodies of James and Emile.

"Poor Emily and her sons," observed Minnie. "They were just as fragile as Gretchen and Ethel."

"What about the other child?" asked Mola.

"I am not lacking in mercy. Let her live."

Minnie and Mola departed. Emily's housekeeper discovered the bodies later that evening.

Twenty-four years passed.

"It's a concealed air-rifle," stated Julius Von Herder in Berlin during 1887. The mechanic was a heavyset man who hooded his eyes like a hawk. Despite being a skilled artisan, Von Herder was blind.

The sightless craftsman handed his invention to his fellow conspirator. The visitor was a member of the Gentlemen of the Night, the principal criminal gang of London. He was an elegantly dressed man. His facial characteristics included a thin nose, a large forehead and a grizzled mustache. His name was Colonel Sebastian Moran.

The object held in Moran's hands look like a walking stick, but it was a gun that silently dispatched bullets.

A few days later, Moran was in Britain. The Gentlemen of the Night was part of a larger European crime syndicate, the Black Coats. When the leaders of that continental organization met in London, Moran planned to arrange an assassination elsewhere.

"Derrick Stewart is the most dangerous man in Asia," emphasized Dr. Antonio Nikola. The statement was made before the High Council of the Black Coats. From 1879 until 1885, the Black Coats had been in a state of civil war. Jim Nemo, the Lord of the Night, had spearheaded a rebellion from London against the All-Father, the supposedly immortal master of the Black Coats. That insurrection had ended with the marriage of Jim's younger brother to Catarina, the daughter of Count Salvatore Corbucci, the All-Father's chief lieutenant. Once Catarina's nuptials were celebrated, the two contentious factions of the Black Coats were strongly united in pursuit of common goals.

The High Council assembled in the London residence of Finola Nemo, the Lord of the Night's wife. Also present were Count Corbucci, his daughter Catarina, Horace Dorrington, Albert Van Klopen, Paul Mascarin and John Macklin. The tall Jim Nemo had the appearance of an ascetic scholar. As a citizen of the United States, Madame Nemo, a slender brunette, was responsible for the Black Coat penetration of North America. Corbucci, a stout man with a bushy mustache, was the leader of the Camorra, the Neapolitan branch of the Black Coats. His daughter, a dark-haired beauty, headed the Brotherhood of the Seven Kings, another secret society of Italy. Dorrington, a muscular man with a military mustache, ran a celebrated private detective agency which clandestinely indulged in theft and murder. The rotund Van Klopen was the most celebrated fashion designer in Paris. Together with the handsome Mascarin, a renowned photographer, Van Klopen controlled a ruthless gang of blackmailers in France. In the recently reorganized Black Coats, Macklin, an albino dwarf, ran all Black

Coat operations in South America, Africa and Asia in partnership with Dr. Nikola.

Absent from this assembly was the All-Father. He lived a reclusive existence in the mountains of Corsica. The exact reasons for his absence were unclear. Conflicting rumors circulated among the rank and file of the Black Coats. One story was that Nemo had reduced the All-Father to little more than a figurehead. Supposedly the All-Father had only a ceremonial role in the Black Coats comparable to that of Queen Victoria in the British Empire. Partisans of the All-Father stated that he merely preferred to maintain a concealed role in the operations of his illegal empire. He was portrayed as constantly issuing orders to the Lord of the Night.

One of the All-Father's protégés had been Dr. Nikola. He was a slim man of 31 years. Some years earlier, Nikola had been engaged to Catarina Corbucci. Catarina's infidelity with an Englishman, Norman Head, had led to the dissolution of their betrothal. This development had created the opportunity for Nemo to negotiate the marriage of his brother to Catarina. The decision to post Nikola overseas had partially been intended to mitigate an awkward relationship among the leaders of the Black Coats.

"Derrick Stewart is the elder son of Ju Hai Van Eeden, the matriarch of the Asian black market," continued Nikola. Based in Hong Kong, Madame Van Eeden and her Red Dragon Tong preside over a huge smuggling empire. Prior to her marriage to a Dutch merchant, she had an affair which resulted in Stewart's birth. The exact identity of the father is uncertain. One story is that he was an English officer, Gruesome Clayton. This soldier supposedly seduced the future Madame Van Eeden at the start of the Opium War. However, there is a conflicting rumor that the offspring's father was a Scottish trader known throughout the Far East as the Green-Eyed Devil. The Scottish alias of Madame Van Eeden's progeny supports this belief. Derrick Stewart is very similar to the real name of the Green-Eyed Devil.

"Stewart is a man of considerable intellect. He studied medicine at the American missionary school at Canton. For the last few years, Stewart has been enrolled at the University of Edinburgh. He has just recently earned a medical degree at that distinguished institution of learning.

"Besides being the heir to Madame Van Eeden among the Red Dragons, Stewart has considerable influence with other tongs such as the Chang Li, the Chuen Gin Lou, the Yat Soy, and the Yo Thans. His ultimate dream is to revive the Si-Fan."

"The Si-Fan!" exclaimed Nemo. "That ancient order collapsed 200 years ago."

"What exactly is the Si-Fan?" asked Mascarin.

"Just as the All-Father erected the Black Coats as an alliance of the secret societies of Europe," explained Corbucci, "the Si-Fan was a confederation of the cults of Asia. I often wonder if the All-Father was inspired to create the Black Coats by hearing of the earlier Si-Fan."

"In order to resurrect the Si-Fan, Stewart must extend his influence beyond China," concluded Dorrington. "He needs to gain supremacy over the Thugs of India and the Dacoits of Burma."

"Stewart is already halfway there," asserted Nikola. "He is married to the high priestess of Kali. The Thugs have become his minions."

"Stewart is a man of great promise," confirmed Nemo. "Antonio has negotiated an agreement with Stewart to be our main supplier of opium for the next seven years."

"But the Wu Fang Clan has been our principal source of opium!" objected Catarina. "They are close allies of the All-Father!"

"I have convinced the All-Father of the futility of a continued collaboration with the Wu Fang Clan," sternly decreed the Lord of the Night. "Since an alliance with Stewart has great potential, Antonio has invited him here to meet all of us."

"Accompanying Dr. Stewart is Culverton Smith, a former plantation owner in Sumatra," added Nikola. "He will act as Stewart's ambassador to the High Council."

Some minutes later, there was knock on the door of the Nemo residence. Nikola answered it. Two men entered.

Dr. Derrick Stewart was a tall man. He had a high forehead. The lower portion of his face was covered by a small beard. With his eyes shielded by green spectacles and his hands covered by gloves, there was no hint of Asian ancestry in his appearance. An observer easily would have assumed that Stewart was solely of European stock. His companion, Culverton Smith, was a short man with an enormous bald head.

Once Nikola introduced Stewart to Nemo, the two men shook hands.

"Your alias is intriguing," noted Stewart. "Latin for 'no one.' A pirate also used the same *nom de guerre*."

"That earlier Nemo was an Indian with black eyes," said Nemo. "I'm an Irishman with gray eyes. I borrowed my pseudonym from the false identity assumed by the doomed Captain Hawdon in *Bleak House*. Perhaps that pirate was also influenced by Charles Dickens."

"Your rounded shoulders imply years spent in long study. Have you earned any academic degrees?"

"I have a doctorate in mathematics."

While pursuing his medical studies, Derrick Stewart resided with his family in Lauder, a town twenty-seven miles south of Edinburgh. While her husband was conferring with the Black Coats in London, Mrs. Jasmine Stewart remained behind in Lauder. She was 45 years old. Mrs. Stewart had just placed her two young daughters, Karah and Mina, to bed.

Count Negretto Sylvius was an accomplished criminal recently arrived from Paris. He was a big man with a dark mustache, a cruel mouth and a curved nose. The French police had questioned him regarding the recent death of Mrs. Harold, a wealthy English expatriate. No charges had been made against the Count, but he found it prudent to leave France because his name had appeared in the Parisian press. Under the terms of Mrs. Harold's will, the Count was bequeathed the profitable Blymer estate in Scotland. Certain legalities needed to be ironed out before the Count could take possession. Stretched temporarily in his finances, the Count had offered his services to Antonio Nikola. On Nikola's recommendation, the Black Coats had assigned Sylvius to Dr. Stewart to act as his wife's bodyguard.

In a room on the second floor, the Count watched Mrs. Stewart kneel in obsequiously in before an idol of Kali, the four-armed goddess of the Thugs. She was cradling in her arms a *khussee*, the Thuggee pickaxe. It was a three-bladed weapon. The horizontal bar of the pickaxe ended in a hooked edge on each side while the upward tip of the vertical pole was a sharp blade. She placed a *goor*, a wafer of consecrated sugar, inside her mouth and swallowed it. Touching a circular hairpin above her forehead, she sang a hymn to Kali. Mrs. Stewart zealously performed these religious rites every night.

Suddenly the Count and Mrs. Stewart heard a noise downstairs, Sylvius whipped out a gun from the pocket of his jacket.

"We may have a burglar, Madame. I'll take care of him."

Sylvius rushed downstairs. Reaching the first floor, he didn't see the intruder until she stuck. Sylvius howled in agony as a sharp blade slammed into his right arm. The gun fell from his hand. The female attacker pushed the wounded Sylvius to the ground as she kicked the gun far away.

Sylvius recognized the invader from newspaper accounts. She was clad in a black shirt with matching pants and boots. Her V-shaped neckline was outlined in red. Her face was covered by a black cowl with a red skull insignia on the forehead. Her crimson gloves held a Thuggee pickaxe.

"The Revenant!" cried Sylvius. The stricken criminal uttered the name of the scourge of the Parisian underworld.

The response of the Revenant was to slash the Count's legs with the vertical blade of her pickaxe.

"Die in the name of Kali!" yelled Jasmine Stewart at the top of the stairs. Swinging her own pickaxe, she leaped at the Revenant.

The pickaxes of the two female assailants clashed in combat. The Revenant blocked the blows of her adversary, but Jasmine relentlessly struck in the direction of the masked woman. Finally Stewart's pickaxe slammed forcefully into the opposing weapon. The Revenant dropped her pickaxe.

Jasmine opted to gloat over her disarmed rival. Laughing mockingly, she permitted the disarmed Revenant to retreat into a corner of the room.

"There is nowhere to run," said Jasmine raising her pickaxe slowly above her head. "I'm going to brash in your skull."

The Revenant was quicker. She swiftly grabbed a lasso fastened on her belt. Hurling the rope in the air, the Revenant swung the noose over Jasmine's pickaxe. Tightening the lasso, the Revenant yanked the three-bladed weapon out of Stewart's hands. Swinging the entrapped pickaxe in the rope, the Revenant knocked the bottom of the handle into Jasmine's jaw. The stunned Jasmine dropped face forward to the floor. Recovering her senses, Jasmine attempted to raise herself, but her progress was halted as the Revenant struck from behind. The Revenant strung her lasso around Jasmine's throat.

"This is for Emily Caber," whispered the Revenant into Jasmine's ear.

Dr. Archibald MacDonald was the Stewarts' neighbor. He was walking home after having delivered a baby in a house five blocks away. As he approached his house, MacDonald noticed a coach in front of the Stewart residence. Suddenly a masked woman with a pickaxe rushed out of the front door of the Stewart house. She hurried into the coach. Snapping his whip, the driver drove the vehicle speedily away.

MacDonald proceeded into the Stewart home. He heard the groans of the wounded Sylvius, but the physician's eyes were fixed on a gruesome tableau. With the Revenant's noose around her neck, Mrs. Stewart hung from the chandelier. The shoulder of her garment had been torn open. A bloody "V" had been carved into Mrs. Stewart's flesh.

Some miles from the outskirts of Lauder, the coach carrying the slayer of Mrs. Stewart arrived at the camp grounds of Ronder's Circus. Removing her Revenant costume during the ride, the passenger had changed into a stylish dress. Alighting from the vehicle, the killer was revealed to be an attractive blonde woman in her twenties. Her name was Penelope Farthing. She was the leading acrobat of Ronder's Circus.

Two days later, Penelope was conferring with the coachman in her dressing room. He was now dressed in a fashionable suit. He carried a cane.

"My superior is very pleased, Penny," assured Sebastian Moran. "Your impersonation of the Revenant was masterful."

"When will I meet your mysterious chief?"

"After tonight's performance."

Some hours later, Penelope Farthing looked down on the circus audience as she stood on the trapeze pole. Attired in a white leotard with a black "D" emblazoned on the chest. Penelope was billed as "the Death Lady" because she performed dangerous stunts without benefit of a net. She always made a special effort to spot her lover in the crowd. Moran had informed her of the section where he would be seated. By pointing his cane in her direction, Moran made it easier for Penelope to locate him. Finally seeing her lover, Penelope smiled.

Penelope swung on a trapeze. Releasing her hold, she did a double somersault before flying forward with the intent of gripping another trapeze. Moran fired Von Herder's air-rifle from the stand. The bullet severed the second trapeze's rope before Penelope could grab it. Missing the trapeze, Penelope plummeted to her death.

If Jasmine Stewart had been murdered in England, the local chief constable could have asked the London police to dispatch an inspector to investigate. However, the killing occurred in Scotland. Therefore, the authorities of Lauder asked Edinburgh for assistance. Inspector Frederick MacStruan Jr. of the Edinburgh police concluded that Mrs. Stewart was slain by the "deranged" French vigilante, the Revenant. Dr. Derrick Stewart was cleared of any complicity in his wife's death. The police theory was that the Revenant viewed Count Sylvius as a criminal due to the publicity surrounding Mrs. Harold's death. The Revenant allegedly followed her quarry from Paris in order to kill him. Sylvius was visiting Mrs. Stewart when the Revenant attempted to murder him. When Mrs. Stewart tried to interfere, she was butchered by the Revenant. Mrs. Stewart was portrayed as a gallant heroine responsible for preventing the demise of the wounded Sylvius. Newspapers throughout Britain carried details of the Stewart murder. The story was quickly picked up by the French newspapers.

Among the Parisian readers of the Stewart murders was the real Revenant. Framed for murder and treason by the Black Coats, Darlla Rassendyll had assumed the identity of the Revenant to seek revenge. Trained by Erik, the reclusive Phantom of the Opera, the Revenant had conducted a lethal campaign against the criminal cartel. With Erik's death, the Revenant had inherited her mentor's base beneath the Paris Opera House. Secret passageways connected the subterranean sanctuary with the dressing room of Feliciana Sorelli, the Opera's principal ballerina. The Revenant navigated those hidden corridors to visit Feliciana.

The blonde Feliciana was a member of the Black Coats. She was a double agent whose true loyalty was to the Revenant. Under the alias of Lady Leopard, Feliciana also belonged to the Acolytes of the Shadows, the vigilante society founded by the Revenant.

Wearing her costume, the Revenant conferred with her associate.

"It's the old concept of *pay the law*," noted Lady Leopard. "An innocent person must be made the scapegoat for the crimes of the Black Coats. Just as they made you *pay the law* in your real identity, the Black Coats must have now made you *pay the law* as the Revenant."

"Have you discovered anything about this Mrs. Stewart, Leopard?"

"Her husband is rumored to be a new ally of Antonio Nikola. Dr. Stewart is not a member of the Black Coats, but has some nebulous connections to the Chinese tongs."

"Stewart's wife must have participated in his illegal enterprises. Sylvius is a diversion. My impostor's real target was Mrs. Stewart."

"It's been two years since the civil war between the two Black Coat factions ended, Revenant. Yet the Black Coats will always be consumed by internal rivalries. Some member of the High Council must have wanted to kill Mrs. Stewart in order to advance a private vendetta."

Besieged by reporters, Dr. MacDonald felt compelled to sell his Lauder practice. He relocated in the Scottish town of Paisley.

The general belief in Britain was that the Revenant's guilt in the Stewart murder was uncontestable. That view changed when a letter was published in the *London Times* arguing for the innocence of the Revenant. The following is an extract from that letter.

The Edinburgh police would have us believe that the Lauder murder follows the pattern of the Revenant's killings in Paris. In actuality, the killing violates the continuity of the vigilante's documented crimes. The original Revenant murders in Paris always had the victim's body disfigured with a "V" to represent "voleur," the French word for thief At the risk of being pedantic, I shall note that the more proper interpretation of the "V" in the Lauder atrocity would be "voleuse," the feminine form of the French word. Nevertheless, it has been six years since the Revenant has utilized the "V" mutilation. She has butchered scores of alleged criminals in Paris over the following time interval, but she has abandoned the gruesome practice of disfiguring their corpses. Also the Revenant has never left her lasso tied around the neck of her Parisian victims. She has merely left in her wake a corpse with a broken neck.

If Count Sylvius was the intended target, why was his life not taken by the assailant? The Revenant had ample time to extinguish the Count's existence. Instead she wasted valuable time in manufacturing a grisly tableau with Mrs. Stewart's remains.

The logical conclusion is that the Count was deliberately spared. Mrs. Stewart was the primary focus of the attack. The Count was merely wounded in order to act as a convenient witness. The murderer was a Revenant impersonator.

There had long been tales of a French Camorra whose tentacles extend into other nations including Britain. Such an organization would have ample reason for hating the Revenant. This sinister fraternity plotted the death of Mrs. Stewart. Furthermore, the conspirators have hoodwinked the police into concluding that this barbarity was perpetuated by the Revenant.

The author of this document was a private investigator residing in London. He had recently become a celebrity due to his exposure of the Netherland-

Sumatra Company swindle perpetrated by Baron Maupertuis. The letter bore the signature of Sherlock Holmes.

Among the readers of this letter was Dr. Derrick Stewart. Having buried his wife in Lauder, Stewart was preparing to depart for Hong Kong with his two young daughters. Summoning Antonio Nikola to Scotland, he confronted Nikola with the theories expressed in the letter. Stewart removed his colored glasses. His green eyes shone with a bright malignancy.

"Holmes hints that the Black Coats were behind my wife's death. Swear to me, Nikola, that this is untrue."

"My friend, I swear on the grave of my beloved mother that the Black Coats were innocent of your beloved's murder."

Stewart concluded that Nikola's utterance was spoken in true faith.

In his rooms in Baker Street, Sherlock Holmes was preparing to depart.

"I intend to pay Hugh Lawrence a visit, Watson. Do you care to come?"

"Socializing with one of our neighbors is a rare activity for you, Holmes," responded the sleuth's fellow lodger. "Thank you, no. I have some medical journals to consult in order to compose a proper treatment for one of my patients. In addition, a boring discussion with Lawrence over chemistry holds no interest for me."

"Chemistry is not the subject of my visit. I'm interested in the Warrender case. Do you recall it?

"How could I forget Lawrence's vivid account? In 1862, Lawrence was a guest at the Yorkshire household with three young children. One of them, Ethel Thurston, had recently perished. Her demise had been falsely attributed to a seizure. In reality, Ethel had been throttled by her governess, Minnie Warrender. The bloodthirsty governess had also been responsible for the death of a young girl earlier in Germany. Before Warrender could be punished for her crimes, she vanished."

"Still intent on remaining behind, Watson?"

"I'm tempted to go with you, but I really must research my patient's treatment."

Alone Holmes arrived at Hugh Lawrence's flat. Lawrence's apartment was located a few houses away in Baker Street. After exchanging pleasantries with Lawrence, Holmes proceeded to discuss Minnie Warrender.

"The late Mrs. Jasmine Stewart was 45, Lawrence. She was born in the same year as Minnie Warrender. The physical description and Indian ancestry also match. The newspapers also described a hairpin similar to one owned by Miss Warrender. Minnie could be a nickname for Jasmine."

"Miss Warrender's real first name was actually Yasmina, Holmes. She shortened it to Mina or Minnie. Jasmine is an appropriate English substitution for Yasmina."

"The supposed Revenant employed Thuggee weaponry to kill Mrs. Stewart."

"Ah, I was wondering when you would bring up the Thuggee angles of the Warrender case."

"Lawrence, you unearthed that Miss Warrender was the daughter of some Thuggee chieftain."

"Yes, I firmly believe that she was contacted in Yorkshire by one of her father's followers. Together they sought refuge in India."

"But not immediately after Miss Warrender's flight from the Thurston household. There was a sequel in Manchester one year later."

"A woman named Emily Caber was murdered along with two of her children. When I read about the slayings in the newspapers, I contacted the police upon recognizing Miss Warrender's handiwork. It was fortunate that I did. Suspicion was falling on an innocent man."

"Emily's lover and the father of her children. You withheld his name in our previous conversations concerning Miss Warrender."

"That man has suffered enough, Holmes! Rumors surrounding his involvement with the late Emily Caber ruined his career."

"I need to know his name, Lawrence! He's a logical person to seek vengeance against Mrs. Stewart!"

Lawrence reluctantly complied. "He held the Mathematics Chair at the University of Manchester. The Caber scandal forced him to resign his position I've heard that he's currently living in London. He etches out an existence tutoring young soldiers for the officer exams. His name is Professor James Moriarty."

"Moriarty..."

"Does that name mean anything to you, Holmes?"

"No, I've never heard of the fellow before."

In his private study, Professor Moriarty (alias Jim Nemo) received a surprise visit from his younger brother. Noel Moriarty was tall and gaunt like his older sibling. His hair was brushed low on his forehead. Like Derrick Stewart, Noel's eyes were hidden by tinted spectacles. This fact made Noel often difficult to fathom.

"I'm here to offer my assistance, brother," asserted Noel.

"Why should I need your assistance?"

"The letter by Sherlock Holmes is perilously close to the truth. The alliance with Dr. Stewart must be preserved at all costs."

"I don't know what you are talking about. The Revenant was responsible for Mrs. Stewart's death."

"A beautiful bluff, brother. Let me prove to you my grasp of the salient facts. Colonel Moran is your chief of staff. You pay him an annual salary of 6,000 pounds, but you only employ sparingly in extremely important assignments. My wife informs me that Moran was absent from the High Council meeting in London. Consequently, he must have been performing some task for you. From his former military service in India, Moran would be familiar with Thuggee fighting techniques. He could train a woman to impersonate the Revenant."

"And where would Moran find this hypothetical woman?"

"One of our compatriots, Leonard Scot, once recruited a female acrobat from Ronder's Circus to act as a disposable pawn. Moran emulated Scot."

"What leads you to that conclusion?"

"Shortly after the Stewart murder, an aerialist at Ronder's Circus, Penelope Farthing, expired during a performance in the same vicinity. Moran must have arranged that convenient accident to ensure Farthing's silence. Only you and Moran would know the true details of Mrs. Stewart's assassination."

"Your astute deductions complicate the situations. I assume your cooperation in this endeavor has a price."

"There is no price, brother. I once loved Emily. You avenged her and my nephews. If Stewart learned the truth, he might seek retribution against Urania. I would never place the life of Emily's daughter in jeopardy."

"Our father always wanted me to succeed him as Lord of the Night, but I harbored no desire to sit on the High Council. I spurned his entreaties to pursue my academic career. When Emily and the lads were slaughtered, my life was shattered. In order to secure justice, I implored our father for assistance. His help came at a steep price. I placed my entire future in his hands."

"You disappeared for nearly six years, Jim. I still don't know what happened during that period."

"That period of my life must remain a mystery to you. All you need to know is that I searched for Mola Singh and Minnie Warrender. I eventually traced Mola to a remote island. I wrung his neck with one of his own strangling cords. His female accomplice eluded me until recently."

"You always were a gambler, brother. You banked on Stewart still recognizing the value of an alliance with the Black Coats despite our inability to ensure his wife's safety."

"Stewart's dream of a Si-Fan revival is impossible without our support."

"How can I be of service?"

"Dr. Nikola has already repaired the damage caused by the Holmes letter. Of course, Nikola actually believes me innocent of any role in Mrs. Stewart's extermination. He must continue to do so."

"As must my wife and father-in-law."

"You must be placed in a better position to deceive them. I must apologize, Noel, for not recognizing your talents earlier. A man of your abilities needs to be on the High Council. I'm confident that Catarina and Count Corbucci will support your candidacy as well."

Some months later, Chantal Lebrue was reviewing newspapers in a Parisian office labeled the Sure Values Agency. An account of a murder came to her attention. A sailor had been strangled near a locked warehouse along the Seine. Chantal belonged to the Acolytes of the Shadows. In the guise of running a bureau that regularly printed a news summary, it was Chantal's responsibility to find articles in periodicals that would be of interest to the Revenant. With other items clipped from newspapers, Chantal enclosed the report of the murder in an envelope.

In the same building as the Sure Values Agency was a locked office that supposedly was rented by a lawyer named A.L. Lard. The true leaser of this office was Darlla Rassendyll. A. L. Lard was an anagram of Darlla. Leaving the confines of the Sure Values Agency, Chantal approached the Lard office. She deposited the envelope inside the mail slot of the door. Later that same day, Feliciana Sorelli unlocked the Lard office and retrieved the envelope. She personally delivered it to the Revenant in the Paris Opera House.

In her underground sanctuary, the Revenant reviewed the contents. The description of the sailor's murder was of particular interest to her. The body had been found next to a warehouse belonging to Silver Lotus Importers. Eight years previously, the Revenant had learnt that the warehouse was secretly owned by the Wu Fang Clan, a family of Chinese pirates. The warehouse had been used to store an opium shipment from the Wu Fang Clan to the Black Coats. The warehouse had been unused for years, but the sailor's death could indicate that the drug trafficking of the Wu Fang Clan was being revived.

The next evening, a coach arrived not far from the Silver Lotus Importers' warehouse. The driver was Charles Blanton. Under the alias of Lord Charon, he was one of the Acolytes of the Shadows. It was Charon's primary duty to provide transportation for the Revenant throughout Paris.

On many of her missions, the Revenant was accompanied by the most formidable fighter in the Acolytes of the Shadows, the Jade Seraph. That night, the Seraph was absent. She was assisting another Acolyte, Dr. Rolande Cerral, in a scientific experiment. The Seraph's blood had rare recuperative properties. Dr. Cerral was attempting to create a synthetic serum that would duplicate the regenerative powers inherent in the Seraph's blood. Consequently, the Revenant vacated Charon's coach alone.

The Revenant's pickaxe easily broke open the padlock securing the door of the warehouse. She crept into the dark interior.

"Die! Assassin!"

The words were shouted by a hooded man clad entirely in black. He swung at the Revenant with a Thuggee pickaxe. The Revenant blocked the blows with her own three-bladed weapon. The pickaxes clashed together for several minutes. Eventually, a strong swing by the Revenant smacked the pickaxe out of her masked opponent's hands. A swift kick by the Revenant into her disarmed enemy's stomach propelled him against a wall. Moonlight gleamed through a window upon the vanquished man's mask.

"Unmask!" commanded the Revenant pressing her pickaxe's top blade against the chest of her foe.

The man slowly removed his hood. A skeletal face with yellow eyes was exposed.

"Erik!" shouted the Revenant. The man looked exactly like the Phantom of the Opera.

So shocked was the Revenant that she didn't hear the female Thug creeping up behind. The woman slipped her Punjabi lasso over the Revenant's head. As the noose tightened, the Revenant dropped her pickaxe. The Revenant was overcome by oblivion.

When the Revenant awoke, she was sprawled on her back. Her arms were raised over her head. Her wrists were enclosed in leather straps attached to an iron spike hammered into the ground. Her ankles were strapped to another spike. Her mask had been removed. She looked around her surrounding and beheld a huge statue of Kali. Wherever she was, it was no longer the warehouse of Silver Lotus Importers. The room was dimly lit by torches. Smoke came from a small brazier filled with charcoal. Near the legs of the brazier were a copper bowl and a wooden box. A figure walked out of a darkened corridor towards the Revenant.

"You are in a temple of Kali that has been secretly established in Paris," noted the man with the face like Erik. He was clad in a blue robe adorned with a golden scorpion. A blue skull-cap adorned his head. His right hand held a Thuggee pickaxe while his left grasped the Revenant's cowl.

"You have such lovely red hair," he continued. "I shall probably decapitate you after your death. My Emperor will want to preserve your head. It will make a fine companion to his Afghan relic, the skull of Ratina. She led the Kandahar brigands in 1850."

"If I am to perish," responded the Revenant, "let me at least know the name of my executioner."

"You don't know me? Yet you called me Erlik, It's true that isn't my current *nom de guerre*, but I assumed that you had some familiarity with my past."

"I said 'Erik,' not 'Erlik.' You resemble a man that I knew by that name."

"Then I must apologize for my inaccurate sense of hearing. Let me properly introduce myself. Years ago, I was revered as an avatar of Erlik Khan, the God of the Black Throne. Today I am called Fu Hsi."

"You have adopted the name of the legendary first Emperor of China."

"It was bestowed on me by my Emperor. I protested that I was unworthy. If anyone is worthy of the sacred name of Fu, it should be him for the blood of both the Ming and Chi'ng dynasties flows in his veins. However, my liege insisted that I accept this honor."

"I suspect that you're not talking about the current Emperor of China. Who is your Emperor?"

Fu Hsi laughed. "I'll bargain with you. Tell me about your Erik and I'll tell you about my Emperor."

"I never knew Erik's real name. He was born in France around 1830. Ostracized because of his face, he fled to Asia. He spent time among the pirates of Indochina and the Thugs of India. In the mountains of Afghanistan, he was captured by the priests of Erlik Khan. Although they kept him incarcerated, the priests proclaimed their captive to be the modern incarnation of their god. Misunderstanding their cries of 'Erlik,' the wanderer took the name of Erik. Escaping from the Erlik cult, the newly christened Erik spent the next few years in Persia and Turkey. Eventually he returned to France. Erik was skilled in the arts of assassination. His ambition was to bestow his lethal knowledge on a Disciple of Death. He chose me for that role shortly before he died."

"Your information is consistent with facts known to me, Revenant. I can not reveal the identity of the Emperor without elucidating on my own history. Twenty-four years ago, I was born in Yolgan, the Afghan stronghold of the Erlik cult. The priests of Erlik Khan told me that I was the son of Erlik Khan. That was a lie. Your Erik must have been my father."

The Revenant recalled a story that Erik had reluctantly divulged. After drugging him with the Purple Sacrament, the priests of Erlik had left him alone with a woman. Erik had only vague memories of doing something horrible to her in his delirium. He must have raped her. She later gave birth to Fu Hsi.

"I was merely a figurehead for the priests," continued Fu Hsi. "They ruled Yolgan by manipulating me. When I was fifteen, the Emperor came to Yolgan. He had a great dream. For centuries, Asia had feared a powerful convocation called the Si-Fan. In the seventeenth century, the Si-Fan fell into complete disarray. The order had always been ruled by a Lady of the Si-Fan. The last woman to hold that title presided over the Si-Fan from Yolgan. Belonging to the bloodline of Kublai Khan, she was dubbed the Black Star because of an unusual birthmark between her breasts. The Emperor hoped to find a female descendant of the Black Star to become the new Lady of the Si-Fan. In order to trace her whereabouts, the Emperor needed access to the secret archives of the city. He could only achieve this goal by becoming a priest of Erlik. Perusing the old records, the Emperor learned that the Black Star's children had fled to India in the wake of the Si-Fan's destruction. There they carved out a kingdom on the Yamuna River. The Black Star's dynasty survived to rule Thuggee, an offshoot of the Erlik cult. The Emperor was in a quandary. To pursue his quest, he had to leave Yolgan for India. Yet his oath to the cult of Erlik prohibited his departure. The Emperor is a man of honor. He never breaks his word."

"He needed you to release him from his oath," deduced the Revenant.

"I was technically the supreme authority of the Erlik cult. I had become bored with the religious rituals of Yolgan. I wanted to see the world that the priests had hidden from me. In exchange for releasing the Emperor from his priestly duties, he promised to act as my mentor. We fled Afghanistan together. In India, we contacted the Thugs. Some elders of the cult remembered a man with a countenance like mine. We found the Black Star's female descendant. In 1880, the Emperor married her. The Emperor and his bride treated me as if I was their own son." Tears filled Fu Hsi's eyes. "She was like a mother to me! You murdered her in Scotland!"

"Jasmine Stewart! The Emperor is Derrick Stewart!"

"Yes! I knew of your previous attack on the warehouse of the Silver Lotus Importers. The Wu Fang Clan was persuaded to lend us the warehouse to lure you here."

"You had that sailor murdered to act as bait."

"That is not true!" asserted a female voice. A dark-haired woman emerged from the shadows. A black fur coat covered a dark ensemble consisting of a tunic, pants and boots. A gold necklace was looped around her neck. A black cap with a fur brim crowned her head.

"That sailor tried to rob me of my necklace. I merely defended myself." The woman opened her coat revealing a Punjabi lasso tied to her belt. "Like you, Revenant, I am proficient with Thuggee weapons."

"Permit me to introduce Renee Zayata," contributed Fu Hsi. "Her French relatives are merchants in India as well as members of the Thuggee cult. In India, she earned the sobriquet of Bagheela, which means 'panther.' I have been her instructor in the arts of Kali as Mrs. Stewart had been mine. Bagheela is just as deadly as her namesake. As you learned to your discomfort in the warehouse, Revenant, she is quite adroit in strangulation."

"I could have easily twisted your neck," said Bagheela, "but I knew my Lord wanted to prolong your death."

"Bagheela hadn't any prohibitions about the felonious sailor," informed Fu Hsi. "When she told me about the assassination, I saw the possibilities of using his corpse to entice you into the warehouse. And now you shall pay for killing my Empress!"

"I'm innocent" protested the Revenant.

"Enough of your lies!" decreed Fu Hsi. "Lingering death requires a woman's touch. Bagheela, outline to our prey the nature of her demise."

Bagheela bent down next to the Revenant's head. The brunette stroked the redhead's cheek as she spoke softly.

"The Emperor has met several creative people. One such individual was Yuan Li of the Mekong valley. He devised this punishment."

Moving towards the brazier, Bagheela lifted the copper bowl from the floor and brought it closer to the Revenant. Attached to the bowl were straps made of chainmail. There was a buckle at the end of each strap.

"Let's see if this will fit," said Bagheela. She pulled up the Revenant's shirt exposing her stomach. Fitting the bowl downwards over the Revenant's exposed flesh. Bagheela hooked the straps underneath the Revenant back to see if the buckles would reach.

"Perfect," purred Bagheela, but she didn't latch the straps. Bagheela showed the bottom of the bowl. She pointed to a large indentation. "This will hold a small lump of blazing charcoal from the brazier, Revenant." Placing the bowl aside, Bagheela retrieved the wooden box from the other side of the brazier. As the brunette brought it closer, the Revenant could see that the box was really a cage. Inside the cage a shadowy form squealed.

"This is a rat from the Pagoda of the Chang Li Society," explained Bagheela. "I will put him on your stomach. He won't bite you initially because he's been well fed. The bowl will be placed over the rat. I will buckle the straps around your body. The charcoal will be placed on the indentation in the bowl. The heat from the charcoal will drive the rat wild with frenzy. In order to escape the heat, the rat will have no choice but to gnaw a tunnel through your body."

"I didn't kill Jasmine!" exclaimed the Revenant. "The Black Coats used an impostor to make me *pay the law*! Sherlock Holmes proved that!"

"I'm very familiar with the rambling of that mountebank," interrupted Fu Hsi. "The Black Coats had no reason to murder the Empress. They had just concluded a lucrative agreement with the Emperor. Proceed with the execution."

Bagheela removed the huge rat from the cage.

"The Black Coats are divided into two factions!" yelled the Revenant.

The rat was deposited on the Revenant's stomach,

"They were involved in a power struggle that Nemo won!"

The bowl was placed over the rat.

"The All-Father became a mere figurehead!"

The straps were positioned underneath the Revenant.

"The All-Father wants to regain his power!"

The straps were buckled.

"The All-Father wanted Nemo to be blamed for a great failure!"

Bagheela rose towards the brazier.

"The All-Father wanted your Emperor to blame Nemo's for failing to protect his wife!" shouted the Revenant. "The Emperor was expected to break the agreement!"

Bagheela reached inside the brazier to grab a set of metal pincers.

"Nemo would lose face!" wailed the Revenant.

The pincers gripped a chunk of blazing charcoal.

"The Black Coats would restore the All-Father to power!"

Bagheela was about to position the charcoal on top of the bowl when Fu Hsi raised his hand. "Stop, Bagheela! Return the charcoal to the brazier. Unlatch the bowl and put the rodent back in the cage."

After complying with Fu Hsi's directives, Bagheela examined the Revenant's stomach. There were no bite marks.

"You have manufactured a very plausible scenario, Revenant," concluded Fu Hsi. "While the Emperor has returned to Asia, he left an Englishman to serve as his ambassador to the Lord of the Night. I am in regular communication with my English confederate. In his opinion, the Black Coats are currently structured like the Japanese Shogunate. Real power lies in the hands of the Lord of the Night, a modern Shogun, while the All-Father functions solely as an Imperial sovereign in name only."

"She still may be lying," interjected Bagheela. "We should interrogate the other prisoner. He may contradict her story."

"Have Ali Khan bring him before me!" ordered Fu Hsi. Bagheela left to carry out her master's dictates.

"Other prisoner?" asked the bound Revenant.

"My Thugs found a coachman suspiciously waiting near the warehouse. He was easily overcome."

Bagheela and a massive Thug entered the chamber. They escorted a blindfolded Lord Charon. His hands were tied behind his back.

"Remove the prisoner's blindfold!" ordained Fu Hsi.

The burly Ali Khan untied the blindfold. Once the obstruction was removed from Charon's eyes, he stared at Fu Hsi in disbelief.

"Master…" muttered Charon. "You're alive!"

"You mistake me for my father. You must have known him as Erik."

"Yes. He was the greatest man who ever lived."

"You were his loyal servant. What is your name?"

"I am called Charon. Your father saved my life. I swore to serve him faithfully. The day that he died was the saddest moment of my life."

"How did my father perish?"

"He loved a woman unworthy of him. She broke his heart. He withered away pinning for her."

"Was she the woman?" Fu Hsi pointed to the Revenant on the ground.

"No, her name was Christine. The Revenant truly loved your father, but his infatuation for Christine blinded him. The Revenant was the one woman who could have made your father happy."

Fu Hsi turned his attention to the captive Revenant. "Does Charon speak the truth? Did my father die of a broken heart?"

The Revenant looked into Fu Hsi's yellow eyes. She burst into tears. "I can't lie to the son of my one true love! Forgive me, Charon! I lied to you! When I learned that Erik was dying from his love for Christine, I ran to console him. His separation from Christine had thrown him into a murderous rage. Erik was going to kill another woman. I had to save her. Erik and I fought with pickaxes. I stabbed him."

"You killed the Master!" howled Charon. "Liar! Murderess! *I'll kill you!*"

"Unbind Charon's hands!" said Fu Hsi to Ali Khan. Once Charon's hands were free, Fu Hsi addressed him."

"Vassal of my father, take this pickaxe. I deputize you to decide the fate of the Revenant. Free her or slay her. The choice is yours!"

Seizing the pickaxe, Charon advanced towards the prostrate Revenant, He raised the pickaxe high in the air.

"Forgive me!" pleaded the Revenant. "Erik was going to kill Lady Leopard! I had to stop him!"

Charon hesitated briefly before he stuck. The pickaxe smashed into the leather straps that bound the Revenant's wrists. A second blow of the pickaxe cut the throngs around her ankles. Charon helped the Revenant to her feet.

"I understand, Revenant. You had to rescue Leopard."

"Let me congratulate you, Revenant," declared Fu Hsi. "Your veracity has been confirmed. You risked your life to tell the truth of my father's death. Your unwillingness to lie about that tragedy proves your denial of any role in the assassination of the Empress."

Fu Hsi paused. He gazed at the Revenant thoughtfully. Taking her gently by the arm, Fu Hsi motioned the Revenant away from Charon. Erik's son returned the Revenant her cowl.

"My father was a fool. He should never have spurned you. You are a woman of strength...a woman of vigor. You were my father's Disciple. I make you an offer. Be my equal. Become my bride."

Before the Revenant could reply, a groan issued from Charon. Bagheela had looped her lasso around his throat.

"I won't allow you to elevate this upstart over me!" screeched Bagheela, "Revenant, I challenge you to a duel to a death. Accept or your servant dies."

"I accept your challenge!" answered the Revenant. In preparation for battle, the Revenant donned her mask.

Bagheela removed her lasso from Charon's neck. "You're a fool to accept my challenge," she taunted. "These furs I wear are from Indian panthers slain by my pickaxe. Once you are dead, Revenant, I shall construct a belt from the skin of your carcass."

In another part of the temple, the Revenant and Bagheela stood with Fu Hsi before a circular pit twenty feet deep and fifteen feet wide. At the bottom squirmed a score of spotted snakes. Both women held pickaxes and Punjabi lassos. Some distance behind them stood Lord Charon and Ali Khan.

"Below are Indian swamp adders." divulged Fu Hsi. "A single bite from any of them is fatal." Fu Hsi pointed towards hooks in the ceiling. "You will each throw one end of your lassoes around your assigned hook. The other end you shall be tied around your left hand. Swinging back and forth over the pit, you shall fight with the pickaxes grasped in your right hand. Charon and Ali Khan will act as your respective seconds. Their duty will be to assist the victor to safety once the duel is concluded."

"The combatants must assume their positions!" bellowed Fu Hsi. Within seconds, both combatants were suspended over the pit. "Let the battle begin!"

Swinging across the pit, the female gladiators slashed at each other. For several minutes, their weapons clanged together. Then the Revenant changed her tactics. Instead of her pickaxe, she struck with her legs. As Bagheela raised her pickaxe to attack, the Revenant delivered a kick with her left leg into her rival's right forearm. The force of the blow caused Bagheela to drop her pickaxe into the mass of squirming reptiles. Swinging once more into her enemy, the Revenant raised her legs to encircle Bagheela's waist. The Revenant's pickaxe cut though Bagheela's rope. Still tied to Bagheela's wrist, the rope hung downwards.

Her legs gripping Bagheela, the Revenant swirled over the pit of vipers.

"Surrender or I'll drop you!" demanded the Revenant.

Bagheela response was to throw her severed lasso around the Revenant neck. The rope twirled around the vigilante's throat.

"We'll die together!" predicted Bagheela as he tightened the lasso.

Grasping for breath, the Revenant squeezed her thighs close together. Bagheela yelped in pain before lapsing into unconsciousness. Her adversary rendered senseless, the Revenant pulled the lasso from around her neck.

"Charon, help me!"

Swinging to the side, the Revenant was caught by Charon. He disentangled the slumbering Bagheela from the Revenant's legs. After depositing the female strangler safely on the ground, Charon caught the oscillating Revenant once more. Once the Revenant slipped her wrist out of the lasso, Charon lowered her to the ground.

"Why did you spare Bagheela?" asked Fu Hsi.

"Because she suffers like I did," said the Revenant.

"I don't understand."

"Can't you see that you're repeating your father's mistake? Bagheela loves you. I can see it in her eyes. Just as your father ignored me, you ignore her. You and Bagheela have chosen a dark path. It is fraught with death and destruction. Your time on this earth may be brief. Do not squander a chance at finding a moment of true love."

"Your advice merits contemplation. There are certain conditions regarding your release. The location of this temple must remain secret. My servitors transported Charon's coach to this location. It waits outside. Both you and Charon shall be blindfolded and placed inside the coach. You shall be transported back to the vicinity of the warehouse where we initially met. Ali Khan will drive Charon's coach. You must give me your word that neither you nor Charon will remove your blindfolds during the journey. You must also promise not to follow Ali Khan after he relinquishes the coach to you."

"You have my word. The next time we met, Fu Hsi, it may be as enemies."

"Hopefully that day shall never come. I will be returning to Asia. Ali Khan, arrange for the departure of my guests. I wish to be alone with Bagheela."

Once the others had left, Fu Hsi knelt beside the dormant Bagheela. He rubbed her cheek gently "Awaken, my Disciple."

Bagheela opened her eyes. "The Revenant vanquished me, Lord. I merit death."

"No, Bagheela, you merit life." Fu Hsi kissed her on the lips. She passionately returned his caresses.

The next day, the Revenant was alone with Feliciana Sorelli in her dressing room. The erstwhile Lady Leopard was fully briefed on The Revenant's encounter with Fu Hsi.

"Did the All-Father really orchestrate Mrs. Stewart's murder?" wondered Lady Leopard.

"The All-Father was just a convenient scapegoat," disclosed the Revenant. "His exact relationship to Nemo is actually unclear to me. I honestly have no idea who in the Black Coats conspired to kill Mrs. Stewart. Hopefully I have fatally sabotaged the alliance between the Black Coats and this self-appointed Emperor of Asia."

When Fu Hsi arrived in Hong Kong, he immediately conferred with Dr. Stewart. Since leaving Scotland, Stewart had shaved his beard and ceased using tinted spectacles to hide his slanting green eyes. His long fingernails were no longer covered by gloves. He was dressed in a plain yellow robe and a black mandarin's cap. His slender hands stroked a marmoset.

Stewart was seated in a room where was stored one of his most precious possessions, the rare black lotus. It was proof of Stewart's membership in the Chang Li Society, also known as the Brotherhood of the Lotus.

On a chair next to Stewart was one of his closest allies in the Chang Li Society, Huan Chow Lee. A much shorter man than Stewart, Huan was a direct descendant of Confucius as well as a Cambridge graduate.

After Fu Hsi described the events surrounding his capture of the Revenant, Stewart asked Huan for his opinion.

"The Revenant clearly spoke the truth," volunteered Huan. "I have heard many stories of this All-Father. He puts his own miserly greed above the interests of his organization. A man totally without honor, he has often sabotaged the plans of his subordinates. He has even murdered his own offspring. We are fortunate indeed to be dealing with men as trustworthy as Jim Nemo and Antonio Nikola."

"My wife's soul cries out for justice," insisted Stewart.

"I counsel patience, my friend. Our agreement with the Black Coats is essential for the resurrection of the Si-Fan. We promised to cooperate with them for seven years. We must honor that pledge. When our treaty with the Black Coats expires, your hands will be free to strike at the All-Father."

"My precious Yasmina will be avenged in 1894," swore Stewart. "When that year arrives, the All-Father shall suffer the most agonizing death ever devised by man!"

"For years, I suspected a clandestine force behind the criminal classes of London," confessed Sherlock Holmes. "Finally a clue emerged to enable me to identify this subterranean overlord. The clue was the Stewart murder. I can finally put a name on this Caesar of Crime. His name is Professor James Moriarty."

These words were uttered at the Diogenes Club in London. Sherlock Holmes was haranguing his older brother. To the outside world, Mycroft Holmes was a minor auditor in a government agency. In reality, he served in a major clandestine role that shaped the foreign policy of the British Empire.

"Moriarty's malign influence apparently extends even into France," added Mycroft.

"His usage of the Revenant as a red herring implies as much," observed Sherlock. "She may be the key to dethroning Moriarty. What do you know about the Revenant?"

The obese Mycroft replied briefly to his brother's query.

"Other than the location of her secret headquarters in the Paris Opera House, her usage of the nearby A. L. Lard office, her employment of Feliciana Sorelli and Julia de Trémeuse as agents, her disguise of Augustine d'Erlette, and her true identity of Darlla Rassendyll, I really know very little about the Revenant."

A Bullet for the Colonel

"Die, Seraph!" shouted the Pallid Mask.

The sickle of the male assailant narrowly missed the Seraph's head. The hands of the female vigilante unhooked the metal belt around her thighs. She swung it in the air. The chain belt looped around the sickle.

A momentous battle was transpiring late one night on a rooftop in Paris during the summer of 1888. The Pallid Mask was emerging as the principal assassin of the Black Coats, the European crime syndicate. His name was derived from a notorious verse play, *Le Roi en Jaune.* The killer's face was covered by a white hood-like mask in the shape of an inscrutable face with high cheekbones and thin lips. The wearer's naked ears protruded from slits in the mask. A long dark cape flowed from his shoulders. A black suit with gloves finalized his costume.

The Jade Seraph belonged to the Acolytes of the Shadows, a small band dedicated to the destruction of the Black Coats. Her face was green. This was not due to makeup, but the result of exposure to a rare South American poison. Her raven hair was styled upward like a bouffant. A narrow forelock speared downward. Her eyebrows were slanted upward. Her body was encased in a green leotard with black gauntlets and boots. A pendant in the image of a six-winged angel hung around her neck.

Their weapons locked, the two combatants engaged in a tug of war. Each sought to dislodge the opposing lethal instrument out of the opponent's hand. The Pallid Mask broke the stalemate by delivering a vicious kick to the Seraph's midriff. Losing her footing, the Seraph fell sideways. Still clutching her chain, she slid backwards down the roof. As she skidded, her chain unwound from around the sickle. The Seraph dropped off the side of the roof. Her fall from the three story building was broken by a canopy over the entrance to a grocery store. She rolled off the canopy into the sidewalk. The Seraph lay unconscious on the pavement.

When the Pallid Mask reached the street, the Seraph was nowhere in sight. The assassin was approached by a statuesque woman. She had short blonde covered by a crimson cap. Her attire was a white blouse and a black skirt.

"The canopy broke the Seraph's fall," said Dr. Tanja Samuel. "She got up and ran into the night."

"How could anyone walk away from such a fall!" objected the Pallid Mask.

"The Seraph is no ordinary human. She has partaken of the Purple Sacrament."

The Pallid Mask accepted his associate's diagnosis.

"Let us continue to our destination, Tanja. Corbucci must be growing impatient."

The duo walked towards a hearse a few blocks away. As a front for her criminal activities, Tanja ran a funeral parlor. Her primary duty for the Black Coats was to dispose of corpses in an acid vat. The Pallid Mask had delivered the cadaver of a recent victim to her mortuary earlier. Tanja had volunteered to drive the Mask to his superior, Count Corbucci, at a disreputable tavern, *L'Epi-Scié*. The Mask needed to report the success of his assassination. While Tanja had driven the horse-drawn hearse, the Mask had sat in the back with an empty coffin. Three blocks from *L'Epi-Scié*, the Mask had looked out the hearse's window. He spotted the Seraph lurking in an alley. Since the Black Coats had literally placed a price of 10,000 francs on the Seraph's head, he immediately signaled Tanja to stop the hearse. Exiting the carriage, the Mask had chased the Seraph to the rooftops.

Back inside the hearse, the Mask secreted his sickle in a large pocket inside his cloak. He removed his white hood. The handsome face of Antoine Boucher, a young man of 21 years, was revealed. Arriving at *L'Epi-Scié*, Boucher alighted.

"Shall I wait for you?" asked Tanja

"That won't be necessary. Corbucci will provide transportation."

Tanja drove the hearse back to her parlor. Upon her arrival, she opened the lid of the supposedly empty coffin. Inside was an unconscious Jade Seraph.

The Jade Seraph lived in a secret sanctuary underneath the Paris Opera House. Her companion was the leader of the Acolytes of the Shadows, Darlla Rassendyll alias the Revenant. When the Seraph failed to return, Darlla took emergency measures the next day. She traversed a secret passage to the dressing room of Feliciana Sorelli, the leading ballerina of the Opera. Feliciana was the Acolyte called Lady Leopard. After being briefed by her superior, Feliciana left the Opera House for an office building on the Rue de Provence. There Feliciana entered the offices of the Sure Values Agency, a news bureau run by her fellow Acolyte, Chantal Lebrue. As Lady Invisible, Chantal handled all newspaper transactions for the Revenant. Feliciana instructed Chantal to place a personal advertisement in tomorrow morning's edition of *L'Epoque*. The ad read as follows:

Meeting of the Retribution Society at 3:00 this afternoon. All members are expected to attend.

The same afternoon, Tanja visited *L'Epi-Scié*. The blonde took another of the alehouse's female patron aside after a game of billiards.

"I have a business proposition for you. Come to my funeral parlor tonight."

The other woman, a fashionably dressed brunette of 29 years, was called La Richarde ("the Rich One"). She supposedly was Paris Mason, a fugitive from American justice. Her primary source of income was allegedly a regular remittance from her wealthy relatives in the United States. This whole background was false. In reality, La Richarde was Francis Clampin, the daughter of a former head of the Sûreté. She was a member of the Acolytes of the Shadows. Since her father had the nickname of Pistolet, she was known to her fellow Acolytes as Lady Pistolet.

La Richarde visited the Samuels Funeral Home that evening. She was greeted by Tanja. The female doctor was dressed in her customary garb with the exception of her red cap. She invited La Richarde to drink some La Frenaie wine in the reception room. Tanja related yesterday's events.

"You captured the Jade Seraph!" said La Richarde.

"She was lying dazed on the pavement," continued Tanja. "Luckily I always carry a bottle of chloroform in my hearse. It was child's play to overpower her. I hid my prize in the coffin in order to fool the Pallid Mask."

"Why was it necessary to trick him?"

"I have two reasons. First, I intend to collect the 10,000 bounty. Second, I need to make the Seraph a subject in my Great Experiment."

"What are you talking about, Tanja?"

"Since the Reign of Terror, doctors have speculated that a severed head doesn't always die instantly at the moment of decapitation. During a beheading, most victims perish immediately from shock. It has been theorized that a supply of oxygen can allow a human head to cling to life for minutes. I have long sought to prove this premise."

"I don't understand how the Seraph figures in your Great Experiment."

"For years, I've tested on human subjects, Richarde. I found beggars on the street and brought them here, but none of them survived after the physical separation. The Jade Seraph is unique. She has been exposed to the Purple Sacrament. As a consequence, her powers of recuperation have been enhanced, If anyone stands a chance of lingering after decapitation, it's the Seraph."

"The Seraph's still alive?"

"Yes, her demise has been delayed for a very practical reason. If I killed the Seraph last night and presented her head to Corbucci for the bounty, the Pallid Mask would have suspected my ruse. No, the head must be delivered to Corbucci a day later by someone other than me."

"You wish me to bring the head to Corbucci?"

"You were once a bounty killer. You're the logical candidate."

"We shall split the bounty equally. 5,000 francs each."

"You are being exceptional greedy, Richarde. I've done all the hard work. Your share will be only 3,000 francs."

"You drive a hard bargain, Tanja, but I agree."

"A freshly severed head will be the most effective evidence to fool the Pallid Mask. Will you assist me in the extermination of the Jade Seraph?"

"Of course."

"Follow me to the basement, Richarde."

"I'm surprised that you didn't try to make a deal with Ida Similor. She'll do anything to kill the Seraph."

"I want nothing to with that redheaded harpy. She mauled poor Kate Cusack."

Tanja was referring to her former pool partner. Ida had severely beaten Kate outside *L'Epi-Scié*. Since La Richarde hadn't seen Kate since, she assumed Tanja's friend had perished as a result of the thrashing.

From previous visits to the mortuary, La Richarde was aware that Tanja kept her acid vat in the cellar. After they descended the stairs, La Richarde paused in front of a wall mirror. She was a vain woman constantly admiring her own reflection. As Tanja indulged in her moment of narcissism, she spoke to La Richarde.

"Do you like my little device? It once belonged to the Countess de Clare. She used it to eradicate the Maynottes."

La Richarde's eyes beheld a guillotine. Lying on a bench was the Jade Seraph. She was face forward with her wrists handcuffed behind her back. Identical shackles bound her ankles. Her head was in the circular stock of the guillotine. A padlock prevented the stock from being opened. The blade of the deadly machine reclined high above the Seraph's neck. Some distance from the guillotine was Tanja's acid vat.

Filled with anxiety for the Seraph's plight, La Richarde approached the front of the guillotine. The tortured eyes of the Seraph gazed at her fellow Acolyte. La Richarde knew that the Seraph was suffering. The green-skinned vigilante was very sensitive about her neck. Nine years ago, the Seraph had been thrown into a coma due to a severe neck injury.

"Why is her mouth gagged?" asked La Richarde.

"She proved a most difficult subject," answered Tanja. "She's constantly screaming. Such behavior will deplete the reservoir of oxygen in her skull."

"Would it be better for your experiment if the subject was calm?"

"Yes."

"Could you let me try to calm her down?"

"Try whatever you wish."

"Seraph, if I remove the gag, do you promise not to scream?"

The Seraph nodded in response to La Richarde's question. La Richarde untied the gag. The Seraph emitted a large scream.

"Gag her again!" ordered Tanja.

"No!" begged the Seraph. "I'll behave."

"Would you like to lie on your back?" asked La Richarde.

"Yes, please."

"Tanja, could you unlock the stock?"

Reacting to La Richarde's request, Tanja opened a cupboard and took out a ring of keys. Unlocking the padlock, Tanja lifted the stock. La Richarde flipped the Seraph on her back.

"Thank you, I'm comfortable now," acknowledged the Seraph.

"You're comfortable enough," decided Tanja as she turned the lever that released the guillotine's blade. La Richarde seized The Seraph and yanked her backwards. The blade missed the captive's head. Tanja leaped at La Richarde.

"You ruined my Great Experiment!"

Tanja's hands encircled La Richarde's throat. Seizing her blonde opponent's wrists, the brunette pried the choking hands off her neck. La Richarde pushed Tanja away. The blonde directed a punch toward the brunette's head. Ducking the blow, La Richarde grabbed Tanja's arm. The brunette twisted it behind the blonde's back. La Richarde pushed Tanja towards the large acid vat. The blonde's head slammed against the side of the vat. She slumped senseless to the ground.

Grabbing Tanja's keys, La Richarde removed the Seraph's handcuffs. The Seraph hugged La Richarde.

"Thank you, Pistolet!"

"You're the Disciple of Life, Seraph. You can't see what's about to happen. Please wait upstairs."

Tanja Samuel's slumbers were interrupted by strange sensation. As the blonde rested on the ground, she was examined closely by La Richarde. The brunette was relieved that her defeated opponent was still breathing. La Richarde had been concerned that Tanja had succumbed outright to a death blow. Tanja's eyes flickered indicating that she was about to revive. La Richarde removed the mirror from the wall and held it in front of Tanja's face.

"Behold your reflection, Tanja. I beheaded you with the guillotine while you slept! Your Great Experiment is a success!"

Tanja tried to scream, but no sound left her mouth. She had no vocal cords. As the oxygen left her brain, Tanja succumbed to death.

Driving Tanja's hearse, La Richarde transported the Seraph to the Paris Opera House. Once the Seraph disembarked, La Richarde took the hearse back to the funeral parlor. After spending hours at the mortuary, La Richarde exited carrying a hat box. She took a cab back to her apartment.

The newspaper ad placed by Lady Invisible had been a call for the gathering of the Acolytes of the Shadows. "The Retribution Society" was a code name for the Acolytes. The alias stemmed from the secret motto of the Acolytes: "Retribution to the Black Coats."

Their meeting was a mansion belonging to Dr. Rolande Cerral, alias Lady Scalpel. She was a brown-haired woman in her forties. All the other females attending the meeting were in their twenties and thirties. Besides Lady Pistolet, the blonde Lady Leopard and the dark-haired Lady Invisible, the Acolytes included the brown-haired Angelique LaSalle, alias Lady Tocsin. Also present was the blonde Julia de Trémeuse, alias Lady Judex. She had been the first Acolyte recruited by the Revenant. Now a married woman with children, she had technically been inactive since 1881. However, she attended the Acolytes' meeting to offer advice.

All of these Acolytes were dressed in black leotards with a black belt and a hood tucked inside. Gloves covered their hands. They had been trained in fighting techniques by the Jade Seraph and the Revenant. With the exception of Lady Judex, the female Acolytes normally wore these costumes under their clothes during the day. The active Acolytes never knew when they might be called upon to assist the Revenant or the Seraph in physical combat against the Black Coats. Judex only wore her leotard when attending a conference of the Acolytes.

In the early days, the Acolytes wore black capes and domino masks. Upon the recommendation of the Seraph, the black leotard became the garb of the Acolytes in 1884.

Three attendees were dressed differently from the other Acolytes. There were the Revenant, the Jade Seraph and Charles Blanton alias Lord Charon, the only male member of the Acolytes. Charon drove a coach that transported the Revenant and the Seraph throughout Paris. A tall muscular man, Charon was attired like a regular coachman. He had driven the Revenant and the Seraph to Lady Scalpel's residence.

Because she was framed for murder and treason by the Black Coats, the Revenant could not appear in public in her real identity of Darlla Rassendyll. Therefore, she disguised herself as an elderly spinster named Augustine d'Erlette. Upon her arrival at Lady Scalpel's, Darlla removed her Augustine disguise and switched into her Revenant costume. As the Revenant, Darlla wore a black shirt whose V-shaped neckline was outlined in red. She wore black pants and boots. In loops in her belt were holstered a three-bladed pickaxe and a Punjabi lasso. Scarlet gloves covered her hands. Although the Revenant normally wore a black hood with a red skull insignia, she appeared to her Acolytes unmasked. A tall redhead, the Revenant had world-weary eyes and a cruel mouth.

Valorie Varno, alias the Jade Seraph, had escorted the Revenant to the conclave. Valorie had hidden her Seraph costume underneath a veil and a heavy dress with wide sleeves. Like the Revenant, the Seraph had doffed her disguise at Lady Scalpel's.

Seated in front of all the Acolytes were the Revenant and the Seraph. The Revenant was holding her pickaxe like a scepter. The Seraph was seated to the right. Judex, Tocsin and Leopard were seated together on a couch. On an adjacent coach were Invisible, Pistolet, and Scalpel. Pistolet was tossing a small golden object in her right hand. Since he had been seated during the coach ride, Charon preferred to stand.

"We are the Acolytes of the Shadows," proudly proclaimed the Revenant. "My Ladies and my Lord, what is our goal?"

"Retribution to the Black Coats!" answered the Acolytes.

"The original purpose of this meeting was to react to the disappearance of our Disciple of Life," continued the Revenant. "Fortunately, the actions of Pistolet render such a topic moot. Not only did Pistolet rescue the Seraph, but she also rendered justice on a depraved murderess. Tanja Samuel is no more. She has been fed to her own guillotine."

"Tanja's death might make the Black Coats suspicious of your La Richarde identity, Pistolet," noted Leopard. "How did you dispose of the body?"

"I dump Tanja's headless body on her acid vat, but I embalmed her head. It resides in a hatbox in my apartment."

"I don't see the wisdom of preserving such a ghoulish relic," declared the Revenant.

"With your permission, Revenant, I intend to employ Tanja's head to deceive the Black Coats."

"Does this involve the bounty of 30,000 francs that the All-Father placed on my head four years ago?"

"Yes. The All-Father was afraid that one of his hired killers might defraud him by killing a random woman and putting her severed head in a Revenant mask. Therefore, it was stipulated that the bounty killer must present your head personally to the All-Father to collect the reward. The All-Father thinks that he can infallibly tell whether someone is lying. If I present Tanja's head as yours to Count Corbucci, he'll arrange a meeting between me and the All-Father in Corsica."

"But Corbucci will recognize the head as Tanja's," objected Tocsin.

"The Black Coats are unaware of the Revenant's true identity," stated Pistolet. "I'll claim that Tanja was really the Revenant."

"And if you are granted an audience with the All-Father in Corsica, what good will that accomplish?" asked Invisible.

Pistolet stopped tossing her golden keepsake. She held it up for all to see. "Seven years ago. I promised my father to slay the All-Father with this golden bullet. I intend to kill the overlord of the Black Coats."

"You'll never get close to the All-Father with a gun," predicted Judex.

"Not with an ordinary gun," said Scalpel. Her right hand displayed a fountain pen. "This is my latest invention. It looks like one of the new pens developed by Waterman. It actually is a single-shot pistol."

"My trip to Corsica might take a month or longer," estimated Pistolet. "During that time, Revenant, you must not attack the Black Coats in your costume."

"I can fight our enemies in other guises," said the Revenant.

"Don't you all realize how insane this proposal is?" cried the Seraph. "Pistolet will be all alone in Corsica with no one to aid her."

Judex shook her head. "Your objection is easily remedied. All our information indicates that the All-Father's base is somewhere in the vicinity of Sartène. My wealthy parents owned a house in that city. I could easily stay there to assist Pistolet if necessary."

"You rarely play a major role in our activities," observed Invisible. "Why are you volunteering now?"

"I'm a Corsican," affirmed Lady Judex. "My maiden name is Orsini, but my great-grandfather was Mathieu d'Arx. He was strangled in 1823 by the All-Father's minions. Mathieu's daughter was my grandmother. In 1854, she was nearly strangled by the All-Father. Her life was saved by Joseph Clampin, the original Pistolet. I'm honor bound to assist his daughter and namesake."

"The All-Father of today can't be the same man who killed your great-grandfather," professed Invisible.

"The All-Father is the immortal Colonel Michele Bozzo-Corona," said Judex. "He's almost 150 years old. If you have any doubts about his longevity, ask the Seraph. She has met him."

"I only saw him in a black robe and hood," contributed the Jade Seraph. "He boasted that he was the original Colonel, but he could easily be an impostor."

"If the current All-Father lays claim to the Colonel's identity, then he inherits his sins as well," replied Judex.

"I know that the All-Father is evil incarnate, but we must abandon Pistolet's plan," insisted the Seraph. "We can't be plotting an assassination. Adopting such a course will make us as monstrous as the Black Coats. Revenant, as your Disciple of Life, I humbly beg you to reject this plan."

"Judex is clearly in favor of Pistolet's plan and the Seraph is opposed," remarked the Revenant. "Before I make my decision, I wish to hear from all my Acolytes."

"My sister was killed by the Black Coats," said Tocsin. "Their leader must die."

"Now that he has made peace with Monsieur Nemo, the All-Father has grown more powerful," affirmed Leopard. "We may never get another chance to kill him."

"I dislike assassination," said Invisible, "but then I remember this maniacal bounty placed by the All-Father on the heads of the Revenant and the Seraph. Let it be his undoing!"

"I use the surname of Cerral, but my real name is Lenoir," confessed Scalpel. "My family went into hiding due to the persecution of the Black Coats. Our protector was Joseph Clampin. I support his daughter."

Charon was appalled. "You're letting revenge blind your judgment. If Pistolet goes to Corsica, the Black Coats will kill her."

The Revenant raised her pickaxe in the air. "Lady Pistolet has performed courageously as an Acolyte for four years. She has saved both my life and the Seraph's. Her petition is granted."

When Antoine Boucher entered the "Confessional," the upstairs conference room of *L'Epi-Scié*, he was startled by the sight of Tanja Samuel's embalmed head lying on a table in front of a seated Count Corbucci. Next to the severed head were a pickaxe, a lasso and a Revenant costume. Standing nearby was La Richarde.

"Repeat what you told me, Richarde," commanded Corbucci, a stout man with a heavy mustache.

"During a billiard game at *L'Epi-Scié*, Tanja related the battle between the Pallid Mask and the Jade Seraph. Her account sounded fishy to me. She could have easily hidden the Seraph in the empty coffin in her hearse. I decided to spy on her funeral parlor last night. I saw the Jade Seraph leaving the mortuary. It must have taken her a day to recover from the fall. I picked the lock of the funeral home. Searching the house, I found Tanja dressed as the Revenant. She was about to put on her mask when I surprised her. That blonde witch tried to brain me with her pickaxe. Luckily I had this."

La Richarde reached into her purse and pulled out a circular disk with a barrel sticking out from it. It was an assassin's weapon popularly called a "squeeze gun."

"I shot her in the right breast. I used the top blade of the pickaxe to cut off her head. After stripping off the Revenant's clothes, I disposed of the body in the acid vat in the basement." La Richarde patted Tanja's blonde curls. "Since I didn't want my trophy to rot, I embalmed it."

Boucher examined the Revenant costume. He found a bullet hole in the left chest area. There was a noticeable red stain. The stain was produced by blood ironically contributed by the Jade Seraph. For years, Rolande Cerral had been experimenting with samples of the Seraph's blood in an attempt to isolate the recuperative properties bestowed by the Purple Sacrament. Before departing that afternoon as Augustine d'Erlette, Darlla Rassendyll had left her Revenant paraphernalia at Dr. Cerral's. La Richarde, alias Lady Pistolet, had shot a bullet through the shirt. Dr. Cerral, alias Lady Scalpel, sprinkled one of the Seraph's blood samples over the bullet hole.

Boucher asked La Richarde for her squeeze gun. She surrendered it. Opening the cartridge chamber, he saw that one bullet had been fired.

"Tanja's father was a member of the High Council," said Boucher. "How could she be the Revenant?"

"Wasn't her father always plotting against the All-Father?" asked La Richarde. "Maybe she was carrying on some family vendetta."

Boucher lifted up Tanja's head by its hair. "You filthy slut! You killed my darling Meaghan!" Boucher spat in Tanja's face.

Meaghan Cullen had been a bounty killer for the Black Coats. Boucher mistakenly believed that Meaghan had been drowned by the Revenant. In reality, La Richarde had slain Meaghan.

"I understand your feelings, young man, but you must not damage the All-Father's prize," admonished Corbucci. "Antoine, you will escort La Richarde and the Revenant's head to Corsica."

Since she was being shepherded to Corsica, La Richarde didn't risk taking her Acolyte leotard with her. With a hatbox housing Tanja Samuel's head, La Richarde and Antoine Boucher traveled to Toulon. There they took a ship for Ajaccio, the capital of Corsica. In Ajaccio, they rode in a coach bound for Sartène.

When Boucher was seventeen, he had been La Richarde's lover before deserting her for Meaghan Cullin. During their journey together, La Richarde and Boucher rekindled their romance. They spent many nights wrapped in each other's embrace.

At Sartène, their coach rendezvoused with another coach. A stunningly beautiful woman in a blue dress stepped out of the other vehicle. Her black hair hung down on her shoulders. She possessed alluring blue-gray eyes. Bright red lipstick adorned her lips.

"I'll be leaving you now, my sweet Richarde," revealed Boucher. "This is Desdemona Cullin, Meaghan's cousin. Her carriage will transport you to the All-Father."

"Will you be remaining in Sartène, my love?" asked La Richarde.

"I'll be returning to Ajaccio to catch a ship for Barcelona. I have another commission for Count Corbucci." Boucher gave La Richarde a parting kiss.

La Richarde's luggage was loaded on top of Desdemona's coach with two exceptions. La Richarde carried the hatbox as well as a small purse. Once the two women were inside, the coach started.

"I'm afraid that you won't be able to admire the countryside," said Desdemona. "The windows have been covered by shutters. The All-Father's location is a closely guarded secret. When we arrive at our final destination, I'll have to blindfold you."

"So long as I'm paid the bounty, I'll have no complaints."

"You are American?"

"My real name is Paris Mason."

"Did you know my late cousin Meaghan very well?"

"We were great friends."

"Did she ever tell you about her ancestors?"

"I know her father was a British earl."

"What about her mother's family?"

"They were residents of Magna Sark, an island in the British Channel. Her maternal grandmother was a music hall performer."

"She was my grandmother as well. Meaghan's parents never married. Cullin was my father's name, but it was her mother's. Did Meaghan ever talk about our American grandfather?'

"The Cullins originally came from America?"

"Cullin is actually a corruption of another name. My grandfather changed his surname because of his notorious reputation. He was nearly beheaded for witchcraft in 1840."

"Where did this happen?"

"In the state of Maine."

"You're pulling my leg. Unlike the French, Americans don't behead people. They hang them. Furthermore, there hasn't been a witchcraft trial in New England since the 1690's."

"I speak the truth. Some judge revived an old colonial law. My grandfather's family is one of the wealthiest in Maine. They suppressed all the records of my grandfather's trial. Even though my grandfather was exonerated, he thought it wise to resettle with his British bride in Magna Sark."

"Just as I thought it wise to migrate to France after a little misunderstanding with the law in West Virginia."

"You talk like a lawyer, Richarde."

"My father was a lawyer."

"As was my grandfather. May I hold the hatbox?"

La Richarde handed the hatbox to Desdemona.

"So this is the head of Tanja Samuel," said Desdemona. "I wonder if she became the Revenant to avenge the knifing of her father in 1838. The original Dr. Samuel nearly died from that attack. The All-Father ordered the Marchef to do the stabbing. Have you heard of the Marchef?"

"He was the All-Father's private executioner. His real name was Jean-Francois Coyatier. An ex-soldier, his title of Marchef was military slang for the French equivalent of a quarter-master sergeant. The Marchef died long ago."

"But his legacy lives on. When the All-Father re-emerged in the 1870's, he recruited a Corsican to be his personal assassin. The Corsican was given the title of Marchef. Last year, another member of the All-Father's entourage grew jealous of the Corsican's prestige and challenged him to a duel. When the Corsican was killed, his slayer became the new Marchef. Pray you never meet the Marchef, Richarde."

"Why?"

"Those who meet the Marchef are condemned to a slow and agonizing death."

Desdemona paused. She looked at the hatbox.

"It is doubly ironic, Richarde, for me to hold this relic. I never would have been born if my grandfather had suffered a similar fate as the Revenant. I also hold the head of the woman responsible for my cousin's death." Desdemona's gaze shifted away from the hatbox and stared into La Richarde's eyes. "I never knew the full details of poor Meaghan's death. She was killed by one of the Revenant's Acolytes. Was she not?"

"No, she was killed by the Revenant."

"You make that statement with great certainty. Did you witness my cousin's death?"

"I tried to save your cousin. I even wounded the Revenant with my squeeze gun."

"Ah, your squeeze gun. Do you have it on you?"

"It's in my purse."

"May I see your squeeze gun?"

Taking the weapon out of her purse, La Richarde gave it to Desdemona.

"A handy pistol. I'll return it to you after your session with the All-Father. Do you have any other weapons?"

"No."

"Did this gun kill the Revenant?"

"Yes"

"You avenged my cousin. I owe you a great debt, Richarde. I shall do my utmost to repay it."

The carriage suddenly halted.

"We have reached our destination," declared Desdemona. "I must blindfold you."

The blindfolded Acolyte was led out of the carriage by Desdemona. La Richarde was escorted down a long flight of stairs. Desdemona directed La Richarde through a stream of corridors. Throughout the journey, Desdemona carried the hatbox while La Richarde's purse hung on her wrist. Eventually Desdemona indicated that they should proceed no further.

"Wait here, Richarde. I must leave you now. The All-Father shall be with you shortly."

After five minutes, the silence was broken by an ominous voice. "Remove your blindfold!"

Putting her hands behind her head, Pistolet untied the blindfold. She let it fall to the ground. She beheld a figure seated on throne. He was garbed in a black robe with a raised hood. A dark mask covered his face. Behind his chair was a long black curtain. Before him was a table with a black cloth. It gave the impression of a satanic altar. On top of the altar were two golden jars. The hatbox was open. The bare hand of the personage reached down and grasped the hair of the head inside. The robed character raised the head.

"The daughter of Dr. Samuel! Her father was an untrustworthy lieutenant. It pleases me to own her head. I, the All-Father, thank you!"

"You're welcome, Colonel. May I have the bounty?"

La Richarde, alias Lady Pistolet, knew that it was within her power to shoot the All-Father, but such an action now would be suicidal. She had no avenue of escape. Pistolet would only act once she had properly gauged her surroundings.

"Before I authorize payment," said the All-Father, "I need to rectify a few matters. Monsieur Boucher noticed a slight discrepancy in your accusations against Tanja Samuel."

"Antoine never mentioned this to me!"

"But he conveyed it to Salvatore Corbucci, who told me. It involves Meaghan Cullin. You wounded the Revenant twice on the night Meaghan died. Didn't you?"

"Yes."

"Do you remember where Boucher went after he discovered Meaghan's body?"

"He went to Tanja Samuel's funeral parlor to have Meghan's corpse embalmed."

"And Samuel demonstrated no evidence of having been wounded. Explain this discrepancy."

"Count Corbucci must have told you that I tried unsuccessfully to collect the bounty on the Revenant's head. I was convinced that my two bullets fatally wounded her four years ago. The Revenant must have died that night and been buried secretly by her Acolytes. One of those Acolytes, Tanja Samuel, then assumed the Revenant's identity to fool the Black Coats. I actually slew two different Revenants."

"Why didn't you disclose this information before?"

"I thought it would confuse matters. I've already been denied one bounty. I didn't want to lose another."

"A very credible explanation. Come closer, my dove, I wish to examine your features."

Pistolet positioned herself directly in front of the table. She gazed down on the jars. They were labeled "André" and "Julie." She realized that the jars must contain the heads of the Maynottes, whose decapitated corpses were discovered in 1848. Reaching into her purse, Pistolet gripped the fountain pen. The All-Father rose to his full height. He was much taller than Pistolet had expected.

'You're an extraordinary woman, my dear, almost as pretty as my irreplaceable Desdemona. What's your opinion of her?"

"She's very charming."

"I knew her grandmother. She was an accomplished performer who toured both France and America. I saw her perform at the *Tivoli* in Avignon during the 1830's. Desdemona's grandmother was *'fey'* Do you comprehend the meaning of that English word?"

"It means to have second sight."

"Desdemona's grandmother was a psychic. Desdemona inherited this gift. She can look into a person's eyes and perceive if the subject is lying." The All-

116

Father's hand shot out across the altar and grasped Pistolet's throat. *"Who are you?"*

"I'm Francis Clampin, the daughter of Pistolet!"

Pistolet fired the fountain pen into the breast of the All-Father. He collapsed on his throne. Pistolet pulled back his hood and remove the mask. The face of a gray-haired man was exposed. Pistolet judged his age to be about fifty. His wide mouth was open in death. Pistolet looked inside.

"He has no tongue," she said with a shudder.

The curtain behind the throne was suddenly pulled back.

"Drop your weapon!"

The speaker was Desdemona holding a gun. Next to her was a wizened old man.

Pistolet let the pen fall from her hand.

"I am Colonel Bozzo-Corona," said the old man. "The deceased is Saladin, also known as the Sword-Swallower. In the 1860's, he had the effrontery to usurp my title of All-Father. I enslaved him for his insolence. My punishment was to make him *swallow his last sword*. The consequence was the removal of his tongue. He became my decoy. Hidden behind the curtain, I employed ventriloquism to make him appear to speak. His actions were based on cues in my dialogue. Considering your parentage, my dear, I wish we could spend more time together. However, I promised you to Desdemona."

"Put your hands up and turn around," ordered Desdemona.

Lady Pistolet did as her captor ordered. Desdemona moved directly behind her prisoner.

"You told me a pack of falsehoods in the coach, daughter of Pistolet. You lied when you said my cousin wasn't killed by an Acolyte of the Revenant. She was. That Acolyte can only be you. I do indeed owe you a debt---a debt of vengeance. I intend to collect with interest. You shall meet the Marchef!"

Reversing the gun, Desdemona brought its butt crashing down on the back of Lady Pistolet's skull.

When Pistolet awoke, her arms were extended high above her head. They were chained in two shackles on a crossbar mounted on a chain extending into the ceiling. There was a lock in the middle of the crossbar. Pistolet's dress had been removed. She was only clad in her white undergarments, a corset and a petticoat ending just above the knees. There were no longer any shoes on her feet.

A young girl was laughing at Pistolet. The petite chuckler's brown hair was cut in a short fashion that made her head resemble a monkey's. She wore a military uniform. Her blue coat had three vertical rows of buttons. One row ran down the middle while the others were parallel on the right and left sides. A red ascot was looped around her neck. Her blue skirt was covered by a small white apron. The skirt ended shortly above her ankles. Beneath the skirt could be glimpsed the ends of her black trousers covering boots. White gloves encased her hands. A canteen hung crosswise from her right shoulder.

"Are you the Marchef?" asked Pistolet.

"No, I'm the Marchef's slave. I'm the Cantinière."

Pistolet recognized the term. Cantinières were female quartermasters in the French army. They supplied food and drink to soldiers.

"How old are you, Cantinière?"

"I'm sixteen."

"You shouldn't be a slave. Release me, and we can escape this place together."

"Why should I do that? I belong to the Marchef. Besides I'll enjoy watching you die. Once you're dead, I'll drink your blood!"

"You sick depraved girl! How could you become such a monster?"

"My father was Faustine Cortina. He was the second Marchef. For over a decade, my father served the Colonel faithfully. Four years ago, a devil in human form became the principal advisor to the Colonel. This devil resented my father's influence with the Colonel. The devil challenged my father to defend his title of Marchef. They dueled with those." She pointed to a pair of crossed machetes mounted on the wall. The weapons had blades thirteen inches long. "The devil slew my father. The colonel then gave the devil my father's title and all his possessions including me."

"No one has a right to make you a slave."

"I made myself a slave. The new Marchef offered me a choice. Either die like my father, or sell my soul. To preserve my life, I sold my soul to the Marchef by a rite of baptism. I bathed in the blood of my father."

"The Marchef can't own your soul."

"The Marchef practices witchcraft. If the Marchef were to die, my soul would be sent immediately to Hell. I relish my servitude. I get to see the Marchef torture others to death. So far I've observed forty-five people perish. You will be the forty-sixth. I must finish my preparations."

The Cantinière walked to a downward lever on the wall. She pushed it upward. The chains holding Lady Pistolet rose four feet. Her feet dangling, Pistolet hung in the air.

On a table, there rested an iron bowl. Next to it were a ring with a single key, a barrel with a spigot, and a blank wooden placard with a rope looped around it. The Cantinière took the bowl and placed it under Pistolet's feet.

"When the Marchef interrogates you," said the Cantinière, "your blood shall drip into this bowl. Once you are dead, I shall take the bowl and mix your blood with this La Frenaie wine. "The Cantinière tapped the barrel on the table. "I'll fill up my canteen with the blood-wine. The blood-splattered Marchef and I will then roam the tunnels sipping your blood. They say that Coyatier was so feared that none of the other Black Coats would shake his hand. The other denizens of this place dread my Marchef so much that none will gaze on us during our revelry. Making our way to the surface, we shall take horses from the stables and ride for hours. We shall celebrate your destruction in ways beyond your imagination."

"Are you the Marchef's lover?"

The Cantinière giggled. "Lover? What type of girl do you take me for? The Marchef only has one lover. The Marchef's lover is Colonel Bozzo-Corona."

Desdemona Cullin lied naked in the Colonel's bed. Michele Bozzo-Corona massaged her back.

"You are like a matador, my enchanting Desdemona. You must make love before you kill."

"It's the only time that I have you for myself, Michele. After the death of Francis Clampin, I'll have to share you with my Cantinière."

"Are you satisfied with her, my dove?"

"She fulfills her duties for me adequately."

"But I'm not satisfied with her performance. I find it subpar."

"Perhaps I should replace her. Do you have a candidate in mind?"

"My original Marchef had a granddaughter. Her name is Orianne. She is nearing her twentieth birthday."

"Where is she now?'

"Orianne's in a boarding school near Avignon. She graduates next year."

"If she becomes my Cantinière, I'll have to baptize her."

"Baptize Orianne with the blood of your current Cantinière."

"An excellent suggestion, Michele. Young Clampin will be growing impatient. I must depart for our intimate interview."

Rising from the bed, Desdemona clothed herself in a black outfit. She put on pants and boots. The only thing covering her breasts and midriff was a butcher's leather apron that extended to her knees. She tied the apron's string around her bare back. On her arms were opera gloves that ended just below her shoulders. Looking in a mirror, she painted her lips with vividly crimson lipstick. Desdemona picked up an object from the top of a cabinet. She tossed it in the air.

"What are you playing with?" asked the Colonel.

"I carved this out of Saladin's body. It's a golden bullet."

The Colonel roared with laughter. "Our guest must have heard the false legend that only a golden weapon can kill me. I am Fra Diavolo. I am Bel Demonio. I can never die. Make young Clampin's death particularly excruciating, Desdemona, my Marchef."

Desdemona locked the door of the torture chamber behind her. She gazed upward at the shackled captive.

"Has my Cantinière told you the fate that awaits you?"

"I'm to be your forty-sixth victim," replied Pistolet.

"You're to be my forty-sixth intimate. I prefer the term of intimate over that of victim. Other than the relationship between lovers, nothing is more intimate than the bond between the slayer and the slain. I intend to achieve a level of intimacy with you higher than any I've experienced before. Our intimacy will ascend to the ultimate climax. For us to be intimates, we must address each other properly. Call me Marchef. What shall I call you? Francis? Clampin? Richarde? Paris?"

"I am Pistolet, the daughter of Pistolet! If I swear an oath in my father's name, I shall keep it!"

"A totally accurate statement, Pistolet, but somewhat superfluous."

"As superfluous as drinking the blood of your intimates, Marchef?"

"My ritual stems from a vision that I had while reading an account of Elizabeth Bathory. Are you familiar with her, Pistolet?"

"She was a fiend who sought eternal youth by murdering virgins and bathing in their blood."

"In my vision, I beheld a dark handsome man dressed in the garb of the late eighteenth century. He was feasting on the blood of young women. I knew instinctively that Bathory had been misguided. Drinking blood was the true path to immortality."

"Your lover professes to be immortal. Why not ask him?"

"The Colonel does not share all his secrets with me. Perhaps the man in my vision was one of my ancestors. If I ever visit my grandfather's ancestral home in Maine, I shall scrutinize the family portraits."

Desdemona pointed to the wine keg. "It's poetic justice. You drowned my cousin in La Frenaie wine, and I shall drink your blood laced with the same beverage."

"My only regret concerning your cousin, Marchef, is that I can't arrange your reunion with her in Hell."

"A foolish statement of bravado, Pistolet. You shall pay royally for it by entering a Hell of my own making." Desdemona held up the golden bullet in her right hand. "I can sense a word sometimes in my subject's eyes. I perceive the word 'Father' currently in yours. This pellet was a legacy from your father. After I finish with an intimate, I show my lover their mutilated carcasses. A placard surrounds their necks bearing the final word derived from their eyes. It is scrawled in their own blood. The word has often been 'Hell.' When my lover examines your cadaver dangling from the chains, he'll also find your precious bullet clenched between your teeth."

Desdemona positioned herself next to the mounted machetes.

"These were a gift to the All-Father from Count Corbucci after a trip to Cuba. We must establish the rules of our intimacy, Pistolet. I shall ask you several questions. When you fail to tell me the truth, I shall draw one of the machetes and begin to slice off your flesh. Who is the Revenant?"

"Darlla Rassendyll."

Desdemona stared into the eyes of her prisoner. "You speak the truth. How can Rassendyll be the Revenant? The knife of Feliciana Sorelli was driven into her heart. I saw the photo."

"The photo was faked with a wax effigy. Feliciana is one of the Revenant's Acolytes."

"Who are the other Acolytes?"

"Julia de Trémeuse, Angelique LaSalle, Chantal Lebrue, Rolande Cerral, and Charles Blanton. Valorie Varno, the Jade Seraph, acts as the Disciple of Life."

"Your cooperation surprises me, Pistolet. I must move closer to ensure my powers are not failing me." Desdemona now stood directly in front of Pistolet. "Are you a coward? Are you afraid of torture?"

"No to both questions."

"Then you must me be trying to trick me. What trick are you playing?"

"If you're focused on my eyes, then you aren't watching *my legs!*"

Pistolet jackknifed her body. Her legs seized Desdemona's neck in a scissor hold. Desdemona dropped the golden bullet. She gripped Pistolet's legs in a futile effort to break the stranglehold.

"Cantinière!" yelled Pistolet. "In the name of my father, my next words are true! I can easily snap the Marchef's neck! Throw me the key and I'll release her alive!"

Grabbing the key ring from the table, the Cantinière threw it. Pistolet caught the ring in her right hand. She nimbly maneuvered the key into the lock on the crossbar. The shackles on Pistolet's wrists unlocked. In order not to fall prematurely, Pistolet's hands held on to the open manacles. She relinquished her hold on Desdemona. Gasping for breath, the Marchef tumbled sideways. Releasing her grip on the manacles, Pistolet swung forward and planted her feet firmly on the ground. The iron bowl was behind her.

The Cantinière drew one of the machetes. She hacked at Pistolet. The Acolyte of the Revenant easily dodged the blow. She delivered a devastating leg kick to the Cantinière's face. Rendered insensible, the young girl plummeted smack into the floor. The impact loosened the cap on the girl's canteen. Wine began to leak on the ground.

Pistolet quickly seized the machete from the unconscious Cantinière. A fully recovered Marchef rose from the ground and drew the other machete.

"I underestimated you, Pistolet! Your little ploy will gain you nothing! The Black Coats will hunt down the Revenant and all her Acolytes!"

"You know too much, Marchef! You shall not leave this room alive!"

The two duelists battled across the dungeon. Their blades constantly clashed together blocking each other's assaults,

Pistolet seemed to be getting the upper hand. The Marchef had been forced back towards the locked door, but she then mounted a ferocious attack. Pistolet was pushed back near the empty chains. The heel of Pistolet's left foot stepped in the spilled wine. She slipped and fell on her back. Her machete slid away from her hand. The Marchef's machete slashed downwards. Pistolet avoided her opponent's blow by rolling on the ground. She rolled next to the iron bowl. Pistolet grabbed the bowl. Her arms raised the bowl with the bottom facing upward. The Marchef's machete struck the improvised shield. Pushing her adversary away, Pistolet leaped to her feet. She smashed the bowl into the Marchef's forehead. Still standing with the machete in her right hand, the dazed Marchef swayed back and forth. Casting aside the bowl, Pistolet's hands clutched the staggering Marchef's wrist. Turning the Marchef's hand inwards, Pistolet plunged the blade into her adversary's stomach.

The Marchef howled in agony. Pistolet released the Marchef's wrist. The gloved hand fell limply as the Marchef's legs buckled. Her descent was halted by Pistolet. While her left arm wrapped around the collapsing Marchef's waist, Pistolet's right hand grabbed the imbedded machete's hilt. Cradling the stabbed interrogator, Pistolet stared triumphantly into the Marchef's gaping eyes.

"What do you glimpse in my eyes?" hissed Pistolet.

"Retribution...," muttered Desdemona. Her eyelids flickered briefly before she expired.

Yanking the machete out of her vanquished enemy, Pistolet disdainfully dumped the corpse on the ground. She went over to the senseless Cantinière and gently rubbed her face. The girl was Pistolet's only hope of escape. The Cantinière must be manipulated into shifting her allegiance.

"Awaken, child," said Pistolet.

The Cantinière opened her eyes.

"Where is the Marchef?"

"Your enslaver has fallen in combat." Pistolet helped the Cantinière to her feet. "Look upon the woman who slew your father."

"Hey! If she's dead, my soul should be in Hell!"

"She lied to you. Desdemona Cullin was a false devil. Your soul is your own, child."

The Cantinière kicked Desdemona's corpse.

"Liar! Whore!"

"What is your real name, child?"

"Andreina."

"Andreina Cortina, Desdemona offered you a choice between life and death after she killed your father. Now that she's dead, choose between damnation and salvation. If you stay here, what will be your fate?"

"The Colonel will be angered by the Marchef's death. He'll blame me. He'll *cut the branch*." Andreina ran her finger across her throat.

"You were the Marchef's slave, Andreina. I, Lady Pistolet, the Acolyte of the Revenant, offer you a greater role. The knights of old had squires. Will you be my squire?"

"One job is as good as another. My answer is yes."

"Kneel before me, Andreina Cortina."

Andreina complied. Pistolet raised the bloody machete in the air.

"Do you swear before God to serve me loyally?'

"Yes."

"In return, I, Francis Clampin, the daughter of Joseph Clampin, the man called Pistolet; promise to protect you from all who seek to harm you."

"Arise, Squire."

Andreina stood upright.

"I was blindfolded when I came here," said Pistolet. "Where are we?"

"We are in the catacombs underneath the abandoned Convent of the Brotherhood of Mercy. The Black Coats create the illusion that it is haunted. They masquerade as ghostly monks."

Pistolet had heard of the Convent. In 1843, the French government had mined the entrances to the catacombs. The Colonel must have reopened the passageways decades later.

"Do you know your way through the tunnels, Andreina?"

"Yes."

"Could you take me aboveground to the stables?"

"Yes."

"The Marchef and I have the same shade of hair and similar builds. I'll impersonate her. Help me strip off her clothes. I'll also need your assistance to arrange my hair properly."

Once Pistolet was dressed as the Marchef, she directed Andreina to fill her canteen with La Frenaie wine. "Should I mix it with the Marchef's blood?" asked Andreina.

"We don't drink blood!"

Andreina was dejected. "You don't have to be nasty. I'm only asking. My duties as a squire are new to me. First you kick me in the face, and now you yell at me."

Pistolet realized that Andreina's ego needed to be soothed. "I'm sorry, my faithful Squire." She hugged Andreina. "You're making an excellent transition." Pistolet picked up the golden bullet from the floor. She was going to leave a message for the Colonel.

Guided by Andreina, Pistolet marched through the subterranean corridors. She held the canteen to her mouth to hide her face. She passed numerous members of the Black Coats. Most of them were dressed as monks. They all shielded their eyes when they approached the supposed Marchef and her Cantinière. If any of the Black Coats noticed the blood on the apron worn by Pistolet, they assumed it belonged to the Marchef's latest victim. Inevitably, Andreina brought Pistolet to a flight of stairs which led upward to a trapdoor. Once they reached the surface, the two females went to the stables. They saddled two horses and rode away.

Being a native Corsican, Andreina was very familiar with the countryside. The Orsini estate in Sartène was well known. Andreina was able to direct Pistolet there.

When the Marchef and the Cantinière failed to arrived at his bedchamber after a decent interval, the Colonel decided to investigate. Together with a trio of guards, he went to the torture chamber. Clad in a breechcloth, Desdemona was hanging from her wrists above the iron bowl. Her breasts were covered by a placard tied around her neck. On the placard was the word "Retribution" etched in Desdemona's blood. The golden bullet was clenched between her teeth.

Pistolet had been welcomed by Julia de Trémeuse, alias Lady Judex, at the Orsini residence. Judex had taken the precaution of transporting an extra set of clothes for Pistolet to her parents' domicile. Discarding the apparel stolen from the Marchef, Pistolet slipped into a white dress. Andreina replaced her Cantinière uniform with clothes borrowed from a servant. During the night, Andreina Cortina retired to a guest room while Judex and Pistolet conferred in the kitchen. Pistolet briefed her colleague thoroughly on her experiences in the Colonel's stronghold.

"If I knew you would behave like a reckless gambler," said Judex. "I never would have supported your mission. You have jeopardized all the Acolytes of the Shadows."

"Desdemona Cullin took her knowledge to the grave."

"The tigress is dead, but her young cub still lives."

"Andreina Cortina is no threat."

"Isn't she? I have a husband and two children. I'll kill anyone who endangers them. If the Black Coats connected me with the Revenant, they would exterminate my entire family. That girl knows that I'm an Acolyte."

"Andreina's no longer a Black Coat. She's my Squire."

"You have deluded yourself with thoughts of chivalry, but not that little monster! She's laughing behind your back."

"She's pledged her loyalty to me!"

"Andreina is a natural born turncoat. She allied herself with her father's killer. Before Desdemona's corpse is even cold, she joins you. At the first chance, she'll betray you to the Black Coats."

"She knows the Colonel will kill her."

"Bozzo-Corona is not the only power in the Black Coats. Have you forgotten Monsieur Nemo, the Lord of the Night? He has long been the Colonel's rival. Nemo will harbor no reason to avenge the slaughtering of the Colonel's harlot."

"Have you forgotten the Green Lamia? She was a diabolical murderess. Today she's the Jade Seraph."

"The crimes of this degenerate girl pale before those of the Green Lamia. Andreina was Desdemona's accomplice in scores of murders. She has drunk human blood. Stakes have been driven into the hearts of creatures like her." Judex picked up a carving knife. "This would prove an adequate substitute."

"I've given my word to protect Andreina Cortina."

"But I haven't given mine!"

Running out of the kitchen, Judex slammed the door. Pistolet tried to open the door, but it was locked.

Judex stepped slowly into Andreina's room. The young girl was asleep on the bed. Judex raised the knife high in the air. Suddenly Judex's wrist was held from behind in a grip of steel. An arm encircled Judex's neck.

"I picked the lock," whispered Pistolet into Judex's ear. Pistolet pulled the struggling Judex outside the room.

A series of loud noises awoke Andreina. She got out of her bed. When she looked in the corridor, Andreina saw a moaning Judex sprawled on the ground. An erect Pistolet was wiping the blood from a cut on her lip.

"What happened to Madame de Trémeuse?" asked Andreina.

"We were debating tactics," answered Pistolet. "Go back to bed, my Squire."

As Andreina resumed her slumbers, Pistolet clasped Judex's ankles and dragged her away.

In another room, Judex lied on a couch. Opening her eyes, Judex beheld Pistolet holding the carving knife against her larynx.

"I have no desire to harm you, Judex. Our families have long been allies against the Black Coats. In the name of our ancestors, I offer you a compromise. Desist in your murderous designs, and I will allow the Revenant to decide Andreina Cortina's fate in Paris."

"I accept your compromise."

"Swear by your grandmother."

"I swear in the name of Valentine Pagès."

Pistolet withdrew the knife.

Judex was still defiant. "You have only deferred your blood-drinker's demise. I was the first chosen of the Revenant, her original Acolyte. I helped her extinguish the detestable Cagliostro. She shall listen to my counsel."

Together with Judex, Pistolet and Andreina traveled incognito to Ajaccio. After landing in Toulon, they made their way to Paris. Recognizing that the Black Coats would be searching for her, Pistolet did not return to the apartment rented under her La Richarde alias. Leaving Andreina with El Hichmakani, a Persian sage who advised the Acolytes of the Shadows, Pistolet resided at Lady Scalpel's abode. Both Pistolet and Judex delivered detailed reports into the mail slot of an empty office which the Revenant rented under the alias of "A. L Lard." Once the Revenant read the reports, she arranged through Lady Leopard and Lady Invisible to schedule a conclave at Scalpel's house.

During the meeting, the Revenant permitted both Pistolet and Judex to make their cases.

Lady Tocsin sided with Judex. "The girl has been corrupted beyond comprehension. She must be removed."

"No one is beyond redemption," said the Jade Seraph.

"The Seraph and I have disagreed in the past," admitted Leopard, "but we agree on Andreina Cortina. The Seraph and I once belonged to the Black Coats. Today I spied on them for the Revenant. If the Seraph and I can be members of the Acolytes of the Shadows, so can this girl."

Invisible, Scalpel and Charon echoed the sentiments expressed by the Seraph and Leopard.

The Revenant announced her decision. "Judex argues for Andreina Cortina's removal while her redemption is advocated by Pistolet. Judex is correct. This girl must be removed."

The Seraph was visibly stunned by the Revenant's words.

"But Pistolet is also right," resumed the Revenant. "The girl should be redeemed. Andreina must be removed from France in order to be redeemed. So long as Andreina is in this country, she risks being tempted by the Black Coats. Pistolet, your position in France has also become precarious. Your La Richarde identity is now exposed. Leopard reports that the All-Father has posted a bounty of 50,000 francs on your head. He hates you now even more than me. Soon the deadliest killer of the Black Coats, the Pallid Mask, will return to our country. He has ample motive to desire your death. You have relatives in America. Are you on good terms with any of them?"

"My cousin, King Marley. He lives in Arizona."

"Find refuge with him. Take Andreina Cortina with you to America. Complete her rehabilitation."

"Thank you, Revenant," said Pistolet. "Before I depart for America, I want to apologize to everyone here for putting their lives in jeopardy. I also want to apologize for the failure of my mission in Corsica."

The Jade Seraph had the last word. "If you succeed with Andreina Cortina, her redemption will be worth the death of a thousand Colonels."

Ruination

"You utter incompetent!" shrieked Professor Marguerite Chavain in late December 1887. "All our careful planning for naught! Madame Nemo and I arranged for you to be hired as the Countess of Morcar's maid. Yet you failed to deliver the Blue Carbuncle."

"But I didn't fail, Professor," pleaded Catherine Cusack. "I seduced James Ryder of the Hotel Cosmopolitan staff into stealing the gem for me. I even covered my tracks by making an innocent plumber *pay the law*. I followed the maxim of the Black Coats: Give the courts a *guilty party* for every crime committed."

"Your accomplice was supposed to hide the Carbuncle. Instead Ryder foolishly lost the gem before you could cheat him out of it. When the Carbuncle fell into the hands of Sherlock Holmes, it led him straight to Ryder. Your lover confessed all and implicated you. If Holmes hadn't been moved by the Christmas spirit to let Ryder flee, you would be in jail. Instead, the Countess dismissed you once Holmes informed her of your actions. Leave us, Catherine. Madame Nemo and I have matters to discuss."

Marguerite Chavain stroked her raven hair as Catherine left the room. The confrontation transpired inside Finola Nemo's residence. Finola was a gaunt brunette with black eyes. In a turquoise robe embroidered with golden birds, Finola sat sipping a cup of tea. Attired in a flamboyantly red dress, the gray-eyed Marguerite was also having tea.

Finola was the wife of Jim Nemo, arguably the most powerful member of the Black Coats, the European crime cartel. As the Lord of the Night, Nemo presided over the British branch of the Black Coats. Originally Marguerite had been aligned with Count Corbucci, Jim's rival on the High Council. She had been enticed by Finola to change loyalties. Marguerite was now a leading member of the Neptune Society, the scientific department of the Black Coats. Finola had charge of the Neptune Society's budget, but she was forced to allow her stepdaughter, Urania, full control of the subsidiary's daily activities.

"You misjudged Catherine's talents, Marguerite," pronounced Finola. "Where did you ever find this foolish girl?"

"Her real name is Catherine Emmanuelle Cussac. She was recommended by the headmistress of my former school. Catherine served as a prefect at the Fourneau College alongside Francesca Delacourt and your sister-in-law. I recruited Francesca and Catherine at the same time. When I posted Catherine to London, she adopted the Irish variant of her surname."

"Francesca has proven herself more than competent, Marguerite. She has successfully infiltrated the Second Bureau. A double agent inside the French espionage apparatus suits my husband's plans very well. Catherine is another matter. I have great plans for you, Marguerite. Urania is even more of a bungler than Catherine. I must nurture a protégé to usurp her role in the Neptune Society. This protégé must be both adept in scientific technology and strategic operations. I have chosen you, Marguerite, to be this protégé."

"I am honored, Madame."

"You need not convince me of your operational expertise. It is my husband who must be persuaded. Jim must learn that there is a candidate more qualified to manage the Neptune Society with me. Acquisition of the Blue Carbuncle would have gone a long way to prove your worthiness to Jim. You must learn to choose proper agents to implement your plans."

"I apologize for entrusting Catherine with this delicate mission. Perhaps I should *cut the branch*."

"Your background as a botanist, Marguerite, makes you too prone to eliminate inadequate employees. Rather than view your underlings as plants in a garden, see them as songbirds that need to be taught to chirp properly."

"You envision Catherine as some sort of thrush?"

"An apt analogy. The Black Coats are a hierarchy of thrushes. You and I are among the top birds. Below us are undesirables to be removed and slaves to be subjugated. Catherine requires proper subjugation."

"What are you recommending, Madame?"

"We shall use Catherine as an object of barter. There is another woman almost as disappointing as Catherine. Her name is Ida Similor. My husband had great hopes for her, but she failed to meet expectations. When Jim reorganized the Black Coats in 1885, Jim restricted her duties to supervising a small gang of thieves in Paris. Her cutthroats provided a modest profit until the last quarter. Their activities suddenly became very lucrative. I have traced this improvement to Ida's recruitment of a new subordinate, Lucretia Venucci. I shall convince Jim to transfer Venucci out of Ida's entourage into your own. Ida will demand compensation. We shall give her Catherine."

In February 1888, a pool game was underway in a Parisian tavern, *L'Epi-Scié*. Two pairs of women competed. One duo consisted of Catherine Cusack and a blonde whose short hair was covered by a scarlet cap. She was Tanja Samuel, a doctor who disposed of unwanted corpses for the Black Coats. The other team consisted of La Richarde, an elegantly dressed brunette in her late twenties, and the redheaded Ida Similor.

Catherine approached the table. "If I make this shot, Tanja and I win."

Her pole stuck the white ball. It ricocheted off the side of the table and hit another ball. The ball fell into a pocket.

"Bravo!" shouted Tanja. "Pay up, Richarde."

The sullen brunette paid Tanja the stakes agreed upon. Dividing up the money, Tanja gave half to Catherine.

"You're being incredibly generous, Tanja. We were only playing with your money."

"You earned it, Kate. Let me buy you a beer!"

As the bartender poured their beer, Catherine expressed her gratitude to her companion.

"You're a true friend, Tanja. All the other Black Coats treat me with contempt."

"Those fools are blind to your sterling qualities. However, you have a secret admirer. A man has been asking me about you. "

"Who?"

"Parker."

"The Garotter who does errands for Nemo? He's old enough to be my father!"

"Believe me, Kate, Parker could be just the man to reignite your career." Once their glasses were full, Tanja made a toast. "Friends forever!"

"Friends forever!" echoed Catherine.

"This is your last failure," snarled Ida Similor two days later.

Lying at Ida's feet was a bruised and battered Catherine Cusack. In Ida's hands was a long white scarf. The bottom of the scarf had a piece of metal sewed inside. Ida had just delivered a brutal thrashing to Catherine in an alley close to *L'Epi-Scié*. Putting the scarf around her neck, Ida's right boot kicked Catherine in the stomach. Ida addressed the two men who had been gleefully observing Catherine's punishment.

"Cocotte! Piquepuce! Raise this slut to her feet!"

Each of the men grabbed one of Catherine's arms. They lifted the weakened Catherine upright against the wall.

"Mercy," murmured Catherine.

"Save your pleas of mercy for Landerneau. He's in a jail cell tonight because you failed to give the alarm during our warehouse robbery."

"I warned you as soon as I saw the police."

"I'm tired of your excuses! You've been a millstone around our necks ever since you replaced Lucretia. You have a lot of advantages, Kate. You're 25, three years younger than me. You're tall and slender. Your brown hair is a lovely shade. Sometimes it almost looks red like mine. Many a man had been struck by your beauty." Ida opened her long pink coat revealing ten knives sheathed inside the lining. Removing one of the blades, she held it in front of Catherine's eyes. "No man shall desire you once I slit your nose."

Before she could strike, Ida felt her wrist in a grip of steel.

"You've hurt the girl enough!" said the burly man holding Ida's wrist.

"Parker!" exclaimed Ida. "You have no right to interfere!"

"If you have an objection, you can take it up with Monsieur Nemo! If you know what's good for you, Ida, you'll take your two mates here and leave."

Ida knew that the Lord of the Night had been friends with Parker since they sailed together on a ship in the 1860's. It was in her interests to avoid a confrontation with Parker. She retreated with her two satellites.

Resting against the wall, Catherine's legs buckled. She fell into Parker's arms.

A short man with a mustache, Larry Parker was more than 20 years older than Catherine. He rented an apartment in a Paris. Catherine awoke in Larry's bed. Standing over her was another woman.

"Tanja," murmured Catherine.

"Ida is a monster! How could she do this to you? Rest, Kate. I examined you while you slept. It will take about a month for you to recover from your injuries. Fortunately no bones were broken."

"Where is Monsieur Parker?"

"He's outside. If you need him during the night, he'll be sleeping on the coach outside. Now get some rest." Dr. Samuel departed.

That morning, Parker served Catherine breakfast in bed.

"Monsieur Parker, you saved me from a horrible fate. I don't even know your first name."

"Call me Larry. It's short for Lamar."

After her recovery, Catherine became Parker's mistress. Parker kept her totally divorced from criminal activity. Catherine enjoyed this leisurely existence for weeks before she became bored. In April 1888, she complained.

"I want to commit a crime, Larry."

"You need to lay low, Kate. Landerneau gave your name to the French peelers."

"Did he inform on Ida and the others?"

"No. He only gave you up. But Tanja's watching your back. She's spreading the rumor that you're dead."

"Good old Tanja! She's my best friend."

"Let's take advantage of your sabbatical from crime. You must learn to protect yourself."

"Can't you teach me? You're called the Garrotter for a reason."

"I studied Thuggee in India. I know how to strangle a man with ease."

"Teach me, Larry. Ida also studied Thuggee. That's where Ida got the idea for her scarf."

"Ida? Is that what's bothering you? Forget about her. Needless vendettas are the road to a quick death. Do you want ruination to be your destiny? I'll teach you on one condition. Promise to ignore Ida."

"I promise, darling. You're also pretty handy with a revolver."

"I had some private lessons from Sebastian Moran. If you want to learn how to shoot, I'm your man."

By May, the police had stopped looking for Catherine Cusack. Parker installed Catherine in her own apartment rented under the name of Emmanuelle Cussac.

After her training in the arts of strangulation and gunplay, Parker arranged for Catherine to be instructed in housebreaking and safecracking by Reginald Crawshay, an English cracksman vacationing in Paris. Crawshay took Catherine with him on burglaries while Parker waited outside in a carriage. On their initial outings, Catherine observed Crawshay at work. In later excursions, Crawshay supervised Catherine.

One night in Paris, Crawshay and Catherine broke into the house of a reputedly wealthy art collector, Ludovic Imbert. The two burglars found an immense safe made of iron and steel. It had a combination lock as well as a key slot. Catherine pressed her ear against the safe. She turned the combination and heard the tumblers clicked. Once she had finished, she put a wiry metal tool inside the key slot.

"It's open," announced Catherine. All that was inside was the statue of a black falcon.

Pulling the statue out, the redheaded Crawshay examined it.

"It's a piece of junk," determined Crawshay. "I'm putting it back."

"Surely it must be worth something, Reggie."

"That's the problem with burglary, Kate. We dream of a large bonanza, but we often find useless stuff."

Once Crawshay's lessons had ended, Catherine had another request for Parker.

"Maybe I can learn to throw knives."

"Remember your promise. Vengeance against Ida will lead to a quick death. Do you want ruination to be your destiny?"

"I haven't forgotten. I'm just trying to use Ida as a role model."

"Ida isn't worth emulating, Kate. The Lord of the Night despises her."

"That's because the Jade Seraph made a fool of her."

"How did you learn about that?"

"Ida was always ranting about the Seraph. They used to be in a circus together, The Seraph's real name is Valorie Varno. I never imagined that green skin was real. I always assumed the Seraph used greasepaint."

"The Seraph knows how to fight. Try to be like her. You should learn hand-to-hand combat. The best instructor of fighting techniques is a Japanese expatriate, Shintaro Olaki. He's a master of judo and karate. They say that he only teaches a tenth of what he knows."

"Will he be willing to teach me?"

"For a price. He's expensive, but I have enough money stashed away to hire him. I wouldn't do this for anyone else, Kate."

Catherine's response was to passionately caress her lover.

After a training session of two hours, Olaki and Catherine bowed to each other. Both wore the traditional white karate uniform consisting of pants and a jacket. On the right side of Olaki's jacket was the *shi kanji*, the Japanese symbol of death.

Considering his skills, Olaki was remarkably young. He was the same age as Catherine.

"Your training is complete, my student," decreed Olaki.

"But I've only been your pupil for two months, Sensei," protested Catherine.

"There is nothing more for me to teach you."

"They say that you only teach a tenth of what you know."

"That is true, my student."

"I'm willing to pay for more of your knowledge, Sensei."

"No amount of money will change my mind."

"I'm willing to pay in a medium other than money."

Untying her belt, Catherine removed her jacket and her pants. She stood stark naked in front of Olaki. Catherine needed tutoring in many areas, but she had mastered the art of seduction. Over the course of the next three months, Olaki taught Catherine all of his fighting techniques.

During an October evening, Cocotte and Piquepuce were playing pool at *L'Epi-Scié*. Their game was interrupted by a short stranger. A beard covered his face.

"Excuse me. Is one of you named Cocotte?"

"I'm Cocotte."

"The bartender said that you might be able to help me. I'm looking for Catherine Cusack."

"Catherine? Oh, you mean Kate. I can tell you about Kate, but first you must answer some questions. Who are you?"

"My name is Jacques Cavalier."

"What do you do for a living, Jacques?"

"I'm a porter at the Royal Palace Hotel."

"How do you know Kate?"

"I met her before she came to Paris."

"He must have known Kate in Avignon," said Piquepuce. "Kate told me that she was born there."

"Is that correct, Jacques?" asked Cocotte. "Are you from Avignon?"

Cavalier hesitated. "Yes."

"And why do you want to find Kate?"

"I love her."

"You have answered my questions, Jacques," said Cocotte. "Here's what I know.

You're a liar!" Cocotte knocked Cavalier down with a punch to the jaw. "Your accent betrays you! You do not speak French like a man from Avignon or anywhere else in Provence! You speak French like an Englishman."

Rubbing his sore jaw, Cavalier rose from the floor. He left the tavern.

Larry Parker was completely unaware that his mistress was cheating on him with Olaki. When her sessions with Olaki concluded in November 1888, Catherine was ecstatic.

"I feel like I could beat the Revenant," she purred one night as Parker shared her bed.

Her lover laughed. "Right now, concentrate on tangling with me, my precious."

"I'm serious, Larry. Killing that masked vigilante would be very profitable. I recall those posters in the Confessional at *L'Epi-Scié*. There's a 30,000 franc reward for the Revenant's head and a 10,000 reward for the Jade Seraph's."

"There's now a 50,000 bounty on Pistolet."

"Pistolet? Isn't he dead?'

"This is the daughter of the original Pistolet. Her real name is Francis Clampin. You may have talked to her. She used to hang around *L'Epi-Scié.* Called herself La Richarde."

"The fancy snob with the squeeze gun! She's always tossing a golden bullet."

"That bullet ended up clenched in the teeth of the corpse of the All-Father's mistress. That's why the bounty on Pistolet's head is higher than the Revenant's."

"You should let me go to *L'Epi-Scié* once in a while. I'm missing on all the local gossip. It doesn't matter if Ida's there. Besides I miss playing pool with Tanja."

"There's something that I didn't tell you, Kate. I didn't want to upset you."

"What is it?"

"Tanja died months ago. Pistolet killed her."

Catherine's eyes filled with tears. "Why didn't you tell me? She was my best friend. I should have gone to the funeral."

"There was no funeral. Pistolet beheaded Tanja and threw her body into an acid vat."

"Why did Pistolet do that?"

"Pistolet is one of the Revenant's assistants. They're called the Acolytes."

"The Acolytes! For what they did to Tanja, I want to murder them all!"

The next evening, Parker took Catherine to dinner at the Restaurant Imperial. He had a surprise for her.

"Jim Nemo is organizing a gala ball, Kate. Nearly all the High Council will be there. It's sort of a beauty contest. He wanted me to find a female contestant to compete. I told him all about you. He says you should come."

"Larry, that's wonderful! But doesn't his wife hate me?"

"Don't worry about her. Jim wants to needle his wife back for the little prank that's she playing. Ida Similor told you many things, but she probably held this back. Jim almost had an affair with her. The budding romance fell apart when Ida was beaten up by the Jade Seraph. Well, Madame Nemo put Ida in charge of providing entertainment at the ball."

"Will Ida be competing at the ball?"

"Jim has excluded her from the competition."

"When Ida sees me hobnobbing with the upper crust of the Black Coats, she'll be livid."

"You'll finally have your revenge on that snotty redhead."

"Why wait, Larry? Can't I go to *L'Epi-Scié* and tell her that I'm going to the ball?"

"You'll only cause a fight!"

"I'm more that capable of protecting myself! Olaki taught me how to dodge knives."

"I know, but wouldn't your revenge be sweeter if you defer it to the night of the ball?"

"You're right, Larry."

"There's something else. Jim's concerned about all his attention being focused on Paris. Business in London might taper off. He wants me there for the next few weeks."

"But Christmas is only a month away."

"I should be back in time for the holidays. Just promise me that you won't gloat over Ida in my absence."

"I promise. I don't want ruination to be my destiny."

A few days after Parker's departure, Catherine was overcome by ennui. She visited Shintaro Olaki.

Following a session of sexual intercourse, Catherine had a proposal for her Japanese lover.

"Shintaro, I want you to write me a letter of reference. You're going to claim that I gave you lessons in English from May to October."

"I'll be very happy to do so, Catherine. Why do you need this letter?"

"I'm going to apply for a job. I'm bored. I need to plan a crime."

"What crime are you contemplating?"

"When I worked for Professor Chavain, I orchestrated a robbery as a lady's maid. I intend to infiltrate a wealthy household as a servant."

"I understand. You want to perpetrate a burglary. Your prospective employer may investigate your background."

"When you write your letter, refer to me as Emmanuelle Cussac. My apartment in the Rue de Choiseul has been rented under that name since May."

"You'll need to explain what you were doing before May."

"I've anticipated that. When I worked for the Countess of Morcar, we once stayed overnight at the Maynooth estate. I stole some stationary belonging to the Earl of Maynooth. I'm going to forge a letter of reference from the Earl. The letter will say that I served as a maid in his household from 1885 until the early part of this year. The Earl was recently awarded a governorship in Australia. The letter will state that I gave notice rather than accompany the family to Australia."

"Have you decided what household to rob?"

"I saw an unusual ad in *L'Epoque*. There's a female doctor living in a fashionable district of Paris. She wants a maid who only works mornings and afternoons. There probably aren't too many applicants. Most maids want full room and board."

Armed with her letters of reference, Catherine knocked on the doctor's door. It was opened by a middle-aged woman with brown hair. A gold bracelet was on her right wrist.

"I'm here to apply for the position of maid."

"Please come in. I'm Dr. Rolande Cerral."

Perusing her references, Dr. Cerral had a few questions.

"Were you born in France?"

"Yes, in Avignon."

"How did you come to be in England?"

"I've always been a little adventurous. In Avignon, I was hired as a maid by a noted botanist, Marguerite Chavain."

"I've heard of her. Her work has been published by the Academy of Science."

"When Professor Chavain was hired by a London research firm, I accompanied her to England. Unfortunately, the Professor didn't pay very well. I left her service to work for the Maynooth family."

Rolande began to rotate her neck.

"Are you experiencing cervical difficulties, Doctor?"

"I have a sore neck. I worked very late last night. I fell asleep in the chair in my office."

"I understand. You're suffering from prolonged posture."

"Did you study medicine, Emmanuelle?"

"No, but one of my friends did. I gleamed some medical terms from my conversations with her."

"Emmanuelle, you're just the sort of person I'm looking for. You're adventurous with some exposure to science and medicine. When can you start?"

"Tomorrow, Doctor."

"You must report to work at 10 o'clock. You'll be able to leave at 5. I allow ninety minutes for lunch. One of my rooms is equipped as a gymnasium. I generally exercise for an hour starting at 12:30. You're welcome to join me during your lunch period."

"Thank you, Doctor."

"You'll discover that I spend most of my time in medical research. I have two patients, Madame d'Erlette and Mademoiselle Valeur. They occasionally visit me. Madame d'Erlette is an invalid who walks with a cane. You'll find Mademoiselle Valeur to be extremely eccentric. She suffers from a rare skin disease. Consequently, she wears a heavy veil and gloves. When I'm conferring with them, my office door will be locked."

On her first day as Dr. Cerral's maid, Catherine had lunch alone in the kitchen starting at noon. At 12:30, she went to the gymnasium. Dr. Cerral wasn't there. Catherine went to the doctor's office to see if she intended to follow her regular routine. The door was locked. Catherine knocked on the door.

"Dr. Cerral... Dr. Cerral."

No one answered. Could something have happened to Dr. Cerral? Using a skeleton key given her by Crawshay, Catherine picked the lock.

Opening the door, Catherine cautiously entered. Suddenly she saw an object zooming straight for her head. She quickly dodged the missile as it embedded itself in the wooden door.

"Emmanuelle!" exclaimed Rolande. "I could have hit you!"

"Fortunately, Doctor, the only damage was to the door." Catherine removed the object from the door. It was a dart. Closing the door, Catherine saw a circular dartboard.

Catherine handed the dart to Rolande. "Your projectile, Doctor."

"I'm sorry, Emmanuelle. I thought that I had locked the door."

"I did knock, Doctor."

"It's my fault, Emmanuelle. I tend to ignore distracting noises when I practice dart throwing."

"Based on the position of the darts, Doctor, you are quite proficient."

"My aim has been a little off ever since I began wearing this bracelet." Rolande extended her right wrist.

"I didn't notice that it was inscribed. What does 'Retribution' mean?"

"I belong to a charitable organization called the Retribution Society. My best friend is also a member. Family matters compelled her to travel aboard."

"Your friend has exquisite tastes, Doctor."

"In clothes as well as jewelry. Would you like to see a picture of her?"

"Yes, Doctor."

Rolande went over her desk and opened a drawer. She pulled out an album. Opening the book, Rolande pointed to a photo of her with a younger woman in her late twenties. Both women were smiling in the photo.

Suddenly, Catherine began to cry.

"Emmanuelle, what's wrong?"

"Seeing that photo made me think of my best friend. She died horribly. A gang of ruffians butchered her."

"Is there anything that I can do?"

"Please leave me alone for a few minutes."

After Rolande departed, Catherine stared at the photo. The sadness in her eyes was replaced by hate. "Pistolet," she hissed.

Later that night, Catherine sat alone in the silence of her apartment.

I must tread carefully, she thought. *Pistolet is an Acolyte. Cerral must be an Acolyte as well. It would explain my unusual hours as a maid. At night, Cerral must work for the Revenant. Her Retribution Society could really be a façade for the Acolytes.*

Cerral mentioned a veiled patient with a skin disease. Her name is Mademoiselle Valeur. The Seraph has green skin. The Jade Seraph's real name is Valorie Varno. Valeur could be a variant of Valorie. The Seraph must be Mademoiselle Valeur.

The Seraph is worth 10,000 francs, the Revenant 30,000, and Pistolet 50,000. 90,000 francs for all of them. The only Black Coat that I can trust is Larry. Anyone else would try to cheat me of the bounties. I must confirm my suspicions. I must learn more about these Acolytes. When Larry returns, I'll send all the Acolytes to Hell!

The next day, Rolande Cerral left her house early in the morning to deliver an envelope to a building in the Rue de Provence. The envelope was deposited in the mail slot of a locked office. The empty office bore a placard entitled "A. L. Lard." Rolande returned to her house well before her maid arrived for work.

Around noon, the office was unlocked by Feliciana Sorelli, the leading ballerina at the Paris Opera House. She was secretly Lady Leopard, one of the Revenant's Acolytes. All of the other Acolytes delivered their reports early in the morning to the Lard office. It was the blonde Leopard's duty to retrieve these reports and deliver them to the Revenant. Returning to the Opera House, Leopard locked herself in her dressing room. Her large wall mirror actually concealed a secret passage that led to the underground lake beneath the Paris Opera House. Reaching that lake, Leopard paddled a canoe to the shore on the other side. Leopard had reached the secret sanctuary of the Revenant.

In an underground complex dwelt Darlla Rassendyll, a woman with fiery red hair. Her beautiful face was marred slightly by a cruel mouth. Framed for murder and treason, Darlla had seen her career as a policewoman ruined by the

Black Coats. Forced to live a subterranean existence, Darlla became the masked vigilante known as the Revenant.

Leopard handed the envelopes to the Revenant.

"Don't leave yet, Leopard," ordered the Revenant. "I may have new instructions based on Lady Scalpel's report." Scalpel was the code name utilized by Rolande Cerral.

"Does this involve Scalpel's efforts to recruit a new Acolyte?"

"Yes. Ever since Pistolet was required to leave France, our intelligence has been hampered by the absence of an agent in *L'Epi-Scié*. Scalpel has been looking for a woman with a courageous nature to undertake that task. Using the ruse of hiring a maid, Scalpel hoped to find the proper candidate. She thinks that such bravery may reside in Emmanuelle Cussac, a woman hired two days ago."

The Revenant perused Scalpel's report.

Emmanuelle Cussac will be easy to recruit as an Acolyte. Her best friend was murdered by a vicious gang. Emmanuelle has the right temperament to be an Acolyte. As her previous association with Professor Chavain indicates, she is drawn to highly independent women. She will easily gravitate into your orbit. Although I've had only a single joint exercise session with her in my gymnasium, she has shown herself to be as athletic as the goddess Diana. I suggest that you verify her background based on my previous letter. Enclosed is a sketch that I made of her face. Please show it to Leopard and Tocsin.

Scalpel

The Revenant exhibited the sketch to Leopard. In addition to being an Acolyte, Leopard was a member of the Black Coats. Acting as a double agent, Leopard gave the Revenant valuable information about the activities of the criminal organization in France. Since Leopard only circulated among the elite of high society, she had never seen Catherine Cusack. Thus, she failed to recognize the woman in the sketch.

Discussing Scalpel's reports, the Revenant mentioned Emmanuelle Cussac's connection to Professor Marguerite Chavain. When Chavain was active with the Black Coats in France, the crime syndicate was divided into two warring factions. Leopard had been aligned with Jim Nemo while Chavain had been allied with his rival, Count Corbucci. This schism prevented any contact between Leopard and Chavain. Once peace had been negotiated between Nemo and Corbucci, Chavain had been transferred to London. Leopard was unaware of Chavain's membership in the Black Coats. Like Scalpel, Leopard believed Chavain to be a reputable botanist.

The Revenant had new instructions for Leopard, "When you retrieve the reports tomorrow, pay a visit to Lady Invisible. She needs to verify Emmanuelle's background for us."

After another joint workout with Emmanuelle in the gymnasium, Rolande Cerral briefly left her house to buy medical supplies. Rolande had a wall safe in her office. Catherine took advantage of Rolande's absence by burglarizing her safe. Inside the safe was a circular device with a barrel. Catherine recognized it as a squeeze gun. If it was identical to Pistolet's, then the weapon was equipped with a silencer. There were also technical designs for several weapons, as well as a notebook detailing experiments with the blood of a patient identified only as "V." Also inside were six vials of a purple serum. Catherine scrupulously returned the objects to the safe.

There was a locked storage closet in the house. Picking the lock, Catherine discovered a life-side mannequin. A placard hung around the figure's neck. Written on the sign was "Nemo."

During her employment as a maid, Catherine made sure to always inspect the mail before Rolande. Hoping to find some clue to Pistolet's whereabouts, Catherine steamed open every letter. After resealing the letters, she delivered them to Rolande. So far, Rolande's mail had included only insignificant communications.

The Revenant resided in her sanctuary with the Jade Seraph. The Seraph's skin was green due to a South American poison employed by the Black Coats. Her regular attire was a green leotard with black gauntlets and boots. Her thighs were encircled by a metal chain. Her dark hair was raised in a bouffant. A narrow stroke of hair divided her slanted eyebrows. Her height was five feet and four inches.

One of the Seraph's nightly duties was to contact Lady Tocsin, another of the Revenant's Acolytes. Under her real name of Angelique LaSalle, Tocsin was employed as a waitress at *L'Oreille Cassée,* a bar just as disreputable as *L'Epi-Scié.* Tocsin was a petite woman with brown hair.

Micheline Roget, the manager of *L'Oreille Cassée,* always allowed her barmaids to take a break of ten minutes. During this interval, the Seraph and Tocsin conferred. The Seraph had brought Rolande's sketch to the meeting.

"The face of this Cussac woman is unknown to me," admitted Tocsin, "but her surname is similar to Cusack. When Pistolet was stationed at *L'Epi-Scié,* we regularly shared information. Pistolet gambled on pool games. She lost money regularly to an associate of Ida Similor. Her name was Kate Cusack."

"I'm worried, Darlla," said the Jade Seraph in the Opera House sanctuary. "My old enemy could be using one of her cronies to infiltrate the Acolytes."

"I haven't forgotten the trap that Ida set for you years ago, Valorie," declared the Revenant. "Ida can be a cunning adversary. I vaguely remember Pistolet mentioning Kate Cusack in her reports."

"Did you record Pistolet's information in our index of Black Coat members?"

"Of course." The Revenant opened a large book full of handwritten entries. Quickly locating an entry, she read it and then showed it to the Seraph.

Cusack, Kate – Of Irish extraction. A minor functionary with a history of bungling assignments. Joined Ida Similor's gang of thieves in January 1888. Arguably the best pool player at L'Epi-Scié. Frequent pool partner of Tanja Similor. Disappeared in February of the same year after being brutally beaten by Ida outside L'Epi-Scié. Wanted by the police for her role in a botched robbery. Believed to be dead.

"It's inconceivable that Emmanuelle Cussac and Kate Cusack are the same person," concluded the Revenant. "If Cusack still lives, Ida would never use her to spy upon us."

"Scalpel's maid could still be Kate Cusack," argued the Seraph. "We should send an Acolyte to Avignon to verify Emmanuelle's past."

"There is not enough evidence to warrant the expense of a trip to Avignon, but there is a way to verify whether Emmanuelle is a native of Provence. I shall request the help of Lady Judex."

In the morning, Rolande Cerral requested her maid to make her a cup of tea. Catherine delivered it to Rolande in her office. Seated behind her desk, the doctor was reading a newspaper.

"There's an editorial here about the Revenant, Emmanuelle. The writer condemns her for being a bloodthirsty vigilante."

"Frankly, Doctor, I admire the Revenant, She eradicates the scum of the Earth. France needs more women like her. Have you read what's happening in London?"

"You must be referring to the Ripper Murders."

"It's not safe for a woman to walk the streets of London. If Jack the Ripper ever came to Paris, the Revenant would protect the female population by killing him."

The first Acolyte recruited by the Revenant was Lady Judex. Born Julia Orsini in Corsica, she was now married to Pierre de Trémeuse. Since her marriage, she rarely participated directly in the activities of the Acolytes. Judex was a diminutive woman with blonde hair. Her alias was the Latin word for "judge."

Madame de Trémeuse was entertaining Augustine d'Erlette. Since Darlla Rassendyll could not appear in public in her true identity, she disguised herself as the elderly Augustine.

"I need your help, Judex," said Augustine. "You've always had a fine ear for dialects. You're also familiar with Avignon. I want you to visit Scalpel's house and talk to her maid. She purports to be from Avignon, but she may really be from the British Isles."

During her next visit to the Rue de Provence, Lady Leopard went to the floor above the Lard office. Located there was the Sure Values Agency, a firm whose single employee was Chantal Lebrue. To the outside world, this brunette produced a weekly news digest gleamed from other periodicals. Chantal was really the Acolyte referred to as Lady Invisible. Her primary duty was to search newspapers for information that would assist the Revenant's war on crime. Invisible also occasionally adopted the guise of a reporter.

Leopard delivered the Revenant's orders

"Invisible, you must substantiate the references of Scalpel's new maid."

That afternoon, Chantal visited the boarding house where Catherine resided as Emmanuelle Cussac. Chantal pretended to be a journalist writing a story on independent women living alone in Paris. Interviewing Catherine's landlady, Invisible asked her how many single female boarders were residing in the house. The Acolyte then maneuvered the conversation into a discussion of those boarders. The landlady, Madame Vabre, was a talkative gossip. She disclosed that Emmanuelle had lived in her apartment since May.

That evening, Chantal Lebrue had dinner with an old friend, Sigismond Trottier. He was a reporter knowledgeable about the European aristocracy. He confirmed the Earl of Mayntooth's existence and his recent posting to Australia.

"Did you ever hear of the Mayntooth family employing a maid named Cussac?" asked Chantal.

"That surname sounds familiar. There was some English Countess whose maid had a name like that. It probably was the Earl's wife, the Countess of Mayntooth."

Trottier had actually confused the Countess of Mayntooth with the Countess of Morcar.

The followers of the Revenant were very active in the course of the next day. The only male member of the Acolytes was a coachman, Charles Blanton. As Lord Charon, it was his function to transport the Revenant and the Seraph around Paris. His coach pulled up in front of Rolande Cerral's house. Inside were Judex and the Jade Seraph disguised in a dress with a veil and gloves. The pair alighted from the coach. Judex knocked on the door. It was answered by Catherine.

"You must be Mademoiselle Valeur," said Catherine. "I'm Emmanuelle, Dr. Cerral's new maid."

"This is my friend, Madame de Trémeuse," replied the Seraph. "I was feeling very weak today. Madame de Trémeuse kindly volunteered to accompany me here. Could you please see that she is comfortable while Dr. Cerral examines me?"

"As you wish, Mademoiselle."

After escorting the veiled Seraph to Dr. Cerral's office, Catherine returned to Judex in the living room.

"Are you native to Paris, Emmanuelle?"

"I'm from Avignon, Madame."

"Avignon! What a lovely city! I went there on my honeymoon. I remember the Notre-Dame des Doms. It's amazing how much bigger it is than the nearby Palais des Papes. And the Pont Saint-Bénezet! I walked across that bridge to Villeneuve-lès-Avignon."

"Madame, your memories have been clouded by time. The Palais des Papes dwarfs the Notre-Dame des Doms. You couldn't have crossed the Pont Saint-Bénezet because most of that bridge was swept away by a flood in 1668."

Inside her office, Rolande Cerral showed the Seraph one of the purple vials from her safe.

"I've finally been able to replicate the regenerative powers inherent in your blood, Valorie."

"I've never been comfortable with your experiments to copy the Purple Sacrament. That drug accelerated my body's ability to heal, Rolande, but constant exposure turned me into a maniacal lunatic."

"I prefer to call my derivative the Purple Serum," replied Rolande. "I gave the drugs to rabbits. Their recuperative powers were intensified, but they showed no signs of hysteria."

"You have yet to test this on a human being."

"I would only risk that if my patient was seriously wounded. There are some wounds that required more than a scalpel."

Rolande's left hand touched the golden bracelet on her right wrist. She pulled out a thin object that had been cunningly sheathed in the bracelet. It was a scalpel with a golden handle.

On the ride back from Dr. Cerral's, Judex informed the Seraph of her conversation with Lady Scalpel's maid.

"Not only does Emmanuelle speak with a Provencal accent, but she's highly intelligent. She'll be a valuable asset to the Revenant."

Chantal Lebrue interviewed Shintaro Olaki. She pretended to be writing a story on Japan.

"You speak French very well, Monsieur Olaki," observed Chantal. "Do you know any other European languages?"

"I know English."

"I'm looking for an English tutor. Is there any person whom you would recommend?"

Olaki had studied English in Japan, but Chantal's question made him suspicious. Could this woman be checking on Catherine's references? Therefore, he lied.

"I learned English from a charming Frenchwoman. Her name is Emmanuelle Cussac."

Two days passed. The Revenant had evaluated all her Acolytes' reports. She made her decision, As Augustine d'Erlette, the Revenant was driven in Lord Charon's carriage to Dr. Cerral's residence.

As Augustine exited the vehicle, she carried a large black bag. Her Revenant paraphernalia was inside. Augustine was greeted at the door by Catherine.

"I'm Madame d'Erlette," said the Revenant.

"Please come in, Madame," replied Catherine.

As Catherine closed the door, she noticed that the driver of the carriage was the same man who transported the Seraph. Madame d'Erlette must be an Acolyte!

Madame d'Erlette was accompanied by Catherine into Dr. Cerral's office.

"Emmanuelle, I left my medical bag in my bedroom," professed Rolande. "Please fetch it for me."

Retrieving the bag, Catherine re-entered the office. She dropped the bag in shock. Standing in front of Catherine was a woman wearing a black cowl with a red skull emblazoned on the forehead. Her outfit consisted of a black shirt with matching pants and boots. A thin red line delineated her V-shaped neckline. Her gloves were crimson. A lasso and a Thuggee pickaxe hung from her belt. Her crimson gloves gripped a Thuggee pickaxe.

"The Revenant!" exclaimed Catherine.

"Emmanuelle Cussac, you are a woman of courage and intellect. Your employer, Rolande Cerral, is my Acolyte. As, Lady Scalpel, she fights alongside me in the cause of justice. Will you too be my Acolyte?"

"YES!"

"Kneel before me."

Catherine followed the vigilante's command. The Revenant unsheathed her pickaxe. Looking upward, the Revenant raised the pickaxe.

"We are the Acolytes of the Shadows! We are the dispensers of justice! We are the punishers of the guilty! We are the executioners of the sinful! Yet we must remember one fundamental truth. We must never become as monstrous as the criminals we chase!"

The Revenant looked into Catherine's eyes.

"You were born Emmanuelle Cussac. As an Acolyte of the Shadows, you must adopt a new name. Just as I, the Supreme Acolyte, call myself the Revenant, you must choose a name that strikes fear into the souls of the wicked."

"I join your organization for one reason. My best friend was slaughtered by savage killers. It is my destiny to bring ruination to those killers. I choose the name Ruination."

"Arise, Lady Ruination. Your initiation will be complete once you meet your other fellow Acolytes tonight."

Inside Dr. Cerral's living room was seated the masked Revenant. She held her pickaxe like a scepter. Seated to the right of the Revenant was the Jade Seraph. In front of the Revenant and the Seraph were two couches. Judex, Tocsin and Leopard were seated on one couch while the other held Invisible and Scalpel. They all wore black leotards and gloves. A black belt encircled each of their waists. A hood of the same hue was tucked inside the belt. Scalpel wore her bracelet over her costume. Although the women were seated, Charon preferred to stand.

"We are the Acolytes of the Shadows," trumpeted the Revenant. "My Ladies and my Lord, what is our goal?"

"Retribution to the Black Coats!" shouted the Acolytes.

"We have a new member," resumed the Revenant. "We owe Lady Scalpel a debt for bringing this talented woman to our attention. Scalpel, please escort your protégé into our presence."

Rising from the coach, Scalpel walked to the door that led to her office. After Scalpel opened the door, Ruination walked into the room. She was clad like the other female Acolytes.

"Approach me, Acolyte."

"I call upon the other Acolytes, to reveal their names and titles."

"Julia de Trémeuse, Lady Judex."

"Angelique LaSalle, Lady Tocsin."

"Feliciana Sorelli, Lady Leopard."

"Charles Blanton, Lord Charon."

"Chantal Lebrue, Lady Invisible."

"Rolande Cerral, Lady Scalpel."

"Disciple of Life," said the Revenant, "state your name and title."

"Valorie Varno, the Jade Seraph."

"The new Acolyte will state her name and title," decreed the Revenant.

"Emmanuelle Cussac, Lady Ruination."

"Ruination, our battle cry is 'Retribution to the Black Coats.' Do you know who the Black Coats are?"

"No, Revenant."

"They are the men behind most of the crime in Europe. They are the men who thrive on murder and extortion. They are the men who enslave women in prostitution and other vices. Do you now know who the Black Coats are?

"Yes, Revenant."

"It is up to women like us, Ruination, and men like Charon to fight the Black Coats. Proudly raise your head and proclaim our battle cry."

"Retribution to the Black Coats!"

"Do you have any questions before your initiation is complete?"

"No, Revenant."

"The Black Coats always have the innocent blamed for their crimes. In their own parlance, they make others *pay the law*. I was one of those scapegoats. All the others know my true face. You do not. Let me reward your faith in me." The Revenant removed her mask. "My name is Darlla Rassendyll."

Ruination was visibly stunned.

"Do you know my story, Ruination?"

"Yes, Revenant. I read about you in the newspapers."

"You probably thought that I was guilty. Do you now accept my innocence?"

"Yes, Revenant."

"You told me and Scalpel that your best friend was murdered. Her assassins remain at liberty. Are you ready to tell us about your loss?"

"Not yet, Revenant. My friend died horribly. It's difficult for me to discuss her demise. Please give me a few days."

"When you are ready, you can describe the tragic fate of your friend in one of your reports."

"My reports?"

The Revenant explained how the A. L. Lard office functioned in her operations. She even disclosed the location of her base underneath the Paris Opera House.

"Now that you understand our methods of communication," continued the Revenant, "we shall train you to defend yourself against the Black Coats. Lord Charon, please fetch Nemo."

"Nemo?" asked Ruination. "Are you using the Latin word for 'no one,' Revenant?"

"A little joke. Leopard will explain."

"Jim Nemo is the most dangerous Black Coat in London," elucidated Leopard. "We gave his name to a dummy that we pretend to kill."

Charon returned with the mannequin that Ruination had discovered before she became an Acolyte.

"Lady Judex, please demonstrate for Ruination," requested the Revenant."

Rising from the coach, Judex removed her belt.

"You'll find yourself, Ruination, in circumstances where you shall have no choice but to kill your enemy," said Judex. "Strangulation is a silent and effective way to dispatch an enemy." Judex positioned herself behind the mannequin. With both hands gripping her belt, Judex swung it over the effigy's head. The belt encircled the figure's neck. "You must pull very hard to break the neck."

145

Judex yanked hard on the scarf. She then removed it from the neck of the bogus Nemo.

"Now you try, Ruination," commanded the Revenant.

Unbuckling her belt, Ruination easily duplicated Judex's demonstration.

"Excellent!" complimented the Revenant. "You mastered garroting."

"Isn't it time for the Seraph to beat up the other ladies?" asked Charon.

"Indeed it is," confirmed the Revenant. "Acolytes, we shall reassemble in Scalpel's gymnasium."

As they walked to the gymnasium, Ruination questioned Charon.

"What's happening?"

"The Seraph is our society's most formidable fighter. She shall instruct you and the others in self-defense."

Mats covered the floor of the gymnasium.

"Ruination, you must learn how to fight," asserted the Seraph. "I shall be your teacher. My students begin each session by attacking me individually. This enables me to determine if any of them have improved since our previous session. The rules of engagement are as follows. I commence each bout by telling the student to attack me. The bout ends when one of us yells 'I yield.' Acolytes, let us begin."

Ruination whispered to Charon. "Has the Seraph ever been beaten?"

"Never."

"Do you get to attack the Seraph?"

"I'm a coachman, not a fighter."

Judex was the first to attack the Seraph. She quickly yielded. Attacks by Tocsin, Invisible and Scalpel followed. They all yielded. Leopard's attack was the longest and the most ferocious. Even she was forced to yield.

"Now it's time for me to show you something new," said the Seraph.

"Excuse me," interrupted Ruination. "Don't I get a turn?"

"But you've never been instructed by me before?"

"I still want to try."

"Be my guest. It's your Waterloo."

"I told you that Ruination was courageous," whispered Scalpel to the Revenant.

The Seraph and Ruination position themselves on opposite sides of the mat.

"Attack me!" ordered the Seraph.

Ruination rushed towards the Seraph. Ruination raised her arm to deliver a karate chop, but the Seraph seized it with both hands. The Seraph turned around in order to flip the taller Ruination over her shoulder. However, Ruination's left arm shot around the Seraph's neck. Caught in a crushing stranglehold, the Seraph relinquished her grip on Ruination's right arm. The Seraph's fingers struggled futilely to break the chokehold. Ruination tightened her hold by placing her liberated right arm on top of the Seraph's head.

"Stop it," gasped the Seraph. "I..." The Seraph never finished her sentence. She ceased moving. Her arms fell limp at her side. Ruination released her hold. The Seraph tumbled forward on the mat.

"I believe that the Seraph has yielded," said Ruination.

The Revenant and Scalpel rushed to the Seraph's side. "She's all right," diagnosed Scalpel. "She's merely dazed."

"Acolytes, return to the living room," dictated the Revenant. "Your combat training is over."

In the living room, Ruination found that she was now the center of attention.

"Will you teach me that hold?" asked Leopard.

"I'll be happy to," replied Ruination.

"Where did you learn to fight like that?" questioned Tocsin.

"I know," interjected Invisible. "It was from that Japanese gentleman to whom you gave English lessons."

"Quite correct," said Ruination.

The Revenant entered the room with Scalpel and a revived Seraph.

"Acolytes, please take your seats."

The women did as the Revenant had bidden. As was his custom, Charon continued to stand. The Revenant and the Seraph also resumed their seats.

"Ruination taught us all an important lesson today," confessed the Seraph rubbing her neck. "Never underestimate an opponent."

"Ruination, you have passed your initiation with flying colors," said the Revenant. "The other Acolytes shall now explain to you their roles in our organization."

Ruination discovered how all the other Acolytes gathered information. She was stunned by the revelation that Leopard was also a member of the Black Coats.

"Monsieur Nemo recently ordered me to seduce General Boulanger," divulged Leopard. "For unknown reasons, Nemo wants to scuttle Boulanger's career. I deliberately bungled the assignment. Without Boulanger, France will never be able to recover Alsace-Lorraine from the Germans."

"Nemo must have received a commission from the German military," surmised Judex. "He's been aligned with them in the past."

The Revenant wanted to make her new Acolyte feel a valued member of the organization. She felt that Ruination had the potential to outshine all her other followers.

"Ruination, now that you've familiar with our operations, do you have any suggestions on how they might be improved?"

"Revenant, every time you slay a Black Coat, the police come under pressure from the press to arrest you. You must disguise your killings. Give the courts a *guilty party* for every killing you commit. Make it appear that another Black Coat slew your victim. Make the Black Coats *pay the law*."

"An excellent suggestion," said the Revenant. "Ladies, put on your hoods for the toast."

The forehead of each hood was different. Judex's mask had embroidered an axe surrounded by a bundle of wooden sticks, the Roman symbol of justice. Tocsin's symbol was a bell. A spotted jungle cat was Leopard's motif. Scalpel's emblem was a sharp surgical blade. The Japanese symbol of death was etched into Ruination's cowl. Befitting her name, Invisible's mask was unadorned. If Pistolet had been present, her insignia would have been a derringer.

The Revenant restored her own hood before speaking.

"It has always been our custom to conclude these meetings with a toast. It has also been traditional for the most junior member of the Acolytes to retrieve the wine bottle and the glasses. In the past, that responsibility fell on Lady Scalpel because she was the last inducted. You must now assume that role, Ruination."

"Gladly!" replied Ruination.

She went to the kitchen. When she returned, she was carrying a tray with wine bottle and nine glasses. Putting the tray down on a table, Ruination poured the wine into each glass. After giving a glass to each of her colleagues, Ruination poured the wine into her own glass.

"There is one Acolyte who is absent, Ruination," declared the Revenant. "Francis Clampin, Lady Pistolet. When her identity was exposed by the Black Coats, Pistolet was forced to leave the country. You were recruited to assume her duties."

"Are any of you in communication with Pistolet?" asked Ruination.

"I am," admitted Scalpel. "I received a letter from her at my Post Office box this morning."

Scalpel has a box at the Post Office, thought Ruination. *That's why I didn't see the letter!*

"You all will be happy to hear that Pistolet has found sanctuary abroad," said Scalpel. "For reasons of security, only I and the Revenant know Pistolet's new address."

"You showed me the letter when I visited you as Augustine," revealed the Revenant. "You locked it in your safe. It would be safer if you burnt the letter after committing Pistolet's address to memory."

"I'll burn it tomorrow morning," promised Scalpel.

"Very good," pronounced the Revenant. "I now deputize you, Lady Scalpel, to propose the toast."

"The toast shall be to two extraordinary individuals. The first is our absent comrade, Pistolet. She's never far from my thoughts. I wear this bracelet to remember her. The second is to the remarkable woman who has joined our ranks. I'm proud to be her sponsor. To Pistolet and Ruination!"

"To Pistolet and Ruination!" shouted the Acolytes of the Shadows.

Once the Acolytes were dismissed, Lady Ruination returned to the apartment where she resided as Emmanuelle Cussac. Ruination realized that this would be her best opportunity to locate Pistolet. The treasonous Acolyte decided to burglarize Scalpel's safe before the letter could be destroyed.

Some hours later, Lady Ruination left her apartment. Under her street clothes was her Acolyte costume. It was the perfect outfit to commit a late night robbery. When Ruination reached Scalpel's house, the time was shortly after three o'clock in the morning. She stripped off her street clothes and left them tied in a bundle in an alley. Putting on her hood, she picked the lock on the front door. She made her way softly to Scalpel's office. Scalpel should be sleeping softly upstairs. Ruination opened the safe.

"You won't find any letter in the safe because it never existed," said Lady Scalpel. "If you try to escape, I'll shoot you."

Scalpel had entered through the doorway. In her hand was a squeeze gun. Following her were Judex, Tocsin, Leopard and Invisible. They were all dressed in their Acolyte leotards and masks.

"Light the gas, Judex," commanded Scalpel. "I want to see the traitor's face. Tocsin, Invisible, seize her."

Grabbing Ruination's arms, the other Acolytes pushed her back against the wall. Scalpel reached over and pulled off Ruination's hood.

"You're unworthy to wear this mask," said Scalpel. "You are a greedy thief only interested in the bounty on Pistolet."

"Unworthy!" screamed Ruination. "You pious hypocrites! Your oath is a sham! 'We must never become as monstrous as the criminals we chase!' You're no better than the Black Coats!"

"We avenge their victims!" argued Judex.

"You also have victims! I wasn't lying about my best friend! She was butchered by a real gang of ruffians! The Acolytes of the Shadows! My friend was Tanja Samuel!"

"You're Kate Cusack!" deduced Tocsin.

"You nearly had us all fooled," said Leopard, "but you made one mistake. You claimed to be totally ignorant of the Black Coats, but you paraphrased the Black Coat maxim: 'Give the courts a *guilty party* for every crime committed.' When you left the room to get our drinks, the Revenant asked if any of us had mentioned it to you when she and Scalpel were attending to the Seraph. When none of us spoke up, our leader concocted this little test of your loyalty. We were hiding in the shadows outside when you broke into the house."

"We have your clothes," said Judex throwing the tied bundle on the floor. "You won't be wearing them when you leave. Corpses don't need clothes."

"I'm surprised that the Revenant and her precious Seraph aren't here!" growled Ruination.

"The Seraph is our Disciple of Life," professed Invisible. "She can't be part of your execution."

"I jeopardized all the Acolytes by sponsoring you," said Scalpel. "I convinced the Revenant to delegate your interrogation to me."

"Give her to me!" demanded Leopard. She pulled out a knife that had been tucked in her belt. "I'll make her talk!"

"You haven't studied anatomy, Leopard," admonished Scalpel. "I know where to strike."

With Invisible holding her right arm and Tocsin gripping her left, Ruination faced Scalpel. Menacingly pointing her squeeze gun, Scalpel icily stated her terms.

"Ruination, this gun contains ten bullets. I can strategically place all of them so that you painfully bleed to death or dispatch you quickly with a single bullet. If you answer my questions truthfully, your death will be swift and merciful."

"If I am to die, let it be quick. Ask your questions."

"Did you share your information with anyone else in the Black Coats?"

"No. I was worried that the other Black Coats might try to cheat me out of the bounties."

"If you disappear, who would miss you?"

"Only my lover, Larry Parker."

"Where is Parker now?"

"England. He'll be returning to Paris in four days."

"Tocsin, do Ruination's revelations make sense?"

"Parker often visited *L'Oreille Cassée*. I spied on his conversations. He bragged about a beautiful mistress that he had hidden away. He also said that Nemo needed him in London during November."

"You kept our bargain, Ruination," said Scalpel. "Your demise shall be swift. A fatal wound to the heart will be your reward."

"No!" objected Judex. "Ruination is the first traitor in our ranks. Ruination should be hanged like all traitors."

Scalpel shifted her gaze briefly away from her intended victim towards Judex. "Silence!" voiced Scalpel in anger. Scalpel's distraction was the opportunity that Ruination had been waiting for. Her right leg shot upward to bash Scalpel in the jaw. As Scalpel toppled backwards, her hand squeezed her pistol. A bullet whizzed into the wall just above Tocsin's head. Momentarily shaken, Tocsin loosened her hold on Ruination's arm. Breaking free of Tocsin's grip, Ruination's left arm reached across and grabbed Invisible by the back of the head. Ruination smashed Invisible's skull into Tocsin's. The two Acolytes plummeted to the ground.

Judex's hands grabbed Ruination's throat. Grabbing Judex's wrists, Ruination pried loose the blonde's hands. Ruination swung Judex face forward into the wall. The senseless Judex slid downward.

Leopard tried to stab Ruination. Dodging the blow, Ruination seized Leopard's arm and flipped her over her shoulder. Leopard's back slammed into

Rolande Cerral's desk. Sprawled motionless on the desk, Leopard's feet hung over the back of the desk while her head and arms hung over the front. Her fingers holding the knife loosened. The knife dropped on the ground.

All five loyal Acolytes were unconscious.

Ruination laughed. "The Acolytes have fallen."

"You've forgotten the Supreme Acolyte!"

In the doorway stood the masked Revenant. In deference to Scalpel, the Revenant has remained outside the office while her deputy entrapped Ruination. The vigilante threw her pickaxe at Ruination. Moving sideways, Ruination dodged the pickaxe. The Thuggee weapon embedded itself in the wall. Dropping to the ground, Ruination reached for Scalpel's gun. Unloosening the lasso from her belt, the Revenant threw it over Ruination's head. The noose tightened around Ruination's throat. A mere yank by the Revenant would have broken her enemy's neck, but Ruination's hand held the pistol. She shot at the rope. As it broke in two, Ruination fired six bullets at the Revenant in quick succession. Four bullets pierced the Revenant's arms. The others shattered her kneecaps. The bleeding Revenant fell forward.

The triumphant Ruination removed the dangling lasso from around her neck. She tucked the squeeze gun inside her belt. Holding the severed rope, she walked towards the vanquished Revenant. With a flick of her foot, Ruination flipped her masked opponent over.

"Once upon a time, there was a powerful Queen," said Ruination. "The Queen sent her five Pawns against a lone Knight. The Knight defeated the Pawns forcing the Queen to reveal herself." Lady Ruination reached down to remove the Revenant's mask. "The Knight dethroned the Queen and stole her crown.

"You rightfully hate the Black Coats, Darlla Rassendyll, but your pompous ceremonies blind your followers from seeing a fundamental truth. The Acolytes of the Shadows are no different from the Black Coats. You and I are much alike. We both imagine ourselves to be avengers. I have proven to be the superior avenger."

"It isn't over," feebly whispered the Revenant. "There's still the Seraph."

"I've already shown my physical superiority over her."

"But not your moral superiority."

"The Seraph is a sincere idealist, but she serves as a virtuous veneer to excuse your butchery. She lacks your harsh realism. You have two other followers. Charon is of no consequence. The absent Pistolet doesn't frighten me. I look forward to confronting her. She shall prove to be as weak a combatant as she was a pool player.

"I deliberately refrained from damaging your head, Darlla. It's very precious to me. 30,000 francs to be exact. The time has come for you and your Acolytes to atone for the murder of Tanja Samuel. As you lay powerless, watch me throttle your five Acolytes. Your lasso shall be their passport to eternity.

Once your lackeys are extinguished, you shall be beheaded with your own pick-axe. Your first minion to expire shall be Lady Scalpel."

Ruination strolled over to the slumbering Scalpel. She was resting on her back. Ruination positioned her legs on each side of Scalpel's torso. Kneeling down, Ruination straddled Scalpel. After removing Scalpel's hood, Ruination looped the Punjabi lasso around her fellow Acolyte's neck. Ruination pulled slightly. Scalpel opened her eyes. She saw the smiling face of Ruination,

"You promised me a quick death, Scalpel, but yours shall be slow. I know far less anatomy than you, but I fully comprehend the neck. I know where to strike."

As the noose tightened, Scalpel gasped for breath. Her left hand pulled out the scalpel hidden in the bracelet on her right wrist. She stabbed Ruination in the thigh. Ruination's angry response was to tighten the noose. Overwhelmed by agony, Scalpel relinquished her hold on the object that matched her name.

"Is that the best you can do?" asked Ruination. "Olaki taught me to resist pain! A pinprick like that could never send me to a quick death!"

Suddenly Ruination felt dizzy. She couldn't hold the noose any more. She fell sideways rolling off Scalpel. Struggling to breathe, Scalpel untangled the noose around her throat. She twisted her body sideways in order to face the prostrate Ruination.

"What...did...you...do?" murmured Ruination.

"I cut your femoral artery," answered Scalpel. "Very soon you'll be unconscious. Death normally follows within three to five minutes."

The last thing Ruination felt before falling asleep was Scalpel's spittle on her cheek.

"Help me, Scalpel," moaned the Revenant.

"Forgive me, my liege, but first I have to keep my bargain with Ruination."

Scalpel pulled out her namesake from Ruination's thigh. Ruination's departure from the land of the living was greatly accelerated once Scalpel stabbed her in the heart.

During the battle with Lady Ruination, Lord Charon had patiently waited in his carriage several blocks away from the Cerral residence. He was surprised to only see Lady Leopard approaching.

"Where's the Revenant?" asked Charon.

"She's been wounded. You must take me to the Opera House immediately."

Beneath the Opera House, Leopard briefed the Seraph on the fiasco that transpired at Dr. Cerral's.

"Scalpel is busy operating on the Revenant," explained Leopard.

"I must go to the Revenant at once," said the Seraph.

"You are to stay here. Scalpel's orders."

"Scalpel is not the Supreme Acolyte!"

"She is now. Before she went under the anesthesia, the Revenant transferred all her authority to Scalpel. Judex, Tocsin, Invisible and I witnessed the Ceremony of Transfer."

"But a transfusion of my blood saved the Revenant when she was shot in the past!"

"Scalpel believes that the Purple Serum will have the same results."

"But it's untested!"

"We have to take that risk. Ruination may be dead, but she's left a trail that could potentially expose all our identities to the Black Coats or the police. You are the most conspicuous of us all when it comes to travelling during the day. We can't have rumors circulating about a veiled lady. Ida Similor and other Black Coats know that you've used that disguise in the past."

"Can't we just bury Ruination secretly?"

"If Emmanuelle Cussac vanishes, her landlady will report her disappearance to the police. At the very least, the authorities will investigate Emmanuelle's current employer."

"We could let the police discover the body."

"In its present state, an autopsy will conclude that Ruination's femoral artery was severed. The police would know that the killer had anatomical knowledge. Scalpel would again be in jeopardy."

"What can I do, Leopard?"

"Prepare the sanctuary to receive the Revenant. She'll be arriving here tomorrow."

"You're going to move the Revenant in her wounded condition?"

"We have no choice. If Scalpel's plan works, the police will be visiting her house in two or three days."

"What is Scalpel's plan?"

"We're following Ruination's advice. The Acolytes of the Shadows are going to make a Black Coat *pay the law*."

"Who?"

"Ida Similor. Her expertise with knives shall be her downfall."

Lady Scalpel, the acting Supreme Acolyte, coordinated her agents brilliantly over the next few days.

Lady Invisible burglarized the apartment rented by Emmanuelle Cussac. Invisible found an envelope bearing this inscription: "To Be Opened in the Event of My Death." It contained a detailed summary of Ruination's information on the Acolytes of the Shadows. Invisible burned it. Invisible also typed a story entitled "Emmanuelle: an Independent Woman." It was published in the weekly news digest of the Sure Values Agency,

Lady Tocsin and Lady Judex cleaned up all the bloodstains in Dr. Cerral's office. They also repaired the holes in the walls left by Scalpel's squeeze gun and the Revenant's pickaxe. They burned Ruination's street clothes and leotard. The two Acolytes moved the Nemo dummy, the squeeze gun and Scalpel's notebooks to Judex's house.

Lord Charon and Lady Leopard made two trips during one night to the Cerral residence. First, they secretly transported the Revenant and all the remaining vials of the Purple Serum to the Opera House. On the second trip, they took a naked corpse and dumped it into the Seine River.

The police found a woman's nude body in the morning. Her face had been horribly slashed. The lower portion of her torso was mutilated. The mutilations resembled those inflicted on a woman who had died two weeks earlier in London's East End. The other victim's name was Mary Jane Kelly. Her death was attributed by Scotland Yard to Jack the Ripper.

"The press will run rampant with this murder." said Commissioner Mifroid of the Sûreté. He put the case in the capable hands of Chief Inspector Jacques Lefevre, the man who had successfully solved the Bluebeard Strangulations. The immediate need was to identify the victim.

The next day, a woman reported her maid missing. Her name was Dr. Rolande Cerral. The police had Dr. Cerral examine the body in the morgue. Due to a birthmark on the arm of the corpse, Dr. Cerral identified the victim as her maid, Emmanuelle Cussac.

According to Dr. Cerral, a journalist named Chantal Lebrue had visited her home three days earlier hoping to find Emmanuelle and interview her for a story concerning independent women in Paris. Dr. Cerral had invited Chantal to have dinner with her and Camille that evening. After dinner, Chantal and Emmanuelle had left the house.

The police interviewed Chantal. She proved to be a legitimate journalist who owned the Sure Values Agency. Chantal showed the police her recently published article. The story claimed that Chantal had learned of Emmanuelle from two different sources, the maid's landlady and Shintaro Olaki. Both Madame Vabre and Olaki corroborated Chantal's assertions.

In the middle of the newspaper furor, Larry Parker returned to France. Reading of his lover's death, he felt it prudent to retreat back to London. If anyone learned of his connection to the murder victim, he would immediately become a suspect. Worse yet, the police might even imagine Parker to be Jack the Ripper due to his English nationality. The fact that Catherine had been sadistically mutilated with a knife led Parker to believe that Ida Similor had killed her. Catherine must have broken her promise and pursued a vendetta against Ida.

The autopsy on Catherine concluded that she had died from a wound to the heart. Due to the mutilations elsewhere on Catherine's body, it was never determined that her femoral artery had been cut prior to her death.

With Dr. Cerral's permission, Lefevre searched her house for clues. Nothing was found to assist his inquiries. However, Dr. Cerral performed three great services for Lefevre. First, she drew a sketch of Emmanuelle's face. Second, she gave him the letters of references that Emmanuelle had given her. Third, she informed Lefevre that Emmanuelle professed to be a native of Avignon. The woman in the sketch was recognized by Lefevre's colleague, Francois Le Villard, as being Kate Cusack, a felon sought as an accomplice in a warehouse robbery. Cooperation between Scotland Yard and the Sûreté was very difficult in 1888 due to strained relations between the British and French government. Luckily, Le Villard corresponded with a renowned consulting detective, Sherlock Holmes. Le Villard wired Holmes asking if he had any information on a "Kate Cusack" or an "Emmanuelle Cussac" being employed by the Earl of Mayntooth. The message also included a description of Cusack. Holmes wired back that the murdered woman was Catherine Cusack, the Countess of Morcar's former maid and an instigator of the Blue Carbuncle robbery. She had romanced a man named James Ryder to purloin the gem. Furthermore, Cusack had never been employed by the Mayntooth family but she had visited their ancestral estate. The Avignon police confirmed the existence of a Catherine Emmanuelle Cussac who had graduated from a nearby school in 1884.

Lefevre formed a theory of the case. Catherine Emmanuelle Cussac was a scheming woman who posed as a maid to commit robberies. Catherine was probably intending to rob Dr. Rolande Cerral. The treacherous maid must have been killed in a dispute with one of her criminal cohorts. The murderer then attempted to mislead the police by making the crime look like the work of Jack the Ripper.

A police raid on *L'Epi-Scié* resulted in several known felons being rounded up for questioning. Among these "usual suspects" was Cocotte. Under probing by Lefevre, Cocotte told of his encounter with Jacques Cavalier, an Englishman pretending to be a Frenchman.

On a sheet of paper, Lefevre recorded the name "Jacques Cavalier." Since Jacques was also his own Christian name, Lefevre knew the English equivalent. The police official wrote "James." Although the French word Cavalier has an exact English equivalent, there was another way in which it could be translated. Lefevre write the English word "Rider." A variant of "Rider" was the surname Ryder. Jacques Cavalier was James Ryder, Catherine's partner in the Blue Carbuncle robbery.

At the Royal Palace Hotel, James Ryder (alias Jacques Cavalier) was arrested by Chief Inspector Lefevre. Ryder was charged with Catherine's murder. Lefevre argued that Ryder had slain Catherine in a lovers' quarrel.

The truth was very different. After being deserted by Catherine in London, Ryder had futilely searched for her. His quest had brought him to Paris. He had foolishly hoped to rekindle their romance.

At the Sure Values Agency, Feliciana Sorelli discussed the Ryder arrest with Chantal Lebrue.

"Ryder is innocent!" protested Chantal. "We can't allow him to be sent to the guillotine!"

"He's not that innocent!" responded Feliciana. "Ryder was quite willing to let an innocent man, John Horner, rot in jail for the Blue Carbuncle robbery. It's poetic justice that he *pays the law*."

"But Scalpel expected the police to arrest Ida Similor!"

"Ryder will serve our purposes just as much as Ida."

In the sanctuary below the Paris Opera House, Darlla Rassendyll was asleep in her bed. She was undergoing a lengthy convalescence under the care of the Jade Seraph.

"Darlla, what's happening to us?" asked the Seraph as she watched over her slumbering friend. "We're becoming as corrupt as the Black Coats."

Sherlock Holmes testified for the defense at Ryder's trial. Holmes maintained the innocence of the defendant. He skillfully portrayed Ryder as a weak man laid astray by a conniving woman. The detective maintained that Ryder was too frightened to commit another crime after nearly being jailed for the Carbuncle robbery.

The dashing prosecutor, Maître Forrestier, forced Holmes to admit that he had put himself above the law by refusing to surrender Ryder to Scotland Yard. In his closing remarks, Forrestier made a devastating argument.

"This haughty Englishman took it upon himself to function as Ryder's judge and jury. His misguided clemency permitted Ryder to continue his criminal rampage. If Ryder had gone to prison, Catherine Cussac would be alive today. We in France respect the law. One woman is dead. We cannot risk another atrocity by the defendant."

James Ryder was beheaded for the murder of his former lover.

It took the Revenant three months to fully recuperate from her wounds. She was able to regain full usage of her limbs due to doses of the Purple Serum. Because of the Revenant's incapacitation, the Acolytes of the Shadows were temporarily thrown into disarray. Consequently, the Acolytes did not discover that the Black Coats organized an unusual gala ball in February 1889.

The body of Catherine Cussac would have been consigned to a pauper's grave, but Dr. Rolande Cerral insisted on paying for the interment of the corpse in the Montmartre cemetery. The inscription on the headstone of Dr. Cerral's former maid reads as follows:

CATHERINE EMMANUELLE CUSSAC
(1863-1888)
RUINATION WAS HER DESTINY

The Brigand Princess

That night in March 1889, Sophy Kratides cried on the bed. Her lover had shown himself to be a merciless monster. He had poisoned her older brother six months ago. Since that time, she had been a prisoner transported across Europe. Now in Hungary, Sophy was about to endure a brutal beating.

Another woman knocked on the door of the Budapest residence.

The door was opened by a short middle-aged man with rounded shoulders. He examined his visitor critically through eyes covered by glasses. She was a tall woman with a derby hat perched on her head. She wore a gray shawl and dress. Black gloves adorned her hands. Her right hand clutched a black cane. Its handle was a white skull.

"You must be Wilson Kemp," she pronounced. "I represent Monsieur Nemo."

"*Will there be daylight?*" asked Kemp.

"*It will be daylight from midnight to noon if it is the will of the Father,*" she replied.

"Please come in," requested Kemp. "Remove your hat. I must examine your features. Also smile. I need to inspect your mouth. Kratides has perfect teeth."

The woman complied. She has short black hair parted down the middle.

"The resemblance is not perfect, but it is close enough to fool the trustees in Athens," concluded Kemp. "Do you know Greek?"

"I was born in Croatia. I'm fluent in Greek and other Balkan languages. Where is Kratides?"

"She proved somewhat rebellious today. Harold and I had no choice but to restrain her. My colleague is currently in the upstairs bedroom persuading her to be cooperative."

"Could his disciplinary session be interrupted? Our employer has a message for both of you."

Kemp mounted the stairs to the upper level. He knocked on the door. It was opened by a handsome young man carrying a riding crop. Inside the room, the dark-haired Sophy laid on the bed with her arms and legs bound.

"Nemo's emissary is here, Harold," revealed Kemp. "She needs to talk to both of us."

The young man followed his companion downstairs.

"Ah, the attractive Mr. Latimer," intoned the brunette. "I am Petra Donevitch."

She extended her gloved right hand. Harold Latimer gently held it. He lowered his head to kiss her hand.

"You have instructions from the Lord of the Night?" asked Latimer.

"Last year, the Black Coats commanded you to plant a seed that would grow into a tree bearing fruit," answered Petra. "The tree is healthy, but some branches are barren. *Cut the branches*."

Petra's right hand rapidly pulled the handle of her cane. A sword was revealed. Before either man could react, she slew them. Kemp was stabbed in the stomach; Latimer in the heart. Leaving the two corpses, Petra ran up the stairs to the bedroom.

"Sophy," declared Petra, "your brother's murderers are dead."

Petra used her blade to slash open the ropes around the prisoner's wrists and ankles.

"Who are you?" asked the liberated Sophy Kratides.

"My mother was your father's sister, Xenia. I'm your cousin."

Asenath Pons had been a fighter all his life. It was a misfortune of birth that thrust this destiny upon him. His father had received a large inheritance from a spinster aunt. The elder Pons had sworn to name his firstborn child after his departed Aunt Asenath. Even though the child was male, the pledge was fulfilled.

Growing up with a girl's name in England had been the bane of the young boy's childhood. Pons had suffered constant taunts when he had been enrolled in the Wrykyn Preparatory School. There he had befriended another boy with an unfortunate first name, Duckworth Dreux. Their friendship would endure throughout the years as they were both recruited as agents by Her Majesty's Secret Service.

Nominally, Pons was an assistant official at the British Consulate in Prague. Dreux, the son of a French father and an English mother, was a roving trouble shooter throughout Europe. In April 1889, Dreux had arrived in Prague to steal a secret treaty detailing the policies of the Triple Alliance towards the British Empire. Dreux had been successful in his mission. It was imperative that Pons get Dreux aboard a coach to transport the valuable document across the Austro-Hungarian border.

At a relay station near Prague, Dreux and Pons rushed towards the coach. They passed two women moving towards a different coach. One lady was dressed in plain clothes and a veil. Because she was holding two suitcases, Dreux judged her to be a servant. The other female was attired in a bowler hat. She carried a cane.

Dreux stopped momentarily.

"Pons, that woman in the derby! She's Sophy Kratides!"

"Are you sure?"

"She's the spitting image of the photo sent us by M.!"

"You can't afford to waste time, Dreux! Board the carriage! I'll handle this myself!"

As Dreux took his seat in the coach, Pons approached the two women.

"Excuse me," said Pons to the woman in the derby. "Are you Sophy Kratides?"

"Yes, I am," answered Petra Donevitch. She turned to her veiled companion. "Wait in the carriage, my dear. This should only take a moment."

Petra motioned Pons to follow her into an alley.

"We need to talk in private, sir. My life is in danger."

"I'm well aware of the perils you face. I know all about your abduction by the Gentlemen of the Night. I represent the British authorities, I am empowered to-"

Pons never finished his sentence. The blade from Petra's sword cane plunged into his forehead.

Abandoning the corpse in the alley, Petra rejoined the other woman inside the coach.

"Is anything wrong?" asked the veiled Sophy Kratides.

"That man was one of Nemo's agents. I was forced to kill him. We won't be safe until we reach Paris."

Four months later, Sherlock Holmes deciphered a communiqué in Baker Street. He read the coded message before him:

Nemo will be in Paris on August 20. He intends to conclude the Kratides affair.

Fred Porlock

Holmes was pleased. His correspondent had given him valuable information. He left immediately to confer with a relative at the Diogenes Club.

Feliciana Sorelli was the leading dancer at the Paris Opera. As Lady Leopard, she was also an agent of the Revenant, the female vigilante waging a brutal war on the French underworld. One of Feliciana's duties was to retrieve messages prepared by the Revenant's other agents from a building on the Rue de Provence. These reports were deposited in sealed envelopes into the mail slot of a locked office supposedly rented by a lawyer, A. L. Lard. In reality, Monsieur Lard was a fictional creation of the Revenant.

The blonde danseuse returned to her dressing room at the Opera House. Feliciana opened a secret panel covered by her full-length mirror. She moved through a secret passageway. Eventually, she arrived at the underground cellars of the Opera House. Feliciana stood on the shore of a subterranean lake. A canoe with a paddle rested on the edge of the lake. She employed the craft to travel to the other shore of the lake where the sanctum of the Revenant was located.

Dressed in her costume, the Revenant greeted Feliciana. The scourge of Parisian crime wore a black shirt with a V-shaped neckline outlined in red, as well as black pants and boots. Her red-gloved hands received the envelopes from Feliciana.

Although the Revenant was a hooded avenger to the public, she did not wear her mask in her headquarters. She was a statuesque redhead whose facial beauty was slightly marred by a cruel mouth. The Revenant's real identity was Darlla Rassendyll, a former operative of the French police. Years earlier, Darlla had been forced to adopt a clandestine existence when she had been framed for murder and treason. The fictional "A. L Lard" was an anagram of Darlla.

"There was an extra envelope," noted Feliciana. "Have you recruited a new Acolyte, Revenant?"

"No, Lady Leopard. Perhaps one of the Acolytes later delivered a second report."

After Feliciana departed, Darlla retired to her private chamber to examine the messages. One of the missives had surprising contents.

Dear Mademoiselle Rassendyll,
Please pay me the courtesy of having dinner with me at Room 13 of the Royal Palace Hotel at 8 o'clock on Wednesday, August 18th. It would be appropriate if you arrive in your Augustine d'Erlette persona. Do not send one of your Acolytes in your place. What I have to say is for your ears only.

M.

Darlla expressed her shock vocally. "*Mon Dieu!* Who is this M.?"

The clothes encasing Sophy Kratides were not too dissimilar from those that Darlla Rassendyll had flaunted during her conference with Feliciana. The major difference was that Sophy's shirt and pants were gray. Her hands were also gloveless. Her fingers were tightened around a sword identical to Petra Donevitch's. The blade had been a gift from her Croatian cousin.

Petra wore a tan smock that covered an identical gray ensemble with black boots. Standing before an unfinished portrait, she carried a palette and a paint brush in her bare hands. Black gloves were tucked in her belt.

"That's enough posing for today," declared Petra. Covering the painting with a large cloth, she locked it in a cupboard.

"Why won't you let me see it, Petra?"

"I want *The Brigand Princess* to surprise you. I added something from my own imagination. Now it's time for your lesson."

Removing her smock and putting on her gloves, Petra unsheathed the sword from her cane.

"You must learn to fight as proficiently as me, cousin," asserted Petra. "Someday I may not be there to protect you from the Black Coats."

"You've been so kind to me to me, Petra. This is like that famous childhood story, *Cinderella.* A woman is saved from a life of misery by a benevolent relative."

"You probably should call me your Godmother."

Because the authorities sought to arrest Darlla Rassendyll, the fiery redhead had concocted the false identity of Augustine d'Erlette. To the naked eye, Augustine was an elderly spinster who walked with a large cane. A mask of false wrinkles disguised Darlla's face. A gray wig enclosed her hair.

At 8 o'clock, Wednesday evening, Augustine knocked on the door of Room 13 of the Royal Palace Hotel. A stout man in his forties answered the door.

"Madame d'Erlette, how prompt! Please come in."

"Monsieur M., You have me at a disadvantage. You know my real name. Yours remains a mystery to me."

"The 'M' stands for Mycroft...Mycroft Holmes."

"Any relation to the detective who advocated the innocence of my Revenant alter ego in the Stewart murder two years ago?"

"Sherlock is my younger brother. I wholeheartedly supported his conclusions. Please sit down with me and have dinner. The hotel has a wonderful Swiss cook. Monsieur Brenner has produced a scrumptious meal to my specifications."

"I didn't come here for the food. I demand to know why I was summoned."

"I have a manuscript that will answer your question. Before reading it, will you indulge a minor request? There is no need for that ghastly disguise. Please remove your mask and wig."

Darlla Rassendyll did so. Her true face and hair were exposed.

"The famous Rassendyll features. You somewhat resemble your English cousin, Rudolf. In 1887, he got entangled in a scrape in Ruritania. It came to my attention."

Mycroft handed her a typed manuscript of about twenty-five pages. It was entitled "The Adventure of the Greek Interpreter." Its author was John H. Watson. Darlla closely scrutinized Watson's narrative.

It was an account of a case investigated by Sherlock Holmes. An unscrupulous adventurer, Harold Latimer, had seduced a Greek heiress, Sophy Kratides, visiting England. Sophy fled with Latimer to London. Sophy's brother, Paul, came from Athens to find her. Shortly after his arrival in England, Paul had been abducted by Latimer and an accomplice, Wilson Kemp. The intention of the perfidious pair was to coerce Paul into signing over to them the Kratides family fortune. However, Paul did not speak a word of English. Neither Latimer nor Kemp was fluent in Greek. Sophy spoke both languages, but Latimer realized his hold on her would evaporate if she discovered her brother's imprisonment. The two conspirators briefly enlisted the assistance of Melas, an interpreter for the British law courts. Being a fellow member of the Diogenes Club, Melas brought the matter to Mycroft Holmes. Sherlock Holmes was soon brought into the case. Although Sherlock prevented the murder of Melas by Latimer and Kemp, the sleuth failed to thwart the slaying of Paul Kratides. With Sophy still a prisoner, Latimer and Kemp fled the country. Months later, a report of the death of two Englishmen in Budapest reached London. Both had been fatally stabbed. The Hungarian police concluded that the duo had killed each other in a knife fight. The description of the corpses fit Latimer and Kemp.

Once she had finished Watson's story, Darlla Rassendyll made an observation.

"Although Watson never mentions a criminal organization called the Black Coats, this entire sordid affair resembles their handiwork. The Black Coats have long sought to gain control of family legacies."

"I am more familiar with the London branch of the Black Coats, the Gentlemen of the Night, Mademoiselle Rassendyll. For two years, my brother has been investigating their overlord, the man feared as Jim Nemo."

"I've met him. His underlings revere him as the Lord of the Night."

"My brother had enlisted the services of an informant inside Nemo's organization. This turncoat sent Sherlock a message. On Friday, Nemo will be in Paris in order 'to conclude the Kratides affair.' "

"Before we continue any further, there is something that we must settle, Monsieur Holmes. In Watson's tale, Sherlock depicted you as a minor government auditor. Your brother wasn't being totally candid with the good doctor."

"Mademoiselle Rassendyll, what do you imagine me to be?"

"You cited Ruritania, an obscure principality edged in by the German state of Saxony and Austria-Hungary. Only a Foreign Office bureaucrat would be concerned with developments there. You must be involved with matters of espionage. Your sedentary nature clearly prevents you from being an active spy yourself, but you must be a man who coordinates the activities of British spies."

"For the sake of expediency, Mademoiselle Rassendyll, I will not dispute your allegation."

"How did your agents trace me?"

"In 1881, Nihilists tempted to disrupt the Trémeuse wedding reception at the Russian Embassy in Paris. A bomb was removed from the premises under mysterious circumstances. One of my agents, Digby Fell, was then assigned to Paris."

"You're very free with divulging your agents' names."

"Fell has since retired. There is no problem with identifying him. Fell investigated the abortive bombing. He discovered that a woman, Augustine d'Erlette, had mysteriously left the embassy the night before the reception. Furthermore, the bride, the former Julia Orsini, had sent Augustine's luggage to

Feliciana Sorelli, a ballerina at the Paris Opera. Fell surreptitiously followed Feliciana. He discovered her receiving messages from a locked office registered under the name A. L. Lard. Additional inquiries indicated that the Lard office had come into existence in 1879. Fell mistakenly concluded that Augustine, Julia, and Feliciana were members of a Nihilist band of saboteurs. He cabled me for permission to share the details of his investigations with the French authorities."

"You vetoed Fell's proposal. You deduced something else from the Lard alias."

"Precisely, Mademoiselle Rassendyll. Your A. L. Lard pseudonym is an anagram of your first name. I remembered the case of a Darlla Rassendyll who had been accused of committing a murder at the Paris Opera House in the same year that the office was leased by the enigmatic A.L Lard. 1879 was also the year when the Revenant first surfaced. I'll spare you a lengthy discussion of my intellectual processes. You can easily see how I ascertain your identity. I saw no reason for Her Majesty's Government to disrupt a gang of French vigilantes."

"But I have been proclaimed a traitor and a murderess by the French government."

"I am not as foolish as my French counterparts in your Second Bureau. From reviewing the facts reported in the French newspapers, I became a firm believer in your innocence.'

"You summoned me here to request a service. Mademoiselle Kratides must have escaped her abductors in Hungary. Your brother's informant seems to be implying that she's in Paris. Do you want me to rescue her?

"No, Darlla Rassendyll. *I want you to kill Sophy Kratides!*"

"*You can't be serious!*"

"But I am," insisted Mycroft dispassionately. "There are certainly facts with which you are unacquainted. Although I never met Sophy Kratides, I was not unsympathetic to her apparent plight. I circulated a photograph of her to all my agents stationed in Europe. One month after the deaths of Latimer and Kemp, two of my male operatives, Asenath Pons and another fellow, spotted Sophy in Prague. A vital mission caused Pons to be left alone with Kratides. She disappeared, but Pons was fatally stabbed just like Latimer and Kemp."

"Pons was more than just another agent to you."

"Asenath was my second cousin. I was best man at his wedding. I am the godfather of his nine-year old son."

"Are you sure that Sophy is Asenath's killer."

"There could be no doubt. She must have made some deal with Jim Nemo. Originally she was scheduled to inherit an eighth of the Kratides fortune. With her brother's death, Sophy will inherit it all. For all we know, she could have been an accomplice to her brother's own murder. For whatever reasons, Sophy slew Latimer and Kemp. Fearing that Asenath might have her apprehended for those deaths, she slew him as well. Within two months, Sophy will reach her twenty-first birthday. She will only need to appear in front of a board of trustees to claim her legacy."

"You have other agents. Surely one of them could assassinate Sophy on your orders."

"I've already lost one agent in this affair. I won't risk another."

"There's another reason. Isn't there, Monsieur Holmes? Imagine the scandal if a Greek heiress was discovered to have been killed by a British spy."

"Very insightful, Mademoiselle Rassendyll."

"You intend to expose me and my subordinates to the French police if I refuse to act as your executioner."

"There will no penalty if you refuse this mission. By the same token, there will be no reward if you accept."

"I don't understand."

"You have your own reasons for opposing the Black Coats, Darlla Rassendyll. You have your own code of justice. I'm banking that you will undertake this mission because our interests coincide."

"You cited a photograph of Sophy Kratides. Do you have it here?"

Mycroft handed Darlla a picture of a young woman in a white dress and bonnet.

"She looks very young in the photograph," commented Darlla. "How old was she?"

"That was taken two years ago. She was only 19. Watson left out some minor details in his story. Sophy was enrolled as a student at an English boarding school when she was 18. While staying as a guest at a classmate's home two years later, she became involved with Latimer. She hasn't set foot in Greece for the last three years."

"A woman can change in subtle ways during the transition from 19 and 21. Is there a more detailed description of the sighting in Prague by Asenath's colleague?"

"This is a summary of the agent's observations." Mycroft handed Darlla a sheet of paper containing a typed paragraph.

Black eyes and hair. Attired in a gray dress, black derby and gloves. Carried a cane with a skull on the handle (possibly a sword-cane). Accompanied by a veiled female companion who carried their two suitcases. Other woman obviously a servant.

"Well, Mademoiselle Rassendyll, what is your decision?"

"I will bring Sophy Kratides to justice."

"Excellent. I'll be staying here until Sunday. Let us dine before our meal grows cold."

"There is a French saying, Monsieur Holmes. Revenge is a dish best served cold."

"Darlla, how could you make such a bargain!" protested Valorie Varno.

The most notable feature of the raven-haired speaker was her green skin. Her bizarre complexion had been the result of a rare South American drug employed by the Black Coats. As the Jade Seraph, Valorie Varno was the closest of Darlla Rassendyll's associates. While all the other agents were known as Acolytes, Valorie was called a Disciple. The Seraph even resided with Darlla in the underground chambers beneath the Opera House. Valorie had once been an assassin for the Black Coats before Darlla engineered her reformation. In atonement for her earlier brutal acts of murder, Valorie had sworn an oath never to take human life.

"All the evidence points to Sophy being a bloodthirsty murderess."

"She was twenty when Latimer seduced her. I was almost the same age when Leonard convinced me to elope. That act started me on the road to damnation." Clutching her emerald robe with her left hand, Valorie rubbed her neck with her right. "Will you break Sophy's neck as you once did mine?"

"Valorie, not every soul can be redeemed!'

"If you're going to function as Mycroft's executioner, at least make sure you're hanging a guilty party!"

"What are you implying?"

"When I worked for the Black Coats, they had me study the career of Marguerite Sadoulas. She attempted twice to steal the de Clare family fortune. The second time, she replaced an heiress, Clotilde Morand Stuart de Clare, with an impostor."

"There's nothing to suggest, Valorie, that the woman in the derby hat is a false claimant to the Kratides estate."

"Are you sure? There's a major assumption that the veiled woman in Prague was merely a servant. Consider this scenario. The Black Coats deemed Latimer and Kemp to be expendable. They send a female executioner to *cut the branch*. This assassin gained Sophy's confidence by pretending to be her rescuer. This deceiver convinces Sophy that she must pose as her servant to escape pursuit by the Black Coats. Now this murderess has ample opportunity to study Sophy's mannerisms. Additionally, Sophy will confide to her supposed savior all the stories regarding her early years in Greece. Inevitably, the woman in the derby hat kills Sophy and assumes her identity."

"You may be right, Valorie. The real Sophy could have been the veiled woman. We may need to rescue an innocent from the Black Coats."

"Darlla, you're premature in your usage of the word 'we.' I can't function as your accomplice in the execution of the woman in the derby hat. Regardless of her true identity, this killer is too much like I once was."

"I understand, Valorie. You can reside in the sanctuary until this mission is concluded. I will need to confer with Feliciana in her dressing room. She may be able to discover something about Nemo's presence in Paris."

"Can you have Feliciana convey a message to Laurent? I need to see him."

Laurent Remy was the private secretary to the Director of the Paris Opera. He was also Valorie's lover. Darlla realized that her recent actions had disturbed her best friend. Valorie needed to be comforted in the arms of the man she loved.

After crossing the underground lake in a canoe, Darlla Rassendyll traversed the labyrinth of passageways to Feliciana Sorelli's dressing room.

"The Seraph refused to help!" shouted Feliciana. "That ingrate! Her scruples as the Disciple of Life have once again compromised our operations. She was equally reluctant to snuff out Lady Ruination."

"Do not judge Valorie too harshly," advised the Revenant. "She's burdened by her own inner demons. Nemo will be in Paris definitely by tomorrow. Try to trace him."

Feliciana Sorelli was more than just a subordinate of the Revenant. She was a double agent inside the Black Coats. Feliciana had to tread a difficult path. Once she had participated in an elaborate ruse to preserve the Revenant's secret identity. When Monsieur Nemo suspected that the disgraced Darlla Rassendyll was connected to the Revenant, Feliciana pretended to murder Darlla. Feliciana had stuck a knife into a wax effigy of Darlla Rassendyll. The false corpse had then been photographed.

"Nemo never allows his movements to be traced. His minions are merely told when he wants them. A carriage then transports them to Nemo's location. May I peruse Sophy's photograph?"

Darlla gave Sophy's photo to Feliciana.

"Remember, Leopard, we aren't positive that Sophy's the woman in the derby hat."

There was a knock on the dressing room's door.

"What is it?

"A messenger arrived with special letter for you, Mademoiselle Sorelli," volunteered a masculine voice.

"Please slip it under the door," requested Feliciana.

As soon as the envelope appeared in the room, Feliciana opened it.

"It's from Nemo, Revenant. He wants to see me tomorrow. He wants to discuss- *Sacrebleu!*"

"What is it?"

"*Nemo wants to discuss you!*"

"There's no need to worry, Leopard. It's natural for the Black Coats to plot against the Revenant. I remain their implacable foe."

"The message doesn't mention the Revenant! It mentions Darlla Rassendyll!"

Feliciana had been instructed to await a coach in front of the Paris Opera House. The Revenant had seriously considered following the coach, but she realized that such a countermeasure might expose Feliciana's duplicity to Nemo. Darlla merely waited in Feliciana's dressing room for the audience with Nemo to be concluded. Darlla was fearful that Nemo suspected Feliciana's betrayal of the Black Coats. The Lord of the Night may have Feliciana under close surveillance.

The carriage transported Feliciana to a large shop on the Rue de Grammont. A placard on the building had this inscription:

THE REGENERATOR OF FASHION
Van Klopen, tailor for ladies.

Years ago, there had been a violent civil war inside the Black Coats. Jim Nemo had launched a rebellion against the All-Father, the supposedly immortal master of the crime syndicate. Four years ago, a peace settlement had been negotiated between the two factions. To the overwhelming majority of the Black Coats including Feliciana, this agreement was shrouded in mystery. Some claimed that the All-Father was now a nominal figurehead with no more power than the Japanese Emperor under the Shogunate. Supreme power allegedly resided in the hands of Jim Nemo, the Lord of the Night. Other countered that Nemo had been severely chastised by the All-Father. In this version of the tale, Nemo fearfully followed the All-Father's dictates.

Van Klopen, the most prominent fashion designer in Paris, had long been a member of the Black Coats. During the period of internal strife, Van Klopen had sided with the All-Father against Nemo. Once deadly enemies, Van Klopen and Nemo were now ardent collaborators. The fashion designer was 66 years old. His obese face was marred with pimples. He greeted Feliciana as she entered his establishment.

"Greetings, Mademoiselle Sorelli. I'm afraid you must wait. Count Corbucci has just arrived to see Monsieur Nemo. They're in the conference room."

Jim Nemo and Salvatore Corbucci contrasted radically in appearance. Nemo gave the impression of a thin ascetic with a high dome forehead. Corbucci exuded the aura of a corpulent sensualist. While Nemo was clean-shaven, Corbucci had a large moustache.

Also present was Petra Donevitch. She was brandishing her customary bowler hat and skull-faced cane. Rather than a dress, she wore a gray jacket, shirts and pants along with black boots.

"I'm long been an admirer of your novels of the American West, Count Corbucci."

"Thank you, Princess."

"You recognize my title?"

"The Donevitch claim to the throne of Croatia is quite legitimate. It's a disgrace that the effete Elphbergs rule Ruritania while their energetic rivals are denied dominion over Croatia."

"Your knowledge of my family is impressive?"

"I researched Croatia for my novel, *The Undertaker's Big Gun.* As you may recall, the hero was Ignacz Djanko, a Croatian-American gunfighter."

"Exactly what is your role in the Black Coats, Count?"

"I am the All-Father's personal emissary. He's very upset by the Kratides affair. It was badly bungled in the beginning."

"You are not acquainted with the true facts," interjected Nemo. "A year ago, a promising protégé of mine, Harold Latimer, romanced Sophy Kratides, then only a minor heiress. I paid little attention to the matter at the time. I merely introduced Latimer to Wilson Kemp to act as his accomplice. Unexpectedly, a golden opportunity arose for Larimer to gain control of the entire Kratides fortune. Rather than contact me, he embarked on a clumsy ruse to recruit a Greek interpreter. It alerted the authorities. Latimer and Kemp have paid the price for their incompetence."

"I am aware that two branches have been cut," said Corbucci. "You rather cleverly made both victims *pay the law.*"

"If Sophy Kratides were to simply perish," resumed Nemo, "one of her countless Greek cousins would inherit. Impersonation is our only viable option. Sophy's aunt was disowned by her family after she married into the Donevitch clan. Sophy strongly resembles her Croatian cousin. Her Highness is two years older, but she can easily pretend to be younger. Like all the Donevitch family, she is an expert fencer and duelist."

"I have heard that Her Highness is also a painter whose skill rivals Henri Radin," volunteered Corbucci.

"Quite so," Nemo confirmed. "I have commissioned two portraits from her."

"I have Sophy for several months now," added Petra. "I can imitate her voice and hand writing. I know all the important events of her early life. Tonight I snuff out her life. The Kratides inheritance will be mine!"

"And how will you compensate your fellow Black Coats?" asked Corbucci.

"I will allow my associates to use the Kratides shipping companies to smuggle illicit goods throughout the Mediterranean. My family had long dreamed of an independent Croatia. I will purchase armaments for the munitions companies controlled by our cartel. I will launch a rebellion that will reverberate throughout the Balkans. Croatia will secede from Austria-Hungary!"

"The Black Coats will control an entire country!" predicted Nemo.

"The All-Father will be pleased!" exclaimed Corbucci. "You have more than made up for your earlier missteps in this affair. I will inform the Master of your progress."

Corbucci left the room.

"Why permit Corbucci to speak in such a condescending manner?" asked Petra.

Nemo chuckled. "It amuses me to indulge the All-Father's entourage its illusions of power. Have no doubts, Your Highness. Corbucci and his precious Master of Silence hold no sovereignty over me. In the old days, the All-Father would have confiscated nearly the entire Kratides bequest for his miserly treasure trove."

"Why are you so generous with me, my Lord?"

"I'm more interested in altering the map of Europe than feathering my own nest."

A few moments later, Feliciana entered the room. Nemo introduced her to Petra. Feliciana immediately deduced that the woman in the derby was Asenath's killer.

"I have certain arrangements to make with Van Klopen," remarked Nemo. "Please excuse me."

"Monsieur Nemo, didn't you want to talk about Darlla Rassendyll?" said Feliciana.

"Mademoiselle Sorelli, Her Highness wishes to interrogate you concerning Rassendyll. I'll be very upset if she isn't pleased by your answers."

Nemo departed promptly.

"I understand you always carry a knife, Feliciana," purred Petra. "May I see it?"

Feliciana pulled up her skirt. A dagger was strapped in a sheath to her right thigh.

"Hand it to me."

Feliciana sheepishly obeyed Petra's command.

Petra placed the dagger on a table. Drawing her sword, she pointed the blade at Felicana's face.

"You're pretty handy with a knife, Feliciana. Ever use a sword?"

"No, but I'm familiar with many dueling techniques such as the Vautrin thrust."

"Really! The Vautrin thrust is my favorite means of slaying an adversary. A stab to the forehead is so lethal. It's been too long since this sword has tasted blood. Do you like my instrument of death?"

"It's very elegant. The edge of your sword is very close to my eye."

"I need you to examine it closely. Is it as sharp as the knife driven into Rassendyll's heart?"

"No, your sword is sharper."

"I've never killed a woman before. Is it as exhilarating as killing a man?"

"It's even more exhilarating."

"Soon I will know that feeling."

"How soon?" stammered Feliciana.

"At the stroke of midnight. Alas! That is hours away. Thank you, Feliciana. Your answers have been most satisfactory."

Petra sheathed her weapon. She handed the knife to Feliciana, who restored it to the scabbard on her thigh.

"Rassendyll perished eight years ago, Your Highness. Why should she interest you?"

"The Rassendylls are a branch of the Elphberg dynasty. The Elphbergs of Ruritania are the hereditary enemies of the Donevitchs of Croatia. In their ancestral castle in Zenda, the Elphbergs have a portrait celebrating the death of Stefan Donevitch by the hand of the third Rudolf of their line. I wish to commemorate on canvas the death of a female member of this hated family. The photograph of Rassendyll's corpse will permit me to capture her likeness, but I desire to include you in the picture. I envision you gloating triumphantly over your fallen foe. Pose for me, Feliciana. Monsieur Nemo will be upset if you decline my offer."

"I'll gladly pose for you. What is your address?"

Petra handed Feliciana a small sheet of paper. "I've rented a house in the Latin Quarter."

"7 Rue des Quatre Vents," Feliciana read aloud. "You're planning a murder at midnight. Can I watch?"

"Unfortunately, this is purely a family matter. The victim is my cousin."

"Oh! I really wish that I could see it!"

"Don't fret, Feliciana, you'll be able to see my murder tomorrow."

"You're confusing me, Your Highness."

"Ever hear of *The Brigand's Painting*?"

"I'm aware of the legendary portrait belonging to the All-Father. He stole *The Brigand's Painting* from Count Biffi's collection in Rome. It depicts a son murdering his father."

"I'm creating a feminine version for Monsieur Nemo, *The Brigand Princess*. It will immortalize my victory over my cousin. The other portrait celebrating your defeat of Darlla Rassendyll will be a companion piece, *The Acolyte's Execution*. Monsieur Nemo commissioned both portraits in February, but my attentions have been focused on *The Brigand Princess*."

"Why wait for midnight to dispatch your cousin?"

"I have a poetic nature. My cousin has compared herself to Cinderella and myself to her Fairy Godmother. At midnight, Cinderella finally realized that all her Godmother's promises were illusions." Petra stared at Feliciana pensively. "Who is your hairstylist?"

"An employee of the Paris Opera House. Why do you ask?"

Petra removed her hat. "Your hair has been arranged very similar to my cousin's. I'll need to mimic her coiffure."

"I've never met a more diabolical woman. Darlla," claimed Feliciana in her dressing room. "If you don't vanquish her now, she'll butcher more people than Gabrielle Damiens did in the French Revolution."

"Fortunately, Sophy is safe until midnight. With Charon's help, I should reach the Latin Quarter before the fatal hour.

"Can't I go with you? My understudy could take my place in tonight's performance."

"If I end Petra's rampage, Nemo may become suspicious. You need to establish an unbreakable alibi. Is there any way to tell the two cousins apart?"

"Petra's hair is parted in the middle and styled like a bowl cut. Sophy's hair is arranged in a chignon like mine."

At fifteen minutes after eleven, Petra finished *The Brigand Princess*. It depicted Sophy in agony. A sword blade was protruding from her stomach. Standing behind Sophy's image was the smiling form of Petra. She had impaled Sophy from behind.

"My masterpiece is complete, sweet Sophy."

"Why cover the painting? Please let me see it."

"You will have to wait until midnight, my sweet."

"Why, Petra?"

"Because dreams come true at midnight. In the meanwhile, it is time for another fencing lesson."

Petra took off her smock. She put on her black gloves. The lesson should last forty-five minutes. At the conclusion of their mock duel, Petra would take Sophy to view the portrait. Once Petra removed the cloth, she would fatally stab her cousin in the back.

The two cousins fenced back and forth.

Charles Blanton drove the carriage that transported the Revenant across Paris. Under the alias of Lord Charon, he was the only male among the Revenant's Acolytes. His carriage arrived in the Rue des Quatre Vents ("Street of the Four Winds") at 11:30. The Revenant quickly alighted.

The Revenant now wore the mask of her costume. It was a cowl with a red skull emblazoned on the forehead. A Thuggee pickaxe was holstered in a loop on her belt. A Punjabi lasso was tied around another loop.

It was child's play for the Revenant to pick the lock of Petra's front door. As she crossed into the foyer, the Revenant heard noises from the studio located at the back of the house. It was the clang of swords. Petra must be trying to kill Sophy!

Brandishing her pickaxe, the Revenant burst into the studio.

"Petra Donevitch, die for your crimes!"

The keen eyes of Darlla Rassendyll were able to quickly identify both Petra and Sophy. "A Black Coat!" screamed Petra. "Attack her!"

Sophy's sword lunged at the Revenant. "I'm not your enemy Sophy!" yelled the Revenant as she dodged Sophy's thrust. Sophy's sword swung at the Revenant's neck. The Revenant countered with her pickaxe. The tip of the pickaxe smashed into Sophy's sword just in front of the hilt. The blade snapped. The Revenant's right leg kicked Sophy in the midriff. The Greek heiress was propelled backwards.

Suddenly Sophy was seized by Petra. Gripping Sophy from behind, Petra held her blade against her cousin's throat.

"One step further, Revenant, and I'll kill her! *Take off your mask!*"

The Revenant hesitated.

"Obey me! Or I'll cut Sophy's throat!"

Darla's left hand quickly doffed her hood and let it fall to the ground.

"Well, this is a surprise," said Petra. "Darlla Rassendyll! Feliciana's photo was clearly faked. This explains how you knew where to find me. Once I eliminate you and Sophy, I'll exterminate Feliciana!"

"What are you doing?" pleaded Sophy.

The Revenant unveiled *The Brigand Princess.*

"Your cousin plans to kill you!"

Sophy stared at the painting in shock.

"No! This can't be true!

"You insipid fool!" shrieked Petra. "I work for the Black Coats!"

Swiftly removing her blade from her prisoner's neck, Petra raised her sword above Sophy. The Balkan Princess slammed the skull handle into the top of Sophy's head. As the unconscious Sophy slumped in her cousin's embrace, Petra repositioned her blade against her captive's neck.

"Donevitch, if you killed her, I'll tear out your heart!"

"My darling cousin merely sleeps, Rassendyll. Your lineage is almost as prestigious as my own. You're descended from the Elphbergs. The Elphbergs boast that they always keep their word. Is the same true of a Rassendyll?"

"I never break my word, Donevitch!"

"You're also a bit of a gambler. So am I. Agree to two conditions, and I will release my prey. You will have an opportunity to fight for Sophy's life."

"What are your conditions?"

"First, promise to duel me without any weapons. You'll fight barehanded."

"I assume that you'll still have your sword."

"Of course!"

"Agreed!"

"Second, if I lose, you can't take my life. Turn me over to the proper authorities."

"Please clarify the second point. Does it mean that I let a judge decide your fate?"

"Don't play games with me, Rassendyll. That's exactly what I mean!"

"Agreed."

Unlacing her Punjabi lasso, Darlla threw it in a corner. She let go of her pickaxe. Before it hit the ground, Petra launched her assault.

Dropping the senseless Sophy, Petra rammed her sword at Darlla's forehead. Darlla's gloved hands came together in a clap that encircled Petra's sword. The tip of the blade stopped an infinitesimal distance before it could penetrate the Revenant's forehead. With all her strength, Darlla propelled the weapon towards her adversary. Still grasping the sword, Petra's right hand was pushed backward. The skull handle slammed violently into the forehead of the Balkan Princess. An unconscious Petra fell to the floor.

Darlla immediate rushed towards Sophy to verify that she was unharmed.

When Petra Donevitch awoke, she found her hands tied behind her back. The unmasked figure of Darlla Rassendyll towered over her.

"I guessed that your attack would be the Vautrin thrust. You used it to kill Asenath Pons, and you confirmed your mastery of it to Feliciana. Nine years ago, the Vautrin thrust was used against me by your fellow Black Coat, Gloria Scot. Since that time, I've practiced countering that fatal technique."

Petra burst out in laughter.

"I don't see anything amusing in your plight, Donevitch. You lie vanquished at my feet. The shadow of justice threatens you!"

"I've outwitted you!" snarled Petra. "You promised not to kill me! Turn me over to the authorities, and I'll expose your real identity! You have to set me free! You'll never dance over my dead body!"

Darlla smiled. "You're forgetting the clarification you gave me regarding our agreement. I can turn you over to a judge. The blood of kings runs in my veins. My ancestors appointed judges. So do I! *I deputize another woman to judge you! I choose your cousin! Sophy Kratides!*"

Petra suddenly saw Sophy standing next to Darlla. Sophy held Petra's sword in her right hand. Yanking Petra to her feet, Darlla pushed the murderess in front of *The Brigand Princess*. Standing behind her cousin, Sophy grabbed the back of her cousin's hair and forced her to stare at the portrait.

"The Revenant explained everything to me! Our roles in your artistic masterpiece have been reversed, Petra." A clock in the room began to chime.

"No! Sophy! No! I beg you!"

"What was it you told me, cousin? Dreams come true at midnight? So do *nightmares!*"

Sophy plunged the sword into Petra's back.

After Sophy Kratides changed into a dress with a veil, she joined Darlla in Charles Blanton's coach. Underneath a secret recess in the seat of the coach's compartment was the Augustine d'Erlette disguise. Removing her Revenant costume, Darlla quickly transformed herself into the elderly spinster.

At 2:30 in the morning, the sleeping Mycroft Holmes was awoken by a knock on the door of his hotel room. He found himself facing Augustine d'Erlette and a veiled woman.

"I apologize, Monsieur Holmes, for the lateness of the hour," whispered Augustine, "but this is an emergency. The murderer of your cousin is no longer among the living."

"Sophy Kratides is dead?"

"No, this is Sophy. She avenged Asenath's death."

After listening to his two female guests for two hours, Mycroft was fully apprised of the situation.

"In order to protect Feliciana, the Black Coats must learn of Sophy's survival by tomorrow afternoon," explained Augustine. "She must flee the country as soon as possible."

"I can arrange for a boat to transport both myself and Mademoiselle Kratides across the English Channel shortly after dawn," said Mycroft. "In England, I can make the arrangements for the return of Mademoiselle Kratides to Athens."

"I have no desire to go back to Greece," proclaimed Sophy.

"But your inheritance!"

"The Kratides bequest has cursed my life, Monsieur Holmes. It caused the deaths of both my brother and your cousin. I relinquish all claims to my family's finances. I merely wish to live in peace."

"My department is in need of skilled translators. If you're willing, Mademoiselle Kratides, I can secure you employment."

"Thank you, Monsieur Holmes. I will consider your offer."

Feliciana was briefed by Darlla about Petra's demise. The Balkan Princess had wanted Feliciana to pose for a painting commissioned by Nemo. Feliciana visited Petra's abode in the afternoon. Pretending to be shocked to find Petra's corpse, Feliciana informed the Black Coats at the Regenerator of Fashion. Not wishing to be in Paris during Sophy's scheduled murder, Nemo had already returned late last evening to London. One of Nemo's British lieutenants, Horace Dorrington, stayed in Paris to report Petra's progress. Van Klopen and Dorrington investigated Petra's death. They concluded that Sophy must have unveiled the painting prematurely and realized Petra's murderous designs. Believing that the missing Sophy was solely responsible for Petra's liquidation, the Black Coats harbored no suspicions concerning the Revenant. In order to avoid a police inquiry, Van Klopen and Dorrington secretly buried Petra's body in the basement of her Parisian abode. Cognizant that Nemo had authorized Petra's artwork, Dorrington preserved *The Brigand Princess* for his superior's appraisal.

One month later, Feliciana was retrieving the messages at the A. L. Lard office. There was a large manila envelope. She immediately took it to the Revenant's sanctuary. Opening the communiqué, Darlla Rassendyll found several photographs and type-written sheets accompanied by this note.

Dear Mademoiselle Rassendyll,

Sophy is doing fine. My brother wishes to reward you for rescuing the young lady. Enclosed is a copy of his information on the Gentlemen of the Night.

M.

Perusing the data, Darlla found a photograph of a man whom she immediately recognized as Monsieur Nemo. Turning over the photograph, she read these words scrawled on the back: *Professor James Moriarty.*

The Werewolf's Daughter

"The last unicorn on Earth was owned by Andreas of Hungary. He loved his unicorn as if it was his own child. One night Andreas stared at the moon. He fell asleep and forgot to protect his precious unicorn. When Andreas awoke in the morning, he discovered that a wolf had crept into his garden. His beloved unicorn had been butchered. Andreas was overcome by grief."

Once Théophraste Lupin finished his story, he looked at his fifteen-year old listener. Irene had loved this story since she first heard it at the age of five. Théophraste knew that Irene would ask the same question that she always did once the tale was concluded.

"Do you love me as much as Andreas loved his unicorn?"

"Yes, my daughter."

"Will you ever forget to protect me?"

"Never."

"What about me?" interjected Irene's brother, a bright lad of 11 years. "Will you protect me as well?"

"Of course, Arsène."

Irene was actually Arsène's half-sister. Victoire Chupin, Irene's mother, had been Théophraste's lover. Years later, Théophraste had married Henriette d'Andresy. When Arsène was born, Théophraste had arranged for Victoire to be hired as the young infant's nurse. Victoire's employment had been terminated when Henriette had discovered her in Théophraste's amorous embrace. With young Arsène in her custody, Henriette left her husband. Victoire had continued her romance with Théophraste, but eventually she became disgusted with his philandering. When Arsène was six years old, Victoire had reconciled with Henriette. Having taken her maiden lady name, the former Madame Lupin allowed Victoire and Irene to live in her house. The two women raised their children together,

Although Victoire was now fiercely loyal to Henriette, she secretly deceived her. Once a month, she surreptitiously took the children to visit their father at the Montour Academy of Fencing and Boxing in Paris. She also smuggled letters from Théophraste to his children on a regular basis. This was the peculiar situation surrounding the d'Andresy household in 1885.

"We enjoyed your last letter, Papa," mentioned Arsène.

"You must not let your mother ever find my letters," cautioned Théophraste. "It would get Victoire into trouble."

"Don't worry, Papa," assured Irene. "I hide them in a box under the mattress in my room."

"Mama never cleans Irene's room," added Arsène. "Only Victoire does."

"Actually Irene cleans her own room," volunteered Victoire.

"It's still too dangerous to preserve those letters." counseled Théophraste. "Arsène's mother could accidentally discover them. Irene, you should burn them."

Being a dutiful daughter, Irene followed her father's advice when she returned home.

A week later, the d'Andresy residence received a very special visitor. Countess de Dreux-Soubise was visiting the domicile. The Countess and Henriette had both attended convent school together. The aristocrat was a proud woman with auburn hair.

"Remember our former classmate, Natalie Morrell?" asked the Countess.

"She married a school teacher, Roget Fourneau," replied Henriette, "I was the bridesmaid at their wedding. They have three children, a girl and two boys. Natalie and her family moved to Provence after that horrible scandal involving her brother. I haven't had news of her since."

"Provence was a natural sanctuary. Natalie's mother hailed from there. The Fourneaus opened a school for young ladies outside Avignon. Unfortunately, Roget's asthma grew worse. His health deteriorated. Natalie is a widow."

"How dreadful!"

"Roget was a loyal husband. Unlike other women, Natalie married wisely."

That last statement riled young Arsène. He had been patiently listening to the conversation as his mother and her guest sipped tea. The boy correctly interpreted the aristocrat's statement as a disparagement of his mother's decision to marry Théophraste Lupin.

Arsène had long resented the Countess. When his mother had deserted Théophraste, she had sought refuge in the Dreux-Soubise household. Henriette had been treated with contempt by the Countess. Arsène's mother had become a lowly paid servant in the Dreux-Soubise mansion.

Five years ago, when he was only six years old, Arsène had avenged his mother's servitude. The Dreux-Soubise family had owned a diamond necklace of great historical significance. Arsène stole the necklace. With Victoire's help, he gave the necklace to his father. Irene, Arsène's half-sister, had been totally ignorant of her relatives' role in the robbery.

Théophraste Lupin was actually the notorious criminal called Lothaire Stepphun. Under that alias, Arsène's father led the Werewolves, the most daring gang of thieves in Paris. The elder Lupin had converted the diamonds into cash. Falsely falling under suspicion of the theft, Henriette had been dismissed from the Dreux-Soubise domicile. Théophraste arranged for the proceeds of the robbery to be mailed anonymously to Henriette. She mistakenly concluded that the payments were secretly being sent by the Countess. Henriette naively believed that the Countess was making amends for wrongfully terminating the employment of a loyal friend.

Henriette was under the delusion that the Countess was visiting in order to see the fruits of her philanthropy. In actuality, the Countess was motivated by a far different desire. The 1880 theft of the necklace had sparked a series of financial setbacks for the Dreux-Soubise family. Recently their fortunes had vastly improved. The Countess had arrived to flaunt her newfound wealth in front of her former schoolmate. The aristocrat was dressed in expensive dress with a diamond brooch.

Henriette and the Countess were sipping tea poured by Irene Chupin. Victoire was resting in her room after cleaning the house in preparation for the visit of the Countess. After two hours of conversation, the Countess was ready to leave.

Motioning to Arsène, Henriette made a request.

"Raoul, give our gracious guest a goodbye kiss."

Henriette always referred to her son as Raoul. She refused to use the first name that her estranged husband had given to their offspring.

Arsène Lupin, alias Raoul d'Andresy, embraced the Countess as he kissed her cheek.

"What a horrible rainstorm for the summer!" observed The Countess. She nodded in the direction of Irene Chupin, who had poured tea during the visit. "Henriette, dear, have your serving girl help me with my coat?"

"Irene, do as the Countess wishes," said Henriette.

After Irene assisted the Countess, the arrogant lady departed the house and entered her coach. Irene then burst into tears.

"What's wrong?" asked Henriette.

"You treated me like a servant," sobbed Irene.

"Please forgive me, Irene. I didn't want to contradict my benefactor. You're like a daughter to me."

Henriette spoke with great sincerity. Irene was often neglected by her own mother, who was more affectionate towards Arsène. Sensing Irene's fragile sensibilities, Henriette had showered great affection on her husband's illegitimate daughter.

Henriette hugged the weeping Irene. While his mother was preoccupied with his half-sister, Arsène sneaked upstairs into Irene's room. He removed the box from under the mattress of his half-sister's bed. Inside the box, Arsène placed an object. He then replaced the box underneath the mattress.

The object now resting in the box was the diamond brooch of Countess Dreux-Soubise. Arsène had impulsively removed the brooch when he kissed the Countess. Tomorrow he would remove the brooch from its temporary hiding place and have Victoire transport the brooch to his father. As with the necklace, the proceeds of the robbery would be sent anonymously to his mother.

Downstairs, Henriette had succeeded in calming Irene,

"You worked very hard helping your mother with the housework," noted Henriette. "You should go to your room and rest."

Arsène's plans went dramatically awry when the Countess realized that the brooch was missing before the coach brought her home. She immediately ordered her driver to turn the coach around.

Returning to the d'Andresy residence, the Countess confronted Henriette.

"My brooch has been stolen! It must have been that young servant! She took it while she was putting on my coat! Where is she?"

"She's…in her room," stammered Henriette.

"Take me to her!"

Irene was taking a nap on her bed. Her slumbers were interrupted by the intrusion of Henriette and the Countess.

"You stole my brooch!" yelled the Countess.

"I'm innocent!" asserted Irene.

"A search of your room will easily prove your guilt!"

Within a matter of minutes, the box underneath Irene's mattress was unearthed. The Countess triumphantly pulled the brooch out of the box.

"I didn't put it there!" protested Irene.

"Then how did it get there?" demanded Henriette.

Irene paused before answering. Only two other people in the house knew about the box, and only one had opportunity to purloin the brooch.

"Arsène must have put it there."

Henriette viciously slapped Irene.

"You ingrate! You dare to accuse my son! I welcome you into my house and this is how you repay me! Liar! Thief!"

Tears filled Irene's eyes as Henriette and the Countess left the room.

Along with the Countess, Henriette woke Victoire and informed her of Irene's supposed crime.

"Please, Madame, don't send my daughter to prison! It's a horrible place!"

"Countess Dreux-Soubise is the injured party," decreed Henriette. "Only she can decide Irene's fate."

"I will be merciful, Henriette, if you tell me the truth," pronounced the Countess. "I noticed a resemblance between Irene and your own son. Am I correct in assuming that Irene is one of your husband's indiscretions?"

"Yes," admitted Henriette.

"Remember the school managed by Natalie Fourneau in Provence. It specializes in educating young women of such backgrounds. Send her there."

The following day, Victoire informed Théophraste of Irene's punishment.

"It was clearly Arsène who was the culprit," deduced Théophraste. "The foolish lad sought to replicate his success with the necklace."

"What can we do to save Irene?"

"Unfortunately, nothing. The only way to prove her innocence would be to establish Arsène's guilt. If he's revealed to be the thief, then he'll be suspected of the necklace theft. If the police investigation is reopened, both you and I could be implicated."

"But Irene…"

"She'll have to go to Provence. Don't fret, Victoire. How bad can that school be?"

"I'm innocent!" protested Irene in August 1885.

The girl spoke those words in the private office of the headmistress of the Fourneau College for Young Women. Henriette had related to Madame Fourneau an account of the incident of the diamond brooch.

"Mademoiselle Chupin, you must learn to listen patiently to your elders," cautioned Madame Fourneau. "Perhaps it would be prudent for you to wait in another room while I converse with your guardian. After I finish with Madame d'Andresy, I shall listen to your version of these events. Please follow me."

Madame Fourneau rose from her desk. The headmistress was a majestic woman with chestnut hair. She was attired in a dress consisting of a white blouse, a black skirt and a black tie. A ring of keys dangled from her waist.

Irene obediently followed Madame Fourneau down the corridors of the school. In her hands was a book from her home in Paris. Stopping before a door, the headmistress unlocked it. "This will be your chamber of contemplation," said Fourneau opening the door.

"It's a storage closet!" exclaimed Irene.

"The perfect place for an obnoxious girl!" screeched Madame Fourneau as she shoved Irene inside. Fourneau slammed the door shut and locked it.

In the darkness, Irene burst into tears.

Back in her office, Madame Fourneau conferred with Henriette.

"The atrocious behavior of Mademoiselle Chupin must have shamed her mother," observed Madame Fourneau. "We must take measures to protect Madame Chupin's reputation."

"What are you suggesting, Natalie?" asked Henriette.

"Many of my students were also guilty of thievery. Their families had them enrolled here under false names to avoid scandal. We should do likewise with Irene. The girl does not impress me as being particularly bright. Her alias should be something similar to Chupin."

"Victoire Chupin confided in me. She herself was once sent to prison under the surname of Tupin."

"Excellent! Irene Tupin will be the name of my new student. A different name will also assist in Irene's reformation."

"In what way?"

"The newly christened Irene Tupin shall be unable to receive mail from any unsavory friends in Paris."

"That will be a problem, Natalie. Irene's uncle is Victor Chupin. He runs a private detective agency in Paris. He's very close to Irene. Monsieur Chupin shall insist on communicating with her."

"Does he know that she committed a robbery?"

"No, neither Victoire nor I have told him the truth. He believes her study of foreign languages prompted her to come to Provence.''

"Foreign languages? She must be more intelligent than my original impression. What languages does she know?"

"She's fluent in English and is currently learning Spanish and Italian."

"Provence is a perfect place to become familiar with Spanish. Many people here speak that language. In fact, my son Louis insists on being called the Spanish variant of his name."

"What should we do about Monsieur Chupin?

"He will be a special exception. His letters addressed to Irene Chupin will be delivered to Mademoiselle Tupin."

"Victor Chupin will expect Irene to reply."

"That shall not be a problem. All mail coming in and out of this school is read by the leader of my prefects."

"Prefects?"

"My student assistants. Their chief examines all the mail that the other students receive. This prefect also ensures that no libelous gossip defames my school." Madame Fourneau poured a cup for Henriette. "Enough of Mademoiselle Tupin! Let us recall the wonderful days of our youth."

Inside the dark closet, Irene heard the door unlocked. Opening the door, a young girl carrying a lit candle rushed inside. She quickly shut the door. In the candlelight, Irene could see that the girl with long brown hair was wearing a white dress.

"We don't have much time," claimed the visitor. "We need to talk quickly. Mother doesn't know that I stole a set of her keys. I'm Madame Fourneau's daughter. My name is Berenice. What's your name?"

"Irene Chupin."

"Mother doesn't want me to talk to her students. She thinks that they'll give me bad ideas. Are you from Paris?"

"Yes. I'm 15 years old. How old are you?"

"I'm 13. Mother is sending me to a boarding school in Paris. Can I look at your book?"

Irene handed her book to the other girl.

"You won't be able to read it, Berenice. It's in English."

"I know English. *Oliver Twist* by Charles Dickens. Did my mother look at this?"

"She was too busy talking to the lady who brought me here to give it any scrutiny."

"Mother will confiscate this. She hates Dickens because of *A Tale of Two Cities*. Mother became a fanatical defender of the French Revolution due to her friendship with the Blonde Beast."

"The Blonde Beast?"

"Mother's head prefect. She's four years older than me. Last year, Mother took me and my two younger brothers to visit her cousin Corneila in Normandy. Corneila and her husband run a circus. It would have been a great visit if Mother hadn't taken the Blonde Beast along to chaperon me. If only I had been big and strong like my grandmother."

"Your grandmother?"

"My grandmother was Alexandra the Great. You must have heard of her."

"I'm sorry, but the name is unfamiliar to me."

"Alexandra Vadarasse, the Queen of the Woman Wrestlers. She left the circus to marry my grandfather, Gabriel Morrell."

"Why do you want to be like her?"

"My grandmother never let anyone bully her. The Blonde Beast was able to boss me around because she's taller. I have a fantasy. When I get older, I'm going to beat up the Blonde Beast and rip off all her clothes."

"That's not the correct behavior for a lady"

"You need to tutor me about stuff like that. When I go to the school in Paris, I don't want the girls there to look down on me."

"But your mother would never let me talk to you."

"We can meet secretly at night while the other girls are sleeping. Remember I have a set of keys. Can I borrow this book?"

"Yes. It's my favorite book by Dickens. I've read it many times."

"I better leave. Mother will be returning soon. I'll have to relock the door. I'm sorry that you'll be left alone in the dark."

Opening the door, Berenice blew out the candle. "Welcome to the House of Usher," was Berenice's parting farewell to Irene.

Ten minutes later, Madame Fourneau liberated Irene from the closet.

"I hope that you learned your lesson, Mademoiselle Tupin."

"My name is Chupin."

"As punishment for your misconduct, you have been rechristened Tupin. Come with me."

While Irene walked with her, Madame Fourneau made a comment.

"Didn't you bring a book with you?"

"I must have left it in the closet."

"Then it is forfeit to you. Let this be a lesson to you, Mademoiselle Tupin. Hold on to your possessions."

When Madame Fourneau later searched the closet, she didn't find any trace of a book. She falsely assumed that one of her other students must have stolen it.

Late that night, Berenice crept into the large room where all the students slept. She woke up Irene. The two girls snuck off into another room in the school where they conversed for an hour before parting their separate ways. These secret meetings occurred nightly for the next three weeks.

The night before Berenice was scheduled to leave for the Institution Bachelard in Paris, the two friends had their final clandestine meeting.

"Is the Blonde Beast causing you trouble, Irene?"

"She wants me to become a prefect. When I refused, the Beast boasted that she, not your mother, really runs the school. How ridiculous!"

"Don't laugh. My mother refuses nothing to her cherished head prefect. Before you came here, Mother even allowed the Beast to leave the school for a few months. I advise you to be careful."

"I will. I'll miss you, Berenice."

""Even though I've only known you for a short time, Irene, I consider you my best friend. I wish that I could write you from Paris."

"You can. I got a letter from my uncle today. You can write me as well."

"But my mother would punish you if she knew we were secretly friends! All the mail is censored by the Blonde Beast."

"You can pretend to be someone else. Let me think. You can say that you're an English girl whom I befriended in Paris. You can claim to have been given my address by my uncle. That should fool the beastly censor."

"I'll need a pseudonym."

"Use the surname Furnace. It's the English translation of Fourneau."

"And I could use a first name that also begins with the letter B. I'll call myself Blythe Furnace."

"Perfect!"

Berenice paused for a moment. "Your scheme won't work. I can only receive mail at the Institution Bachelard. There is no student there with the name Blythe Furnace. Also the Blonde Beast will become suspicious if you are corresponding with someone at my boarding school."

"We can get around that problem. Your letters must have a false address. Your first letter as Blythe Furnace shall recognize that postage is expensive. Therefore, you recommend that I enclose your letters in the same envelope mailed to my mother. You will have to write my mother and inform her of this arrangement. She'll deliver my letters to you."

"Your mother may not cooperate."

"Imply in your letter that you'll contact my uncle if she refuses. My mother will agree because she deceived my uncle about the real reasons for my exile to Provence."

"Before we separate tonight, I must return this to you." Berenice pointed to an object resting on a table. It was Irene's copy of *Oliver Twist*. "You'll have to hide it from my mother and the Blonde Beast."

Irene lifted the book in her hands.

"Berenice, you shall forever be my friend. Please accept this book as a gift."

"I hope to always be worthy of this gift."

"How could you ever be unworthy?"

"Paris could change me. I dread becoming someone like my mother. It's my greatest fear."

"That will never happen," predicted Irene. "You're too sweet."

"Could you inscribe the book for me?"

Responding to Berenice's request, Irene lifted a pen. Inside the book, she wrote these words: *"Dearest Berenice, pray for my soul, I will pray for yours...Irene."*

"If only I could give you a gift in return."

"You could grant me the keys that you took from your mother."

"I can't. My brother discovered that I was using them to roam at night. He threatened to tell mother unless I surrender them to him just before I leave."

"Philippe did that?"

"Not Philippe. It was my other brother, Louis. Sometimes I wish that little monster had never been born!"

Berenice Fourneau left Provence in September 1885. Two months later, Madame Fourneau and her prefects engaged in a disciplinary action against Irene. The new student was accused of behaving disrespectfully in class.

Irene's blouse had been torn off. She was held down on a bed by a red-haired prefect, Orianne Coyatier. The girl known as the Blonde Beast prepared to deliver the proscribed punishment as Madame Fourneau and the third prefect, the brown-haired Rochelle Moreau, watched.

The Blonde Beast raised a whip high in the air.

Following Irene's advice, Berenice wrote a letter to Victoire Chupin. As a consequence of that communication, Victoire personally delivered Irene's letters to Berenice at the Institution Bachelard. Although the censorship of the Blonde Beast prevented Irene from divulging her difficulties at the Fourneau College, Berenice found veiled ways to disclose her tribulations at the Institution Bachelard. In 1886, Berenice sought her friend's counsel.

Dear Irene,

My life is living hell. A she-devil is tormenting me at my school. Her name is Kaitlin de Winter. She is an uppity aristocrat who delights in persecution. Kaitlin is the daughter of an English Baron. She is a devotee of literature. Kaitlin insists on being addressed as Milady since she is a peer's daughter. Obviously she is mimicking Milady de Winter from The Three Musketeers. *Her affinity for Dumas is matched by her enthusiasm for Poe. Sometimes she employs the nickname of Raven from Poe's poem. I want to write "Nevermore" as her epitaph.*

    Kaitlin has told a horrible joke about me. Nearly all of my fellow students speak English. Kaitlin has said my initials prove that I'm a B. F., a "Bloody Fool," Everyone now calls me B. F. What can I do? You're my best friend. Please advise me.

Blythe

Dear Berenice,
    You must fight back. Create sarcastic nicknames for your enemy. The correct title for a Baron's daughter is neither Lady nor Milady. It's "Right Honorable." Point this out to your fellow students and add the observation that Kaitlin de Winter's arrogance should alter that title to"Right Dishonorable." You can also note that the proper nickname for a bully is not Raven but Craven.
    Have fortitude, my comrade-in-arms.

Irene

The letter made a great impression on Berenice. She felt confident that Irene was successfully resisting her own nemesis, the Blonde Beast. After reading the letter, Berenice reached for her cherished copy of *Oliver Twist* and read the inscription. Berenice said a prayer for her best friend's soul.

The same year saw the death of Henriette d'Andresy from natural causes. In the aftermath of the funeral, Victoire discussed Irene's situation with Théophraste Lupin.

"I grieve for Arsène's saintly mother," professed Victoire, "but her death removes any necessity for Irene remaining in Provence."

"There still remains an obstacle, the Countess de Dreux-Soubise," said Théophraste.

"A year has passed. Surely she's forgotten about Irene."

"She's very vindictive. Have you ever wondered why she was so familiar with Natalie Fourneau's school? I did some investigating. Her husband has an illegitimate daughter named Catherine Lineaire. She's around the same age as Irene. The Count was secretly providing for Catherine's support in Paris. When the Countess learned of Catherine's existence, the poor girl was sent away to the Fourneau College. The Countess and Madame Fourneau are in constant communication with one another."

"But Henriette paid for Irene's tuition! Who will do that now?"

"I will. We can't afford for the Countess to become suspicious."

"It's not fair to Irene!"

"She's enjoying herself at the school. You showed me her letters. She's also taking pleasure in her secret communications with the daughter of the headmistress."

"That Fourneau girl told me the mail was censored!"

"She was exaggerating, Victoire. Madame Fourneau runs a school in Provence not Prussia. She certainly checks the name of her students' correspondents, but it's inconceivable that private letters are read."

"I've seen the letters received by Berenice Fourneau. They pretend that she's this non-existent Blythe Furnace."

"That's merely Irene being overly creative."

In the ensuring years, there were changes at the Fourneau College. One of Madame Fourneau's sons, Philippe, was sent to a boarding school in Switzerland. The other boy, Louis, suffered from asthma like his father. He remained in the Fourneau College supposedly segregated from the female students,

In the late 1880's, Madame Fourneau had ruled the school with four prefects. By 1889, the Blonde Beast and her two junior prefects, Orianne Coyatier and Rochelle Moreau, had graduated. With the departure of the Blonde Beast, her position as head prefect was bestowed on a younger girl whom she had personally trained. The Blonde Beast's successor recruited two other girls to act as her underlings.

The name of the new head prefect was Irene Tupin.

In January 1890, the most popular girl at the Fourneau College was Suzanne Noel. A lottery was regularly organized by Irene Tupin to maintain her domination over the other students. The drawing was done without Madame Fourneau's knowledge. The winner was permitted to have a romantic liaison with Henri, a muscular young man who delivered wood to the school. The lottery was often won by Suzanne for a simple reason. The prefects were not interested in male companionship. They always surrendered their tickets to Suzanne.

After a joyous carnal session in the woodshed, Suzanne had a request for Henri.

"Darling will you do me a favor?"

"I'll do anything for you, my love."

"I want you to mail another letter for me."

"Is this letter going to your relatives, Suzanne?"

"Not this time. It's addressed to the *Tivoli* cabaret in Avignon."

"Who do you know at the *Tivoli*?"

"No one. I didn't write the letter. I'm doing a favor for a friend in trouble."

Mathilde Grévin was a songstress at the *Tivoli*. Although she deeply loved her daughter Teresa, Mathilde had found the girl to be an encumbrance to her career. At the suggestion of her current lover, Pedro Baldie, Mathilde had recently placed Teresa in the Fourneau College for Young Women.

She stared at the letter lying on the bureau in her dressing room. Mathilde had read it once. Now she was reading it again.

Mama,

Help me! This school is worse than a prison! Madame Fourneau leaves the running of the school to a depraved student named Irene Tupin. She whips other girls. She's threatening to have me flogged unless I agree to her unspeakable demands. She wants me to…

Mathilde couldn't read the letter any further. She decided to take immediate measures to liberate Teresa from the school. There was only one man to whom she could appeal for assistance. His name was Dr. Anatole Cerral.

Brechard was the janitor at the Fourneau College. He was sleeping in his hut near the massive gates of the school. He had a very busy day. Madame Fourneau had been in a furor. Another student had disappeared from the school during the previous night. She was the fifth girl to vanish since September. Madame Fourneau assumed that the missing girls had voluntarily run away. During the daytime hours, Brechard had put locks on all the windows and doors.

The janitor's slumbers were interrupted by a commotion of yells coming from the front gates. Someone was demanding to be let in! Who could be arriving at this late hour of the night!

Quickly donning a bathrobe, Brechard grabbed a lantern and his keys. At the gates, he confronted the intruders. Through the bars of the metal gates, Brechard saw a thin man with a beard standing alongside a woman. The duo was standing in front of a coach.

"My name is Cerral," said the man. "I'm a doctor. This is the mother of Teresa Grévin. We're here to liberate her from this accused school!"

"Teresa isn't here! She ran away last night!"

"I insist on seeing Madame Fourneau! Open the gates!"

Brechard did as the doctor requested. Dr. Cerral, Madame Grévin and Brechard entered the coach to take the long path to the boarding school. When the coach reached its destination, the passengers alighted. Brechard unlocked the school's door.

"Madame Fourneau generally works late," volunteered Brechard. "I'll take you to her office."

The trio discovered the office unoccupied.

"She's probably upstairs checking that all the girls are asleep in their beds," concluded Brechard.

"Wait here, Mathilde," said Cerral. "I'll go with the janitor to look for Madame Fourneau."

Cerral and Brechard took the stairs up to the second floor. Before they could reach the bedroom of the students, the air was filled with the piercing screams of a woman.

"It's coming from the attic!" shouted Brechard.

The janitor ran to the stairs that led to the attic. Climbing the winding stairs, Brechard entered the garret. He beheld a cloaked and hooded figure holding a bloody meat cleaver.

"You won't release my mother!" screeched the cloaked apparition.

The assailant swung the axe at Brechard. Dodging the blow, Brechard delivered a massive fist into the face of the maniac. The cloaked attacker fell unconscious to the floor. He removed the hood of the cloak. The face of a sixteen-year old boy was revealed.

Dr. Cerral came into the attic.

"This is Luis, Madame Fourneau's son," said Brechard. "He attacked me with a meat cleaver. He mentioned his mother. She must be here."

"There's a woman lying over there," declared Cerral. He raced to a figure lying slumped against a trunk. "She's too young to be Madame Fourneau," pronounced Cerral. He examined the girl. Blood dripped from a wound in her forehead. When Cerral brought the girl's face into the light, Brechard recognized her.

"It's Irene Tupin! Is she dead?"

"She's still alive."

"Madame!" yelled Brechard. "Are you here?"

The janitor tried the door of a storeroom in the attic. It was locked. He pushed hard against the door until it burst open. Madame Fourneau was lying on her back. Her unmoving eyes were wide open. She wasn't breathing. Madame Fourneau rested at the base of a table. A decaying cadaver rested on the slab. Its body was covered by a blanket, but its unveiled face resembled Madame Fourneau's. Severed limbs and slab of flesh laid piled in a corner. On top of the heap were two small delicate hands.

"It's a charnel house!" howled Brechard.

Cerral had removed his coat. He was ripping off large strips from his shirt.

"What are you doing?" asked Brechard.

"Making tourniquets," replied Cerral. "Irene's hands have been cut off."

In the confines of her Parisian office, Chantal Lebrue of the Sure Values Agency read this article in the front page of *L'Epoque:*

THE COLLEGE GIRLS MURDERS

By Georges Du Roy

The Avignon police department revealed today the details of a shocking se-ries of crimes. Located outside the city is a boarding school called the Fourneau College for Young Women. From September 1889 to January 1890, five teenage girls were murdered inside this school. The police have arrested Louis Fourneau (age 16) for these atrocities. His mother, Natalie Fourneau, was a widow who was the principal of the College.

Louis Fourneau had developed a strange obsession. He wanted to sculpt an effigy resembling his mother. Horribly he chose human flesh to be the mate-rial for his artwork. Dismembering the bodies of his victims, he fashioned a patchwork corpse from their remains in the attic of the school. Once his grisly eidolon was completed, Louis locked his mother in a storeroom with his crea-tion. Her screams summoned two individuals to the attic.

These gentlemen were Pierre Brechard, the school's janitor, and Dr. An-atole Cerral of the Countess Yalta Memorial Hospital in Avignon. Dr. Cerral had accompanied Mathilde Grévin, the mother of a student, to the school. The purpose of the visit was to remove Madame Grévin's daughter, Teresa, from the school. Tragically, Teresa Grévin had been butchered the previous evening by Louis Fourneau.

Brechard succeeded in overcoming Louis Fourneau. It was discovered that Madame Fourneau had suffered a fatal heart attack brought about by the shock of discovering her son's barbarity. Dr. Cerral also discovered Irene Tupin (age 19) who had been knocked unconscious by Louis Fourneau. Mademoiselle Tupin is currently lying in a coma in the Countess Yalta Memorial Hospital. There are unconfirmed reports that both her hands were severed by the killer.

Insanity appears to run in Louis Fourneau's family. His mother's maiden name was Morrell. She was the sister of Gaston Morrell, the Parisian artist who strangled women after painting their portraits. He drowned fleeing the police in 1878.

What prompted Louis Fourneau to embark on this murderous rampage? According to the police, Fourneau rambles incoherently about being inspired by a beautiful goddess. He refers to this imaginary creature as the Muse.

Taking a pair of scissors, Chantal cut the story out of the newspaper. She put the clipping inside an envelope that contained other reports cut from the newspapers. Leaving her office, Chantal walked to a destination located on the lower floor of the same building. Her goal was a locked office whose placard bore the name of A. L. Lard. She pushed the envelope into a slot in the door. An hour later, the Lard office was unlocked by Feliciana Sorelli, the star ballerina of the Paris Opera House.

Chantal and Feliciana belonged to the Acolytes of the Shadows, an under-ground group of vigilantes. The leader of the Acolytes was Darlla Rassendyll, a former member of the Paris police. Darlla had been framed for murder and trea-son by the Black Coats, the dominant criminal cartel in Europe. In order to strike back at her persecutors, Darlla had fashioned the costumed identity of the Revenant. She dwelled in the subterranean sanctuary constructed by the deceased Phantom of the Opera.

The Revenant's Acolytes left their reports at the Lard office. Chantal's major duty was to gather newspaper stories that would interest the Revenant. Feliciana was entrusted with collecting the Acolytes' reports and personally delivering them to the Revenant's base underneath the Paris Opera House.

Reading the newspaper compilation assembled by Chantal, the Revenant felt that she was being haunted by a ghost from the past. The so-called College Girl Murderer was the nephew of Gaston Morrell. One of her closest friends had been strangled by the psychotic artist.

Among the other reports was a letter from Julia de Trémeuse alias Lady Judex, an Acolyte who had virtually retired after her marriage.

Revenant,

Lothaire Stepphun has visited my home in his true guise, He knows your true identity and the entire membership of the Acolytes. You must come to my house at 8 o'clock tonight. Lothaire will be there. Be in the guise that you first met him.

Judex

In the Cathedral of Notre Dame, a young girl not yet 18 years old, knelt in silent prayer. She was Berenice Fourneau.

Dear God, my mother committed many sins but she loved me very much. Now that she's in your hands, please find the compassion to forgive her.

I wish that I could find the same capacity for mercy in my own heart, but I can't. I cannot forgive my brother Louis for his crimes.

My brother Philippe in Geneva must be suffering from this horrible news. Grant him courage.

Divine Creator, I have a special boon to ask you. Let my best friend live! Let Irene live!

As she departed the church, Berenice was observed by a veiled woman dressed in black. Leaving her pew, the woman went outside and hailed a cab. The vehicle delivered the passenger at *L'Epi-Scié,* an alehouse of dubious reputation. Inside the tavern, she removed the veil revealing a brown-haired woman in her early twenties. The woman in black took the stairs to a private conference room on the upper floor. Two other women seated at a table were pouring tea.

"Mademoiselle Moreau! You have returned from your surveillance of Mademoiselle Fourneau. Join me and Mademoiselle Coyatier in a cup of tea."

The speaker was about five years older than her companions. She had black hair and dazzling eyes of a dark blue hue. Born Catarina Corbucci, she had married Noel Moriarty, a former railway master from England.

"Is Mademoiselle Fourneau a pretty girl?" asked Catarina. "She was about 12 years old when I graduated from the Fourneau College. Her mother kept her isolated when I was head prefect. I never saw her."

"She has inherited our former mentor's beauty, Madame," answered Rochelle Moreau.

"Mademoiselle Coyatier has made an intriguing discovery in her inquiries at the Institution Bachelard."

"Berenice has an intense rivalry with a fellow student, Kaitlin de Winter," interjected Orianne Coyatier. "Kaitlin is the daughter of a British diplomat. The two girls despise each other."

"We can use that to our advantage," acknowledged Catarina.

"Madame, will our fellow alumna be joining us in this endeavor?" questioned Rochelle.

"My successor as head prefect is still in Panama," said Catarina. "When our blonde comrade returns to Europe, I'll have other duties for her. Keep her totally in the dark regarding my plans for Berenice Fourneau."

Darlla Rassendyll was an attractive red-haired woman approaching her thirty-seventh birthday. Because she could not appear in public in her true appearance, Darlla had created the false identity of Augustine d'Erlette, an elderly gray-haired woman with a cane. As Augustine, Darlla was driven to the Trémeuse mansion by one of her Acolytes, a coachman named Charles Blanton.

Inside the house, Augustine was greeted by the mistress of the house. Madame de Trémeuse was a petite lady with blonde hair.

"Monsieur Lupin is awaiting you in the study. He wishes to see you alone."

As Augustine entered the study, she beheld the lean handsome face of Théophraste Lupin. She expected to see him smiling in an egotistical manner. Instead his face was grim and serious.

"Revenant, thank you for coming. I apologize for summoning you in such an abrupt manner. A decade ago, you rescued me from the murderous designs of a woman whom I loved. I now must ask you for a favor."

The woman to whom Lupin referred was Joséphine Balsamo, also known as Countess Cagliostro. As a diabolical agent of the Black Coats, Joséphine had destroyed Darlla Rassendyll's reputation and murdered one of her associates. Lupin had been the one man whom Joséphine truly loved. In a campaign of retribution, Darlla had deceived Lupin into believing Joséphine sought to assassinate him. This falsehood had enabled Darlla to fatally stab Joséphine. Maddened by a lust for vengeance, Darlla had lied to the dying Joséphine. Darlla gloated that Lupin had been her willing accomplice in the scheme to ambush Joséphine.

Darlla's nemesis had gone to her grave mistakenly believing that her lover had betrayed her.

"I shall grant no favors, Monsieur Lupin, until you explain your knowledge of my organization."

"Fair enough. As you're aware, I'm a close friend of Pierre de Trémeuse. I was best man at his wedding to Julia in 1881. The wedding reception at the Russian Embassy was interrupted by a Nihilist plot to assassinate everyone present. That monstrous scheme was mysteriously aborted. An English spy, Digby Fell, investigated these events. He suspected that a woman, Augustine d'Erlette, was somehow involved. In order to discover the truth, he needed to recruit a capable Frenchman into Her Majesty's Secret Service. He chose me."

"Besides being a thief, you are now also a spy in the pay of foreigners."

"I am still a patriotic Frenchman. I only give the British information that is not detrimental to the interests of my native land. Nihilists are the enemies of all nations. Fell thought that the enigmatic Augustine was the chief of the Nihilist cell. Having met the lady, I came to a radically different conclusion that I refused to share with him. I suspect that Fell's superior, an eccentric recluse called M., came to a similar judgment when he read our report."

"I have met him. M. told me about Fell's activities. I'm aware that the trail of my Augustine persona led to the A. L. Lard office. Surveillance of that office exposed most of the Acolytes employed by me in 1881. However, M. assured me that he had conducted no further inquiries into my activities. I recruited other Acolytes in the subsequent years. M. is unaware of their existence, but Julia informs me that you know their identities."

"M. did not lie. He terminated the probe into the visitors who drop off envelopes into the Lard office, but I did not. My own organization, the Werewolves, is very effective at gathering information. M. would only have divulged his knowledge of you if he needed a favor. I assume that you granted it."

"Only because the favor suited the cause of justice. I shall not assist you in the commission of any crimes, Monsieur Lupin."

"I would not even consider such a proposal, Revenant. Do you know about my children?"

"I know you definitely have a son. Your former lover, Victoire Chupin, has a daughter. Are you the father?"

"Yes. Irene is my child. The favor concerns her."

"*Mon Dieu!* Irene Chupin! Irene Tupin! Irene's mother went to prison as Victoire Tupin! The girl in the Avignon hospital is your daughter!"

"I must see her, but the police must not learn of my connection to her. I must visit her in disguise. The attending physician is the brother of Dr. Rolande Cerral, one of your Acolytes. On your instructions, she could arrange access."

"I shall grant your request on two conditions."

"Name them."

"First, Rolande and I accompany you to the Countess Yalta Memorial Hospital."

"Agreed."

"Second, you tell me how Irene ended up in a school in Provence."

"Agreed. I must confess that my behavior in the following story is far from commendable. I put the interests of both myself and my son over that of my daughter's. You know all the details of the theft of a famous necklace in 1880. There was a sequel five years later."

Lupin proceeded to tell the Revenant the unvarnished truth.

Two days later, the Revenant as Augustine d'Erlette awaited Théophraste Lupin at the residence of Dr. Rolande Cerral. An elderly man with a moustache and a pince-nez arrived at the appointed hour. He carried a suitcase. The man handed Rolande a business card. She showed it to Augustine. It bore the inscription of "Doctor Poul Heint."

"You indulged your love of anagrams, Monsieur Lupin," maintained Augustine.

"With a name like Théophraste Lupin, it is very difficult to create an anagram," admitted the disguised thief. "Lothaire Stepphun exhausted my imagination. It's far easier to shorten my name to Theo Lupin to manufacture another anagram."

"You are very versatile in your usage of anagrams."

"As are you. After all, A. L. Lard is an anagram of Darlla. I suspect that our employment of anagrams comes from a common source. My former lover taught me how to create anagrams. She hid behind the alias of Gloria Scot, an anagram of her Cagliostro title. I've always assumed that your feud with her prompted the mimicking of her penchant for anagrams."

"The late Joséphine Balsamo had two daughters."

"You're wondering if I'm the father. Joséphine's namesake is not my child, but I fathered her younger sister, Sabine. I see Monsieur Blanton's coach outside. I assume that he will take us to the train station."

Together with Rolande Cerral, a middle-aged woman with brown hair, the supposed Poul Heint and Augustine d'Erlette entered Blanton's vehicle.

On the ride to the station, Poul asked Augustine a question.

"I've often wondered why you never interfered with my robberies."

"Unlike the Black Coats, you draw the line at murder."

"You're forgetting another important distinction, Revenant."

"What's that?"

"The Black Coats believe in *pay the law*. They have innocents punished for their crimes. The concept of *pay the law* is anathema to me. For that reason, I brazenly proclaim my transgressions to be the work of my Lothaire Stepphun alter ego."

At *L'Epi-Scié*, Rochelle Moreau reported to Catarina Moriarty.

"Madame, my uncle has recently come from Avignon. I just had lunch with him."

"The inestimable Bernard Moreau. He enrolled you in the Fourneau College after your father fled Europe in the wake of that vivisection scandal."

"Considering that he was Madame Fourneau's lawyer, it was very easy for him to do so."

"Why is your uncle in Paris?"

"Remember Madame Fourneau's sister?"

"Rosette? She married an Englishman named Trevor. She lives with him in Bristol."

"Rosette Trevor is in Paris. Under the terms of Madame Fourneau's will, a trust fund had been set up for her children. There is enough money there to provide for the education of Berenice and Philippe. Madame Fourneau's son will probably remain in Switzerland, but all the notoriety regarding the College Girl Murders is adversely affecting Berenice. Madame Trevor is hoping to persuade her niece to come to England."

"That development doesn't suit my interests. I have new orders for Mademoiselle Coyatier. She has been busy cultivating Mademoiselle de Winter."

The Revenant and her two companions were registered at a hotel in Avignon. In the room of Poul Heint (alias Théophraste Lupin), the trio was conferring with Victoire Chupin. She had arrived days earlier with her brother.

"Victor had to return to Paris," said Victoire. "He was scheduled to testify at a murder trial."

"Is he suspicious concerning Irene's enrollment at the school under the false name of Tupin?"

"He attributes that surname to an error by the press. Dr. Cerral discovered Irene's real identity when he read Madame Fourneau's records. She's registered at the hospital as Irene Chupin."

"When will Victor be returning?" asked Augustine.

He plans to be back here in February."

"It is just as well," noted Heint. "I prefer that he doesn't see me in my medical guise."

"Dr. Cerral won't let you see Irene. He won't let any other doctor examine her."

"I'll be able to persuade my brother to let Dr. Heint see your daughter," argued Rolande. "I shall introduce him to Anatole as an expert in comas."

"I don't see what good can come from your visit, Théophraste," professed Victoire.

"There is always a special bond between father and daughter," argued Heint. "I hope that the sound of my voice shall awaken Irene."

"Our daughter has suffered terribly during her years at the school," avowed Victoire. "Do you know what Dr. Cerral told me? Irene has scars on her back. Madame Fourneau must have whipped her."

Irene's father was visibly shaken by that revelation.

The Countess Yalta Memorial Hospital had been named after a Russian aristocrat who had been allegedly poisoned by Nihilists in 1880. During her tragic life, the Countess had lost her left hand. After the reading of her will, her heir had used her fortune to finance the construction of a hospital for patients who lost limbs in industrial accidents.

Inside the private office of Dr. Anatole Cerral, Roland introduced her brother to Augustine d'Erlette and Dr. Poul Heint.

"What you suggest is highly irregular, Rolande," objected Anatole. "How can I leave my patient alone with Dr. Heint?"

"I vouch for Dr. Heint's methods at reviving comatose patients," said Rolande. "He performs best when he is unhampered by the observation of colleagues, Besides Dr. Heint will not be alone. Madame d'Erlette will be with him."

Anatole addressed Augustine.

"I don't understand your role in this matter, Madame. You aren't a nurse."

"I'm writing a book on Dr. Heint's methods," explained Augustine.

Anatole remained adamant. "I still refuse to approve this request."

"Be reasonable, my brother," advised Rolande. "Dr. Heint is like you---a man ahead of his times. Remember those controversial theories of yours. They upset all your associates in Paris. Perhaps you and I can discuss your theories while Dr. Heint and Madame d'Erlette examine your patient."

Rolande's words melted Anatole's resistance. "Very well, I agree."

Anatole summoned a nurse. He instructed her to conduct Dr, Heint and Madame d'Erlette to the bedside of Irene Chupin. After the nurse and the others had left his office, Anatole confronted his sister.

"You're playing a dangerous game, Rolande. That man isn't a doctor. That woman is also certainly a liar. I suspect your friends have something to do with the campaign against the Black Coats launched by you and Francis Clampin."

"I too have my suspicions, Anatole. How were you acquainted with Madame Grévin?"

"She's a former patient."

"Has Veronique met her?"

"Leave my wife out of this!"

"There is also the matter of your treatment of Irene Chupin. There are rumors that her hands were severed."

"That isn't true. Her hands were simply bloodied."

"Don't lie to me, Anatole! You didn't want me to discuss your theories in front of my associates! I know the reason why you don't want another doctor to examine her. Your advocacy of limb transplants is still fresh in my mind. *You re-attached her hands!"*

"I could never deceive you---not even when we were children."

"You used that girl as a guinea pig in your experiments!"

"I used her to advance the cause of science!" Anatole paused briefly. "Have you shared your conclusions with your two friends?"

"No. there's no need to do so at the present. However, if the girl dies as a result of your unorthodox methods, I may have to tell them the truth."

On her hospital bed, the slender form of Irene Tupin rested. Her hands were wrapped in bandages. Her father sat beside her. As Augustine watched, the disguised Théophraste Lupin stroked Irene's black hair.

"You always liked me to tell you stories. I still remember your favorite story. Let me tell you it again.

"The last unicorn on Earth was owned by Andreas of Hungary. He loved his unicorn as if it was his own child. One night Andreas stared at the moon. He fell asleep and forgot to protect his precious unicorn. When Andreas awoke in the morning, he discovered that a wolf had crept into his garden. His beloved unicorn had been butchered. Andreas was overcome by grief."

Irene opened her eyes.

"Papa," she muttered. "Papa, everything is so blurry. I can't make out your face."

"But you can hear my voice, darling."

"Papa, why did you lie to me?"

"I never lied."

"You said that I was your unicorn. You promised to protect me. You lied. You made me *pay the law*."

"No," gasped Irene's father.

"Leave me, Papa. *I never want to hear your voice again*."

The face of Irene's father froze in shock. He left the room.

Augustine sat near Irene's bedside.

"Irene, where did you learn that phrase: *pay the law?*"

"Your voice...Berenice...Is that you?"

Augustine lied. "Yes, it's Berenice."

"You always feared to become like your mother. I became like her. Forgive me."

"I forgive you. Where did you learn of *pay the law?*"

"From the Blonde Beast. You warned me about her. I thought that I could fight her. I was wrong. I couldn't let her beat me again. I let her turn me into a prefect."

"Irene, who is the Blonde Beast?"

"I called her the Muse. So did your brother, He invoked her in the attic."

"Who is the Muse? Who is the Blonde Beast?"

"Joséphine Balsamo."

Augustine left the patient's room. Irene's father was not in the corridor. She looked outside a window. He was standing in front of the hospital's entrance. Augustine went to Anatole Cerral's Office. She informed him that Irene was out of her coma but delirious.

"She mentioned the names Berenice and Joséphine Balsamo. Do those names mean anything to you?"

"When I examined Madame Fourneau's records, I saw tuition payments for a daughter named Berenice," said Anatole. "She's studying in Paris. Irene's file mentioned that she had been recruited as a prefect by a student named Joséphine Balsamo."

"Do you know what happened to Joséphine?"

"She left the school last year."

Augustine and Rolande collected their male companion outside the hospital. They took a cab back to the hotel. No one spoke during the journey. When they arrived at their destination, the spurious Dr. Heint scurried off to his hotel room. Augustine went to Rolande's room to have a private talk with her Acolyte.

"Judex told me all about Joséphine Balsamo," said Rolande. "You killed her 10 years ago, Revenant."

"She had a daughter with the same name. She would be over 21 today."

"What does this daughter have to do with the College Girl Murders?"

"Irene identified her as the Muse. She apparently told Louis to perform the killings." Augustine bit her lip. "This may be all my fault!'

"How can that be?"

"I lied to the original Joséphine. I viciously boasted that Théophraste had betrayed her out of love for me. Her body was removed by an accomplice after I stabbed her. If she was still clinging to life, Joséphine could have made her daughter swear vengeance against the Lupin family."

"Didn't Joséphine know your true identity? What if she told her daughter?"

"The younger Joséphine even saw me without the mask, but it doesn't matter. The new Joséphine must be a member of the Black Coats. They all believe that Darlla Rassendyll died one year after the prior Joséphine. My ruse with Erik's corpse and my own wax figure totally duped them "

"Then you're safe from the new Joséphine."

"But Théophraste and her family are in danger. I must go to him."

"You can't tell him the truth! You can't reveal how you manipulated him during the Queen's Necklace Affair! He'll turn against you!"

"I'll tell him a partial version of the truth!"

Exiting Rolande's quarters, Augustine knocked on Théophraste's door.

"Go away!" yelled the occupant inside.

Utilizing a hairpin, Augustine picked the lock. Entering the hotel room, she closed the door and bolted it.

Théophraste was staring at a bottle. He had been drinking.

"What do you want?

The Revenant removed the Augustine mask and wig.

"So that's what you look like. I knew your face from photographs. This is the first time that I'm seeing it in the flesh."

"Théophraste, Irene told me the identity of the Muse after you left. She's Joséphine Balsamo. She must be conducting a vendetta against your family."

"What are you talking about? Joséphine's dead."

"But the daughter bearing her name still lives."

"I'm doubly damned. First, Irene suffered for my role in the theft of the Queen's Necklace. Then she became the casualty of a feud resulting from one of my love affairs."

"Don't blame yourself, Théophraste."

"Why not? I never told Irene the real version of the story of the unicorn and the wolf. I thought the original story was too frightening. Andreas was a werewolf. He killed his precious unicorn because the full moon transformed him into a beast. A werewolf always slays those whom he loves. I'm a werewolf too---a different sort of werewolf, but still a werewolf. I ruined my daughter's life."

Théophraste wept. Darlla Rassendyll embraced the master thief in order to console him. Suddenly Théophraste kissed her on the lips. Darlla didn't resist his embraces.

One night in Avignon, Darlla Rassendyll and Théophraste Lupin became lovers.

When Rolande awoke the next morning, she knocked on the door of the Revenant's hotel room. There was no answer. Rolande went down to the first floor to have breakfast. Everyone was discussing a story in the morning paper. Procuring a copy, Rolande went to Théophraste's room.

"Open the door! It's Rolande."

Théophraste answered her knocking. "Come in, your superior resides within."

Ushered inside, Rolande was surprised to find Darlla Rassendyll there. "Horrible news," said Rolande showing Darlla the newspaper's headline:

VICTIM OF COLLEGE GIRL MURDERER DIES
IN HOSPITAL

Théophraste was overcome by grief. While Darlla remained behind to comfort her lover, Rolande took a cab to the Countess Yalta Memorial Hospital to learn the tragic details of Irene's death. Her brother had a surprise for her when she arrived.

"The story is false, Rolande. Irene's emergence from the coma became twisted into an account of her demise. Some overly zealous reporter must be responsible. I personally informed Irene's mother of the error, and sent a telegram to her uncle in Paris."

"Are you going to publicly refute the story, Anatole?"

"No. Of course, the truth shall inevitably become public. Irene has already endured great hardships. It's probably for the best that the world think her dead. When she finally recovers, Irene will be able to escape all the lurid publicity surrounding her plight."

Silently, Rolande concurred. This misinformation would shield Irene from the murderous designs of the current Joséphine Balsamo.

The Parisian press spread the falsehoods of the Avignon newspaper. Berenice was devastated by the news of Irene's alleged death. With her Aunt Rosette, Berenice went to Sunday Mass to pray for Irene's soul.

While Berenice was occupied at Church, Orianne Coyatier was being entertained by Kaitlin de Winter in her room at the Institution Bachelard.

Orianne was scrutinizing an edition of Edgar Allan Poe's *Tamelane and Other Poems*. The book bore an inscription: *To Kaitlin: A great rarity for a great daughter. Love, Father.*

"Your father in very generous," observed Orianne. "This book is quite expensive."

"So long as I go to Church and behave like an obedient daughter, Father indulges my every whim. Tell me, Orianne, what is your favorite Poe story?"

" 'The Cask of Amontillado.' "

"An intriguing choice. Why do you like it?"

"Because my grandfather once walled up a man alive."

"You're joking."

Orianne smiled. "I like the way Montressor tricks Fortunato. Do you have an enemy like Fortunato---someone who insulted you?"

"I do. Her name is Berenice Fourneau. She's a fellow student. This pretentious plebeian has mocked me on numerous occasions."

"How would you like to punish her for her slights?"

"You could ransack her possessions."

"A superb suggestion, but she locks her door when she goes out."

"I know how to pick locks."

Returning from Sunday Mass, Berenice Fourneau and Rosette Trevor were accosted by another woman as they approached the Institution Bachelard.

"Excuse me," said the newcomer. "Are you Natalie Fourneau's daughter?"

"Yes," affirmed Berenice,

"I came to offer my condolences on the death of your mother. I was one of her students. I am Countess Catarina Corbucci."

"I don't remember my mother ever teaching a Countess, but she did mention a Catarina Koluchy."

"I am she. My father enrolled me under a pseudonym."

"I'm Natalie's sister," said Rosette. "Would you like to join us for tea in my daughter's dormitory apartment?"

"Gladly," remarked Catarina.

Upon arriving at her quarters, Berenice was surprised to find the door unlocked. She was in for a bigger shock. Her room had been vandalized. All her possessions were scattered around the room. Most of them were damaged.

She picked up her copy of *Oliver Twist*. All the pages had been torn out.

"It was a gift from my best friend," sobbed Berenice.

"Who could have been so heartless to do this?" asked Catarina.

"Only one person," replied Berenice. "Kaitlin de Winter."

Although the Revenant had yet to return from Avignon, her Acolytes continued to perform their duties. They gathered information to assist the vigilante's crime-fighting activities. At the Sure Value Agency, Chantal Lebrue clipped this item from *L'Epoque*.

THE COLLEGE GIRL DISAPPEARANCES

By Sigismond Trottier

The brutal College Girl Murders of Provence have had a strange sequel in the metropolis of Paris. Two girls, both not yet 18, have disappeared from the Institution Bachelard, the prestigious boarding school. One of these girls has a direct connection to the College Girl Murderer.

The more prominent of the two girls is Kaitlin de Winter, the daughter of Baron de Winter of the British Embassy. All her possessions, including a valuable collection of Edgar Allan Poe first editions, are missing from her room.

The other girl has a less prestigious pedigree. She is Berenice Fourneau, the sister of the College Girl Murderer, Louis Fourneau, as well as the niece of Gaston Morrell, the Bluebeard of Paris.

Students of the Institution Bachelard have confirmed that an intense animosity existed between the two girls.

To the author of this article, the solution of this mystery is fairly obvious. Berenice Fourneau suffers from the same criminal insanity that afflicted her relatives. She has murdered Kaitlin de Winter and stolen her possessions. Berenice intends to finance her escape by selling Mademoiselle de Winter's Poe collection to unscrupulous collectors.

Professor James Moriarty was the Lord of the Night, the de facto overlord of the Black Coats. He was meeting in his London study with his sister-in-law.

"As you know, Jim, my father helped to create the Pallid Mask, the ultimate assassin of the Black Coats," said Catarina. "I intend to create a feminine counterpart."

"Does this killer of yours have a name?"

"She has adopted the alias of Milady Nevermore."

"Her *nom de guerre* suggests a familiarity with the works of Dumas and Poe."

"Milady is an aficionado of both authors. She is highly cultured and intelligent. Milady shall be our equivalent of the Revenant."

"The Revenant is skilled in Asian assassination techniques. She knows the methods of the Indian Thugs. Do you intend to have Milady trained in the same way?"

"No, Milady will be far more deadly than the Revenant. My new protégé will be tutored by the Iga ninjas of Japan. They are far more lethal than the Thugs. Antonio Nikola is arranging the details."

"How did you gain Milady's loyalty?"

"I employed the traditional Rules of Recruitment codified by the All-Father, Jim,"

"I know the Rules very well. First, have your candidate befriended by a member of our fraternity. Second, discover the candidate's hated enemy. Third, gain the candidate's loyalty with assistance against that enemy. Who was Milady's enemy?"

"A snotty girl at Milady's boarding school. With our help, Milady has punished her insolence."

"Did Milady murder her?"

"Milady conceived a far worse punishment than death. Her enemy has been enslaved by the Black Coats. Milady has a penchant for nicknames. She has bestowed the sobriquet of the Artful Dodger on her enemy."

"Milady has read Dickens?"

"It was one of Milady's jokes. Her enemy had an unusual connection to a copy of *Oliver Twist*."

"I assume that Milady intends to have the Dodger's spirit broken. Will Milady be personally disciplining our new slave?"

"No, that task will be entrusted to two others of my agents. Having been educated at the same alma mater as myself, they are well versed in the art of coercion."

Elsewhere in London, Rochelle Moreau and Orianne Coyatier were leaving a bedroom. Rochelle carried a whip dripping blood,

"That was very nostalgic, Rochelle. I haven't done that since we graduated."

"I have always been impressed, Orianne, by your ability to hold down a struggling captive. It's a pity that our subject doesn't have more stamina. The session would have been more invigorating if it lasted longer."

"Why couldn't I do the flogging? I never get to do it."

"Don't whine, Orianne. This is actually the first time that I employed the lash. Madame Fourneau always reserved that pleasure for Joséphine and Irene. Next time, I'll let you handle the whip."

The girl called the Artful Dodger lay on a bed in the room just vacated by Rochelle and Orianne. She rested face forward. The back of her dress has been torn. On the flesh of her bare back were a series of linear wounds. The battered Dodger moaned as she reached under the mattress to retrieve the object that she hid before the beating. It was a torn page of a book. She looked at the words written in ink on the page: "*Dearest Berenice, pray for my soul, I will pray for yours...Irene.*" The words inspired the Dodger to pray to the Almighty for her deliverance.

Irene Chupin was still delirious in February 1890.

"The King promised to protect me," she muttered on her hospital bed. "He said that I was as precious as a unicorn. The King lied. He abandoned me."

Irene's words were heard by the man standing vigil at her bedside. He was her uncle, Victor Chupin.

"Irene, you are more precious to me than any unicorn," he replied. "I make a solemn promise that can never be broken. I shall always protect you."

Victor kissed his niece on the forehead.

Dance on My Grave

The Great Vampire sometimes employed human disciples to further his schemes of conquest. The two most formidable of these mortal underlings were granted an Amulet of Lilitu. This talisman mentally linked the mind of the recipient to the Great Vampire. If the bearers of the Amulet were slain, the medallion could transform them into vampires under certain conditions. Revelry such as singing or dancing must be performed near the grave of the deceased.

C. M. Loridan, *L'Essence du Dragon* (1866)

In Paris during the Mardi Gras celebration of 1824, the young man was garbed as Chicot the Jester, a famous comedian of an earlier era. He saw a most extraordinary woman wearing the costume of an Amazon. She had luxurious ebony hair and a very athletic physique. She was in the company of a man clad as Apollo. Although the counterfeit god was masked, the Jester could discern Apollo's identity from the flaxen curls of his hair. He was a debauched libertine named Ladeau. He and the Jester had attended the same university together.

"Apollo, I'm surprised that you're paying court to this fair maiden."

"Why are you surprised, Jester?"

"Wouldn't an Adonis be more attractive to you?"

Ladeau swung his right fist at the Jester. Dodging the blow, Lupin grabbed Ladeau's arm and twisted behind his assailant's back.

"We can end this conflict one of two ways," noted the Jester. "I could thrash you, or you could simply leave."

"I'll leave," gulped Ladeau.

Lupin released his hold. His rival scampered away.

The Amazon smiled favorably at the victor.

"Jester, only a true champion such as you could compete against me. I'm a wrestler. I challenge you."

"I accept your challenge on one condition. You must tell me your name."

"Maria Kratides, You have me at an unfair disadvantage for a contestant. I don't know your name."

"I want us to be evenly matched. I am Charles Arsène Lupin."

"If we are to wrestle, we need an isolated area. I suggest we retire to my private coach."

"I heartily agree, Maria. Show me the way to our arena."

As Maria and Charles departed, they were observed by Ladeau and another man dressed as Satan. The two conferred in German.

"Madame Kratides is a truly diabolical woman," noted Ladeau. "She claims to have murdered her husband and abandoned her son to become one of the paramours of the cult's leader."

"She is also a capable strategist," responded the man in the guise of Satan. "She reasoned correctly that Lupin would recognize your hair and be prompted to seduce her away from you. Her alias of Sinistrari is quite appropriate."

"This whole affair sickens me, Friedrich. You should let me tell the police what Sinistrari is planning."

"Absolutely not. Cooperate with Sinistrari to the bitter end. I must have an accurate chapter on the Cult of the Undead for my book."

Charles was quite delighted with Maria. Imagine using a wrestling match as a metaphor for an assignation. A bedroom would be more comfortable than a coach, but the sensual body of the brunette would surely compensate for the surroundings.

Soon after Charles made himself comfortable inside the coach, his alluring companion delivered a brutal punch to his jaw. Charles slumped unconscious in his seat.

"You poor trusting dupe!" proclaimed Maria. "My heart belongs to the Great Vampire!"

The Parisian residence was owned by a recluse called Jean Grimoire. One afternoon, a visitor discovered to her chagrin that Grimoire was absent. Therefore, the caller had no choice but to deal with Grimoire's housekeeper.

"Prove to me that you're the Emissary of the Great Vampire!" shouted the middle-aged housekeeper. "I can sense the Undead! You are mortal!"

The words were addressed to another woman who was 15 years younger. The dark-eyed beauty stared into the blue eyes of her older challenger.

"I know things that only the Emissary would. You are Alexis Duvalier, one of a pair of twins born in Martinique during 1774. As an infant, your mother surrendered you to Jean Grimoire, the high priest of Zukala-Koth. He supervised your initiation in the Black Arts. In 1787, minions of my master sought to initiate a renowned beauty from Martinique, Joséphine de Beauharnais, into the ranks of the Undead. This plan was foiled in Fontainebleau by my liege's enemy, Count Cagliostro. Due to the failure of this enterprise, Joséphine gave birth to Cagliostro's child. Years later, the Great Vampire conspired with Grimoire to strike at Cagliostro through Joséphine. In 1793, a girl of 19 years secured employment as a maid in the de Beauharnais household. A year later, Joséphine was arrested for treason. Joséphine's incarceration resulted from false evidence manufactured by her maid. That girl was you. Is this not so?"

"Yes. Stupid Joséphine trusted me. She would have perished on the guillotine if Robespierre hadn't unexpectedly fallen from power. Instead, that pompous aristocrat was released and eventually became Empress of France!"

"Have I not substantiated my claims?"

"No!" exclaimed Alexis. "You arouse my suspicions even more!"

"How so?"

"You could be Joséphine's daughter by Cagliostro. They call her the White Stalker! She hunts the Undead!"

The other woman laughed. "You accuse me of being the Stalker. Her hair isn't black. She has blonde hair and blue eyes. In fact, she resembles you. Perhaps you're related. Both you and the Stalker's mother hailed from Martinique."

"Joséphine de Beauharnais was no kin of mine!"

"Maybe you are descended from Joséphine's aunt, Andrée Tascher de la Pagerie. She married the scion of a mercantile family. Her son was a womanizer. You could be his daughter."

"Enough of your nonsense! Leave this house!"

"This will convince you of my authenticity," said the brunette reaching into the collar of her blouse. "Cagliostro's daughter could know your past history, but she couldn't posses this."

She had pulled out an ornament that hung from a chain around her neck. The pendant was in the shape of a golden bat.

"The Amulet of Lilitu!" declared Alexis. "The Great Vampire gave that to Armond du Moliere. He was buried alive in an unknown grave centuries ago."

"There are two matching Amulets. I am Armond's successor. The Great Vampire has dubbed me Sinistrari."

"An intriguing *nom de guerre*. Ludovicus Maria Sinistrari was an authority on incubi. Are you Italian?"

"No, I'm Greek."

"Your Amulet confirms your veracity. What does the Great Vampire want of the Carcosa Cult?"

"Have you ever heard of the Seeds of Glyu-Uho?" asked Sinistrari.

"The scrolls of Vathelos the Blind profess that the Elder Gods dispatched the Seeds of Glyu-Uho throughout the universe to accelerate the evolution of the lesser races. The luminous magic inside the Seed amplifies intelligence and physical prowess. Such a Seed landed on Earth nearly 30 years ago. It was mistakenly believed to be a meteor."

"A member of the Cult of the Undead witnessed the event. The Seed released enormous burst of mystical radiance. Can an identical projectile be drawn to Earth?"

"There is a sacrificial ritual to entice a Seed of Glyu-Uho to an exact location on Earth, but the victim must have been touched by a previous Seed. The Red Offering must be someone present at the original landing."

"What about a child born afterwards to a parent affected by the Seed?"

"The child can substitute for the parent in the Ritual of Summoning."

"I have procured such a candidate, Alexis. He's Charles Lupin, a young man of about twenty. His father, a leading police official, was altered by the Seed."

"Idiot! The police must be tearing Paris apart to find your prisoner!"

"Their efforts shall be fruitless. I had Charles moved to Brittany. The police are pursuing a false trail. The elder Lupin has blamed his son's disappearance on an old enemy."

"The Great Vampire doesn't know the Ritual of Summoning to entrap a Seed of Glyu-Uho. You need the Carcosa Cult."

"You have been allied with my master in the past."

"His Cult of the Undead reveres Slidith, the Dragon Lord of the Blood Chalice. I and my colleagues worship Zukala-Koth, the King in Yellow. Our cults only cooperate after a Blood Covenant has been negotiated."

"The Seed of Glyu-Uho only affects the living not the Undead. The Great Vampire has instructed me to assemble 20 human specimens, ten men and ten women, who approach physical perfection. All have pledged allegiance to Slidith. After these mortals have been enhanced by the Seed, they will be transformed into the Undead by my master."

"The Great Vampire will have 20 superior subjects. That shall be of little benefit to the Carcosa Cult."

"We would allow a reasonable number of the Carcosa Cult to be present at the gathering, Alexis. The Seed would augment them as well."

"Aldebaran and the Hyades will only be properly aligned one week from today. The Ritual of the Summoning can only be effective then. These are our conditions, Sinistrari. First, the Ritual of Summoning shall be performed by an Initiate of Zukala-Koth."

"My master always assumed as much."

"Second, two of the Slidith adherents will be chosen by our representative. They shall foreswear all loyalty to the Dragon Lord and pledge fidelity to the King in Yellow."

Sinistrari touched her Amulet and closed her eyes. She seemed lost in a trance.

"This witch has agreed too readily. Master," thought Sinistrari. *"I fear trickery."*

"Your suspicions are groundless, my love," pronounced a voice inside Sinistrari's head. *"I see through the witch's motivations. She would choose a man and a woman to act as a new Adam and Eve. They will spawn a race of super-humans beholden to Zukala-Koth."*

"I don't have time to recruit two more disciples. Your cadre of warriors shall be reduced to 18."

"Actually 19. For you too will be enhanced, precious Sinistrari. The price is acceptable. Agree to her terms."

"As you command, Master."

Reaching inside her purse, Sinistrari pulled out a knife.

"This blade was consecrated to the Dragon Lord centuries ago in Montségur."

Sinistrari sliced a cut across the palm of her right hand. She handed the knife to Alexis, who did likewise to her left palm. The two women pushed their bleeding palms together.

"I swear by the pools of blood where Slidith bathes in Ngoth," pledged Sinistrari.

"I swear by the black stars that hung over Carcosa when Zukala-Koth was born," professed Alexis. "Our bargain is sealed in blood."

When Jean Grimoire returned to his abode that evening, he was briefed by his housekeeper on the meeting with the Emissary of the Great Vampire. To say that Grimoire was outraged would be an understatement.

"You incompetent imbecile! You had no authority to conclude a Blood Covenant! The agreement is only valid if I endorse it. Do you realize the consequences when I refuse?"

"My soul will be ripped to shreds by the Unspeakable Feaster of Hali," concluded Alexis nonchalantly. Seated at a table, she was sketching on a pad.

"You seem incredibly resigned to your fate, Alexis."

"My fate shall be quite different, Jean. You shall validate the pact as soon as you realize its enormous benefits."

"Bah! The creation of an Adam and Eve to spawn a super-race! A project only worthy of a lesser demon! Not Zukala-Koth!"

"I agree. Probably the Great Vampire came to the same false conclusion regarding my ambitions. My real plan is totally different. May I use your Zugite relics to illustrate?"

Grimoire's response was to open a desk drawer and remove a small chest. Jean placed it on the table before Alexis. Putting aside her sketch, she opened the chest. Inside were scores of coins stamped with the countenance of an ancient sorcerer.

"Jean, how many humans beholden to the Great Vampire will be empowered at the Ritual of Summoning?"

"Eighteen."

Counting that exact number of coins, Alexis placed them on the right side of the table

"How many will be servitors of Zukala-Koth?"

"Two."

Alexis placed two coins from the chest on the left side. "You have miscalculated, Jean. Sinistrari will be there." Alexis added a nineteenth coin to the stack on the right. "Furthermore, an Initiate of Zukala-Koth will be present to perform the Ritual." She placed a third coin on the left stack.

"Three," announced the high priest of Zukala-Koth with delight.

"What is the significance of the number three to Zukala-Koth?"

"Surely I don't need to enlighten you. Alexis?"

"Indulge me, Jean. You were very harsh before."

"As you wish. When our master resided on Earth in the citadel of Carcosa-Koth, he recruited three women to be his First Triumvirate of Consorts. In the wars of the Lemurian Era, Zukala-Koth was expelled from our world by the Sages of the Phoenix. The First Triumvirate went into hiding and adopted the identity of the Three Matrons of Darkness. For eons, the Matrons have conducted human sacrifices to return our master to Earth, but their powers are not enough. The King in Yellow has long tried to create an additional trio of Consorts to augment the sorcery of the Three Matrons. Currently there are three vacancies in the Second Triumvirate of Consorts. All the previous members of the Second Triumvirate were either slain by our enemies or executed for failure by the King in Yellow."

"You now have the means to fill those positions with women augmented by the Seed of Glyu-Uho. The Initiate of Zukala-Koth will obviously be First Consort. The choices for Second and Third Consort will be ironic, Jean. The Great Vampire has long slavishly copied the King in Yellow. The Lord of the Undead always recruits three women to act as his lieutenants."

"Ah, yes. The Sisters of the Night."

"No doubt at least three of the Slidith cultists present shall be candidates for the Sisterhood. We shall conscript two of these prospective Sisters for the Second Triumvirate. We can easily guess the identity of one of these prospective Sisters." Alexis held up her sketch. "This is Sinistrari. Her beauty alone qualifies her to be a Consort of Zukala-Koth."

"The Great Vampire has impeccable taste, but surely your agreement rules out such a choice."

"No. The terms permit the Initiate to choose from anyone present."

Grimoire chuckled. "Very clever. You outwitted the Great Vampire. However, there is a flaw in your scheme."

"What do you mean? There should be no difficulty in choosing a Third Consort."

"There is the matter of the First Consort, Alexis. There are no Initiates available to fulfill this role. I must act as Initiate. I shall only be able to create two Consorts, but that is better than none."

"You're forgetting the obvious choice." The housekeeper pointed to herself.

"Alexis, you can't be serious, I evaluated you for the role of Consort 30 years ago. You were found to be lacking."

"Only because you blamed me unfairly for your failure to destroy Joséphine de Beauharnais. Was I responsible for the overthrow of the Robespierre regime?"

"Your complaint has merit, but you were 20 in 1794. You are 50 today. You are far too old to be a Consort of Zukala-Koth."

"You have the appearance of a man of 50, Jean, but your real age is 194."

"Zukala-Koth bestowed on me the gift of longevity when I was 50."

"The King in Yellow must have taught you some means of rejuvenation."

"There is a Rite of Renewal. I can only perform it every 50 years. The ritual would return my physique to that of a man of 20. I would then age normally until the next interval of 50 years."

"Why don't you employ it?"

"I did once. For the last 20 years of the interval, my physical age resembled that of a man between 51 and 70. I found it easier on my body to continually be a man of 50."

"Can you teach me this ritual?"

"Yes. Apparently I have no choice but to instruct you in the Rite."

"Thank you, Jean."

"Don't thank me yet. When I made my pact with Zukala-Koth in 1680, longevity came at a price. I was given 250 years to secure the Tattered King's dominion on Earth. If I fail to accomplish this goal, my body and soul would be devoured by the King in Yellow. I shall impose a similar restriction on you."

"What do you mean?"

"If you fail to achieve the return of Zukala-Koth to our world within the next 75 years, Alexis, you shall suffer the same dire fate awaiting me in 1930."

"Once I am transformed into a Consort, I shall not need 75 years."

In the course of the next three days, three teen-age girls disappeared. Their relatives petitioned the police to search for them, but the authorities were more concerned with conducting a massive manhunt for a dangerous criminal.

The solution to the crime could be found in the basement of Grimoire's house. There were buried the flayed remains of the girls. Each had been skinned alive by Alexis Duvalier in order to consummate the Rite of Renewal.

Ladeau's hands were tied to the back of a chair in an underground chamber. A hood covered his face. The hood was yanked from his head. Ladeau gazed at his interrogator.

"Jacques Collin! But you're in prison!"

"I escaped four years ago," said Ladeau's captor. "You've been a naughty boy. First, you leave my service to consort with that German."

"I had no choice, Jacques. Louis Gondureau apprehended you."

"Now I discover that you escorted a woman to Mardi Gras. Silly boy! Didn't I teach you never to trust women?"

"How could you know that? I was masked!"

"You were dressed as Apollo. Have you forgotten? Apollo was my nickname for you. There are very few men in Paris with your muscular physique and golden curls. It was child's play for my agents to find you."

"What can I do to regain my freedom?"

"Tell me about the woman who was your companion."

"I was with several women at Mardi Gras."

Collin slapped his captive's face.

"Don't joust with me, boy! You know whom I mean! The woman garbed as an Amazon! You left her in the company of Charles Lupin!"

After Ladeau revealed everything he knew, Collin decided to violate one of his cardinal precepts. He had to trust a woman.

The French National Police, the Sûreté, had many former criminals in positions of authority. The most notorious of these ex-felons was Eugène François Vidocq, who founded the Sûreté around 1812. Lesser known was the man nicknamed Bibi-Lupin. His real name was Albert Lupin. By the age of fifty-four, he had led a truly remarkable life. In 1793, he had been sentenced to death by Robespierre's Committee of Public Safety. Narrowly escaping the guillotine, Bibi-Lupin fled to England. In 1802, he returned to France under the terms of First Consul Napoleon Bonaparte's amnesty for émigrés. In the years that followed, Bibi-Lupin served loyally in the French army. Unfortunately, he had a penchant for thievery that resulted in his being sentenced to the French galleys in 1810. In 1813, Bibi-Lupin secured his release by informing the authorities about an escape planned by his fellow inmates. Recognizing Bibi-Lupin's talents, Vidocq recruited him into the Sûreté. As both a criminal and a policeman, he had employed scores of false identities. For example, many of his Sûreté subordinates only knew him as Louis Gondureau.

That afternoon, he received a most unusual visitor. She was a stunning woman of 36 years. Her golden hair crowned an attractive face with a delicate chin, high cheek bones and slightly slanted eyes.

"Sit down, Mademoiselle Balsamo. I can spare you only a few minutes."

"Surely Magistrate de Grandin's letter informed you that my business was urgent."

"It's only out of my high regard for the Magistrate that I am permitting this brief interview."

"I understand your desire for brevity. You want to supervise the ongoing search for your missing son."

"What? How did you learn about that?"

"I was contacted by the man you suspect of engineering Charles's disappearance, Jacques Collin."

"How do you know Collin?"

"When Collin escaped the galleys in 1815, he adopted the alias of Vautrin. Under that name, he sold a dueling technique, a secret known to such famed swordsman as Delapalme and Lagardère – a fatal thrust to the forehead. I purchased the secret of this thrust from Vautrin. Due to our former dealings, the man formerly known as Vautrin chose me to act as an intermediary."

"What ransom does Collin demand for my son's return?"

"He has no demands. Collin has sworn to me that he is innocent of any role in your son's abduction."

"What do you know of my relationship to Collin, Mademoiselle Balsamo?"

"He swore an oath of vengeance against you for betraying your fellow convicts in 1813. His animosity was exacerbated when you arrested him in his Vautrin identity during 1819. He escaped captivity again one year later."

"Collin is my implacable foe. I have every reason to mistrust his word. How does Collin know of my suspicions?"

"Through your actions. Your operatives have been asking if a man of Collin's description was in the same vicinity where your son was last seen."

"You earlier used the word 'abduction.' Did Collin use that word?"

"Yes."

"That fact proves Collin's guilt. I have no evidence that my son was kidnapped. Only his captor would know that!"

"Collin has investigated your son's disappearance and deduced that it was a kidnapping. He unearthed a lead to the perpetrators."

"Why would Collin conduct such an inquiry?"

"Collin has no desire to be a scapegoat for someone else. Your extensive search for him is hampering his movements. Once your son is found, Vidocq will force you to shift your resources away from a needless quest to capture Collin."

"With all due respect, I can't imagine a hardened criminal like Collin acting like a policeman."

"With all due respect, the same statement could be made about you and your superior, Monsieur Vidocq."

"Touché, Mademoiselle! What has Collin supposedly discovered?"

"Collin has a certain proclivity to surround himself with young handsome men."

"I am aware of this eccentricity. It increased the antipathy between us as galley slaves."

"One of Collin's former protégés is a young man named Ladeau."

"I have a file on him. This Ladeau is currently living with a wealthy German."

"Ladeau's German friend has literary ambitions. He hopes to write a book on obscure cults. As a favor for the German, Ladeau joined a satanic coven in order to conduct research for the book. This coven has imprisoned your son. Ladeau has told Collin of the coven's plans for your son. They intend to sacrifice him in Brittany on Thursday."

"That's three days from now! Where is this cult holding my son?"

"Collin has persuaded Ladeau to cooperate. Ladeau hasn't discovered your son's location yet. His instructions are to stay at an inn and await a summons to the place of sacrifice. Ladeau will pass the location to me once he learns it."

"You are asking me to trust the most dangerous criminal in France."

"I disagree with your characterization. Collin's rival, the All-Father of the Black Coats, is far more sinister."

"The Black Coats are a Corsican myth! They don't exist! I have the personal assurance of Monsieur Vidocq!"

"I won't debate the French criminal hierarchy with you, Monsieur. You have a choice. You can either trust Collin and accept my assistance, or let me try to rescue your son alone."

Bibi-Lupin's eyes scanned two documents before him. One was a secret dossier of the Sûreté:

BALSAMO, JOSÉPHINE – Born in Palermo, Sicily, on July 29. 1788. Confirmed to be the illegitimate daughter of Joseph Balsamo (alias Alexandre Cagliostro) and Joséphine de Beauharnais. Presented to Emperor Napoleon at Malmaison in 1806. Adopted alias of Countess Cagliostro in Russia during 1815. Reputed to be former lover of Henri de Belcamp (see DEVIL, JOHN). Rumored to have given birth to Henri's son.

The illegitimate daughter of a confidence trickster and the lover of a notorious criminal, thought Bibi-Lupin. Not much of a recommendation!

Bibi-Lupin then shifted his gaze to a passage from Raymond de Grandin's letter:

...I would trust Joséphine Balsamo with my life. She is a woman of incredible courage and veracity. My friend, I know that you will check the police files. You shall find some scandalous information about her past. Do not let it warp your judgment. Remember that your own past is far from stellar.

Bibi-Lupin looked into Joséphine Balsamo's eyes.
"Mademoiselle, help me save my son!"

One evening at an inn in Brittany, Ladeau vacated his room. He was in the company of five other travelers. Claiming the need to steady his nerves, he briefly excused himself from his companions to purchase a drink at the inn's bar. He secretly passed a note to a woman seated at the bar. She was wearing a large coat with a raised hood that made her appearance difficult to discern. Ladeau passed a note to her. He then boarded a coach with his associates.

Leaving the inn, the woman mounted a white horse in the stable. The name of the mare was La Reine. A cane was shoved into a pocket of the saddle. Its golden handle was carved in the shape of a ram's head. The woman rode to where Bibi-Lupin waited on a horse with a troop of mounted gendarmes.

Riding up to Bibi-Lupin, the woman removed her hooded coat. The form of Joséphine Balsamo was revealed. Her upper torso was clad in a white tunic with wide sleeves. White pants and boots encased her lower limbs. From a white belt around her waist hung a coiled whip whose metal tip was made of silver.

Joséphine informed Bibi-Lupin of the coven's location.

"How will my men know Ladeau?" asked Bibi-Lupin. "I don't want him slain by accident."

"He will be wearing a black armband on his right arm," replied Joséphine.

"You may need this." Bibi-Lupin handled Joséphine a single-shot pistol.

The Pointe du Raz is a remote Breton promontory that juts into the Atlantic. Sinistrari had chosen a high cliff in this barren region to erect her sacrificial altar. It took three coaches consisting of eighteen passengers and three drivers to deliver the entire coven to the site.

All of Sinistrari's 20 disciples wore red robes. The Emissary of the Great Vampire was attired in a totally different fashion. A red cape draped her shoulders. Her upper torso was bare except for a brassiere covering her breasts. Each of her two golden breast plates was decorated with a reptilian crimson eye. These painted designs were dubbed the Eyes of the Dragon Lord. Sinistrari wore red trousers and boots. The Amulet of Lilitu hung from her neck. She carried a staff whose head resembled a dragon.

Clad only in a loin cloth, Charles Lupin laid bound and gagged on the altar.

"We only await the Initiate of Zukala-Koth," Sinistrari informed her followers.

Suddenly a huge gust of wind blew around the assembled coven. After the wind dissipated, Sinistrari and her underlings noticed the inexplicable presence of a robed figure. A raised hood obscured the upper face of the visitant. The yellow robe of the stranger was emblazoned with a black design of a monstrous peacock-like creature.

"I am the Initiate of Zukala-Koth," said a female voice.

"Lower your hood," demanded Sinistrari. "I must inspect your visage."

The Initiate complied.

Upon viewing the face of the Initiate, the black eyes of Sinistrari filled with hate. "Joséphine Balsamo!" Gripping the carved dragon's head, she quickly drew a sword from the staff's outer shell. She pointed the sword's tip against the Initiate's throat.

"Tell me where the real Initiate is, White Stalker, or I'll cut off your head," promised Sinistrari.

The Initiate laughed. "You were right. I do resemble the Stalker. Look closely at my hand, Sinistrari. Would the Stalker bare such a scar?"

"The Mark of the Blood Covenant!"

"I am Alexis Duvalier. The adepts of Slidith are not the only ones capable of renewing their youth."

Sinistrari withdrew her blade. "Time grows short! Prepare the Red Offering!"

During the confrontational meeting between Sinistrari and the Initiate, Ladeau had taken advantage of the confusion to slip a black band over the right arm of his red robe. He was growing impatient. Where was Joséphine Balsamo? Alexis Duvalier had been chanting for several minutes. The blade of Montségur was clenched in her right hand.

Approaching the end of the ceremony, Alexis raised the sacrificial knife high in the air above the helpless Charles Lupin. She would shortly begin to skin him alive.

"In the depths of Hali, living Hastur lies feasting! Ia! Ithaqua rules the winds! Ia! Ai! Sin rules the moon! Ai!"

Riders on horses flooded the scene.

"Die! Spawn of Satan!" screamed Joséphine Balsamo as she fired her pistol.

The bullet slammed into the chest of Alexis. Dropping the knife, she collapsed.

With the exception of Ladeau, the other coven members fiercely resisted Bibi-Lupin's men. In the resulting confusion, Sinistrari ran into the darkness of the night. Still mounted on La Reine, Joséphine Balsamo rode after her. Leaping from her horse, Joséphine landed on her quarry's back and tackled her to the ground. Breaking the blonde's grip, the brunette scrambled to her feet.

"The White Stalker!" snarled Sinistrari.

"We meet again, Sinistrari! This time you won't escape!"

Unsheathing her sword, Sinistrari sliced at the Stalker's belt. The Stalker's sliver-tipped whip fell to the ground.

"You're defenseless, Stalker!"

Joséphine whistled. La Reine moved towards Sinistrari. The steed raised her front legs high in the air. Fearing that the horse had been ordered to trample her, the Emissary of the Great Vampire leaped away from the mare. Lowering her legs, La Reine stopped before her mistress. Joséphine removed the cane from the saddle. Like Sinistrari's staff, the cane concealed a sword. Pulling the blade from its casing, the White Stalker advanced towards her antagonist.

"To the death, Sinistrari!"

The swords of the duelists crashed. Sinistrari's attack was ferocious. Joséphine was forced backwards towards the edge of the cliff.

"You can't win," taunted Sinistrari. "Have you forgotten Moldavia? I was your superior then! I'm your superior now!"

"I've learned a few tricks since Moldavia!"

"So have I!"

As her sword warded off Joséphine's assault, Sinistrari's left hand unhooked the clasp of her cape. Twirling the cape, the brunette threw it on the ground at Joséphine's legs. Her feet entangled in the cape, the blonde fell on her back.

Sinistrari bent forward to drive her sword into Joséphine's heart. Raising herself to a sitting position, Joséphine stabbed upward. Her blade penetrated Sinistrari's forehead.

"The Vautrin thrust!" exclaimed Joséphine

Regaining her footing, Joséphine disengaged her blade. Sinistrari's corpse toppled to the ground. Sheathing her sword, Joséphine restored her cane to La Reine's saddle. She reached down to grab her whip.

"It isn't over, White Stalker! I'm very hard to kill!"

The speaker was Alexis. Her hands grasped her blood-drenched chest. Joséphine raised her whip to strike, but she hesitated upon fully viewing the Initiate's face for the first time.

"It's almost like looking into a mirror," gasped Joséphine.

The White Stalker's hesitation had consequences. Alexis started to sing.

Along the shore the cloud waves break.
The twin suns sink beneath the lake.
The shadows lengthen in Carcosa.

Behind Joséphine, the Amulet of Lilitu glowed on Sinistrari's corpse. The wound on Sinistrari's forehead healed as the voice of the Great Vampire whispered inside her skull.

"Your slumber is disturbed by revelry, my love. Arise as a Sister of the Night! Destroy the White Stalker!"

Sprawled on the ground, Sinistrari smiled exposing a pair of fangs. She opened her eyes. No longer black, they were a brilliant shade of red.

A strong gust of wind caused Joséphine to close her eyes. When she reopened them, Alexis had vanished.

Jumping to her feet, Sinistrari seized Joséphine from behind. Raising the Stalker high in the air, the Sister of the Night threw her over the cliff. The hurtling Joséphine swung her whip. The lash twirled around Sinistrari's neck. The vampire attempted to dislodge the whip, but she howled in agony. The silver tip was burning her flesh. Silver was anathema to the Undead.

With the erect Sinistrari as an anchor, Joséphine hung suspended against the wall of the precipice. She climbed hand over hand up the whip until her feet reached firm ground. She stood facing the vampire. Twisting the whip, she moved sideways, Joséphine forced Sinistrari to turn and become parallel with the cliff.

Weakened by the silver, Sinistrari dropped to her knees in front of the Stalker.

"Mercy," pleaded the Sister of the Night."

"I have no mercy for the Undead. I am the White Stalker."

Joséphine yanked harshly on the whip. Sinistrari was propelled forward. Her face slammed brutally into the earth. With her arms outstretched, she lay on the soil moaning in agony. The White Stalker towered triumphantly over her defeated foe. Still holding the lash, Joséphine moved to the side of the prostrate Sinistrari. With all her might, Cagliostro's daughter kicked the hip of the exhausted vampire. Sinistrari rolled towards the precipice as the whip around her neck untangled. When the silver tip lost all contact with her flesh, Sinistrari plummeted into the sea.

Immersion in running water was a traditional way to slay a vampire. As the salt water clogged her lungs, Sinistrari had one final thought before being obliterated: *"Master, I failed you."*

Joséphine discovered a liberated Charles Lupin together with his father. Ladeau's black armband had ensured his safety during the raid. All of the other coven members had been killed or captured.

From a window in the tower of a Carpathian fortress, a bearded man peered into the night.

"You have crushed another of my slaves, White Stalker. Savor your victory for the moment. My retribution will come, but I can be patient. My retribution can span decades; even centuries. One night, you and your entire bloodline shall endure ruination by my Curse---the Curse of Dracula."

Ladeau informed Joséphine and Bibi-Lupin that the cultist resembling the White Stalker identified herself as Alexis Duvalier. Upon his return to Paris, Bibi-Lupin's inquiries discovered that a woman of that name was housekeeper to Jean Grimoire. When the police raided Grimoire's residence, they discovered the premises vacated. An examination of the basement unearthed the grisly remains of the missing girls. The physical age of the Alexis Duvalier seen at the Pointe de Raz did not match that of the housekeeper. Bibi-Lupin theorized that the younger Alexis was the housekeeper's daughter by Grimoire.

The White Stalker came to a different conclusion. She deduced that Alexis was a sorceress capable of renewing her youth. Researching the background of Alexis Duvalier, the Stalker was stunned to discover that Alexis had been her mother's maid. Further investigation uncovered that Alexis spent her childhood and formative years in Jean Grimoire's household. The Stalker never learned that Alexis had been born in Martinique.

On the deck of a ship bound for England stood a man and a woman.

"You only have 75 years of life left, Alexis. Use them wisely."

"I promise you, Jean, that I shall achieve my two great missions."

"Two missions? What other mission do you have besides the restoration of Zukala-Koth?"

"My revenge on the White Stalker. Joséphine Balsamo and all her family shall die!"

II. The Destiny of a Cagliostro

During the nineteenth century, three different women were known as Joséphine Balsamo, Countess Cagliostro. The first was the White Stalker, the nemesis of the Undead. The second was the Stalker's granddaughter. Also called Gloria Scot, the second Joséphine inherited her grandmother's signet ring. Despite this legacy, she dishonored her noble forebear's name. As a member of the Black Coats, she delighted in murder and betrayal. In 1880, the second Joséphine was fatally wounded by the Revenant, the masked scourge of the Parisian underworld.

This mistress of treachery was survived by two daughters. The younger of these sisters, Sabine was gentle and timid by nature. The older sister bore the name of her mother and grandmother. Inside her chest beat the heart of a warrior. On her deathbed, the second Joséphine had given the Stalker's ring to the heroine's great-granddaughter. The woman feared as Gloria Scot also made her daughter swear a bloodthirsty oath of vengeance against those who supposedly conspire to bring about her destruction. The targets of this vendetta were the Revenant and Théophraste Lupin. The third Joséphine also pledged to ruin the lives of Lupin's children.

In the wake of their mother's death, Joséphine and Sabine became the wards of Arthur Gordon, an American munitions dealer who often vacationed in Europe. He enrolled the young girls in the Marie Gilbert School in Paris. Gordon's policy towards his charges was that of benign neglect. This attitude suited the sisters who enjoyed the benevolent tutelage of the nuns at the school. In March 1883, a meeting transpired which would have severe consequences for the tranquil existence of the Balsamo sisters.

Arthur Gordon was a tall man with mutton chop whiskers. Born in Nantucket during 1817, he had a long and brutal career. Like his cousin, a famous Antarctic explorer, Gordon was consumed by the desire to go to sea. At the age of sixteen, he became a sailor. Gordon eventually jumped ship in Vera Cruz. He led a marauding band of guerillas during the Texas Revolution of 1836. From 1837 until 1842, he captained a ship participating in the illegal slave trade. In 1843, Gordon wedded a French heiress while he was already married to an actress residing in Austin. After the American Civil War, he formed a partnership with a former Confederate gunsmith, Lee Bailey. In the 1870's, Gordon selectively marketed several of Bailey's inventions including a forerunner of the Maxim machine gun. Currently Gordon's primary source of income was selling munitions to the Spanish forces stationed in Cuba.

Gordon was staying in Monaco when he received a summons to come to the Spanish Embassy in Paris. The current Ambassador was Enrique Basilio. He was a short man with a mustache. Gordon was received by Basilio in his spacious office.

Also present was the Countess de Dreux-Soubise, a stunning woman with brown hair and green-blue eyes. Gordon was surprised by her presence. Three years earlier, the Countess and her husband had been nearly impoverished following the theft of their most valued possession, the Queen's Necklace. In order to survive financially, the Count had solicited money from Ambassador Basilio. In exchange for this money, the Count had turned a blind eye when his wife was romanced by Basilio. The Countess had tried to be discreet in her adultery, but Gordon had heard gossip about the affair.

"Señor Gordon, it's a pleasure to see you," said Basilio. "You know the Countess. She has been advising me on a minor matter that we need to discuss. However, there is a more important matter that requires our attention. When we first met, I was stationed in Cuba. Due to my previous experience, the Prime Minister has written seeking my advice. There are considerable budgetary difficulties in Madrid. The government needs to reduce expenditures. Serious consideration is being given to severely cutting our purchase of armaments for our Cuban garrisons. After all, the island is now extremely stable. Don't you agree?"

"Such a judgment would be shortsighted," replied Gordon. "Garcia's revolt only ended three years ago. Even though there is no current insurrection, widespread banditry plagues the entire country."

"The significance of banditry is not lost on me, Señor Gordon. My great-grandfather lost his life in an attempt to apprehend the most notorious bandit in the history of Spanish California. I shall take your arguments into account when drafting my response to the Prime Minister."

Gordon realized that Basilio was toying with him. The wily man from Spain was aware of Gordon's financial dependence on the purchase of munitions for Cuba. This whole conversation had been a prelude to Basilio asking for a favor in exchange for advising the Prime Minister to continue the current Cuban policy.

"You mentioned another matter, Excellency," commented Gordon.

"It concerns the Marie Gilbert School. I understand that you are the guardian of two students there."

"Joséphine and Sabine Balsamo."

"Are you familiar with a recent incident involving them and a fellow student, Raquel Valencia?"

"Sister Daphne, the principal, wrote me about it."

"What is your understanding of the incident?"

"Señorita Valencia made a joke about Sabine walking like a frog. Her sister retaliated by placing a frog in Señorita Valencia's bed. Sister Daphne has punished Joséphine for the prank. May I ask why you're interested in a minor squabble between schoolgirls?"

"Raquel Valencia is the daughter of my sister. The experience of being touched by a scaly creature has severely upset her."

"You have my regrets, Ambassador."

"Joséphine Balsamo should be punished."

"Sister Daphne has already done so. Joséphine was given extra cleaning chores for the next month."

"The punishment is insufficient," interjected the Countess speaking for the first time. "His Excellency asked my advice on the leniency extended by Sister Daphne. Joséphine Balsamo should be expelled. Since Sister Daphne has been overwhelmed by illusions of mercy, it is incumbent on you, her guardian, to impose a penalty."

"Joséphine is very young," noted Gordon. "Surely that fact must be taken into account."

"We are taking it into account," argued Basilio. "We aren't demanding that your ward be sent to prison, but merely to a stricter boarding school."

"Such a school exists in Provence," volunteered the Countess. "The school's headmistress is a personal friend of mine. Her name is Natalie Fourneau."

Gordon saw no choice but to comply with the recommendation of Basilio's mistress. Despite his checkered past, Arthur Gordon was not lacking in compassion for the Balsamo sisters. He believed both sisters to be his biological children. While it bothered him to separate his wards, he justified his decision on the grounds that the continuance of his Cuban revenue enabled him to support the two girls.

Three months later, a history lecture was given by the principal of the Fourneau College for Young Women. Her audience was a classroom of 30 students. Madame Fourneau was an elegant woman with brown hair. She was in the habit of repeating her statements twice in order for her pupils to inscribe them verbatim.

"Joséphine Tascher de la Pagerie was... Joséphine Tascher de la Pagerie was... married twice... married twice ... Her first husband was... Her first husband was... Alexandre de Beauharnais... Alexandre de Beauharnais... He was guillotined... He was guillotined... during the Reign of Terror... during the Reign of Terror... Her second husband was... Her second husband was... Napoleon Bonaparte... Napoleon Bonaparte... She cheated on... She cheated on... both her husbands... both her husbands... Joséphine was little better... Joséphine was little better... than a prostitute... than a prostitute."

Slamming her notebook shut, a 15-year old girl made a loud noise that caught the attention of the entire class. Her right hand was raised defiantly in the air. On her fourth finger was a ring bearing the crest of a golden ram. The blue eyes of the blonde student stared defiantly at the lecturer.

"You wish to contribute commentary, Mademoiselle Balsamo?" asked the headmistress.

"You have defamed one of the greatest women in the history of France!" declared Joséphine Balsamo. "I will not be silent! My ancestor shall not be slandered!"

Madame Fourneau laughed. "Your ancestor! What fantasies are you spreading? Joséphine Tascher de la Pagerie only had two children from her first marriage. Which one do you claim descent from?"

"Neither," mumbled the young girl.

"If your assertions about your ancestry are true, you prove my earlier point about Joséphine Tascher de la Pagerie. You could only be descended from an illegitimate child. Mademoiselle Balsamo, do you admit that in your veins runs the blood of a bastard?"

Advancing quickly from her seat, Joséphine slapped Madame Fourneau.

The headmistress rubbed her cheek. "You insolent girl! Mademoiselle Koluchy!"

A 20-year old student with black hair and dark blue eyes rose from her desk. She was clad in a black skirt and a brown blouse with a black tie.

"Yes, Madame."

"Escort Mademoiselle Balsamo to the isolation room."

The brunette motioned the blonde to follow her. Leaving the classroom, the two girls silently marched up a flight of stairs to an austere room with a bed and two chairs.

The brunette closed the door.

"Joséphine, how could you act so defiantly?"

"Fourneau is a monster, Catarina. Remember when she admired my drawings in art class. She asked me to sketch her in private. As soon as we were alone her office, she began to remove her clothes. I immediately left her office."

Catarina turned away in shame. "Fourneau did the same with me shortly after my enrollment here."

"How can you serve that depraved creature? How can you be her head prefect?"

"I lack your courage, Joséphine."

Catarina left Joséphine alone. About three hours later. Catarina returned with

Madame Fourneau and two other girls. Fourneau's hands were behind her back.

"Mademoiselle Balsamo, I normally grant a recalcitrant pupil the opportunity to avoid punishment by apologizing in front of the entire class. Your brazen misconduct rules out such clemency."

"Spare me your hypocrisy, Madame."

Madame Fourneau exposed her hands. She held a whip.

"Mademoiselle Koluchy, prepare Mademoiselle Balsamo."

"Madame, I'm not feeling well," claimed Catarina. "I humbly beg your permission to be excused."

"This is most unusual, Mademoiselle Koluchy. In light of your years of loyal service, I shall permit it."

"Thank you, Madame."

Catarina vacated the room.

Fourneau addressed the two other girls. "Mademoiselle Delacourt! Mademoiselle Cussac! I shall assume the role normally performed by Mademoiselle Koluchy. Remove the prisoner's clothes."

A whimpering Joséphine sat on the edge of the bed. She was bending forward as the bleeding wounds on her back were washed with a towel by Catarina. The two were alone in the isolation room.

"Listen to me, Joséphine. Your painful humiliation will only intensify if you continue to defy Fourneau. I was once as rebellious as you, but resistance is suicidal in the face of overwhelming force. Learn from the life of Rodrigo Borgia. When Rome was threatened by the French army, Borgia conceded Naples to survive as Pope. You must be as cunning as Borgia."

"What can I do?" cried Joséphine in despair.

"Let me sponsor you to be a prefect."

Catarina conferred later with Natalie Fourneau.

"Our ruse worked, Madame. Balsamo views me as a friend. She has agreed to accept my advice."

"Excellent, Mademoiselle Koluchy. The pretext for this disciplinary action was easy once you told me of the girl's absurd delusions about her pedigree."

"Joséphine's claims may not be false. My father believed in the existence of an illegitimate line stemming from Joséphine Tascher de la Pagerie."

"Our new recruit may indeed have an extraordinary heritage. It would explain her bravado."

"Under my tutelage, the haughty insurgent shall quickly be molded into your docile slave, Madame. I have one regret."

"What is that?

"My pretense denied me the pleasure of inflicting the lash on Balsamo."

"Don't be so bloodthirsty, Mademoiselle Koluchy. Remember to say your prayers before going to sleep tonight."

"I will, Madame."

"Balsamo shall be as pliant as the female envoy of Cyrus. After Pharaoh Khufu had her beaten for insolence, the Cypriote became his second wife. Upon her husband's death, the Cypriote proved her devotion by ordering his tomb sealed with herself inside. I, Natalie Fourneau, shall play Pharaoh to Balsamo's Cypriote."

"With your permission, Madame, I would like to discuss Balsamo's future duties."

"They shall be no different than that of any secondary prefect."

"I would like them to be slightly modified."

"In what way, Mademoiselle Koluchy?"

"As you are aware, I shall be graduating in the spring of next year. I will be returning to my father's villa in the Bay of Naples."

"I shall miss you. I don't understand what this has to do with Balsamo."

"My father wishes me to marry his young business partner. I view such a match with great enthusiasm. I fear my anticipation of this event has caused me to serve you inadequately."

"To be frank, Mademoiselle Koluchy, your recent performance of certain duties has not been up to your usual standard."

"Madame, I have a modest proposal. Remove the burden of those duties from me and shift them totally on Balsamo. Being young and vibrant, she can amuse you longer."

"Your suggestion is acceptable, Mademoiselle Koluchy."

When Catarina graduated in the spring of 1884, she recommended that Joséphine Balsamo succeed her as the chief prefect. Madame Fourneau accepted Catarina's recommendation even though Francesca Delacourt and Catherine Cussac were older and more experienced prefects.

As the months progressed, Joséphine's influence over Madame Fourneau intensified. The students of the Fourneau College had always been forbidden to travel beyond the confines of the school. Joséphine was exempted from this restriction on two occasions.

Natalie Fourneau was a widow with three children. She kept her progeny segregated from all contact with her pupils. Natalie's mother had been a circus performer named Alexandra Vadarasse. Alexandra's niece, Cornelia, had married César Cascabel. The Cascabels ran a circus in Normandy. Cornelia invited Natalie and her family to stay with her during the summer of 1884. The oldest of the Fourneau children, Berenice, was an unruly girl of 12 years. Since Natalie would be preoccupied with caring for Berenice's younger brothers, she enlisted Joséphine to chaperon Berenice. Resenting Joséphine, the headstrong Berenice called her "the Blonde Beast" behind her back. Berenice was particularly resentful that her cousin, Sandre Cascabel the contortionist, was infatuated with Joséphine.

Months after her return to Provence, Joséphine demonstrated signs of an illness. She was frequently nauseous in the morning. Madame Fourneau permitted Joséphine to stay with the Cascabels in Normandy until all signs of the apparent illness dissipated.

With the graduation of Delacourt and Cussac in the spring of 1885, Joséphine quickly enticed two students, Rochelle Moreau and Orianne Coyatier, to replace them as assistant prefects. Joséphine soon grasped the opportunity to ensnare another student in her web of domination.

In August 1885, a girl of 15 years was registered at the Fourneau College for Young Women. Her name was recorded in Madame Fourneau's records as Irene Tupin. Joséphine quickly recognized Irene as the daughter of Théophraste Lupin. Joséphine recalled the advice of her dying mother regarding Théophraste's children:

"...Pretend you view Arsène and Irene with affection. Slowly bend them to your will. Entangle them in your schemes. When the moment is right, cast them aside just as pawns are sacrificed in chess to protect the Queen."

As Catarina Koluchy conspired with Madame Fourneau to coerce Joséphine into becoming a prefect, Joséphine plotted with the headmistress to impose the same fate on Irene. Just as Joséphine's spirit was broken, so was Irene's. A similar confrontation was arranged during a lecture with the same appalling aftermath. Unlike Catarina, Joséphine did not excuse herself during the chastisement of Irene. Joséphine handled the lash with extreme expertise.

Another dissimilarity between the two incidents at the boarding school involved the duties imposed on Irene. Whereas Catarina shifted certain of her chores to Joséphine, the so-called Blonde Beast continued to jealously conduct those same entertainments for Madame Fourneau. Instead Irene was instructed to cater to Joséphine in the same manner that the senior prefect was catering to Madame Fourneau. This unique relationship prospered for nearly four years.

Professor James Moriarty was the Lord of the Night, the de facto ruler of the European crime syndicate called the Black Coats. His marriage was a closely guarded secret. Finola Moriarty (alias Madame Nemo) lived in a separate London residence with Trickie, their young daughter. The Professor occasionally utilized his wife's abode to meet with his associates. In November 1888, the Moriarty were being visited by a most unusual guest.

At the age of twenty-one, Antoine Boucher was viewed as the most formidable assassin in the Black Coats. In the guise of the Pallid Mask, Boucher dispatched his victims ruthlessly with a sickle. Without his white mask, Boucher was an extremely handsome man with black hair.

The Moriartys had another guest. She was a striking woman with full red lips. Her black hair was cut short like a page of the Renaissance era. Boucher judged her to be around his own age.

"This is Leontine," said the Professor. "She's been helping Trickie with her history studies."

"For a girl of 13, Trickie is remarkably bright," emphasized Leontine. "Trickie, could you explain the differences between the three Napoleons?"

The eyes of the dark-haired Trickie opened wide with excitement as she began her recitation.

"After his defeat at Waterloo, Emperor Napoleon I had abdicated in favor of his son, Napoleon II, then only four years old. The Emperor's son never assumed the throne of France. Napoleon II lived as a virtual prisoner in Austria until his death in 1832. With Napoleon II's alleged death, his cousin, Louis Napoleon Bonaparte proclaimed himself the heir to his uncle's legacy. In 1851, Louis became dictator of France. He formally adopted the title of Emperor Napoleon III a year later. The Second Empire was proclaimed. In 1870, Napoleon III abdicated after a humiliating military defeat by the Prussians. The Third Republic, the current constitutional democracy of France, replaced Napoleon III's regime."

Boucher applauded. "I commend you, Miss Moriarty, on your rendition of the facts."

"Come, Trickie, it's time to practice the piano," said Finola. "Leontine and Father need to talk to Mr. Boucher."

The mother and daughter left the room.

"Why did you summon me, Professor?" asked Boucher.

James Moriarty stared firmly into Boucher's eyes.

"Leontine was one of triplets born in Brittany during 1867. Her two siblings were boys. She is your sister, Antoine."

Boucher was stunned. "How did you learn the secret of my birth?"

"Let me acquaint you with my knowledge," declared the Professor. "In April 1814, Emperor Napoleon Bonaparte realized that he was about to be deposed. He summoned three officers, Brigadier Gerard, Colonel Despienne and Captain Tremeau, to embark on a vital errand. The Emperor had secreted valuable documents regarding his family. The three soldiers were told that the papers included proof of the Emperor's divorce from Joséphine, his legal marriage to Marie Louise of Austria, and the birth of their son. The officers were instructed to retrieve the papers. In the course of their mission, two of the officers perished. Only Gerard survived to deliver the papers to the Emperor. In Gerard's company, Napoleon buried the documents in an abandoned pigeon-house not far from Fontainebleau. The records remained there even during Napoleon's brief restoration in power during 1815. During his exile in St. Helena, Napoleon tried multiple times to secretly dispatch a letter to Gerard. These efforts to contact Gerard ended with Napoleon's death in 1821.

"In 1832, Gerard was saddened by the reports of Napoleon II's death in Austria. An ardent Bonapartist, Count Bertrand, contacted Brigadier Gerard. Bertrand had a startling revelation. In 1814 with his wife's compliance, Napoleon I had replaced his young son with an impostor. The real child was entrusted to Bertrand's care. Napoleon II was still alive! Documents proving this subterfuge were with the other papers buried by Gerard. Bertrand and Gerard unearthed the records. They presented them to the genuine Napoleon II.

"It was Bertrand's hope that Napoleon II would claim his birthright. However, Napoleon II declined. He felt his father had thrown Europe into a series of unnecessary wars. Napoleon II decided to live in obscurity under a false name.

"The real Napoleon II married twice. The first marriage ended without issue. When Napoleon II was a widower in his fifties, he fell in love with Anne-Marie Gerard, the Brigadier's granddaughter. She became his second wife.

"Rumors of Napoleon II's survival had reached the ears of the corrupt secret police of the Second Empire. Viewing Napoleon II's existence as a threat to Emperor Napoleon III's legitimacy, the secret police located the true heir to the Imperial throne. They murdered him in 1867, but his wife escaped. She sought refuge with her parents. Anne-Marie Bonaparte gave birth to triplets, two boys and a girl. In order to protect her offspring from the secret police, Anne-Marie decided to split up the children. Each son was given to the descendants of Brigadier Gerard's comrades from 1814. One brother was given to the Despienne family and the other to the Tremeau family. Anne-Marie kept custody of her daughter. She was raised under her mother's maiden name. As an extra precaution, the Despiennes were given all the documents proving the Napoleonic heritage of the triplets as well as Anne-Marie's engagement ring. The Tremeaus perished during the Prussian siege of Paris in 1870. Their foster son was consigned to an orphanage. When the foster son of the Despiennes was 16, he was accused of theft. Rather than face prosecution, he fled with all the documents proving his lineage.

"Ann-Marie's daughter was recruited as a model for a prosperous dressmaking firm. Can you guess which one, Antoine?"

"The Regenerator of Fashion. Its owner, Van Klopen, is on the High Council."

"Leontine told Van Klopen the story of her birth." resumed the Professor. "Another man might have dismissed her story as absurd, but Van Klopen wisely passed the information to me. I verified Leontine's ancestry. I have yet to trace the brother consigned to an orphanage, but I was delighted to find the other brother hiding under my own nose, Monsieur Boucher, or should I say Bonaparte."

"I prefer Boucher," said the young man. "It was through my mother's ring that you traced me."

"Her diamond engagement ring was very distinctive. It had a gold setting adorned with the eagle and bee from the Napoleonic coat of arms. You gave that ring to Meaghan Cullin. Your late fiancée showed the ring to Count Corbucci and Antonio Nikola, my associates on the High Council."

"You must have summoned me here to surrender the documents. What will the Black Coats do with them? Make me Emperor of France?"

"No, my dear brother," interjected Leontine. "The Black Coats shall make me Empress of France!"

"I won't have my birthright stolen, sister!"

"Be practical, Monsieur Boucher," advised the Professor. "To prove your true identity, you would have to answer to a charge of theft. You have squandered your own birthright."

"In exchange for the documents, I must be royally compensated," demanded Boucher.

"I intend to literally do that," promised the Professor handing Boucher a sheet of paper. "I have outlined a plan to replace Archduke Juan North of Heisse-Weimar with an impostor. I intend for the counterfeit Archduke to be you."

Boucher scrutinized the plan for several minutes before speaking. "Your price is acceptable. The documents are not in London. I will need a week to retrieve them."

The Professor smiled. "That interval is acceptable."

"I must compliment you," acknowledged Boucher. "You have surpassed the All-Father. He only trafficked in men pretending to be Louis XVII. You deal in genuine Napoleonic claimants."

After Boucher's departure, Madame Nemo rejoined the Professor and Leontine.

"There is still the matter of my other brother," said Leontine. "We can't have a rival heir."

"Once we have learned his whereabouts, he shall be assassinated," assured the Professor.

"There is also the matter of General Boulanger," observed Leontine. "Many in France view him as a military genius equal to my grandfather. As Minister of War, he conquered Indochina and outwitted Bismarck in the Schaebele Incident. Although he is no longer in the French Cabinet, support is growing for him to stage a coup."

"Leontine's fears are justified," confirmed Finola Moriarty. "A Napoleonic heir will be a viable alternative to a civilian government but not to a military dictatorship. We must ruin Boulanger's career."

"I have already factored in the threat of Boulanger," said the Professor. "I ordered Feliciana Sorelli to seduce him."

"But he proved totally resistant to her charms," countered Finola. "It will take a special woman to melt Boulanger's heart."

"There is an obvious solution," suggested Leontine. "I shall romance Boulanger."

"Too risky," objected the Professor. "You must remain in the background until the foundations have been laid for your political movement."

"I have a proposal," said Finola. "Let me organize a gala ball and invite female members of the Black Coats. This way you could pick the perfect temptress from multiple candidates."

"A wonderful idea!" exclaimed the Professor. "We can hold it in Paris."

"Marguerite can help me prepare the guest list," said Finola.

"Involve both Urania and Catarina as well," insisted the Professor. "I want peace in the family."

"I'll need someone to help with the decorations," noted Finola. "Evangeline Bramwell! She's a brilliant designer as well as an architect!"

"It's a pity that Evangeline is so near-sighted," complained the Professor. "Without her spectacles, she would probably be as alluring as the late Gloria Scot. A woman like Gloria would be the obvious choice to entrap Boulanger."

Finola resumed her musings. "I'll also need a person in charge of entertainment. Ida Similor can fill that role."

The Professor glared at his wife with disapproval. Finola was needling him. Six years ago, he had considered making Ida his mistress.

"Ida's a bungler! Ever since she failed to capture the Jade Seraph, I've relegated her to minor tasks."

"She may be a third-class criminal, but she's a first class entertainer," argued Finola.

"Your point is valid," conceded the Professor.

"I assume that I'm not invited to this ball." said Leontine.

"Correct," confirmed the Professor. "At this stage, only a few Black Coats must know of your existence."

Finola was consoling. "Don't be upset, Leontine. When you're Empress of France, you'll be running your own gala balls."

The ball was scheduled for early February. Due to her earlier failure to woo Boulanger, Feliciana Sorelli was not invited. Perusing the final guest list, the Professor noted a slot allocated without a name.

"Who is this mystery guest?" asked Professor Moriarty of his wife.

"Your sister-in-law insisted on an open slot. Catarina's in the process of hiring a new assistant."

In January 1889, Catarina Moriarty was staying at the Villa Corbucci in the Bay of Naples. A gold ring in the shape of a snake adorned her hand. It was a family heirloom. Her ancestors had worshipped the serpent god Set. She was fluent in the obscure Aklo language preserved by the cult of Set. Catarina kept a secret journal written in Aklo. This is an excerpt from that journal:

My life was ruined in 1879. My mother had been murdered by my father's enemies in the Camorra. I and my sister barely escaped with our lives. To guard against further assassination attempts, my father secreted me and Carolina in different locations. Carolina was the lucky one. She was sent to Texas to reside with my mother's relatives. Unfortunately, my father opted to keep me in Europe.

I was sixteen and hopelessly in love. My heart shall always belong to Antonio, the young man whom my father had adopted in Cuba. I remember when father first brought him into our ancestral home. Antonio was twelve, and I was five. From my first glimpse of him, I felt destined to be his wife.

Marguerite Chavain of the Black Coats advised my father to send me to the Fourneau College for Young Women. She was a graduate of that infernal institution. It is impossible for me to fathom Marguerite's motivations. Does she hate me? Does she have some grievance against my family? Or is she just committing wanton acts of cruelty?

When I became a student at the College, my noble surname of Corbucci was replaced by the alias of Koluchy. It was a precautionary measure to protect me from my father's enemies. I soon found myself the target of endless harassment by Madame Fourneau. Through simply using threats, she transformed me into her minion. For the rest of my life, I will always feel tarnished by the unspeakable acts that she perpetrated on my person.

After four years of a hellish vassalage, I found the means to alleviate my subjugation. Joséphine Balsamo came to the school. It was easy to direct Fourneau's attention to this youthful siren. Balsamo soon replaced me as Fourneau's personal slave.

I harbor no regrets regarding Balsamo's degradation. Her mother and namesake had been an enemy of my father. The elder Balsamo may even have played a hidden role in my mother's murder.

When I returned to Naples, my shame prompted me to keep quiet about Madame Fourneau's depravity. I asked to be married to Antonio immediately. My father declined on the grounds that an elaborate wedding needed to be planned. In order to sate my growing restlessness, my father entrusted me with a formidable task. I was placed in charge of one of the Neapolitan branches of the Black Coats, the Brotherhood of the Seven Kings. Inside the Brotherhood, I met Norman Head.

My ordeal at the Fourneau College caused me to doubt my own sexuality. I had nightmares that Antonio would find me inadequate on our wedding night. Although I possessed no affection for Norman, I felt compelled to have an assignation with him in order to prove my femininity. To my everlasting despair, my fiancé learned of my liaison. Antonio broke our engagement.

My squandering of Antonio's love had consequences. Like Lucretia Borgia, I became a pawn in dynastic politics. In order to secure our family's influence in the Black Coats, my father arranged my loveless marriage to Noel Moriarty, the brother of the Lord of the Night.

My efforts to reshape the Brotherhood continue. To achieve this goal, I need competent subordinates. I have decided to induct Balsamo into the Black Coats. Despite her arrogance, she has proven herself to be a competent seductress. In correspondence with Madame Fourneau, I have arranged for Balsamo to graduate early. Balsamo falsely believes that her role will be governess to my young son.

My father is opposed to this decision. His resentment towards Balsamo's mother hasn't mitigated. He fears that Balsamo shall betray me. I have suggest-

ed a compromise. Antonio will interview Balsamo when she arrives at the Villa Corbucci. He'll determine whether Balsamo can be trusted.

If Antonio rules against Balsamo, she would merely be given some duties as governess for the next few days to occupy her attention. After that short interval, my father would have Balsamo discretely killed.

When Joséphine disembarked at the Bay of Naples, she was met by a carriage which transported her to the Villa Corbucci. The driver, Stefano Baldi, escorted her into a private study.

Seated at a desk was a dark-haired man with a pale complexion and black eyes. On the smallest finger of his right hand was a ring similar to that worn by Catarina Moriarty.

"Signorina Balsamo, let me welcome you to the Villa Corbucci. I am Dr. Antonio Nikola, the family physician. I also serve as an unofficial councilor to His Excellency, Count Corbucci."

Joséphine extended her hand which Antonio gracefully kissed. He motioned for his guest to take a seat before returning to his desk.

"I'm somewhat confused, Doctor. What does the Corbucci family have to do with Signora Moriarty?"

"For his daughter's safety, the Count registered her at the Fourneau College under a false name. Catarina's maiden name is not Koluchy but Corbucci."

"I see. Signora Moriarty has already approved my employment. Why must I be interviewed by her father's representative?"

"His Excellency wishes assurances that you are the proper person to educate his grandson."

"I meet the requirements for a governess outlined in Signora Moriarty's letter. I am fluent in both Italian and English."

"It is not your qualifications that are in dispute, but your attitude towards the Corbucci family."

"Upon her graduation, Signora Moriarty sponsored me to be her successor as chief prefect. Why should I resent her?"

"Signora Moriarty briefly told me that you had to be reprimanded for unruly behavior at the College. As chief prefect, I assume Signorina Moriarty played some role in disciplining you."

"Any difficulties that I had with Signorina Moriarty in our student days were solely the fault of the school's headmistress."

"In what way?"

"Madame Fourneau liked to manipulate her students to compete against each other."

"When you knew Signorina at the College, you were unaware of her association with the Corbucci family. Have you ever heard of her father?"

"When I was very young, I heard my mother mention him."

"What did she say about His Excellency?"

"My mother spoke about Count Corbucci in unflattering terms. I assumed that His Excellency was a business competitor."

"Do you share your mother's animosity towards His Excellency?"

"Before I answer, may I ask you a few questions, Doctor?"

"In light of your frank responses, your request is extremely fair."

"Is your mother alive?"

"No. She died during my youth in Cuba."

"How did she perish?"

"From starvation."

"Do you hold anyone responsible for her demise?"

"Don de Silvestre, the governor of Cuba."

"I've heard of him. Don de Silvestre was killed by an assassin. You must view the assassin favorably."

"I do, Signorina."

"My mother was brutally butchered. I live only to avenge her. Whatever adversarial relationship Count Corbucci had with my mother, he bears no responsibility for her death. My hatred is solely reserved for those who murdered my mother."

"And if Count Corbucci or his daughter could help you achieve your vengeance?"

"They would have my undying loyalty."

Dr. Nikola raised no objections to Joséphine's induction into the Black Coats. He swiftly arranged a meeting between Catarina Moriarty and Joséphine. Catarina informed Joséphine of the real position that she was being offered. Accepting Catarina's proposal, Joséphine proposed an elaborate scheme to destroy Madame Fourneau.

"We both have reasons to extinguish Madame Fourneau," admitted Catarina. "She abused both of us horribly. However, there are certain factors that must be taken into account. Are you familiar with Professor Marguerite Chavain?"

"Madame Fourneau praised her constantly," noted Joséphine. "The stellar graduate of the College! An accomplished botanist! Essays published by the Academy of Science!"

"Chavain is an influential member of the Neptune Society, the scientific branch of the Black Coats. She has hired other graduates of the College. They have even created an unofficial Alumnae Association. I am a member of this Association. It would be prudent for you to join it."

"Chavain would violently object to the annihilation of Madame Fourneau. Is Chavain a member of the High Council?"

"I and Madame Nemo are the only women on the High Council. Madame Nemo is Chavain's patron."

"The wife of the Lord of the Night! Her husband use to give me candy when he visited my mother. What exactly is Chavain's relationship with Madame Nemo? Has Madame Nemo supplanted Madame Fourneau on the botanist's heart?"

Catarina grinned. "The alliance between Chavain and Madame Nemo is purely professional. The Neptune Society is jointly managed by Madame Nemo and her step-daughter. The two women are constantly at loggerheads. Chavain cultivates my sister-in-law by supporting her against my niece."

"Madame Nemo is your sister-in-law!"

"Monsieur Nemo's real name is Professor James Moriarty. He is Noel's brother."

"Tell me more about your niece."

"She uses her late mother's surname. She's called Urania Caber. She inherited her father's brilliance but not his ruthlessness. In fact, Urania is somewhat squeamish. She has degrees in medicine and astronomy. Urania recently authored a book on the stars, *Luminary Leeway*."

"Do you have a copy of this book?"

"Yes."

"Please loan it to me. I want to read it."

"Why?"

"I intend to befriend Urania. She might be a useful ally against Chavain."

"A clever stratagem, but we must not antagonize Chavain openly. We will defer implementation of your plan against Madame Fourneau for the time being. There's another issue to discuss."

Catarina handed Joséphine a photograph. It was of a corpse with a skeletal face.

"Who is this?" asked Joséphine.

"He is the first Revenant, the man who slaughtered your mother. The Black Coats uncovered proof of his demise. Unfortunately, a female Revenant emerged after he died."

Joséphine didn't believe this assertion. She had seen the face of the "first" Revenant. It had been the countenance of a woman with red hair. The "first" Revenant had been a male impersonator. The Revenant must have faked the death of her masculine alter ego and then pretended to be a feminine successor. There must be only one Revenant. Rather than divulge her suspicions to Catarina, Joséphine opted to remain silent.

"There is one final matter, Joséphine. You must be measured for a gown. You'll be attending a gala ball in February."

The gala celebration held in Paris became famous in criminal annals as the Ball of the Black Coats. A large banquet hall was rented for the evening. Nearly every member of the High Council was present. Two notable absentees were Count Corbucci and Antonio Nikola. Detained by business in Naples, Count

Corbucci had tried to persuade Antonio to attend. Corbucci perceived Antonio as a surrogate son. Ever since the dissolution of his engagement to Catarina, Corbucci had hoped that Antonio would find another woman to bring him happiness. This gala ball would be the perfect opportunity for Antonio to pursue a romance. Antonio's absence fueled the rumor that he was a misogynist.

Since Antonio declined, Corbucci arranged for his nephew, Bruno Relli, to attend. Relli was a leading member of the Camorra, one of the Neapolitan subsidiaries of the Black Coats, Acclaimed as a music composer, he was a dashing bachelor with thick black hair. Catarina was pleased that Relli was attending. She hoped to play the role of matchmaker for her cousin. To Catarina's delight, Relli became immediately infatuated with one of her friends at the ball. In fact, Relli composed an ode to this lady and played it on the piano.

The object of Relli's affection was Evangeline Bramwell. She seemed to be around the age of 35. She wore large tinted spectacles of an azure hue. Her hair was blonde. Besides having a degree in architecture, she had designed the decorations at the gala. Although her glasses marred her facial beauty, Relli was impressed by both her wit and artistic talent.

The female criminals at the ball were dressed in elegant gowns. The notable exception was Petra Donevitch. Her attire was singularly masculine. Clad in pants, boots, a frilled shirt and a dress jacket, she resembled a modern version of Beau Brummel. Clutched in her gloved hands was a cane whose handle was carved in the image of a skull. Parted down the middle, her black hair was styled like a bowl cut.

Petra instantly became the subject of gossip among two other brunettes at the ball.

"Has that Croatian woman lost her mind?" asked Finola Moriarty.

"Actually her clothes suit her very well," replied Marguerite Chavain. "Notice how all the men are clustering around her. She seems to have favored Horace Dorrington. The two are going off somewhere."

"Dorrington is actually escorting Petra to see my husband. She is a versatile painter. Jim has an artistic commission for her."

Ida Similor was the only woman whose attire resembled Petra's. However, her garb resembling that of a ringmaster was viewed as appropriate to all the participants. To entertain the guests, Ida had imported a group of young boxers to compete against one another. The red-haired Ida functioned as both the announcer and referee in the boxing ring. Unlike regular prizefights, there were no formal rules of engagement. The contestants wore no gloves. They were allowed to kick, gouge and bite. The only similarity to a regular boxing competition was that a fallen combatant was declared defeated after a count of ten.

The hosts of the gala celebration took bets on the fights. The main match pitted Steve Dixie against Sam Merton. Dixie was of African descent. Because most of the attendees were racial bigots, it was inconceivable to them that a black man could defeat a white man. The betting was heavily on Merton. This proved to be a costly miscalculation. Merton was nearly beaten to a pulp by Dixie. Professor Moriarty, alias Monsieur Nemo, was quite pleased with the substantial profit made from all the betting on Merton.

While the majority of the guests were watching the final round of fisticuffs, one of the assistant hostesses left the match to get a glass of sherry. At the bar, she was accosted by a woman wearing an elegant green gown.

"Excuse me. Do you know where I can find Catarina Nemo?"

"She's watching the boxing matches."

"A boxing match! I've read about them in the newspapers. Are they following the Queensbury rules?"

"There are no rules in these matches. I didn't see you when I was helping Madame Nemo greet the guests."

"I just arrived. My gown from Van Klopen's was delivered late. My name is Joséphine Balsamo."

"I am Urania Caber."

"The author of *Luminary Leeway*?"

"The same."

"I loved your book!"

What followed next was an intensive discussion of constellations and asteroids. Urania was delighted to meet someone who shared her interest in astronomy.

"I need your advice, Urania. I understand you're a medical practitioner."

"Yes. Is something ailing you?"

"No. My sister Sabine wants to become a doctor. Do you know a medical school that wouldn't be prejudiced against female applicants?"

"My alma mater, St. Swithin's, is very open-minded. Does your sister speak English?

"Yes, Sabine's very studious. She skipped a grade at the Marie Gilbert School."

"I assume that your sister is still studying in France."

"Yes. She's in her second year of college."

"Her chances of acceptance of St. Swithin's would be better if she spent her final two years at an English college. One of my Neptune Society colleagues is the Chancellor of Brichester University. He could easily arrange your sister's transfer."

"Thank you, Urania. Please excuse me. I must tell Catarina that I'm here."

As Joséphine was walking towards the boxing ring, she passed a couple. A mustached man of military bearing was conversing with a flamboyantly dressed brunette holding a photograph.

"This photograph will be a superb basis for one of your paintings, Petra."

"Monsieur Nemo has provocative tastes, Horace."

Hearing Professor Moriarty's alias, Joséphine glanced over Petra's shoulder. The photograph showed a dead woman with a dagger in her heart. Joséphine recognized the corpse's face. It was the face of the Revenant!

Joséphine impulsively grabbed the photograph out of the brunette's hand. With her right hand, Petra pulled the skull on her cane. A sword was revealed. With extreme alacrity, Petra pointed her blade at Joséphine's forehead.

"Unless you want your brains punctured, I suggest returning my property," snarled Petra.

Joséphine extended the photograph. Petra seized it. Her sword remained in its threatening position.

"We have not been formally introduced, my pretty thief. I am Princess Petra Donevitch."

"I am Joséphine Balsamo."

The dark eyes of Petra Donevitch narrowed.

"There was an earlier woman with the same name. They called her the White Stalker."

"I am her great-granddaughter."

"There is a chapter on your great-grandmother in a book entitled *Nameless Cults*. It tells of a feud between your ancestor and an accomplished duelist, Maria Kratides. Your ancestor was easily defeated by Maria in a sword duel in Moldavia. The only reason that the original Joséphine survived was because her sister interfered. Maria and Joséphine crossed blades again in Brittany. This time your ancestor was victorious. After slaying Maria, Joséphine performed acts of revelry over her corpse. Rather than give her fallen adversary a decent burial, your ancestor kicked Maria's body into the sea."

"The British translation of Von Junzt's *Nameless Cults* is riddled with inaccurate summarizations of the German passages," maintained Joséphine. "Your version of Maria's death is false."

"The Dusseldorf edition is impossible to find."

"My later mother owned a copy which I read."

"Can you produce this Dusseldorf edition of *Nameless Cults*?"

"My mother sold it to pay her debts."

"How convenient."

Petra's sword continued to threaten Joséphine's forehead. Since the last boxing match had concluded, a crowd began to gather around the female antagonists.

"Do you recognize my dueling technique?" asked Petra.

"It's the Vautrin thrust. My great-grandmother mastered it."

"She used it to slay Maria. That fact prompted me to learn it."

"Why are you obsessed with Maria Kratides?"

"Maria was my great-grandmother. There is a blood debt between our two families, Joséphine Balsamo. I intend to collect it!"

"Princess Petra!" yelled a masculine voice. "Cease and desist! Return your sword to its scabbard."

The speaker was Professor Moriarty.

Petra sheathed her blade. "As you command, Monsieur Nemo!"

Moriarty scrutinized the blonde woman involved in the disturbance.

"You must be the daughter of Gloria Scot. You greatly resemble your mother."

"Like my great-grandmother, my mother's real name was Joséphine Balsamo. I am proud to bear the same name."

Moriarty turned towards Petra. "Princess, you owe Mademoiselle Balsamo an apology."

Joséphine raised her hand bearing the ring formerly owned by the White Stalker.

"That won't be necessary, Monsieur Nemo. Even if this self-styled Princess rendered me an apology, I would refuse to accept it."

Removing the glove from her left hand, Petra slapped Joséphine's face.

"Joséphine Balsamo, I challenge you to a duel."

"Petra!" shouted Moriarty.

"Please do not intervene, Monsieur Nemo," requested Joséphine. "I fight my own battles. Petra Donevitch, I accept. As the challenged, it is my right to choose the weapons for our contest."

"Choose what you wish," replied Petra. Putting her hands on her hips, she leaned forward and pushed her face close to Joséphine's. "I have expertise in all forms of combat."

"I choose fisticuffs," said Joséphine. "We have here a boxing ring, a proven referee and established rules of engagement. There is no reason to delay."

Before the bout began, there was a demand from the crowd to bet on the contest.

"We can't take bets, Jim," cautioned Finola. "Everyone will bet on Petra Donevitch. All our profits from the Merton-Dixie fight won't cover our losses."

"I shall cover all bets," decreed Professor Moriarty.

As Finola predicted, all the bets were on Petra Donevitch. The largest bet was made by Horace Dorrington.

Petra Donevitch removed her jacket before entering the ring. She handed it and her cane to Dorrington. Joséphine was still wearing her expensive gown.

Ida Similor stood in the middle of the boxing ring.

"Ladies and Gentlemen of the Night! This is an unscheduled bout. In this corner is Princess Petra Donevitch of Croatia, the Balkan Tigress!" Huge applause and cheers erupted from the spectators. "In this corner is Joséphine Balsamo of France, the Blonde Brawler!" Only Urania Caber clapped.

"May the two contestants come to the middle of the ring," requested Ida.

The two adversaries positioned themselves on either side of Ida.

"Do either of you have anything to say before fighting begins?" asked the referee.

"I think we need to discuss the rules," stated Joséphine with great trepidation in her voice

The crowd laughed.

Placing her hands on her hips, Petra leaned forward and pushed her face close to Joséphine's. "Fool! There are no rules!"

Joséphine delivered a vicious uppercut into the jaw of her overconfident opponent. Petra staggered backward. Joséphine delivered two more punches to Petra's face. Petra fell backwards against the ropes. Joséphine delivered a devastating series of punches to Petra's midriff. Grabbing Petra's black locks with both hands, Joséphine pulled her off the ropes. Joséphine dragged her woozy enemy to the center of the ring. Extending her legs backwards, Joséphine dropped to the ground taking Petra with her. The brunette's face slammed into the ground. Joséphine rose to her full height leaving a senseless Petra on the floor.

Ida began the count. "One...Two..."

"I protest!" roared Dorrington. "The match never officially began!"

"Petra said there were no rules!" shouted Urania.

Ida was nearing the end of the count. "Eight...Nine...Ten!" The redhead raised the blonde's hand in victory. "I declare Joséphine Balsamo to be the winner!"

"France has conquered Croatia!" yelled Joséphine. She danced the Can-Can around the prostrate Petra. Joséphine concluded her performance by kicking Petra's hip. The unconscious brunette rolled under the ropes of the raised platform. She would have landed on the floor if Dorrington hadn't caught her.

"Remove the Princess!" ordered Professor Moriarty.

"She'll be extremely angry when she wakes up." replied Dorrington.

"I'll deal with that later," answered Moriarty. He approached Urania. "You appear to have become very friendly with Joséphine. Please bring her to my private conference room."

Joséphine Balsamo was alone with Professor Moriarty.

"Your late mother utilized a title inherited from her grandmother," said Moriarty. She would want me to address you by that title. You are Countess Cagliostro."

"Thank you, Monsieur Nemo."

"You're welcome. Dorrington informed me that your dispute with Petra Donevitch involved a photograph. Why are you interested in this photograph?"

"I've seen the face of the dead woman before."

"Under what circumstances?"

"It was before my mother's death. The woman was wearing a Revenant's costume."

"I can explain what you saw. I have deduced the origin of the first Revenant. Your mother left a woman, Darlla Rassendyll, to drown in the underground lake beneath the Paris Opera House. She was rescued by a recluse with a skeletal face. This hermit has been dubbed the Phantom of the Opera. Romancing the Phantom, she convinced him to seek vengeance on your mother and the Black Coats. The Phantom became the first Revenant. Using the alias of the Acolyte, Darlla sometimes assisted the Revenant. When I and your mother first encountered the original Revenant at Colonel Bozzo-Corona's tomb, the Acolyte confused us by also wearing a Revenant costume. Eventually, the Revenant became infatuated with an opera singer, Christine Daae. A jealous Darlla slew her philandering lover. The death of the first Revenant was witnessed by one of my agents. That agent stabbed Darlla in the heart. Another member of the Black Coats photographed the corpses of the Revenant and the Acolyte."

"How do you explain the existence of the present female Revenant?"

"When the female vigilante first appeared, she claimed that the first Revenant had multiple Acolytes. She identified herself as one of these Acolytes. Possibly the second Revenant was recruited by the Phantom of the Opera to assist him and Darlla in the original campaign against us. Our intelligence indicated that the current Revenant has several Acolytes to support her."

"Including the so-called Jade Seraph, the woman who abducted me as the Green Lamia."

"You can ask Ida Similor about the Seraph. Ida was the referee in your boxing match. She knows the former Lamia very well, Countess. According to Leonard Scot, you saw the Lamia defeated in combat by a woman. Was Rassendyll the woman?"

"Yes."

"I had falsely concluded that it was the woman who became the second Revenant," confessed Nemo.

"Can I have the names of Darlla Rassendyll's killer and the photographer?"

"That information is classified. You don't have the proper clearance yet."

"What must I do to gain the proper clearance?"

"You must perform three tasks successfully for me. I already have the first for you."

"I report to your sister-in-law in the Brotherhood of the Seven Kings, Monsieur Nemo."

"There will be no difficulty in gaining Catarina's cooperation. You are to seduce General Boulanger. You shall be provided with a Parisian residence and a false identity. Your great-great-grandfather sometimes posed as Count de Fenix. You can be Countess de Fenix."

"I will need a maid in my new identity. Can Ida Similor assume that function?"

"Yes. Servitude suits her."

Following his interview with Joséphine, Moriarty inquired about Horace Dorrington. He was informed that Dorrington had taken the slumbering Petra to a bedroom to recover from her thrashing.

When Moriarty entered the bedroom, he discovered that Petra was awake. Furthermore, she was naked in bed with Horace Dorrington.

"My apologies for interrupting, Princess Petra," said Moriarty. "I merely came to issue an order. Do not engage in any retaliation against Joséphine Balsamo. Congratulations on your speedy recovery. Your recuperation has permitted a wrestling bout with Monsieur Dorrington. I declare you the victor. It's clear that you have your opponent pinned to the mat."

Soon after Joséphine was installed as the Countess de Fenix, she interviewed her new maid. Ida Similor was almost eight years older than her employer.

"Your mother would be proud of you, Countess," said Ida.

"You knew my mother?"

"I had indirect dealings with her. Your uncle acted as an intermediary."

"Leonard Scot isn't really my uncle. I lost all contact with him during my time in Provence. Do you know where he is?"

"He lives in London." Ida wrote on a sheet of paper. "This is his address."

"Thank you, Ida. I'm informed that you are both a fire eater and a knife thrower. Do you have any experience with swords?"

"I'm an experienced fencer."

"Excellent. The Fourneau College for Young Women doesn't include fencing in its curriculum. My recent encounter with Petra Donevitch had made this gap in my education a liability. One of your duties will be to train me in sword fighting. Are you familiar with the Vautrin thrust?"

"Only by reputation, Countess."

"We shall both learn the thrust. I have my mother's dueling manual. She described the technique in great detail."

Weeks later, a special delivery package arrived at the Fenix household. Ida took it to her employer who was busy putting on her makeup. Opening the package, Joséphine took out a sword cane made exactly to her specifications. The head of the cane was a golden ram.

In April 1889, a major political event transpired in France. The French government decided to arrest General Boulanger on charges of conspiracy. The evidence against Boulanger was very weak. If Boulanger had bravely faced the charges, he could easily have been acquitted. Such a victory would have made him more powerful than ever. Instead, Boulanger fled the country to the shock of his supporters. As a consequence, his political movement totally collapsed.

It is generally believed that a woman prevailed upon Boulanger to flee. Many believe that this woman was Boulanger's mistress, Madame de

Bonnemains. However, the legend persists that Boulanger had briefly deserted his mistress for an enigmatic woman called the Countess de Fenix. It became impossible to verify this rumor because both the Countess and her maid vanished from their residence in Paris.

In May, Joséphine was at Noel Moriarty's house in Pavia. With the disgrace of Boulanger, she was again receiving her orders directly from Catarina Moriarty. The two women were discussing personnel issues in the Brotherhood of the Seven Kings.

"A handful of students will be graduating from the Fourneau College soon," observed Catarina. "I would rather see them inducted into the Brotherhood than ushered into the Neptune Society by Chavain."

"There are two graduates worthy to be your lieutenants," said Joséphine. "Both were my junior prefects at the College. Their names are Rochelle Moreau and Orianne Coyatier."

"Moreau was the name of Madame Fourneau's lawyer."

"Rochelle is his niece. She is a naturally born organizer."

"Orianne's surname is intriguing. The All-Father employed an assassin named Coyatier."

"She was very circumspect about her background, but her personality is that of a killer. Orianne's as cold-blooded as a fish. Her hobby is taxidermy."

"Both will be valuable additions to our ranks. Now that we have concluded business, we can discuss pleasure. You and I have been invited to a wedding in Naples!"

"Who's getting married?"

"My cousin Bruno. His fiancée, Evangeline Bramwell, has just arrived from England. She insisted that you be invited to her wedding."

"But I've never met Mademoiselle Bramwell."

"Very strange. Evangeline seems to be very familiar with you."

During the wedding celebration at the Villa Corbucci, the spectacled Evangeline took Joséphine aside. The two blondes met privately in Evangeline's quarters.

"You're probably wondering why you were invited, Joséphine. When I saw you win the boxing match, I was immediately struck by the resemblance."

"Resemblance?" questioned Joséphine. "Did you know my mother?"

"I never had the pleasure."

"Then you must have seen a portrait of my great-grandmother."

"I'm extremely familiar with the White Stalker, but I've never seen any artistic rendering of her,"

"Then who are you talking about?"

"My own great-grandmother. There is a portrait of her in the family estate in England. She was born in Martinique during 1774. As a young girl, she was hired as a servant by a wealthy family. In 1795, she traveled with her employers to New England. There she married a wealthy American. Unfortunately, her bigoted father-in-law resented her humble roots. My great-grandparents felt compelled to leave for England. In the 1870's, I traveled to Martinique and America to research my ancestral roots. In Martinique, I found my great-grandmother's employment contract."

Evangeline retrieved a document from a nearby desk. There were two signatures

"Do you recognize the august name of the Countess who hired my great-grandmother?"

"This Countess was the daughter of Andrée Tascher de la Pagerie!" gasped Joséphine. "Andrée was the aunt of my great-great-grandmother, Joséphine Tascher de la Pagerie."

"It was a common practice for the nobility to hire as servants illegitimate children sired by family members. My great-grandmother could easily have been the Countess's niece."

"I would love to see the portrait of your great-grandmother."

"I could do better than that, Joséphine." Evangeline removed her heavy spectacles. "I resemble my great-grandmother."

"You look like..."

"Like you. Many people would mistakenly assume that I'm your older sister, Joséphine. You must be around 21. I'm 35."

"35," muttered Joséphine. "That was my mother's age when she died."

The Black Coats had given Joséphine Balsamo a house in Pavia. Her household staff now included a butler. He was the man called Leonard Scot. Joséphine has very warm feelings towards Leonard. She loved him like a father.

"This Evangeline Relli bothers me," said Leonard.

"Why?" asked Joséphine. "She's very sweet."

"Remember your family legends? Have you forgotten Alexis Duvalier?"

"The immortal witch shot by my great-grandmother."

"The White Stalker never found her body. Evangeline could be Alexis or even her descendant."

"But I saw the employment contract of Evangeline's great-grandmother. Alexis Duvalier was in the Grimoire household when that young maid was hired."

"The maid may have existed, but there's no corroboration of the rest of Evangeline's story. That whole American episode sounds like a Gothic melodrama."

"There's only one way to be sure, Leonard. You must travel to the United States and verify the existence of Evangeline's great-grandparents."

At an orientation meeting for the two newest members of the Brotherhood of the Seven Kings, Rochelle Moreau and Orianne Coyatier, Catarina had an announcement.

"I shall be utilizing the alias of Madame Koluchy. Henceforth, all my subordinates without exception shall address me as Madame."

Joséphine Balsamo was assisting in the orientation. "May I bring up a related matter, Madame?"

"Yes, Mademoiselle Balsamo."

"Your brother-in-law, the Lord of the Night, has graciously recognized my title of Countess Cagliostro. It is only fitting that my colleagues in all the branches of the Black Coats address me as Countess."

"Your point is well taken," acknowledged Catarina. "Of course, as your superior, I shall call you Joséphine."

"Of course, Madame."

It was July in Paris when Petra Donevitch received a message to meet Evangeline Relli at the house of a man named Johann Grimm. Petra was dressed only slightly less provocatively than at the Ball of the Black Coats. Her ensemble comprised her sword cane and a black derby. Her gloves and boots were also black, but her shirt, jacket and pants were gray.

When she knocked on the door, it was answered by a man whose age seemed around 50. Introducing himself as Johann Grimm, he directed Petra towards a drawing room. Hanging over the fireplace was a painting of a brunette holding a sword. She was garbed in red pants and boots. A brassiere with designs of crimson eyes shielded her breasts. An amulet in the image of a golden bat was chained around her neck. A red cape draped her body. The portrait bore a signature: *Alexis Duvalier*.

"Maria Kratides!" uttered Petra.

"Your likeness is uncannily close to your ancestor's, Princess," remarked Evangeline Relli still wearing her spectacles. "Do you recognize the signature on the painting?"

"Alexis Duvalier was an ally of my forebear. According to *Nameless Cults*, Alexis was shot by the White Stalker."

"She was only wounded. Alexis later returned to the Pointe du Raz." Evangeline opened a drawer and pulled out an object. "She found something that had washed ashore."

"Maria's amulet," announced Petra.

Evangeline handed the amulet to Petra. "Your veins contain the blood of Maria Kratides. You are the rightful owner."

"What is your connection to Alexis Duvalier?"

"She was the twin sister of my great-grandmother. You must never tell this to Joséphine Balsamo."

"That blonde strumpet! I have no reason to confide in her. A Donevitch always pays her debts. If you ever need a favor, you have only to ask."

The female duelist left the house. Evangeline was joined in the drawing room by Johann Grimm.

"I don't understand why you waste your time, Evangeline, in these petty intrigues," said Grimm. "You only have a decade left to bring the King in Yellow to Earth."

"The Black Coats are the key to the second coming of Zukala-Koth! I must rise high in their ranks. The High Council is meeting at Van Klopen's Regenerator of Fashion. My husband has just become a member of the Council."

"I don't see how Petra fits into all of this."

"I haven't forgotten my pledge to decimate the Cagliostro family. Petra will become a thrall of the Great Vampire. He will use her to destroy the current Joséphine Balsamo."

"And if Petra fails?"

"I have deluded Joséphine into believing that I am her cousin. My odd resemblance to the White Stalker is working to my advantage."

"Surely Joséphine knows that her great-grandmother had an enemy who looked like her. Joséphine could deduce that you're really Alexis Duvalier."

"Fortunately, I had a twin sister. I told Joséphine that I visited the Western Hemisphere in the 1870's. I really went there in 1842. I discovered that my sister had two children by her American husband. In 1840, my nephew and niece left England to visit their father's relatives in Maine. My sister's children then disappeared from history."

"Do you have any idea what happened to them?"

"They announced their intention to return to England. My suspicion is that the ship transporting them was lost at sea."

"Your American relatives were nothing like you, Evangeline. They weren't the sort of people who would be associated with witchcraft and vampirism."

"Precisely. Posing as my niece, I returned to England. When I performed the Rite of Rejuvenation in 1874, I pretended to be my niece's granddaughter."

"You're so diabolical, Evangeline. If only I had another servitor like you. I should have persuaded your mother to give me both her daughters in Martinique."

"You probably would have been disappointed by my sister. By all accounts, she was a naïve weakling ill-suited for scheming."

"At least she would have looked exactly like you."

"Don't be so sure, Johann. Not every pair of twins is identical. There could have been significant differences in our features."

In a conference room at the Regenerator of Fashion in Paris, the High Council of the Back Coats was in session. Two men had just been formally inducted into the Council. One was Bruno Relli. The other was Herbert de Lernac, a resourceful French assassin. After the initiation ceremony, the Lord of the Night addressed the Council.

"With the disgrace of Boulanger, we move to the next phase of our plan to control France. All of us made considerable profits by manipulating the stock of Ferdinand de Lesseps's Panama Canal Company. Not only did we bribe French regulators to withhold information about the Company's precarious financial status, we also bribed French and Colombian politicians to issue false reports about the progress of the canal. In February of this year, the bankrupt Panama Canal Company was liquidated. As the years progress, this financial crisis shall escalate into a cause célèbre. Over a hundred members of the French Parliament shall be discredited. The atmosphere will exist for a coup proclaiming Leontine Bonaparte the Empress of France!"

As she went to bed, Petra Donevitch felt the urge to wear her great-grandmother's talisman. In her dreams, she found herself in a land of mists. She beheld a bearded stranger with fiery eyes.

"Come, Petra, enter a world without death; a world where all your desires are satiated; a world where all your cravings for carnage and conquest become real."

The bearded man embraced Petra. His hands caressed her body. His lips touched her flesh. In this realm of illusion, Petra reached levels of canal pleasure far beyond those she had experienced in the waking world.

"What is your name, my love," asked Petra.

"You know my name."

"Yes. There can only be one name for a man like you."

"Say my name."

"*Master.*"

The bearded man haunted Petra's dreams in the weeks that followed. No matter what attire she wore, Petra always kept the talisman on her person. Beneath her clothes, the amulet rested hidden against her skin.

The Alumnae Association of the Fourneau College congregated at Marguerite Chavain's domicile in Paris. Among the ladies present were Catarina Koluchy, Joséphine Balsamo, Rochelle Moreau and Orianne Coyatier.

"Madame Fourneau's birthday is in September," said Marguerite. I expect everyone to contribute towards a gift.'

Marguerite passed a small collection basket around. All the women donated money.

"I will be personally delivering our gift to Madame Fourneau at the College on her birthday. This Association is composed of representatives of the Neptune Society and the Brotherhood of the Seven Kings. I am the most senior member here of the Neptune Society. It would be fitting that a person of equal rank represents the Brotherhood."

"Alas, Professor Chavain, I will be dining with my brother-in-law and his wife on that day," claimed Catarina.

"Excuse me, Madame," interrupted Joséphine. "I will be happy to go as your deputy."

"You have my permission," replied Catarina, "but Madame Fourneau must remain ignorant that her former students are a growing clique inside the Black Coats. Madame Fourneau falsely believes that you are merely my governess. That pretense must continue."

"Exactly my intention, Madame," professed Joséphine.

Joséphine and Catarina were alone in a dressing room at the Regenerator of Fashion. They were trying on dresses.

"You only wear green or gray," commented Catarina. "You really should diversify, Joséphine."

"It was a green dress that Madame Fourneau had torn off my body before she flogged me. Remember the plan that I proposed in January?"

"This would be the perfect time to implement it. You would be planting the seeds of Madame Fourneau's downfall right under the nose of her toadying Marguerite!"

"Do I have your authorization?"

Catarina extended her right hand. *"Will there be daylight?"*

"It will be daylight from midnight to noon if it's the will of the Mother," replied Joséphine. She kissed Catarina's snake ring.

"I've seen many corpses," said Dorrington, "but none more beautiful than her."

"Her vibrant existence was snuffed out much too early," contended Albert Van Klopen, the acclaimed fashion designer. "Her death is a major loss to the Black Coats."

Petra Donevitch was lying dead at their feet. Minus her jacket and derby, Petra was dressed exactly as she had been on the day of her visit to Evangeline Relli. Someone had impaled Petra from behind with her own sword cane,

Dorrington was a blackmailer who posed as a private inquiry agent. In a perverse way, he had the mind of a detective. To Dorrington, the identity of Petra's slayer was obvious. Petra had been living in the Latin Quarter with her cousin, Sophie Kratides. Sophie was a Greek heiress whose surviving relatives had seen her for years. The Lord of the Night had ordered Petra to kill Sophie and usurp her identity. Control of the Kratides fortune would be a major asset for the Black Coats.

Petra was a virtuoso in two arts, murder and painting. Professor Moriarty had admired her portraits so much that he had commissioned two works by her.

Petra hadn't even started *The Acolyte's Execution,* a commemoration of the alleged assassination of Darlla Rassendyll, but the talented Croatian had finished *The Brigand Princess,* a portrait predicting the liquidation of Sophie Kratides, The painting depicted Petra driving her sword into Sophie from behind. *The Brigand Princess* rested on a stand next to Petra's carcass.

Dorrington and Van Klopen had learned of Petra's death from Feliciana Sorelli whom Petra had intended to use as a model in *The Acolyte's Execution.* Feliciana maintained that she had found the body after arriving for her first posing session.

"It's clear what transpired," argued Dorrington. "Sophie stumbled upon *The Brigand Painting* and realized Petra's homicidal intentions. Sophie then stabbed Petra and fled."

"We have to bury the body," said Van Klopen. "We can use the basement."

"She won't be buried like this," insisted Dorrington. He yanked the sword out Petra's back. "She had an Amazon's soul. Let her blade be buried by her side."

Van Klopen noticed a bulge under Petra's clothing. "There's something under her shirt. The dressmaker reached under Petra's collar. He pulled out the Amulet of Lilitu.

"This is solid gold."

"Put it back!" demanded Dorrington. "She once was my lover. I won't have her remains pilfered."

The two criminals buried Petra Donevitch in the basement of the house. Dorrington removed *The Brigand Princess* in order to deliver it to Professor Moriarty.

Petra Donevitch's painting hung in the London residence of Finola Moriarty. The Professor showed it to his dinner guests in September. The guests were Mr. and Mrs. Noel Moriarty, Mr. and Mrs. Bruno Relli, and Herbert de Lernac. The Professor informed his guests of Petra's fate. The evening conversation soon turned to another matter.

"Louis Caratal has emerged as a major threat to our Napoleonic project," said the Professor. "Caratal is an examining magistrate. Having heard of the Black Coats during his youth in Corsica, Caratal is convinced that our confederacy is behind the Panama Canal Scandal. He is orchestrating inquiries in Paris."

"No one would believe Caratal's ravings," contended Bruno.

"Not without evidence," added Noel. "The danger is that Caratal's inquiries may gather proof of the true sources of the bribes."

"I know that I'm not a member of the High Council," admitted Evangeline, "but can I make a proposal."

"Your opinion is valued, Evangeline," assured the Professor.

"This situation reminds me of the crisis that menaced the Black Coats in the 1830's. Another magistrate with roots in Corsica accumulated evidence against the Black Coats. The All-Father used a woman to neutralize the magistrate. Perhaps a woman could be used to checkmate Caratal."

"Do you have any particular woman in mind, Evangeline?" questioned Herbert.

"Joséphine Balsamo," replied Bruno's wife.

"An excellent suggestion," avowed the Professor.

"If Joséphine gets close to Caratal, she could warn us if his investigation ever bears fruit," predicted Herbert.

"Where is Joséphine now?" asked the Professor.

"She's visiting her former teacher in Provence," disclosed Catarina.

"Telegraph her to come to Paris." dictated the Lord of the Night.

"Joséphine will need somewhere to stay in Paris," said Evangeline. "Since Petra Donevitch's domicile in the Latin Quarter is now vacant, Joséphine could stay there."

The Professor indicated his approval. "Another excellent suggestion. Bruno, your wife's contributions to our discussions have been extremely beneficial. Please pay tribute to her with the composition bearing her name."

Acceding to the Professor's request, Bruno walked over to the expensive piano that the Professor and Finola had purchased for their daughter. The room was soon filled with the entrancing notes of *Ode to Evangeline*.

The Fourneau College for Young Women had a room reserved for the exclusive use of its prefects. The current head prefect had entertained her predecessor there for the last ninety minutes.

Irene Tupin sat in a chair in front of a mirror. She had just finished buttoning her brown blouse. Irene was knotting her black tie as her dark hair was being tied in a French braid by Joséphine Balsamo.

"You never could keep your hands away from my hair," said Irene. "I didn't displace any of your lovely curls."

"That's because your hands were busy elsewhere," joked Joséphine.

"Actually I was afraid of dislodging your hairpin. Is the pin's head a golden ram?"

"Yes, it is." Removing the pin from her hair, Joséphine held it in front of Irene's eyes.

"Is the rest of the pin silver?"

"You truly have an artist's eye." Joséphine returned it to her hair. She briefly continued to work on Irene's hair. "Your braid is finished."

As Irene rose from the chair, she brushed off her black shirt.

"I'm glad that you came with Professor Chavain, Joséphine. Once Madame Fourneau saw her, she lost all interest in you. I hated it when I was forced to share you with her."

"Madame Fourneau created many obstacles for us. When we first met, she manipulated me into persecuting you. I still can't forgive myself for what I did to you, Irene."

"I forgave you long ago, my Muse."

"But the scars! I can still feel them on your back."

"The scars on my soul were more important. Your favor healed them, my Empress. I will forever be your loyal handmaiden."

Joséphine curtsied. "I accept your fidelity."

"We better hurry. Madame Fourneau and Professor Chavain are expecting us for tea."

"I need you to lie to them, Irene. Tell them that I feel weak after the trip from Avignon and need to rest for a half hour."

"Why must I lie?"

"I need to see Luis."

"Luis! I never understood your interest in him!"

"I explained my motivations years ago. It's my revenge on Madame Fourneau for her mistreatment of us. She wants to keep her son uncontaminated from contact with girls like us. I totally flouted her wishes by a harmless flirtation with him. Luis just stares at me and mumbles childish drivel."

"I refuse to do this for you! You're lying to me! You must care for this boy."

"You call me your Muse because I inspire you. I am your Muse and no one else's, Irene, have you forgotten my gift?"

"It's my most cherished possession. I generally don't wear it because the other girls might try to steal it."

"My gift symbolizes our angelic sisterhood, a bond that will endure for all eternity. I shall always protect you, my little sister. You remain foremost in my heart. By seeing Luis now, I am protecting you. You can't be made to *pay the law*."

"Pay the law? I don't understand."

"It means to suffer for someone else's misdeeds. Luis will hear all about my visit. If I don't see him today, he'll be upset. He may even tell his mother about our earlier meetings. You distracted Madame Fourneau in order to prevent her from interrupting those meetings. If she learns about those meetings, Fourneau will quickly deduce that you were my accomplice. At the very least, Fourneau will strip you of your prefect's rank. She might even order you flogged again. I don't want you to be a scapegoat for my mischievous pursuit of Luis."

"I'm sorry, Joséphine. You have my interests at heart."

"But I needlessly upset you, Irene. Let me make it up to you. Remember when we practiced together in ballet class? You always relished me dancing the role of Giselle."

Joséphine proceeded to dance as she hummed the ballet music of Adolphe Adam.

"You are my Muse, my inspiration."

The words were voiced by a deeply disturbed boy of 16 years in his private chambers. Although his real name was Louis, he preferred to be called by the Spanish variant of his first name. The beautiful enchantress had visited him on many occasions. She insisted on being called the Muse.

The nude Muse stroked the boy's brown hair.

"Do you love me, Luis?"

"Yes, my Muse."

"Your mother forbade me to see you. She says I'm unworthy of you."

"I hate my mother! She wants me to marry a girl just like her!"

"Would you like to punish your mother?"

"Yes, my Muse."

"Did you read the book that I gave you before I left for Naples?"

"You mean *Frankenstein*?"

"Yes, my love."

"I read it."

"Mary Shelley was vague about how Victor Frankenstein created the body of his creation. Do you have any theories over how he did it?"

"He must have robbed graves. Victor must have stitched together pieces from different corpses."

"Very clever, my love. Is your mother a monster?"

"Yes, my Muse."

"What did Victor try to give his monster?"

"A bride."

"Doesn't your monster of a mother deserve a bride? She rants about a girl just like her. Make this girl for your mother."

"But I can't, my Muse. Mother never let me leave the grounds. I can't rob any graveyards."

"Make your own graveyard, my love. Your mother always says her students are worthless trash. Kill them and use their bodies."

"My mother will wonder what has happened to the girls."

"She will assume that the girls ran away. Girls have run away from this school in the past."

"The police will arrest me, my Muse."

"You will make your mother *pay the law*."

"What do you mean?"

"When your mother is shown your creation, she will lose her mind. She won't be able to defend herself. Tell the police that she killed the girls. They will lock her up in an asylum."

"I will obey you, my Muse. One of the girls has hands like my mother. Her name is Irene. I'll start with her."

"No, my love. You shall end with Irene. I am a girl just like my mother. Irene's father helped kill my mother. There is a special fate reserved for her. Don't kill Irene. Just cut off her hands."

"Why can't I kill her?"

"Irene is a painter. She dreams of being an acclaimed artist. When she loses her hands, she'll also lose her sanity. Your mother needs company in the asylum. My self-styled handmaiden came here because she was accused of thievery. Let her bear the Arabian mark of a thief for the rest of her existence."

Madame Fourneau was in her office having tea with Marguerite and Irene.

"That's a lovely piece of jewelry, Mademoiselle Tupin," said Marguerite.

On Irene's brown blouse was a brooch in the shape of a pentagram. "It's a gift from Joséphine. She gave it to me before she left to become a governess. I only wear it on special occasions."

Once again fully clothed, Joséphine entered the office of Madame Fourneau.

"Are you feeling better?" asked Madame Fourneau.

"Yes," said Joséphine. "I apologize to you and Professor Chavain for my tardiness."

Irene interrupted. "Madame, could you and the Professor retrieve my little surprise?"

"Of course, Mademoiselle Tupin." Fourneau and Chavain left the room.

"Do you notice anything different about me, Joséphine?" asked Irene.

"You're wearing my gift."

"When I learned about your visit, I wanted to give you a gift in return. I use to draw pictures of you with a pencil. They were merely precursors to what you are about to see, my Muse."

Carrying a large-scale framed painting, Fourneau and Chavain returned. The artistic rendition bore Irene's signature. The painting was of a blonde woman in a green dress.

"Irene truly captured your beauty, Joséphine," said Madame Fourneau.

Joséphine burst into tears.

Upon her arrival at the Paris train station, Joséphine Balsamo was met by Rochelle Moreau and Orianne Coyatier. A coach had been hired by Rochelle to transport Joséphine to her new home in the Latin Quarter.

"Ida Similor will be arriving later with your possessions from your house in Pavia," said Rochelle. "Here are your sealed orders from the High Council, Countess. You are only to open it after Orianne and I depart."

Joséphine took the large envelope without response.

"I was surprised to see that large rectangular package in your luggage," declared Orianne. "It looks like a portrait."

"It is, Orianne."

"Did you buy it in Provence?" asked Rochelle.

"It was a gift from a friend, Rochelle."

Joséphine Balsamo barely spoke for the remainder of the trip.

After Joséphine and her luggage were deposited at Petra's former home, Orianne and Rochelle discussed their colleague.

"The Countess wasn't very talkative tonight," noted Orianne.

"She was also acting oddly," said Rochelle. "She called us by our first names. She hadn't done that since we were students at the College. Normally the Countess uses formal modes of address in imitation of Madame Fourneau and Madame Koluchy."

Joséphine had not unpacked. Her luggage remained in the living room. Her sword cane was tied to the outside of one of her trunks. She withdrew the blade in order to use it as a letter opener. Joséphine sliced open the envelope. Inside was a detailed dossier on Louis Caratal. There was also a note.

The High Council orders you to seduce Monsieur Caratal. Keep me regularly informed of his investigation into the Panama Canal Company. Follow Caratal wherever he goes. This counts as your second task for me.

You will be pleased to learn that the Balkan Tigress is no more. Her body lies buried in the basement of your new home.

The Lord of the Night

Petra Donevitch was dead! Had she been executed by Moriarty? Or had she been killed by an enemy of the Black Coats? Joséphine shook her head. It didn't matter. The internal feuds of the Black Coats no longer concerned her. Joséphine restored her sword to her sheath, She was about to make a momentous decision.

Her wrapped portrait rested against a wall. The base of the picture touched the floor. Joséphine gently removed the wrappings. She then began to talk to the painting as if was a living person.

"When I look at you, I don't see a reflection of myself. I see the creator of this masterpiece. I see her hands...the hands that captured my likeness for all eternity...the hands that held me...the hands that comforted me...the hands that soothed me...How can I destroy those hands?

"I thought that I only fell in love once...that time in Normandy...with the father of the child I abandoned...I now realize that there was a second time...a love even more beautiful than what I shared with Sandre...Irene, you are my one true love.

"For years, I lied to myself. I hardened my heart against you. I became obsessed with my mother's vendetta. Your father may be responsible for her death, but you are blameless. I've allowed myself to become trapped in an insane dream of blood and fury. I will forsake that nightmare. I will desert the Black Coats. I will return to Provence. I will call off the maniac of my own making. I will persuade you to leave the College with me. We will flee as far as necessary from a land engulfed by crime.

"Irene, you cannot hear me. You cannot see me. But I shall perform the dance of Giselle one more time for you."

As Joséphine danced, she hummed loudly the music of Adolphe Adam. The sound of Joséphine's joy swept throughout the house. It even reached the depths of the basement.

Beneath the earth the decaying flesh of a corpse began to regenerate. A voice spoke inside a brain that had been dead.

"Revelry disturbs your sleep, my love. The celebrant is of the tribe that has long plagued me. Arise! Petra, Arise! Become a Sister of the Night! Avenge your earlier defeat! Exterminate the vermin called Joséphine Balsamo!"

A woman's hand burst out of the earth.

Joséphine had reached a level of contentment long denied her. She was at peace with herself.

"There is a legend that if you dance on an enemy's grave, your enemy will be resurrected," voiced an intruder.

Joséphine was shocked to see Petra Donevitch standing in the doorway to the basement. Her face and clothes were covered with dirt. Petra's right hand grasped her sword. She slowly raised it to strike.

"You will never get another opportunity to dance on my grave!"

Petra swung at Joséphine. The blonde leaped aside as the brunette's blade slashed opened Irene's masterpiece. Joséphine yanked her sword out of its sheath. The swords of the two combatants crossed.

"So the Blonde Brawler has learned to fence!" growled Petra.

"I'll have your head stuffed and mounted, Balkan Tigress," promised Joséphine.

The adversaries parried each other's attacks. Petra lunged with the Vautrin thrust. Joséphine leaped sideways dodging the blow. The force of her thrust propelled Petra pass Joséphine. As Petra swirled by, Joséphine stabbed her raven-haired rival in the back of the head. Joséphine's sword was jerked out of her hand as Petra fell on her face. As Petra lied motionless on the floor, Joséphine's sword stood vertically in the air.

Joséphine positioned herself in front of her fallen foe. "They say that the dead only return if they have unfinished business. Your unfinished business was to fight a sword duel with me. The matter is now settled. Revel in Hell, Petra Donevitch."

Petra's right hand seized Joséphine's ankle. The blonde collapsed. The brunette's hands reached behind her head to pull out the sword. Petra rose to her full height. Breaking Joséphine's sword with her bare hands, Petra threw the two pieces to a remote corner of the room. Gazing down on the sprawled Joséphine, Petra smiled disclosing her fangs.

"A vampire!" cried Joséphine.

"Not just any vampire," asserted Petra as she reached inside her shirt to expose the Amulet of Lilitu. "I am the Emissary of the Great Vampire. If we exchanged blood, I would transform you into a being like myself. That would be a mistake. We would compete for the Great Vampire's favor just as we contended for Moriarty's. You shall merely be my nourishment."

Grabbing Joséphine's shoulders, Petra lifted her rival from the ground. Petra's teeth bit into Joséphine's throat. As she felt her life ebbing away, Joséphine's right hand gripped her silver hairpin. She plunged it into Petra's neck. The vampire wrenched her teeth out of Joséphine's flesh. Petra howled in pain. Plucking the pin out of Petra's throat, Joséphine jabbed it into the vampire's heart. Petra toppled backwards as blood gushed out of mouth. Petra writhed on the floor.

"You bear my seal!" shrieked the squirming Petra. "You are my slave! Pull out the silver! I command you!"

The teeth marks on Joséphine throbbed. The weakened Joséphine reached down and touched the pin.

"No one commands a Cagliostro!"

Joséphine pushed the pin deeper into Petra's heart. The vampire screamed. Finding Petra's sword, Joséphine lifted it high in the air. Petra was still screaming when Joséphine lopped off her head.

Leonard's trip to Maine confirmed the existence of the couple identified by Evangeline Bramwell Relli as her grandparents. This pleased Joséphine because she deeply wanted to trust Evangeline.

One month after she settled in the Latin Quarter, Joséphine had Evangeline over for lunch.

"You've really done wonders with the house," observed Evangeline. "It's a pity that you have to travel to Panama with Caratal. You were settling in here nicely."

"I did have a bad experience when I first moved in," replied Joséphine. She proceeded to tell Evangeline the full story of her encounter with the revived Petra Donevitch.

"How frightening!" commented Evangeline. "Did it take long for your neck to heal?"

"The marks disappeared after I beheaded Petra."

"What did you do with the body?"

"Mademoiselle Moreau and Mademoiselle Coyatier were kind enough to help me incinerate it."

"What happened to the golden bat?"

"I had it melted down into a lump of metal. I use it as a paperweight."

"What an unusual trophy!"

"I have an even better trophy. Let me show you."

Evangeline followed Joséphine to a locked room in the house. Joséphine opened the door with a key.

"Fortunately, Evangeline, Madame Coyatier is a resourceful taxidermist."

"But you said the body was cremated!"

"Only the headless corpse. I made a promise to Petra Donevitch, and Countess Cagliostro always keeps her promises."

Mounted on a plaque was Joséphine's trophy with an inscription underneath: "Balkan Tigress."

In Panama, Louis Caratal found evidence proving that officials in the Colombian government had been bribed by three members of the High Council, Count Corbucci, Dr. Nikola and John Macklin. Fearful that the Black Coats would assassinate him, Caratal thought it prudent not to return to France directly, but to travel a circuitous path that took him through England. Traveling with him was his mistress, Countess Cagliostro.

Caratal and the Countess landed in Liverpool during June 1890. He insisted that the Countess travel separately through England to France for her own safety. Alerted to Caratal's plans, Herbert de Lernac and Noel Moriarty made sure that the French investigator never reached his native country. Being a railway master in the west of England, Noel Moriarty devised a plan to divert the train carrying Caratal to an unused series of tracks that led to a mine shaft. The train literally vanished off the face of the earth. Caratal's disappearance was a mystery that even baffled Sherlock Holmes.

Joséphine took advantage of her presence in England to visit her sister, who was now a student in Brichester University under the alias of Sabine Absalom. Sabine told Joséphine of the monstrous College Girl Murders reported in the newspapers. The atrocities had occurred at Madame Fourneau's school. Over a period of four months, Louis Fourneau had murdered six girls. Madame Fourneau had died from a heart attack shortly after learning of her son's crimes. Luis had been incarcerated in an asylum where he babbled about a bewitching Muse.

The newspapers issued contradictory reports about Louis Fourneau's last victim, a young woman named Irene. Some periodicals gave her surname as Tupin while others printed it as Chupin. All the news stories professed that Irene perished from her wounds in an Avignon hospital.

Upon her return to Paris, Joséphine went to the Montmartre cemetery. She visited a grave which bore this inscription:

JOSÉPHINE BALSAMO
(1845-80)
DEVOTED MOTHER

"When you died, Mother, I made you a solemn promise. Forgive me! I nearly broke that promise. Consumed by sentimentality, I was going to abandon the path of retribution. I was overcome by a romantic obsession for Irene Tupin.

"Before I succumbed to my maudlin delusions, I was attacked by a vassal of our hereditary enemy. In the exhilaration of my victory, I remembered my true destiny! I am not a foolish woman. I am a Cagliostro! Just as the White Stalker hunted the Undead persecutors of our family, I must mercilessly obliterate our human enemies. I purged my soul of any compassion for Irene.

"I have taken the first step in avenging your brutal murder. The daughter of Théophraste Lupin is dead. Her father and brother will inevitably follow.

"The original Revenant may be dead, but the legacy of that masked enigma continues. The reigning Revenant and her followers shall feel my wrath.

"Théophraste Lupin shall die! Arsène Lupin shall die! The Revenant and her Acolytes shall die! All shall die!"

Afterword
Influences and Inspirations

The major inspiration for these stories is the Wold Newton Universe of the late great Philip José Farmer (1918-2009). He created the concept of a vast universe of literary crossovers. I have tried to follow in his footsteps.

Since my childhood, I was a fan of *The Untouchables*, the TV series that ran from 1959 to 1963. Although I watched this series primarily for the portrayal of Eliot Ness by Robert Stack, I was always fascinated by the gangster conferences featuring such notables as Al Capone, Frank Nitti and Jake Guzik. In my stories, I have similar meetings in which the likes of Sir Arthur Conan Doyle's Professor Moriarty and Guy Boothby's Antonio Nikola launch elaborate conspiracies.

The Black Coats, a criminal gang created by Paul Féval in the 19th century, seemed the perfect vehicle to bring the great masterminds together. Féval's series of seven novels about the evil syndicate has recently been translated from French into English by Black Coat Press with these titles: *'Salem Street, The Invisible Weapon, The Parisian Jungle, The Companions of the Treasure, Heart of Steel, The Cadet Gang* and *The Sword-Swallower*. Féval did not write the novels chronologically and there were major loose ends hanging in the time period that separates *The Cadet Gang* and *The Sword Swallower*. Furthermore, *The Cadet Gang* cavalierly mentioned the murder of the heroes of *The Parisian Jungle* and *Heart of Steel*. I have attempted to answer these mysteries with the events depicted in "The Heir of Pistolet."

Féval's chronology was not always consistent. *Heart of Steel* originally concluded in early 1843. A prequel, *The Companions of the Treasure*, suggested that the conclusion of *Heart of Steel* be moved forward to 1844. Although Black Coat Press published the novels in chronological order, I recommend that new readers read them in the order in which they were originally written: *The Parisian Jungle, Heart of Steel, The Sword-Swallower, 'Salem Street, The Invisible Weapon, The Companions of the Treasure* and *The Cadet Gang*. Read in this order, the reader is more able to follow the somewhat contradictory presentation of this sprawling saga. Both the translator of the Black Coat Press editions, Brian Stableford, and the publisher share this view.

There is also the confusing relationship between Amadine Canada (introduced in *The Sword-Swallower*) and Leocadie Samayoux (introduced in *The Invisible Weapon*). They are both circus performers with the same attributes. Both women are romantic interests for a character named Echalot. *The Companions of the Treasure* implies the two women are synonymous by having

Leocadie assume the name of Madame Canada, but *The Cadet Gang* suggests that Leocadie died before the final 1866 events involving Madame Canada in *The Sword Swallower*. *The Sword Swallower* contains scenes detailing how Madame Canada and Echalot ran a circus together in 1852. *The Cadet Gang* shows Echalot in a bachelor's existence looking mournfully at Leocadie's umbrella during 1853. Echalot and Madame Canada are married in the 1840's (*The Companions* of the *Treasure*), but unmarried in the 1860's (*The Sword Swallower*). I have decided to make the two women the same person and explain the reference to Leocadie's death in *The Cadet Gang*.

Other novels by Paul Féval figure into my mythology. Delapalme and Lagardère are swordsmen from *Le Bossu*. Henri de Belcamp is from *John Devil*.

Anatole and Rolande Cerral are the father and aunt of the surgeon from Maurice Renard's *The Hands of Orlac* (1920). Renard derived the name of Cerral by reversing the syllables of the surname of the real-life Alexis Carrel, a winner of the Nobel Prize for Medicine. I have the Lenoirs from *Heart of Steel* and *The Cadet Gang* create the surname Cerral by manipulating the surname of an earlier historical Carrel.

A running in-joke in my stories is stories is that Count Corbucci, the villain from E. W. Hornung's Raffles stories, wrote novels that paralleled the spaghetti westerns of Sergio Corbucci. In "The Fate of Faustina," Count Corbucci had an underling named Stefano. I gave Stefano the surname of Baldi because Sergio Corbucci had a protégé, Ferdinando Baldi, who also directed spaghetti westerns. Among Baldi's westerns is *Viva Django* (1968, also called *Django, Prepare a Coffin*), a sequel to Sergio Corbucci's

Django (1966). Bruno Corbucci, Sergio's brother, was also a director. This fact prompted me to create Bruno Relli, Count Corbucci's nephew. Evangeline Bramwell Relli, Bruno's wife, first appeared as Eva Relli in "Corridors of Deceit" from *Tales of the Shadowmen 4* (Black Coat Press, 2008). That story was revised for *Sisters of the Opera: The Cagliostro Curse* (to be published by Black Coat Press) to resolve certain continuity issues.

I have Count Corbucci criticizing a fictional author named Jon Dest. The name is an anagram of J. T. Edson, a British writer who wrote westerns nearly a century after the non-existent Dest supposedly did. Edson sabotaged his escapist fiction by lacing it with outrageous political opinions and historical falsehoods. For example, Edson claimed that the American Constitution explicitly granted the right of secession to the states. The accurate view is that the Constitution neither explicitly forbade nor sanctioned secession. One of Edson's recurring characters was Belle Boyd, a real-life Confederate spy whose background was altered to fit the author's prejudices.

The Protector "squeeze" gun actually exists. The Protector anachronistically appeared in two spaghetti westerns set before its creation, *Johnny Yuma* (1966) and *Return of Sabata* (1971). A bounty hunter named Marley appeared in another spaghetti western, *His Name Was King* (1971).

Other villains from escapist fiction were drafted into the ranks of the Black Coats and other criminal conspiracies. These felons include Madame Koluchy from *The Brotherhood of the Seven Kings* (1899) by L. T. Meade and Robert Eustace, Francesca Delacourt from *The Lost Square* (1902) by the same two authors, Horace Dorrington from Arthur Morrison's *The Dorrington Deed Box* (1897), John Macklin from Guy Boothby's *In Strange Company* (1894), Reginald Crawshay from E. W. Hornung's "The Return Match," Ludovic Imbert from Maurice Leblanc's "Madame Imbert's Safe," Van Klopen (granted the first name of Albert by me), Paul Violaine (alias Paul Mascarin) and Arthur Gordon are from Emile Gaboriau's crime novels. The Croatian surname of Donevitch comes from Rex Stout's *Over My Dead Body* (1939). The Pallid Mask is supposed to be an earlier identity of Fantomas, the master criminal created by Pierre Souvestre and Marcel Allain. The activities of Gabrielle Damiens during the French Revolution were told in Baroness Orczy's *Mam'zelle Guillotine* (1940). Bibi-Lupin and Jacques Collin (alias Vautrin) are from Balzac's "The Human Comedy" stories. The story of Marcus Huret's former partners in Mexico can be found in the movie *Run, Man, Run* (1968). Jack Capper is a descendant of a character from Robert Louis Stevenson's *The Black Arrow*.

The Asian villains led by Derrick Stewart are largely inspired by Sax Rohmer's *The Golden Scorpion* (1919). The Chinese tongs in "The Face of Fu Hsi" are all from pulp fiction. The Chang Li is from Robert J. Hogan's Wu Fang novels. The Chuen Gin Lou can be found in Donald E. Keyhoe's *The Mystery of the Golden Skull* (July-August 1936). I also cited two names coined by Robert E. Howard, the Yat Soy (from "Lord of the Dead") and the Yo Thans ("The Sign of the Snake").The Red Dragon Tong was in the film *The Terror of the Tongs* (1961). Olaki, the Japanese martial artist, is from *Bulldog Drummond* (1920) by H. C. "Sapper" McNeile. Master Chun, the weapons designer, was inspired by the movie *Chamber of Horrors* (1966).

The presentation of the history of Thuggee in my stories conflates elements from books and films. My literary inspiration are Doyle's "Uncle Jeremy's Household," the works of Sax Rohmer and Robert E. Howard, *The Deceivers* (1952) by John Masters, and Walter Gibson's Shadow novel, *The Crime Cult* (July 1932). I was also influenced by these films: *Gunga Din* (1939), *The Prodigal* (1955), *The Brigand of Kandahar* (1965), and *Indiana Jones and the Temple of Doom* (1984).

Yuan Lai's torture is from George Fielding Eliot's "The Copper Bowl." Eliot's tale was first published in the December 1928 issue of *Weird Tales*, and recently reprinted in Otto Penzler's anthology, *The Big Book of Adventure Stories* (Vintage Books, 2011). The same barbaric method was depicted in Robert E, Howard's "Black Talons" (also known as "Talons in the Dark"). There are many allusions to Howard's works in my stories including the usage of the fictional *Nameless Cults* (from "The Black Stone"), and the Indian name of Wolf

Hunter ("Graveyard Rats"). Other Indian names came from the films *McLintock!* (1963) and *The Gatling Gun* (1973).

I also utilized characters from the works of Sir Arthur Conan Doyle including Colonel Sebastian Moran, Von Herder, Parker the Garotter, and the Earl of Mayntooth ("The Adventure of the Empty House"), Miss Warrender and Hugh Lawrence ("Uncle Jeremy's Household"), Culverton Smith ("The Adventure of the Dying Detective"), Harold Latimer and Wilson Kemp ("The Adventure of the Greek Interpreter"), Catherine Cusack and James Ryder ("The Adventure of the Blue Carbuncle"), Count Sylvius and Sam Merton ("The Adventure of the Mazarin Stone"), Steve Dixie ("The Adventure of the Three Gables"), Louis Caratal and Herbert de Lernac ("The Lost Special"), Dr. Archibald MacDonald ("Our Midnight Visitor"), Lucretia Venucci ("The Adventure of the Six Napoleons"), Fred Porlock (*The Valley of Fear*) and Francois Le Villard ("The Sign of Four"). The ill-fated Salazars from "The Heir of Pistolet" are relatives of Isadora Klein from "The Adventure of the Three Gables."

The fictional artists in my stories include Joseph Bridau from Balzac's "The Human Comedy" series, Gaston Morrell from the film *Bluebeard* (1944), and Henri Radin, a character with an unusual history. Radin was created by Robert Bloch in his teleplay for "The Grim Reaper," a 1961 episode from Boris Karloff's *Thriller* TV series. Bloch radically reworked a story by Harold Lawlor, "The Black Madonna" (*Weird Tales*, May 1947). Chief Inspector Jacques Lefevre also comes from *Bluebeard*. The surname Forrestier comes from Cole Porter's musical, *Can-Can*.

My repertory of fictional journalists includes Leon Fauchery from Emile Zola's *Nana* (1880), Georges Du Roy from Guy de Maupassant's *Bel Ami* (1885), and Sigismond Trottier from Mary Elizabeth Braddon's *Wyllard's Weird* (1885). The supernatural elements from "Dance on My Grave" owe a debt to Howard's "Dig Me No Grave" and *Devils of Darkness* (1965), a film featuring a vampire called Count Sinistre. The concept of Bram Stoker's Dracula manipulating cultists around the world was first explored in "All Predators Great and Small" from *Tales of the Shadowmen 5* (Black Coat Press, 2009).

Ludovico Maria Sinistrari was a real-life author occasionally cited in Cthulhu Mythos fiction such as Henry Kuttner's "The Hydra" and August Derleth's "The Peabody Heritage." His best known work was *De Daemonialitate et Incubis et Succubis* (*Demoniality: Or, Incubi and Succubi*).

I sprinkle my stories with various connections to the Carcosa Mythology of Ambrose Bierce and Robert W. Chambers as well as the Cthulhu Mythos tales of H. P. Lovecraft, Robert E. Howard, Lin Carter, August Derleth, Clark Ashton Smith and Ramsey Campbell. For example, La Frenaie wine is from Smith's Averoigne series.

Readers of my stories in *Tales of the Shadowmen* will recognize Irene Tupin and Joséphine Balsamo. Irene first appeared in *La Residencia*, a 1969 Spanish film directed by Narciso Ibáñez Serrador. The movie was released in the United States as *The House That Screamed*. Irene was portrayed brilliantly by Mary Maude. In the same film, Madame Fourneau (Lilli Palmer) briefly mentioned a graduate who was an accomplished botanist. The Egyptian story cited by Fourneau in "Dance on My Grave" was a somewhat distorted rendition of the film *Land of the Pharaohs* (1955).

Joséphine Balsamo is a creation of Maurice Leblanc. Her canonical adventures by Leblanc were collected in *Arsène Lupin vs. Countess Cagliostro* (Black Coat Press, 2010). The same volume contained a pastiche, "The Death of Countess Cagliostro" by Jean-Marc and Randy Lofficier. In this story, Joséphine had an affair in Normandy that resulted in the birth of an illegitimate child. It took some clever correspondence between me and Jean-Marc to reconcile this Normandy episode with my earlier stories placing Joséphine in a tyrannical boarding school in Provence. "The Death of Countess Cagliostro" also features a circus family from Jules Verne's *César Cascabel*.

Joséphine Balsamo was the name of three different women in Leblanc's fiction. The last two were criminals, but nothing negative was indicated about the first Joséphine. Since the Mexican horror film, *The Bloody Vampire* (1962), presented the Cagliostro family as vampire hunters, I have made the original Joséphine the archenemy of the Undead. My version of this Joséphine is essentially a female version of the hero from Brian Clemens's film, *Captain Kronos, Vampire Hunter* (1974). Joséphine the White Stalker was also influenced by Zorro, Carl Kolchak and Buffy the Vampire Slayer. The Stalker's friend, Raymond de Grandin, is descended from Ramon Nazara y de Grandin of Languedoc, an adversary of werewolves in Seabury Quinn's "Fortune's Fools" (*Weird Tales*, July 1938). The story was reprinted in *The Other Seabury Quinn Stories: Susette and Weird Tales* (The Battered Silicon Dispatch Box, 2007).

When I first discovered the third Joséphine Balsamo in Leblanc's Arsène Lupin series, I was struck by her similarities to Angelique from *Dark Shadows*, the gothic soap opera from 1966-71. For this reason, I always write Joséphine as if she's being played by Lara Parker. Besides delivering an unforgettable portrayal of Angelique, Ms. Parker has also written two enthralling novels about her *Dark Shadows* character, *Angelique's Descent* (1998) and *The Salem Branch* (2006).

Currently I'm writing two series, as well as some standalone stories, with a shared continuity in different time periods. It isn't easy keeping the Revenant series with the Irina Putine series. Therefore, I have to utilize a plot device that I first saw done on *Dark Shadows*. On the soap opera, the writers had embellished the storyline with various references to the life of Barnabas Collins in the eighteenth century. When it was decided to have a time travel story about Barnabas's origins, the writers wanted to go off in a different direction. To reconcile discrepancies, it was revealed that the accepted history of the Collins family contained inaccuracies and distortions. Author James Clavell employed similar trickery when he wrote his "Asian Saga" novels about the Struan family. There-fore, some events in my stories may be recalled inaccurately years later.

Here's an example. In a story published in *Tales of the Shadowmen #7* (Black Coat Press, 2011), "Will There Be Sunlight?," the All-Father in 1934 alluded to the murder of Mrs. Stewart: "In 1887, Mrs. Stewart was killed by a sniper acting under Moriarty's orders." The sniper was meant to be Colonel Sebastian Moran. This statement implied Moran shot Mrs. Stewart. In "The Face of Fu Hsi," it is revealed that Moran supervised Mrs. Stewart's death by another assassin. Later, Moran used his talents as a sniper to silence his accomplice. The All-Father's statement in 1934 wasn't totally accurate, but it wasn't totally false. It is true that Moran, a sniper, arranged the slaying of Mrs. Stewart. The All-Father simply gave an imperfect summarization of events that transpired 47 years ago.

I am a big fan of the pulp fiction of Walter Gibson, the creator of The Shadow. One of the agents of The Shadow was Chance Lebrue. My Chantal Lebrue pays homage to Gibson's earlier character.

Among Gibson's favorite writers was Edgar Wallace. The Six Vigilant Men from "The Heir of Pistolet" are supposed to be the fathers or grandfathers of Wallace's Four Just Men. Their usage of razors was inspired by *Sweeney Todd, the Demon Barber of Fleet Street*.

Meaghan and Desdemona Cullin are relatives of Monk Cullin, the villain from Lester Dent's "The Sinister Ray." Monk Cullin was an early forerunner of Monk Mayfair from Dent's Doc Savage novels. "The Heir of Pistolet" contains vague testimonials to two Doc Savage novels, *The Sea Magician* (November 1934) and *Bequest of Evil* (February 1941). La Richarde's libel about the Cullin ancestry is derived from H. P. Lovecraft's "Facts Concerning the Late Arthur Jermyn and His Family."

The Pallid Mask's alias of Antoine Boucher is a tribute to Anthony Boucher, the noted mystery writer and critic. Anthony Boucher's anthology, *Four-&-Twenty Bloodhounds* (1950), contained biographies of fictional sleuths by their creators. That book identified Sir Digby Fell and Asenath Pons as the respective fathers of John Dickson Carr's Gideon Fell and August Derleth's Solar Pons.

The idea that Mycroft Holmes was an earlier M. of the British Secret Service goes back to a least John Lescroart's *Son of Holmes* (1986), a book with which I intend no continuity. An early forerunner of Ian Fleming's James Bond was Duckworth Drew from William Le Queux's *Secrets of the Foreign Office* (1903). The son of a French father and an English mother, Drew's real name was Dreux. I made Dreux/Drew a graduate of Wrykyn Preparatory School from P. G. Wodehouse's stories.

"The Fire Eater" cited a unique relationship between Marguerite Blakeney and her husband's mistress. Marguerite was the wife of Sir Percy Blakeney from Baroness Orczy's Scarlet Pimpernel novels. Her relationship to Sir Percy's mistress is explored in Win Scott Eckert's "Is He in Hell?" from Michael Croteau's *The Worlds of Philip José Farmer: Protean Dimensions* (Meteor House, 2010). The story can also be found in *Tales of the Shadowmen 6* (Black Coat Press, 2010).

In writing these stories, I draw upon theoretical articles in my books published by Altus Press: *Rick Lai's Secret Histories: Daring Adventurers* (2008), *Rick Lai's Secret Histories: Criminal Masterminds* (2009), *Chronology of Shadows: A Timeline of The Shadow's Exploits* (2007) and *The Revised Complete Chronology of Bronze* (2010). I sometimes discover that a theory needs to be modified to work in a fictional context. For example, I proposed a relationship between Minnie Warrender and Count Sylvius in "The Legacy of Hanoi Shan" from *Rick Lai's Secret Histories: Criminal Masterminds*. This relationship was presented differently in "The Face of Fu Hsi."

Professor Moriarty's scheme to seize control of France is based on Doyle's "How the Brigadier Was Tempted by the Devil." Joséphine Balsamo's secret role in the Boulanger and Panama Canal controversies was suggested by Maurice Leblanc. Doyle's "The Lost Special" also hinted at some deep conspiracy behind the Canal scandal. The final and concluding volume of *Shadows of the Opera* will deal with the effect of Moriarty's grand scheme on the destinies of the Revenant and Sherlock Holmes.

Cast of Characters

Character (In Alphabetical Order) - Source

Absalom, Sabine (see Sabine, Balsamo)
Acolytes of the Shadows - Rick Lai
Ai - August Derleth and Mark Schorer
Albino Ape Priestess, The - H. P. Lovecraft
Alexandra the Great (see Vadarasse, Alexandria)
All-Father, The (see Bozzo-Corona, Colonel)
Andreas - Sam Hall, Gordon Russell and Violet Welles
Badoît, Francis - Paul Féval
Bagheela - Rick Lai
Bailey, Lee - David Haft, Burt Kennedy, Ian Quicke and Bob Richards
Baldi, Stefano - E. W. Hornung
Baldie, Pedro - Narciso Ibañez Serrador and Juan Tébar
Balsamo, José Alejandro - Miguel Morayta
Balsamo, Joseph - Alexandre Dumas (based on history)
Balsamo, Joséphine (I) - Maurice Leblanc
Balsamo, Joséphine (II) - Maurice Leblanc
Balsamo, Joséphine (III) - Maurice Leblanc
Balsamo, Sabine - Rick Lai
Balsamo, Sharita - Rick Lai
Basilio, Enrique - Based on Robert Bloomfield
Belcamp, Henri de - Paul Féval
Bel Demonio (see Bozzo-Corona, Colonel)
Bibi-Lupin - Honoré de Balzac
Biffi, Count - Paul Féval
Black Coats, The - Paul Féval
Black Silk Bonnet Club, The (see Black Coats, The)
Black Star - Robert E. Howard
Blake, Jillian - Philip José Farmer
Blakeney, Marguerite - Baroness Orczy
Blanton, Charles- Emile Zola and Walter Gibson
Bonaparte, Leontine - Rick Lai
Boucher, Antoine (see North, Juan)
Bouchère, La (see Cullin, Meaghan)
Bozzo-Corona, Colonel - Paul Féval
Bozzo-Corona, Michele (see Bozzo-Corona, Colonel)
Bramwell, Evangeline (see Duvalier, Alexis)
Brechard - Narciso Ibañez Serrador and Juan Tébar

Brenner, Monsieur - Based on Rex Stout
Bridau, Joseph - Honoré de Balzac
Brotherhood of the Lotus, The (see Chang Li Society, The)
Brotherhood of the Seven Kings, The - L. T. Meade and Robert Eustace
Brothers of Ajaccio, The - Arthur Conan Doyle
Burtoni, David - Rick Lai
Caber, Emile - Rick Lai
Caber, Emily - Rick Lai
Caber, James (1) - Rick Lai
Caber, James (2) - Lord Dunsany
Caber, Urania - Philip José Farmer
Cadet Gang, The (see Black Coats, The)
Cadet-l'Amour - Paul Féval
Cagliostro, Count (see Balsamo, Joseph)
Cagliostro, Countess (see Balsamo, Joséphine (I thru III))
Canada, Armadine (see Samayoux, Leocadie)
Cantinière (see Cortina, Andreina)
Capper, Jack - Based on Robert Louis Stevenson
Caratal, Louis - Arthur Conan Doyle
Carradine, Linus Jerome - Fernando Di Leo, Romolo Guerrieri, Sauro Scavolini
and Giovanni Simonelli
Cascabel, César - Jules Verne
Cascabel, Sandre - Jules Verne
Cavalier, Jacques (see Ryder, James)
Cerral, Anatole - Based on Maurice Renard
Cerral, Rolande - Based on Maurice Renard
Cerral, Veronique - Rick Lai
Chancellor of Brichester University, The – Based on Ramsey Campbell
Chang Li Society, The - Robert J. Hogan
Charon, Lord (see Blanton, Charles)
Chavain, Marguerite - Narciso Ibañez Serrador and Juan Tébar
Chicot the Jester - Alexandre Dumas
Chuen Gin Lou, The - Donald E. Keyhoe
Chun, Master - Stephen Kandel and Ray Russell
Chupin, Irene (see Tupin, Irene)
Chupin. Polyte - Emile Gaboriau
Chupin, Victoire - Maurice Leblanc
Chupin, Victor - Emile Gaboriau
Clampin, Francis - Rick Lai
Clampin, Joseph - Paul Féval
Clare, Clotilde Morand Stuart de - Paul Féval
Clare, Comtesse de (see Sadoulas, Marguerite)
Clare, Joulou du Bréhut de - Paul Féval

Clare, Nita Fitzroy de - Paul Féval
Clare, Roland Fitzroy de - Paul Féval
Clay, John - Arthur Conan Doyle
Clayton, Gruesome - Philip José Farmer
Cocotte - Based on Paul Féval
Collin, Jacques (see Vautrin)
Companions of Silence, The - Paul Féval
Corbett, Stanley (see Corbucci, Salvatore)
Corbucci, Catarina (see Koluchy, Catrarina)
Corbucci, Carolina - Rick Lai
Corbucci, Salvatore - E. W. Hornung
Cortina, Andreina - Based on Maurice Leblanc
Cortina, Faustine - Based on Maurice Leblanc
Coyatier, Jean-Francois - Paul Féval
Coyatier, Orianne - Rick Lai
Crawshay, Reginald - E. W. Hornung
Cullin family, The - Lester Dent and Art Wallace
Cullin, Desdemona - Rick Lai
Cullin, Meaghan - Rick Lai
Cusack, Catherine ("Kate") - Arthur Conan Doyle
Cussac, Catherine Emmanuelle (see Cusack, Catherine)
Cypriote, The - William Faulkner, Harry Kunitz and Harold Jack Bloom
Daae, Christine - Gaston Leroux
Damiens, Gabrielle - Baroness Orczy
d'Andresy, Henriette - Maurice Leblanc
d'Andresy, Raoul (see Lupin, Arsène)
Daphne, Sister - Rick Lai
d'Arx, Mathieu - Paul Féval
d'Arx, Rémy - Paul Féval
Delacort, Francesca- L. T. Meade and Robert Eustace
Delapalme - Paul Féval
d'Erlette, Augustine (see Revenant)
Despienne, Colonel - Arthur Conan Doyle
Dest, Jon - Based on J. T. Edson
Devil, John (see Belcamp, Henri de)
Dixie, Steve - Arthur Conan Doyle
Django (I) (see Djanko, Ignacz)
Django (II) (see North, Juan)
Djanko, Bartol - Rick Lai
Djanko, Ignacz - Sergio Corbucci, Bruno Corbucci and Franco Rosetti
Donevitch, Petra - Based on Rex Stout
Donevitch, Stefan - Based on Rex Stout
Donevitch, Vladimir - Based on Rex Stout

Donevitch, Xenia Kratides - Based on Arthur Conan Doyle
Dorrington, Horace - Arthur Morrison
Dracula, Vlad - Bram Stoker and Peter Tremayne
Dreux, Duckworth- William Le Queuex
Dreux-Soubise, Comtesse de - Maurice Leblanc
Du Roy, Georges - Guy de Maupassant
Duvalier, Alexis - Based on Sam Hall, Gordon Russell, Ron Sprout, Violet Welles and Lara Parker
Echalot - Paul Féval
Elder Gods, The - August Derleth and Mark Schorer
Elphberg family - Anthony Hope
Erik - Gaston Leroux
Erlik cult - Robert E. Howard
Farthing, Penelope - Rick Lai
Fauchery, Leon - Emile Zola
Fell, Digby - John Dickson Carr
Fenix, Count de (see Balsamo, Joseph)
Fenix, Countess de (see Balsamo, Joséphine (III))
Forrestier, Maître - Cole Porter
Fourneau, Berenice - Rick Lai
Fourneau, Louis ("Luis") - Narciso Ibañez Serrador and Juan Tébar
Fourneau, Philippe - Rick Lai
Fourneau, Natalie - Narciso Ibañez Serrador and Juan Tébar
Fourneau, Roget - Rick lai
Fra Diavolo (see Bozzo-Corona, Colonel)
Fu Hsi - Sax Rohmer
Gailhard, Pedro – Historical
Garrotter, The (see Parker, Lamar)
Gentlemen of the Night, The - Paul Féval
Gerard, Anne-Marie - Pierre Souvestre and Marcel Allain
Gerard, Leontine (see Bonaparte, Leontine)
Gerard, Brigadier - Arthur Conan Doyle
Gondureau, Louis (see Bibi-Lupin)
Gonsalez, Raymond - Based on Edgar Wallace
Gordon, Arthur - Emile Gaboriau
Grandin, Raymond de - Based on Seabury Quinn
Great Vampire, The (see Dracula, Vlad)
Green-Eyed Devil, The - James Clavell
Green Lamia, The - (see Varno, Valorie)
Gretchen - Arthur Conan Doyle
Grévin, Mathilde - Narciso Ibañez Serrador and Juan Tébar
Grévin, Teresa - Narciso Ibañez Serrador and Juan Tébar
Grimm, Johann (see Grimoire, Jean)

Grimoire, Jean - Robert E. Howard
Gunsight Eyes - Renato Izzo and Gianfranco Parolini
Harold, Mrs. - Arthur Conan Doyle
Hastur - August Derleth and Ambrose Bierce
Head, Norman - L. T. Meade and Robert Eustace
Heint, Poul (see Lupin, Théophraste)
Henri - Narciso Ibañez Serrador and Juan Tébar
Hickmakani, El - Richard Francis Burton and Gaston Leroux
High Priestess of Astarte, The - Joseph Breen, Samuel James Larsen and Maurice Zim
Holmes, Mycroft - Arthur Conan Doyle
Holmes, Sherlock - Arthur Conan Doyle
Horner, John – Arthur Conan Doyle
Huan Chow Lee - Sax Rohmer and Walter Gibson
Huret, Marcus - Based on Pompeo De Angelis and SergioSolima
Imbert, Ludovic - Maurice Leblanc
Invisible, Lady - (see Lebrue, Chantal)
Ithaqua - August Derleth
Jade Seraph, The - (see Varno, Valorie)
Judex, Lady (see Trémeuse, Julia de)
Kemp, Wilson - Arthur Conan Doyle
Khan, Achmet Genghis - Arthur Conan Doyle
Khan, Ali - Sax Rohmer
King in Yellow, The - (see Zukala-Koth)
Kratides, Maria - Rick Lai
Kratides, Paul - Arthur Conan Doyle
Kratides, Sophy - Arthur Conan Doyle
Ladeau - Robert E, Howard
La Frenaie, Comte de - Clark Ashton Smith
Lagardère - Paul Féval
Landerneau - Based on Paul Féval
Lard, A. L. (see Revenant)
LaSalle, Angelique - Based on Frank L. Packard
Latimer, Harold - Arthur Conan Doyle
Lawrence, Hugh - Arthur Conan Doyle
Lebrue, Chantal - Based on Walter Gibson
Lecoq - Paul Féval
Leferve, Jacques - Pierre Gendron, Arnold Phillips
and Werner H. Furst
Lenoir, Abel - Paul Féval
Lenoir, Anatole (see Cerral, Anatole)
Lenoir, Julien - Paul Féval
Lenoir, Rolande (see Cerral, Rolande)

Lenoir, Rose - Paul Féval
Leopard, Lady (see Sorelli, Feliciana)
Lernac, Herbert de - Arthur Conan Doyle
Le Villard, Francois - Arthur Conan Doyle
Lilitu - Robert E. Howard
Lineaire, Catherine - Narciso Ibañez Serrador and Juan Tébar
Loridan, Charles Maurice - Rick Lai
Lupin, Albert (see Bibi Lupin)
Lupin, Arsène - Maurice Leblanc
Lupin, Charles Arsène - Based on Maurice Leblanc
Lupin, Théophraste - Maurice Leblanc
MacDonald, Archibald - Arthur Conan Doyle
Macklin, John - Guy Boothby
MacStruan, Frederick Jr. - Based on James Clavell
Manchot, Le - Paul Féval
Manfred, Leonard - Based on Edgar Wallace
Marchef (see Coyatier, Jean-Francois)
Marley, Dora - Based on Lester Dent
Marley, King - Renato Savino
Marriott, Jabez - John Gilling
Mascarin, Paul - Gaboriau, Emile
Mason, Paris - Rick Lai
Mason, Randolph - Melville Davisson Post
Mason, Smith and Mason (law firm) - William G. Bogart
Maupertuis, Baron - Arthur Conan Doyle
Maynotte, André - Paul Féval
Maynotte, Julie - Paul Féval
Mayntooth, Earl of - Arthur Conan Doyle
McGinty, Brendan - Based on Arthur Conan Doyle
Melas - Arthur Conan Doyle
Merton, Sam - Arthur Conan Doyle
Mifroid, Commissioner - Gaston Leroux
Mohicans of Paris, The - Alexandre Dumas
Mola Singh - Arthur Conan Doyle
Moliere, Armond du - Lyn Fairhurst
Montour - Robert E. Howard
Moran, Sebastian - Arthur Conan Doyle
Morcar, Countess of - Arthur Conan Doyle
Moreau, Bernard - Narciso Ibañez Serrador and Juan Tébar
Moreau, Dr. – H. G. Wells
Moreau, Rochelle - Based on Narciso Ibañez Serrador and
Juan Tébar
Moriarty, Catarina (see Koluchy, Catarina)

Moriarty, Dominick Damien - John Buchan
Moriarty, Finola - Rick Lai
Moriarty, James - Arthur Conan Doyle
Moriarty, Noel - Arthur Conan Doyle and John Buchan
Moriarty, Trickie - Based on Laurie King
Morrell, Gabriel - Rick Lai
Morrell, Gaston - Pierre Gendron, Arnold Phillips and Werner H. Furst
Morrell, Natalie (see Fourneau, Natalie)
Nemo, Captain - Jules Verne
Nemo, Jim (see Moriarty, James)
Nemo, Madame (ee Moriarty, Finola)
Neptune Society - Based on Henry Sharp and John W. Bloch
Nevermore, Milady - Based on Alexandre Dumas and Edgar Allan Poe
Nikola, Antonio - Guy Boothby
Noel, Suzanne - Narciso Ibañez Serrador and Juan Tébar
North, Juan - Pierre Souvestre and Marcel Allain
Olaki, Shintaro - H. C. McNeile
Oracle of Benares, The - Guy Boothby
Order of the Serpent Heart, The - H. Rider Haggard
Orsini, Julia (see Trémeuse, Julia de)
Pagès, Leocadie - Rick Lai
Pagès, Maurice - Paul Féval
Pagès, Valentine - Paul Féval
Pallid Mask, The (see North, Juan)
Parker, Lamar ("Larry") - Arthur Conan Doyle
Pattu, Captain - Based on Paul Féval
Pavia, Julius (see Moriarty, Noel)
Phantom of Truth, The - Robert W. Chambers
Piquepuce - Based on Paul Féval
Pistolet (I) (see Clampin, Joseph)
Pistolet (II) (see Clampin, Francis)
Poiccart, Georges - Based on Edgar Wallace
Pons, Asenath - August Derleth
Popinot, Cesarine - Honoré de Balzac
Porlock, Fred - Arthur Conan Doyle
Prinn, Ludvig - Robert Bloch
Puma - Based on James Edward Grant
Radin, Henri - Robert Bloch
Rassendyll, Darlla (see Revenant)
Rassendyll, Rudolf - Anthony Hope
Ratina - John Gilling
Red Dragon Tong, The - Jimmy Sangster
Reine, La - Rick Lai

Relli, Bruno - Based on Dario Argento and Daria Nicolodi
Relli, Evangeline (see Duvalier, Alexis)
Remy, Laurent - Gaston Leroux
Revenant, The - Rick Lai
Reynier - Paul Féval
Richard, Firmin - Gaston Leroux
Richarde, La (see Mason, Paris)
Roget, Micheline - Rick Lai
Ronder - Arthur Conan Doyle
Rudolf III of Ruritania - Anthony Hope
Ruination, Lady (see Cusack, Catherine)
Ryder, James - Arthur Conan Doyle
Saladin - Paul Féval
Sadoulas, Marguerite - Paul Féval
Sages of the Phoenix, The - Robert E. Howard
Salazar, Isidore - Rick Lai
Salazar, Jacinta - Rick Lai
Samayoux, Leocadie - Paul Féval
Sales, Marie de - Rick Lai
Samuel, Dr. - Paul Féval
Samuel, Tanja - Rick Lai
Savage, Colonel - John Masters
Scalpel, Lady (see Cerral, Rolande)
Scot, Gloria (see Balsamo, Joséphine (II))
Scot, Leonard - Maurice Leblanc
Set - Robert E. Howard
Si-Fan, The - Sax Rohmer
Silvestre, Don de - Guy Boothby
Similor, Ida - Rick Lai
Sinistrai (see Kratides, Maria)
Sin - August Derleth and Mark Schorer
Sisters of the Night, The - Bram Stoker
Slidith - Lin Carter
Smith, Culverton - Arthur Conan Doyle
Sorelli, Feliciana - Gaston Leroux
Stepphun, Lothaire (see Lupin, Théophraste)
Stewart, Derrick - Sax Rohmer
Stewart, Jasmine (see Warrender, Minnie)
Stewart, Karah - August Derleth
Stewart, Mina - Robert E. Howard
Sylvius, Count Negretto - Arthur Conan Doyle
Tascher de la Pagerie, Andrée - Based on Lara Parker
Three Matrons of Darkness, The - Dario Argento and Daria Nicolodi

Thurston, Ethel - Arthur Conan Doyle
Tocsin, Lady (see LaSalle, Angelique)
Tremeau, Captain - Arthur Conan Doyle
Trémeuse, Julia de - Arthur Bernède and Louis Feuillade
Trémeuse, Pierre de - Arthur Bernède and Louis Feuillade
Trevor, Rosette - Based on Guy Boothby
Trottier, Sigismond - Mary Elizabeth Braddon
Tupin, Irene - Narciso Ibañez Serrador and Juan Tébar
Tupin, Victoire (see Chupin, Victoire)
Two-Knife - Based on Mark and Joseph Van Winkle
Unspeakable Feaster, The (see Hastur)
Vabre, Madame - Emile Zola
Vadarasse, Alexandria - Based on Jules Verne
Vadarasse, Cornelia - Jules Verne
Valencia, Raquel - Based on Walter Gibson
Valeur, Mademoiselle (see Varno, Valorie)
Van Eeden, Ju Hai - Philip José Farmer and Philip Pullman
Van Klopen, Albert - Emile Gaboriau
Varno, Garth - Rick Lai
Varno, Marta - Rick Lai
Varno, Valorie - Rick Lai
Vathelos the Blind - Robert E. Howard
Vautrin - Honoré de Balzac
Vennucci, Lucretia - Arthur Conan Doyle
Von Herder, Julius - Arthur Conan Doyle
Von Junzt, Friedrich - Robert E. Howard
Warrender, Sarah - L. T. Meade and Robert Eustace
Watson, John H. - Arthur Conan Doyle
Werewolves, The – Rick Lai
White Stalker (see Balsamo, Josephine (I))
Winter, Kaitlin de- Alexandre Dumas and Arthur Conan Doyle
Winter, Milady de - Alexandre Dumas
Wolf Hunter - Based on Robert E. Howard
Wu Fang Clan, The - James Clavell and Robert J. Hogan
Yalta, Countess - Fortune du Boisgobey
Yasmina (see Warrender, Minnie)
Yat Soy, The - Robert E. Howard
Yiggurath - H. P. Lovecraft, Zealia Bishop and Robert Bloch
Yo Thans, The - Robert E. Howard
Yuan Li - George Fielding Eliot
Zayata, Renee (see Bagheela)
Zeck, Armand - Based on Rex Stout
Zukala-Koth - Robert E. Howard and Robert W. Chambers

SF & FANTASY

Henri Allorge. *The Great Cataclysm*
Guy d'Armen. *Doc Ardan: The City of Gold and Lepers*
G.-J. Arnaud. *The Ice Company*
Charles Asselineau. *The Double Life*
Cyprien Bérard. *The Vampire Lord Ruthwen*
Aloysius Bertrand. *Gaspard de la Nuit*
Richard Bessière. *The Gardens of the Apocalypse*
Albert Bleunard. *Ever Smaller*
Félix Bodin. *The Novel of the Future*
Louis Boussenard. *Monsieur Synthesis*
Alphonse Brown. *City of Glass; The Conquest of the Air*
Emile Calvet. *In a Thousand Years*
André Caroff. *The Terror of Madame Atomos; Miss Atomos; The Return of Madame Atomos; The Mistake of Madame Atomos; The Monsters of Madame Atomos; The Revenge of Madame Atomos; The Resurrection of Madame Atomos*
Félicien Champsaur. *The Human Arrow; Ouha, King of the Apes; Pharaoh's Wife*
Didier de Chousy. *Ignis*
Michel Corday. *The Eternal Flame*
Captain Danrit. *Undersea Odyssey*
C. I. Defontenay. *Star (Psi Cassiopeia)*
Charles Derennes. *The People of the Pole*
Georges Dodds (anthologist). *The Missing Link*
Harry Dickson. *The Heir of Dracula*
Jules Dornay. *Lord Ruthven Begins*
Alfred Driou. *The Adventures of a Parisian Aeronaut*
Sâr Dubnotal *vs. Jack the Ripper*
Alexandre Dumas. *The Return of Lord Ruthven*
Renée Dunan. *Baal*
J.-C. Dunyach. *The Night Orchid; The Thieves of Silence*
Henri Duvernois. *The Man Who Found Himself*
Achille Eyraud. *Voyage to Venus*
Henri Falk. *The Age of Lead*
Paul Féval. *Anne of the Isles; Knightshade; Revenants; Vampire City; The Vampire Countess; The Wandering Jew's Daughter*
Paul Féval, *fils. Felifax, the Tiger-Man*
Charles de Fieux. *Lamékis*
Arnould Galopin. *Doctor Omega; Doctor Omega and the Shadowmen* (anthology)
Judith Gautier. *Isoline and the Serpent-Flower*
Léon Gozlan. *The Vampire of the Val-de-Grâce*
G.L. Gick. *Harry Dickson and the Werewolf of Rutherford Grange*
Edmond Haraucourt. *Illusions of Immortality*
Nathalie Henneberg. *The Green Gods*
V. Hugo, P. Foucher & P. Meurice. *The Hunchback of Notre-Dame*
Romain d'Huissier. *Hexagon: Dark Matter*
Michel Jeury. *Chronolysis*
Gustave Kahn. *The Tale of Gold and Silence*

Gérard Klein. *The Mote in Time's Eye*
Fernand Kolney. *Love in 5000 Years*
Louis-Guillaume de La Follie. *The Unpretentious Philosopher*
Jean de La Hire. *Enter the Nyctalope; The Nyctalope on Mars; The Nyctalope vs. Lucifer; The Nyctalope Steps In; Night of the Nyctalope*
Etienne-Léon de Lamothe-Langon. *The Virgin Vampire*
André Laurie. *Spiridon*
Gabriel de Lautrec. *The Vengeance of the Oval Portrait*
Alain le Drimeur. *The Future City*
Georges Le Faure & Henri de Graffigny. *The Extraordinary Adventures of a Russian Scientist Across the Solar System* (2 vols.)
Gustave Le Rouge. *The Vampires of Mars; The Dominion of the World* (w/Gustave Guitton) (4 vols.)
Jules Lermina. *Mysteryville; Panic in Paris; To-Ho and the Gold Destroyers; The Secret of Zippelius*
André Lichtenberger. *The Centaurs; The Children of the Crab*
Jean-Marc & Randy Lofficier. *Edgar Allan Poe on Mars; The Katrina Protocol; Pacifica; Robonocchio; Tales of the Shadowmen 1-9*
Xavier Mauméjean. *The League of Heroes*
Joseph Méry. *The Tower of Destiny*
Hippolyte Mettais. *The Year 5865*
Louise Michel. *The Human Microbes; The New World*
Tony Moilin. *Paris in the Year 2000*
José Moselli. *Illa's End*
John-Antoine Nau. *Enemy Force*
Marie Nizet. *Captain Vampire*
C. Nodier, A. Beraud & Toussaint-Merle. *Frankenstein*
Henri de Parville. *An Inhabitant of the Planet Mars*
Gaston de Pawlowski. *Journey to the Land of the 4th Dimension*
Georges Pellerin. *The World in 2000 Years*
Ernest Pérochon. *The Frenetic People*
Pierre Pelot. *The Child Who Walked on the Sky*
J. Polidori, C. Nodier, E. Scribe. *Lord Ruthven the Vampire*
P.-A. Ponson du Terrail. *The Vampire and the Devil's Son; The Immortal Woman*
Henri de Régnier. *A Surfeit of Mirrors*
Maurice Renard. *The Blue Peril; Doctor Lerne; The Doctored Man; A Man Among the Microbes; The Master of Light*
Jules Rengade. *Voyage Beneath the Waves*
Jean Richepin. *The Wing; The Crazy Corner*
Albert Robida. *The Adventures of Saturnin Farandoul; The Clock of the Centuries; Chalet in the Sky; The Electric Life*
J.-H. Rosny Aîné. *Helgvor of the Blue River; The Givreuse Enigma; The Mysterious Force; The Navigators of Space; Vamireh; The World of the Variants; The Young Vampire*
Marcel Rouff. *Journey to the Inverted World*
Han Ryner. *The Superhumans*
Brian Stableford. *The New Faust at the Tragicomique;The Empire of the Necromancers (The Shadow of Frankenstein; Frankenstein and the Vampire Countess; Frankenstein in*

London); *Sherlock Holmes & The Vampires of Eternity; The Stones of Camelot; The Wayward Muse.* (anthologist) *The Germans on Venus; News from the Moon; The Supreme Progress; The World Above the World; Nemoville; Investigations of the Future*
Jacques Spitz. *The Eye of Purgatory*
Kurt Steiner. *Ortog*
Eugène Thébault. *Radio-Terror*
C.-F. Tiphaigne de La Roche. *Amilec*
Théo Varlet. *The Golden Rock. The Xenobiotic Invasion; The Castaways of Eros; Timeslip Troopers* (w/André Blandin); *The Martian Epic* (w/Octave Joncquel)
Paul Vibert. *The Mysterious Fluid*
Villiers de l'Isle-Adam. *The Scaffold; The Vampire Soul*
Philippe Ward. *Artahe*
Philippe Ward & Sylvie Miller. *The Song of Montségur*

MYSTERIES & THRILLERS

M. Allain & P. Souvestre. *The Daughter of Fantômas*
A. Anicet-Bourgeois, Lucien Dabril. *Rocambole*
A. Bernède. *Belphegor*; *Judex* (w/Louis Feuillade); *The Return of Judex* (w/Louis Feuillade); *The Shadow of Judex*
A. Bisson & G. Livet. *Nick Carter vs. Fantômas*
V. Darlay & H. de Gorsse. *Arsène Lupin vs. Sherlock Holmes: The Stage Play*
Séamas Duffy. *Sherlock Holmes in Paris*
Paul Féval. *Gentlemen of the Night; John Devil; The Black Coats ('Salem Street; The Invisible Weapon; The Parisian Jungle; The Companions of the Treasure; Heart of Steel; The Cadet Gang; The Sword-Swallower)*
Emile Gaboriau. *Monsieur Lecoq*
Goron & Emile Gautier. *Spawn of the Penitentiary*
Rick Lai. *Shadows of the Opera: Retribution in Blood*
Steve Leadley. *Sherlock Holmes: The Circle of Blood*
Maurice Leblanc. *Arsène Lupin vs. Countess Cagliostro; Arsène Lupin vs. Sherlock Holmes (The Blonde Phantom; The Hollow Needle); The Many Faces of Arsène Lupin*
Gaston Leroux. *Chéri-Bibi; The Phantom of the Opera; Rouletabille & the Mystery of the Yellow Room; Rouletabille at Krupp's*
Richard Marsh. *The Complete Adventures of Judith Lee*
William Patrick Maynard. *The Terror of Fu Manchu; The Destiny of Fu Manchu*
Frank J. Morlock. *Sherlock Holmes: The Grand Horizontals; Sherlock Holmes vs Jack the Ripper*
Antonin Reschal. *The Adventures of Miss Boston*
P. de Wattyne & Y. Walter. *Sherlock Holmes vs. Fantômas*
David White. *Fantômas in America*
Pierre Yrondy. *The Adventures of Thérèse Arnaud*

SCREENPLAYS

Mike Baron. *The Iron Triangle*
Emma Bull & Will Shetterly. *Nightspeeder; War for the Oaks*
Gerry Conway & Roy Thomas. *Doc Dynamo*

Steve Englehart. *Majorca*
James Hudnall. *The Devastator*
Jean-Marc & Randy Lofficier. *Royal Flush*
J.-M. & R. Lofficier & Marc Agapit. *Despair*
J.-M. & R. Lofficier & Joël Houssin. *City*
Andrew Paquette. *Peripheral Vision*
Robert L. Robinson, Jr. *Judex*
R. Thomas, J. Hendler & L. Sprague de Camp. *Rivers of Time*

NON-FICTION

Stephen R. Bissette. *Blur 1-5. Green Mountain Cinema 1; Teen Angels*
Win Scott Eckert. *Crossovers* (2 vols.)
Jean-Marc & Randy Lofficier. *Shadowmen* (2 vols.)
Randy Lofficier. *Over Here*

ART BOOKS

Jean-Pierre Normand. *Science Fiction Illustrations*
Raven Okeefe. *Raven's L'il Critters; Rave's Faves*
Randy Lofficier & Raven Okeefe. *If Your Possum Go Daylight...*
Daniele Serra. *Illusions*

HEXAGON COMICS

Franco Frescura & Luciano Bernasconi. *Wampus*
Franco Frescura & Giorgio Trevisan. *CLASH*
L. Bernasconi, J.-M. Lofficier & Juan Roncagliolo Berger. *Phenix*
Claude Legrand, J.-M. Lofficier & L. Bernasconi. *Kabur*
Franco Oneta. *Zembla*
L. Buffolente, Lofficier & J.-J. Dzialowski. *Strangers: Homicron*
Danilo Grossi. *Strangers: Jaydee*
Claude Legrand & Luciano Bernasconi. *Strangers: Starlock*